PRAISE FOR RACHEL WILSON'S NOVELS:

## *My Wild Irish Rose*

"A beautifully descriptive tale."

—*Scribes World Reviews*

"An amusing historical romance . . . delightful characters . . . a warm, humorous tale that is simply fun to read."

—Harriet Klausner, *Affaire de Coeur*

## *Spirit of Love*

"A warm, wonderful and tantalizing tale of love . . . Ms. Wilson has written yet another great romance."

—*Under the Covers*

"Gifts the readers with a package bound in humor, wrapped in romance, and tied with love . . . Delightful."

—Kathee S. Card

*continued on next page . . .*

## Bittersweet Summer

"With elements of intrigue enhancing the fast-paced, genuine-feeling story line, readers will find it impossible not to finish this novel in one sitting . . . superb."　　　—Harriet Klausner

"*Bittersweet Summer* features likable main characters and a ghost who provides comic relief, but the main focus of this book is the healing power of truth and love . . . enjoyable."

—*Bookbug*

## Heaven's Promise

"A delightful story [that will] entertain readers long into the night . . . Guaranteed to keep readers guessing right until the end."　　　—*Rendezvous*

"If you're in need of a fun and relaxing read, then Rachel Wilson has definitely created a wonderful book for you. Complete with a forty-year-old mystery, *Heaven's Promise* is filled with intensely humorous moments, touching scenes, and a sweetly satisfying romance that will have you turning the pages eager for more . . . wonderful character development, an excellent mystery, and plenty of the paranormal."　　—*Under the Covers*

## Restless Spirits

"Rachel Wilson pens an interesting supernatural romance."

—*Affaire de Coeur*

"*Restless Spirits* surprised me like waking up to find a present given for no particular occasion. Wherever the author gets her characters, I hope she goes back and gets some more. I love this story and I am ready for more by Rachel Wilson!"　—*Bookbug*

# HEAVEN SENT

## RACHEL WILSON

JOVE BOOKS, NEW YORK

HEAVEN SENT

A Jove Book / published by arrangement with
the author

PRINTING HISTORY
Jove edition / September 2001

Visit our website at
www.penguinputnam.com

ISBN: 0-515-13181-4

A JOVE BOOK®
Jove Books are published by The Berkley Publishing Group,
a division of Penguin Putnam Inc.,
375 Hudson Street, New York, New York 10014.
JOVE and the "J" design
are trademarks belonging to Penguin Putnam Inc.

PRINTED IN THE UNITED STATES OF AMERICA

10  9  8  7  6  5  4  3  2  1

This is Linda Kruger's book, for sure—
with a little left over for Monster,
my mom's cat, who maneuvered his way into her
life last Christmas in spite of everything she
tried to do to prevent it.

# PROLOGUE

**Santa Angelica, California, August 1897**

Miss Callida Prophet finished her simple supper, washed her dishes, and sat in her late father's comfortably padded rocking chair. Monster, her aptly named black cat, jumped onto her lap as soon as he figured she was set for the evening and commenced purring.

With no more thought than she might have given to watering a flower, Callie opened the letter little Becky Lockhart had addressed to her mother in heaven. Tampering with the U.S. Mail was a felony but Callie, rural postal carrier for Santa Angelica, California, wasn't worried. All Callie cared about was that, by reading and answering Becky's letters to her dead mama, she might be helping the poor girl cope with her terrible loss.

Anyhow, Mr. Wilson, the Santa Angelica postmaster, had sanctioned Callie's intention to respond to Becky's letters. The entire town of Santa Angelica knew how huge a blow the loss of Anne Lockhart had been to Anne's daughter.

*Dear Mama,* had been written in Becky's firm, though somewhat lopsided printing.

*I miss you lots. Papa dint come down to brekfist
today. He dint eat his dinner yesterday. I miss you. I
miss Papa. He says he will hire a nany for me. Is a
nany like a mama? I want a kitty or a puppy.*

*Love, Becky*

The word "nany" gave Callie pause until she realized
Becky had been trying to write "nanny."

"So. He's hiring a nanny for his child, is he?"

Callie didn't know what to think about that. Becky's letters told her what she'd already guessed: Becky missed her
mother terribly.

Worse, she missed her father, though he still resided in
the house in which Becky lived. But Becky's father, the rich
Mr. Aubrey Lockhart, seemed to have become mired in grief
somewhere along the road leading from his wife's illness and
death to the present. He was wallowing in the slough of
despondency to this day, a year later. He'd clearly withdrawn
from his daughter, who needed him now more than ever.
Often when she read Becky's letters to her mother in heaven,
Callie wished she could shake Mr. Aubrey Lockhart until his
teeth rattled and his brain started functioning again.

Callie knew exactly what Becky was going through because she'd lost her own mother when she was six years old,
the same age as Becky. But Callie, unlike Becky, had had
two wonderful sisters, a compassionate older brother, and a
loving father to comfort her.

Poor Becky sometimes wrote about how nice the Lockhart
housekeeper, Mrs. Granger, was, but the only messages her
letters ever contained about her father were that he was hiding out somewhere in his own personal hell and ignoring
Becky. She didn't use those words, of course, but Callie
could read between the lopsided lines.

And that, in a nutshell, was the reason Callie had started
answering Becky's letters to heaven with letters of her own
and signing them "Mama." *Somebody* had to pay attention
to a little girl's loneliness and distress. *Somebody* needed to
reassure her that her mother had loved her beyond anything.

*Somebody* had to persuade the child that life could be good, even when one did lose the person one loved best in the world. And, since Becky's father didn't seem inclined to interrupt his own selfish suffering to offer assistance to his daughter, Callie tried her best to do the job for him.

"Stupid man," Callie grumbled. It shouldn't take a genius to understand that he and Becky could be of enormous help to each other in coming to terms with Mrs. Lockhart's death.

Anne Lockhart, the mama Becky missed so much, had been sick for a long time, suffering from some sort of wasting illness that had eaten her up inside and sapped her strength until she'd at last been confined to her bed. She'd been the talk of the small village of Santa Angelica for almost two years before her ultimate demise. She was still talked about, with sad shakes of heads and dolorous sighs.

The whole town had mourned her death. Most Santa Angelicans had attended her funeral, Callie among them. Anne Lockhart had, by all reports, been a truly good person.

Everything Callie had ever heard about Anne bespoke a generous, gentle, good-natured, loving woman who had adored her husband and daughter. Surely she wouldn't want them to suffer like this from her death. She would especially hate it that Mr. Lockhart had forsaken his daughter just when she needed him most.

Callie sat in the chair, stroking Monster, and wondering if there wasn't something she could do for Becky. Something more than answering her letters to heaven. Becky's father was beyond Callie's reach, so she'd never be able to tell him to his face that she thought he was an idiot to retreat from his own daughter. Still, there might be something . . .

Her gasp of insight startled Monster into lifting his head and scowling at her. A stunning—no, a *brilliant*—idea had occurred to her. She wasn't sure she dare try it.

"But why shouldn't I, Monster? After all, I'm perfectly qualified for the position. Besides, what do I have to lose?"

Monster evidently didn't know because he didn't answer. He did resume purring after a few seconds, though, so Callie guessed he approved.

She lifted Monster gently off her lap and set him on the

rocking chair as she went to the desk to pen a response to Becky's letter.

> *My darling Becky, I hope you get your kitty or your puppy. A little girl needs a pet to play with. And then, when all the grown-up people around you are busy, you could talk to your pet. Pets are good for that. I hope your papa hires a nice nanny to take care of you, dear. He loves you very much. And so do I.*
>
> *Love, Mama*

It irked Callie to tell Becky that her father loved her, but she knew Becky needed to read it. And the man probably did love his daughter. That he was unable to tear himself away from his own unhappiness and demonstrate his affection was not to his credit, but it didn't mean he didn't love his child.

As she folded the letter and sealed it, Callie turned and murmured to the sleeping cat, "Well, Monster, it looks like I'm going into another line of work."

Monster only purred more loudly.

# 1

Aubrey Lockhart sat with his head in his hands, staring at his desk blotter, wishing he were dead. It wasn't an uncommon pose for Aubrey, and it certainly wasn't an uncommon wish. He'd gotten into the habit of doing both somewhere between the onset of Anne's illness and her death. He was only adhering to tradition.

He sighed heavily. Why had this happened to him? *Why?* Had he irked the gods so much that they'd decided to punish him? Why couldn't they have taken him instead of Anne? Aubrey didn't think he'd mind dying. Hell, he'd greet death with open arms, if that was the only way to see Anne again.

But that would be even more unfair to Becky than he was already being.

He felt very guilty about Becky. He knew he ought to be holding her, talking to her, reading to her, going for walks with her, as he used to do. Before Anne left them.

But now, every time he saw Becky, he saw Anne. Becky had Anne's bright blue eyes and peaches-and-cream coloring. Becky's hair was lighter than Anne's had been, but that was only because she was so young. When she grew up, she'd be the very image of her mother.

No. Aubrey couldn't bear being around Becky. For one thing, she brought Anne's loss into sharp focus, which was excruciating. Worse, he couldn't quell a new fear that if he loved Becky too much the gods would take her, too.

"Ass." Aubrey had also become accustomed to calling himself names, much as he'd become accustomed to basking in his unhappiness. Both behaviors were habit with him now, not unlike his habit of breathing. Or his habit of avoiding his daughter, who didn't deserve it.

He shoved his chair away from his desk, let his head loll back, and stared at the ceiling.

"Why can't I just get over it?" he asked himself, not for the first, or even the hundredth, time.

Anne had been dead a year last week. He shouldn't still have this terrible ache in his chest. He shouldn't still feel this awful emptiness, this deep hole in his life. He shouldn't—

A sharp knock at the library door jerked him upright in his chair. "Yes?"

The door opened without a creak. Mrs. Granger, his housekeeper, wouldn't allow hinges to creak in *her* house, God bless her. Figgins, Aubrey's butler, entered the room slowly and said, "Mr. Lockhart, there's an applicant in the drawing room."

"An applicant?" Aubrey's mind, a cumbersome organ determined to be of as little use as possible to him lately, finally paid attention. "Oh. An applicant. For the position advertised in the *Santa Angelica Post*, I presume?"

"Yes, sir." Figgins, who Aubrey sometimes thought looked as though he'd been stuffed by an exceptionally talented taxidermist, came forward. He looked much more regal than any of the Lockharts ever had, and he bore a silver tray in his white-gloved hand. A small card rested on it.

With a sigh, Aubrey picked up the card. "Miss Callida Prophet."

"Yes, sir. I had her remain in the drawing room."

"Right." Aubrey shoved his chair back farther, rose, plucked his coat from where he'd flung it over the sofa, and accompanied Figgins out of the library, shrugging into the coat as he went.

He was glad he'd thought of hiring a nanny. Since he was of no earthly good to Becky, he ought at least to hire someone who would be.

Guilt gnawed at his insides, nibbling along the edges of the blotch of grief residing there.

But, hell's bells, he couldn't take care of a child. He was a man. Becky needed a woman to care for her. Some gray-haired granny perhaps. Maybe an old maiden aunt who missed taking care of her now grown-up nieces and nephews.

Aubrey could picture the two of them in his mind's eye: Becky, smiling happily as she walked hand-in-hand with a small, graying, elderly woman wearing a silly flowered hat and, perhaps, spectacles. They'd both be smiling. Maybe talking to each other in low voices, exchanging the innocent secrets of the very old and the very young. The nanny would probably walk with a cane. Or carry one of those frilly old-fashioned parasols. She would be like a grandmother to Becky.

Yes, indeed. Once he found the right nanny for her, Becky would finally get the love and care he knew she needed. Aubrey had begun to smile slightly by the time he reached the drawing room.

His smile died when he saw the applicant. Before he could stop himself, he barked, "Who on earth are you?"


Callie Prophet had been staring at the portrait of Anne Lockhart hanging over the fireplace, thinking that the artist had captured Anne's fragile beauty and air of gentle humanity very well. She didn't hear the door open at her back.

She heard Aubrey's question, though, loud and clear. Wheeling around, her heart pounding like a war drum, she saw him standing at the door, Mr. Figgins a few feet behind him. Mr. Lockhart glowered at her. Mr. Figgins merely looked aloof.

Aubrey's brusqueness fired her temper, as she'd done

nothing to deserve it. "I," she said in a cold, dignified tone, "am Miss Callida Prophet. Didn't you receive my calling card?" She stared pointedly at the fingers of his right hand, which had the card in a death grip.

"Of course, I got your card. Figgins said you came to apply for the job as nanny to my daughter."

She made herself smile. "Yes, I have, Mr. Lockhart." She narrowed her eyes and squinted. "You *are* Mr. Lockhart, correct?" If he didn't have enough manners to introduce himself properly, she'd just ask him.

Aubrey jerked and appeared disconcerted. "Er, yes. Yes, I'm Mr. Lockhart. Please be seated, Miss Prophet." He waved at a fatly stuffed, comfortable-looking chair squatting beside an equally chubby, comfortable-looking sofa.

Callie chose instead to seat herself in a prim, straight-backed chair next to a piecrust table. She was, after all, applying for the position as nanny to this man's child. She wasn't a guest in his house.

Aubrey's frowning gaze took in this gesture. He turned to his butler. "You may leave us, Figgins. Tell Mrs. Granger to bring some tea."

"That's not necessary, Mr. Lockhart."

Callie could have bitten her tongue as soon as the words left her lips. It wasn't so much that Aubrey scowled at her for countermanding one of his orders; it was because she didn't want any blasted tea and resented it being foisted upon her. She also knew it wasn't her place to say so. She waved a hand in an airy gesture. "I beg your pardon. Bring on the tea, Mr. Figgins."

She'd known Figgins ever since he'd moved with the Lockharts from San Francisco to Santa Angelica almost ten years ago. According to people in the village, he'd worked for the Lockhart family in San Francisco since Aubrey was a boy. Also according to village gossip, Figgins looked a good deal more stuffy than he really was.

Figgins bowed deeply and scooted off on his silent butler feet. Callie watched him go and wished she'd held firm on the tea issue. She didn't really want it, and with Figgins's departure she felt as if she were marooned on a desert island with a hungry shark lurking not far offshore.

But that was silly. She sat up straighter, laid her little green reticule in her lap, and folded her hands on top of it. She gazed with what she hoped passed for serenity at Aubrey Lockhart.

His gaze was anything but serene. He hadn't yet stopped frowning at her. His elegant black trousers and morning coat didn't do much to relax her, either. He looked rich and remote. And miles and miles above her socially.

With a mental smack on the side of her head, Callie reminded herself that she lived in the egalitarian United States of America, and that things like wealth and social standing shouldn't matter. The United States didn't distinguish its citizens by class or caste. Unfortunately, the recognition of her social equity didn't help to calm her jitters.

She knew her appearance was at least adequate, and probably a good deal more than that. While it was true she was rather young—a mere twenty-four—it was also true that she was a mature, responsible woman, who had been fending for herself for several years. Well, three years, anyhow. She'd subdued her curly strawberry-blond hair into a tight bun and covered it with a prim straw hat adorned with one yellow flower. She'd worn her newest alpaca shirtwaist dress in a sober dark green that brought out the green in her eyes. That she'd chosen the fabric for that very reason needn't be a consideration. The color of a nanny's eyes was a moot point, or should be.

Her credentials ought to be adequate, as well, if she could only stop being nervous long enough to relate them to Aubrey Lockhart. She'd graduated from college in 1893, thereby rendering her better educated than the majority of her peers.

Thus, even though she was anxious in the face of Aubrey Lockhart's continued owlish and unfriendly scrutiny, she knew she shouldn't be. She was as good as anyone, and better suited to be Becky's nanny than most, since she not only possessed a college degree, but she already knew—and

loved—the child. She lifted her chin to show Aubrey she
wasn't intimidated, even though she was.

He paced the room for a minute or two, not taking his
gaze from her face. She wondered if he was trying to dis-
concert her or if he acted like a rude bully to everyone who
came calling. He stopped pacing suddenly, right in front of
her.

Staring down at her with eyes fairly radiating disapproval,
he snapped, "Have you held paid employment before?"

"I certainly have."

He turned as abruptly as he'd stopped, marched to the
straight-backed chair on the other side of the piecrust table
and sat. Good heavens, the man was precipitant.

Laying her calling card on the table, he said, "What kind
of employment?"

Callie cleared her throat. "I've been the carrier on the
Santa Angelica postal route for three years, Mr. Lockhart. I
handle the rural route. Mr. Philpott delivers mail within the
village limits."

"You're a postman—er, -woman?" Aubrey's sooty eyebrows arched like rainbows above his dark brown eyes.

"Yes, sir." She wondered if she should tell him she'd met
his daughter while driving her route, but decided to save this
piece of information until later. She might need a weapon.

"Do you have any education?"

"I do. I graduated with honors from the Brooklyn, New
York, Teaching Seminary for Young Ladies in June of
1893."

His eyes narrowed further. "Why'd you go all the way to
New York to attend school?"

As if that were any of *his* business. However, Callie re-
plied to his question calmly. "My uncle is the dean of students. He recommended the college to my parents. I applied,
and was granted admission."

"Hmm."

"I was *not*," Callie added, feeling defensive, "granted anything else. I mean, I was given no special consideration, but
was admitted on my own merits and my academic record. I
earned a scholarship based on my academic achievements,

as well." She was darned proud of that scholarship.

"Hmm."

Callie wanted to jump out of her chair, dash over to Aubrey Lockhart, and batter the *hmm*s out of him. They were rude, and they made her edgy.

He squinted narrowly. "Why aren't you teaching, if you have a degree in it?"

That was none of his business, either. She said, "My family lives in Santa Angelica. Santa Angelica didn't need any teachers when I returned home from college. I needed some type of employment, and since there was an opening for a mail carrier at the post office, I applied. I would, of course, rather be teaching, but I do enjoy my postal route." *So there.*

"Do you have written references?"

"No, sir. You may feel free to call upon Mr. Wilson, the postmaster in Santa Angelica. He can vouch for my dependability and moral character. Miss Myrtle Oakes, the Santa Angelica schoolmistress, is a good friend of mine and can also vouch for my character. I can supply verification of my employment and education. I have a diploma, of course."

"Hmm." He stared at her some more, his brows drawn straight over his eyes. He looked formidable; cold, aloof, annoyed, and unfriendly. Callie stared back, doing her best not to frown.

"Have you ever cared for children in your vast work experience?"

Oho, so he was going to be sarcastic, was he? Well, Callie would just show *him* who was capable and who wasn't—and she wouldn't have to resort to sarcasm, either. "I not only possess a teaching degree, I've also had a good deal to do with my sisters' and brother's children, Mr. Lockhart. I care for them often when my family needs help."

"That's far from the same as being a nanny to a six-year-old girl."

She inclined her head a quarter of an inch. "Perhaps you don't know as much about six-year-old girls and their needs as you think you do."

His head jerked up so fast that Callie was surprised not to hear his neck snap. "Is that so?"

She hated to do it, but she apologized. "I beg your pardon, Mr. Lockhart. I have had abundant experience caring for children, but I shouldn't have been impertinent."

"Indeed." He squinted at her again. "How old are you?"

Well! In any other circumstances, Callie would have told Mr. Aubrey Lockhart what he could do with himself if he were sufficiently dexterous. However, she cared enough about Becky to hold her tongue. "I shall be twenty-five years old in May, Mr. Lockhart."

"You don't look it."

Whatever did that mean? Did he mean she looked like a crone, or that she looked like a child?

"You're too young," he announced after several pregnant seconds, during which it was all Callie could do to keep from kneading her hands in anxiety. His frown deepened. "You're too young, too immature, and you have no experience with this kind of work. What the devil do you think you're doing, applying for a job for which you're clearly unfit?"

That was enough of *that*. Callie stood up, straightening her frame to show off her whole five feet, five inches. "I am fully fit to be a nanny to your daughter, Mr. Lockhart. I love children, I've cared for them many times, and if you think an older woman could do a better job than I, you're mistaken. Your daughter, Mr. Lockhart, needs someone in whom she can confide. Someone who will take care of her and who will make her feel special. She needs someone to love her! *You* certainly seem to have abdicated from the position!"

"*What?*"

If Callie hadn't been so angry, Aubrey's roar might have demoralized her. As it was, she stood her ground indomitably. "You heard me. You've abandoned your own child, Mr. Lockhart, and you ought to be ashamed of yourself. That poor little girl needs you. If she can't have you, she needs *someone*!"

"Why, you—"

The door opened, and Becky Lockhart barreled into the room, rushing right past her father and over to Callie, who barely stooped in time to catch her up in her arms. She straightened and glowered at Aubrey, whose mouth hung open as he stared at Callie and his daughter, her arms around Callie's neck.

"What the—?"

Becky's blue eyes twinkled happily. "Oh, Papa, isn't it wonderful that Miss Prophet has come to be my nanny? She's ever so nice!"

"Wh-what are you . . .?" He stared at his daughter. Callie was pleased to note that his expression softened considerably.

"Oh, Papa," Becky went on, evidently not worried about her father's frown. "I'm oh so fond of Miss Prophet. Please say that you'll let her be my nanny."

He fastened his attention on Callie. "And how, pray tell, did you get to know my daughter?" His voice cut like a knife.

Becky's smile faded. Callie, sorry to see it go, made sure she didn't sound as furious as she felt when she answered Aubrey's question. "Becky and I met while I drove my mail route, Mr. Lockhart. We've become quite good friends."

"Yes," Becky confirmed. "Oh, please hire Miss Prophet, Papa. She's my *best* friend."

Callie felt like crying.

Aubrey, plainly irate and also clearly believing that Callie had somehow hornswoggled him, opened his mouth and shut it twice before anything came out of it. Callie knew how much he wanted to snatch his daughter from her arms and then kick her down the Lockhart mansion's grand marble front porch steps.

She was pleased when he did neither, but only sucked in a breath and held it for a moment. When he let it out, he looked calmer. Thank God.

"Becky, would you please leave Miss Prophet and me alone for a minute? We won't be long."

Becky looked doubtful. "But . . . isn't Miss Prophet going to come live with us, Papa?" Her eyes were so eloquent, Callie wouldn't have been able to deny her anything. She feared Becky's papa was made of sterner stuff, however.

"We're going to talk about it now, sweetheart," Aubrey said. "We won't be long."

"All right." Becky nodded somberly at her father, then gave Callie a quick hug.

Callie lowered Becky to the ornate Chinese rug decorating the drawing room floor and dropped a kiss on her pretty blonde curls. "I'll see you later, Becky."

"Promise?" Becky looked worried.

Callie smiled at her. "Promise."

"Well . . . All right." Becky left the room much more slowly than she'd entered it.

As soon as the door closed, Callie returned her attention to Aubrey. She braced herself, expecting to be tossed out of his house and told never to return. It would kill her to know that Becky would be living in this sterile household without a mother *or* a father, or anyone else to love her.

"I don't know how you managed to finagle your way into my daughter's good graces, Miss Prophet, but I suppose I'm going to have to give you a chance."

Callie's heart nearly jumped out of her chest. Her eyes opened wide.

Aubrey sneered. "Yes, you might well stare. However, while I'm willing to hire you on a contingent basis, I want you to understand absolutely that if you do anything—anything at all—to upset my daughter, my servants in general, or me in particular, you'll be thrown out on your ear."

"Oh!" She gulped. "Yes. I understand."

"Good."

Swallowing the hot words his attitude provoked in her, Callie said, "Thank you, Mr. Lockhart."

"When can you start?"

She lifted her arms in a gesture of befuddlement. "Er, well, it doesn't matter. Anytime."

"Good. Bring your things tomorrow. I'll have Mrs. Granger prepare a room for you."

"Thank you." Callie bobbed a curtsy, but he didn't see it because the door had opened again and he'd turned, scowling. Callie imagined he expected to find Becky, come to see if they were done talking yet. Time went very slowly for six-year-olds.

It wasn't Becky. It was Mrs. Granger, with a tray holding

tea things. Aubrey sent her away. The last Callie saw of her, Mrs. Granger was glancing back over her shoulder at the two of them, curiosity writ large on her elderly features.

As for Callie herself, she walked home on a cloud.

# 2

Aubrey left his drawing room feeling rather as if he'd been run over by the Santa Angelica mail wagon. He didn't like it.

He did, however, manage to smile at Becky and pick her up when she ran down the hall to him, her face as eager as if she were anticipating Christmas.

"Will Miss Prophet come to live with us, Papa?"

The usual reserve Aubrey had come to expect from his daughter seemed to have vanished under the influence of Miss Prophet's anticipated arrival into the Lockhart home. Aubrey's heart hitched. He'd been so unfair to Becky these last couple of years. "Yes, Becky. Miss Prophet will move her things in tomorrow. Perhaps you can help Mrs. Granger pick out a bedroom for her to use."

He was sorry he'd made the suggestion as soon as Becky wriggled to get down. It had been a while since he had held her, and he had forgotten how good it felt. It especially irked him that all this enthusiasm was for Callida Prophet. He knew he shouldn't mind. After all, what had he done lately to win his child's affection? Not dashed much.

"Oh, thank you, Papa! I know e*zack*ly what room I want her to have!"

At least she deposited a quick kiss on his cheek before she darted off to find the housekeeper. Aubrey sighed as he stared after her.

Before Anne got sick, he had been on top of the world. He'd exuded confidence and competence, and for good reason. He'd started his own Chinese imports business when he was barely out of college, and had made a million dollars by the time he was twenty-five, Miss Prophet's age. He'd attained his life's ultimate goal when he'd married the woman he loved: the sweet and beautiful Miss Anne Harriott. It was Anne for whom he'd worked so hard. He'd wanted to be worthy of her. When Anne had given birth to Becky, he'd thought he'd never want for anything again.

Not any longer. Now he faced each day with dread and loathing. He was still rich—once the wheels of progress had started, it took a lot to slow them down—but everything else in his life had gone straight to hell. He entered his library, which doubled as his office, shut the door, flopped down in the chair he'd vacated when Callie had arrived to be interviewed, and stared at nothing. "Why, Anne? Why did you have to leave us?"

No answer to the question had occurred to him by the time Figgins rang the antique Chinese gong for dinner.

C̲allie bumped along on the passenger seat of her brother George's utility wagon, the one he used when he was transferring supplies for his successful Santa Angelica hardware store. She held the handle of the wicker picnic basket sitting on her lap. Irate and terrible yowling sounds came from inside the basket. Callie was especially grateful that George had thought to tie the lid of the basket down with some rope before they left the house.

"I still say you're out of your mind," George said, for perhaps the fiftieth time.

"Fiddle. She's a sweet little girl."

"Sweet little girl be hanged. She's not your responsibility."

George, who had two children of his own as a result of his marriage to his childhood sweetheart Marie, sounded more severe than he really was.

"Perhaps not, but I remember what it was like to lose our mother when I was her age." Callie felt stupid when she had to brush a tear from her cheek.

George reached over and patted her knee. "I know. It was hard on all of us. But we all pulled through it eventually."

If he hadn't been driving, Callie would have hugged him. "Exactly. But poor little Becky doesn't have any wonderful brothers or sisters to help her. And her father seems to have taken up residence on some other planet. She deserves to know that someone cares about her and how she feels."

George heaved a sigh. "I'm sure her father cares."

"He doesn't act like it." Callie sniffed.

"How do you know?"

"Because I—" Recalling that she'd not filled George in on Becky's sweet and emotionally devastating letters, Callie stopped herself just in time. "Um, because I got to know her on my postal route."

George nodded but didn't jump in to agree with her, as he usually did. Callie eyed him sideways, wondering what had given her brother pause. After a moment, he said, "Well, he was hurt, too, you know. That doesn't mean his behavior is acccptablc, but it does make it more understandable."

She heaved an aggrieved sigh. She didn't want to understand Aubrey Lockhart; he had treated her horribly, and Callie wasn't ready to forgive him for that yet. "Of course he was hurt, but he's a man."

George offered her a grin. "Are you saying men don't feel?"

"Of course I don't mean that men don't feel!"

"It's a good thing, because if anything happened to Marie, I don't know what I'd do."

"Oh, George, I'm sorry." Callie, who knew George loved his family with all the vigor in his strong body, felt a pang of guilt until she noticed her brother's satisfied expression. "Why, you beast!"

George grinned, obviously enjoying his sister's consternation. "Got you that time, didn't I, Callie-Coe?"

She huffed. Then she grinned, too. Then she giggled. She couldn't stay mad at her brother, no matter how hard she tried. He was too jolly and joyful for anyone to be angry at for long. George and her sisters, Florence and Alta, were the three finest human beings in the world and, in Callie's opinion, their respective spouses ranked as the three second finest.

George eyed Callie's basket. "I don't know what Mr. Lockhart's going to think about you bringing Monster with you, though."

"That's *Mister* Monster to you, George."

"Fudge. He's a monster, and you know it."

"Just because he likes to nibble your boot laces doesn't make him a *real* monster. I only named him Monster because he's so big."

"He's big and spiteful and tried to kill Miss Naomi, you mean."

"I do not. Miss Naomi got to like him. After a little while."

"Pooh. She gave up, is what you mean."

Callie imagined he was right. Miss Naomi, the Prophet family cat for years, took things as they came. "Fiddlesticks. They used to curl up and purr together until she died. And then Monster was terribly sad."

"I'll just bet."

But she knew he was joshing in order to take her mind away from how much she despised Aubrey Lockhart. And he was right to do so. She couldn't very well enter into employment and overtly demonstrate her contempt for her employer; not if she wanted to keep her job for long. She hadn't even started it yet and already the miserable cad had threatened her tenure.

Realizing she'd just undone her brother's good intentions, she detached her mind from Aubrey Lockhart, to which it seemed to want to cling like a leech, and returned it to the cat in the basket. "Besides, Becky wants a kitty or a puppy. She said so." She hadn't revealed to her family that she'd been writing Becky, pretending to be the little girl's mother in heaven.

"That cat," said George in a crisp tone, "is *not* a kitty. It's a damned big cat. And a mean one."

"Monster isn't mean," Callie crooned, leaning over the basket—but happy she wasn't within scratching distance. "He's a love."

"Right."

They'd come to the entrance to the Lockhart mansion. The main iron gate in front of the long drive stood open and was, according to the Santa Angelica gossip mill, never locked. Callie guessed that, at one point, this had been intended as an indication of the family's sociability. However, now it seemed to be more of an old habit or a relict of bygone, happier days. Because Aubrey had chosen to isolate himself from the rest of the world, no one visited the Lockharts any longer. Which was one more pity to add to the growing heap.

George maneuvered the horse around the corner and onto the well-tended driveway. Azaleas bloomed alongside the drive, and Callie could see a rose garden in the distance.

"Aubrey Lockhart aside, I'm glad I thought of applying for this job," Callie said, not bothering to suppress the excitement in her voice. "I'm sure I can help Becky."

"You really like that kid, don't you?"

When she turned her head, she saw George watching her curiously. "Yes. Yes, I do. I love her. She's a sweet child, and she's suffered a tremendous loss."

"She reminds you of you, in fact."

"Well—yes." Callie sighed. "I can't help it, George. I just want to help her."

"You're an amazing young woman, you know that, Callie?" George smiled affectionately at his youngest sister. "A bit crazy, but amazing nonetheless."

Callie giggled, glad her brother was there to lighten her mood and soothe her nerves. She was gazing at the roses and thinking how lovely the blooms were when George said, "But all joking aside, there's something else I'm worried about, Callie. You quit your job. What happens if this one doesn't work out?"

Callie had wondered the same thing. She'd talked about it to Mr. Wilson, in fact. He'd told her she could have a job at the post office anytime she wanted one, although she might have to wait for a position to open up. It wasn't a guarantee, but at least it was *some* kind of insurance. "I've already talked to Mr. Wilson. He said he'd be happy to rehire me."

"Well, that's something."

Exactly what she'd thought.

George stopped the wagon at the kitchen door of the mansion at Callie's request and hopped out. Mr. Lockhart already didn't like her. If she dared to walk through the front door as if she were an honored guest, she was pretty sure he wouldn't appreciate it.

George walked over to Callie's side of the wagon and held out his hand. Taking his hand and shinnying down over the big dusty wagon wheel, Callie muttered, "Thanks, George. I think I'd better see if anyone's home before we unload."

She was happy that Mrs. Granger not only seemed to have been expecting her, but even greeted her with a wide smile. "Oh, Callie, I'm so glad that you're here and you're going to be Becky's nanny. I told Mr. Lockhart you'll be good for that poor mite."

"You did?" She hadn't anticipated Mrs. Granger's commendation, but she appreciated it. "Thank you."

"You're ever so welcome, dearie. That dear child has been lost since her mother died. As has her poor papa," she added conscientiously. Callie suppressed a sniff. "We all try to give her as much attention as we can, but we have our other jobs to do."

"I see. I'm glad to be here."

Monster took that opportunity to let out a howl. His howls reminded Callie of stories she'd read about banshees on Irish moors. Were there moors in Ireland? Well, never mind. The shocked expression on Mrs. Granger's face needed attending to before the banshees did.

"Er, I took the liberty of bringing my cat, Mrs. Granger. I hope that won't cause a problem. He's a lovely cat, really. He's a little nervous at the moment, because he's come all this way in a basket in a bumpy wagon."

Mrs. Granger eyed the basket doubtfully. "Well . . ."

"Becky told me she wanted a cat," Callie told her, feeling desperate.

It was the right thing to have said. Mrs. Granger's doubt faded into a sad frown. "Yes. I know the darling girl wants a pet. I hope Mr. Lockhart won't be upset about it."

So did Callie. "I'll keep him in my room at first. Until he gets used to his new home. And I'll fix him a sandbox."

With a slow nod, Mrs. Granger said, "Yes. That's the best thing to do."

Although she didn't say so, Callie imagined Mrs. Granger would have liked to add that perhaps it would be best to keep the cat in her room forever. But Callie was an optimist by nature, and she gave the housekeeper a big smile. "Wonderful! I'm very excited about this new job, Mrs. Granger. I'm very fond of Becky already, and I'm hoping I can be of some help to her."

Mrs. Granger gave her shoulder a pat. "I'm sure you can, dearie. Here, come along inside." She leaned out the door and smiled at George, who had grown up and gone to school with her own boy. "Come on in with her bags, George. We have a pretty room all fixed up for your sister."

"Right-oh."

The ever-agreeable George picked up Callie's two small pieces of luggage—a bandbox and a carpetbag—and toted them into the kitchen. He stopped and sniffed the air. "Smells good in here."

"We're having one of Becky's favorites tonight." Mrs. Granger gave Callie a confiding look. "The sweet child. She asked if we could have chicken and dumplings for special, because you were coming to live with us."

Callie told herself not to get emotional over every little thing. But it was considerate of the little girl to want to feed Callie a special meal on her first night in her home, even if Callie didn't particularly care for chicken and dumplings. "That's very nice of her."

The housekeeper heaved a huge sigh. "She's a darling. She's just like her late mother."

"Yes. I've heard that. She looks like her, too."

"Oh, my, yes. Mr. Lockhart, he's so dark and all. But

Becky has her mother's blond hair and blue eyes. Why, they look like they were molded by the same hand."

How poetic. Callie murmured, "Yes, indeed," as she followed the housekeeper up the back stairs. She and George exchanged a glance, and George winked at her. She felt good about this job. Confident. Secure.

Well, perhaps not secure. But she was absolutely confident that she could be of some assistance to Becky, and that was the important thing.

At the top of the stairs, Mrs. Granger spoke again. "Most of the servants sleep on the third floor, but Becky asked especially that you be allowed to have the room next to hers."

"That was kind of her."

The older woman heaved a dolorous sigh. "She's been awfully lonely these past few months." Shaking her head, Mrs. Granger indicated the closed door of a bedroom to her right. "This is her room here." With another confidential expression, she said quietly, "And you ought to see it, too. It's a dollhouse of a room, Callie. All pink and white and frilly. It's just beautiful. Her mother and father went to great pains to pick out everything just the way they wanted it."

This news surprised Callie. "Her father helped?"

"Oh, my, yes. Why, the poor man used to dote on his wife and Becky. He indulged their every whim. He even took them to San Francisco to pick the fabrics for little Becky's tester and bedspread—all pink-and-white gingham checks, don't you know, with white cotton lace edging it all. Mrs. Lockhart's death crushed him."

It must have. "I had no idea."

The housekeeper sighed soulfully. "There ought to be three or four little children playing in this grand house. Then Becky wouldn't be so lost and alone and neither would her papa. But it pleased the good Lord to call Mrs. Lockhart to a new home." She shook her head.

Perhaps, Callie thought, she ought to go a little easier on Aubrey Lockhart. At least until she got to know more about the family as a whole.

On the other hand, Callie didn't think she could ever really

forgive him for abandoning his daughter. She didn't doubt
for a minute that his wife's death had hurt him and broken
his spirit. But he owed it to his wife's memory and his still-
living daughter to be of solace to the child, blast it.

Her firm and negative opinions about Mr. Aubrey Lockhart flew smack out of her head as soon as Mrs. Granger
opened the door to the room Becky had picked for Callie.
"Good heavens!"

Mrs. Granger beamed. "Lovely, isn't it?"

Callie swallowed and slowly entered the room. "It certainly is." She set Monster's wicker basket down next to the
fireplace. The animal set up a yowl that faded into a hiss of
fury, but Callie paid him no mind.

"Jumping cats, Callie, this is a sight better than anything
you've ever lived in before." George stomped into the room
and dumped her luggage on the bed.

Darting over and retrieving the two small bags, Callie
whispered, "George! Don't put them there!"

He laughed indulgently. "Callie-coe, sweetheart, your two
little bags aren't going to ruin that counterpane, even if it is
a fine one."

She set the bags on the magnificent blue-and-white Chinese rug laid before the fireplace, precipitating a low grown
from Monster, next to the bags. "I suppose not, but . . . well,
it seems like sacrilege to me." She laughed at herself and her
silliness.

So did George. Mrs. Granger looked sort of shocked. Callie hastened to reassure her that the two Prophets weren't
complete heathens. "I'm sorry, Mrs. Granger. It's only that
I've never even seen a room as beautifully furnished as this
one. I never expected to be sleeping in one, and that's a fact."

Her words seemed to soothe Mrs. Granger's feelings. She
folded her hands under her apron and beamed as her gaze
swept the room. "I know. Isn't it something?"

"It is, indeed."

Callie's gaze went from the spectacular Chinese rug before
the fireplace to the equally lovely and much larger one that
covered most of the rest of the polished cedar floor. Evidently Mr. Lockhart's Chinese imports weren't all sold to

create income, but many of them had been diverted to his own home. Callie was glad of it. She wasn't going to mind in the least being able to live in the middle of such luxury and only hoped she wouldn't get too used to it. She sure liked it so far.

The furniture was all made of a gleaming dark wood, covered with ornate carvings. The pearl inlays in the dressing table and mirror accented the beautiful designs worked into the wood.

"Lord love us, Callie, you'll never want to go home again," George said.

Detecting a slight edge to his words—or perhaps the edge was in his voice—Callie dragged her attention away from the blue-and-white goddess residing on the mantelpiece and focused on him. He looked worried.

"What's the matter, George?"

He shrugged. "Nothing, I guess. I just—" He stopped speaking suddenly.

Bemused, Callie said, "You what? Come on, George, spit it out."

He grinned. "Spit? In this place?" His smile disappeared as quickly as it had appeared. "I just hope you don't get too accustomed to this kind of living, Callie. It might be hard to come back to the real world if you get too used to this one."

"George! Do you really think I'm so petty as to be swayed into neglecting my family by wealth and overt displays of opulence? I know what matters in this life, George Prophet. Believe me." Because it was true, and because George had hurt her feelings, she added, "You, of all people, ought to know that my family is more important to me than anything else on earth."

With two giant steps, Callie's brother had her in his arms and was giving her a bear hug. "I'm sorry, Callie-coe. I know you won't let your head get swelled by this stuff. It's just that we Prophets have to stick together."

"You bet," Callie said—somewhat thickly since there was a lump in her throat and her mouth was buried in George's flannel shirtfront.

A low sniffle from Mrs. Granger separated the Prophet

siblings. Callie was shocked to see the housekeeper dabbing at her eyes with a handkerchief. "Mrs. Granger! Are you all right?"

The older woman nodded. "Oh, yes, Callie. It's only that you two are so close, and I think it's wonderful. Sometimes I wish Becky could belong to your family."

"My goodness." Callie was surprised that her own family's closeness should inspire such appreciation from a person who wasn't a member of the Prophet clan, although she'd often wished much the same thing for the lonely little Lockhart girl. She stepped away from her brother, took a deep, refreshing breath, and said, "So, now . . . Well, thank you, George. I'll let you know how things go. Give my love to Marie and the children."

He saluted smartly. "Will do. Take care of yourself, Callie."

"I will." The mention of Marie, George's darling, plump wife, and of their adorable children brought something to mind. "Say, George, after I get settled in and know what's what, perhaps Becky and I can come to visit the children."

George shrugged. "Sure. Don't see why not." He gave her another breathtaking hug. "Let us know if you need anything."

As if she'd need anything now that she was living here. Another glance around the room she'd be occupying nearly left Callie speechless. Nothing could render a Prophet speechless for long, however, and she smiled at her brother and said, "Will do. Thanks for bringing me, George."

"Right-oh. See you later, Callie. He tipped his hat at the housekeeper. "Mrs. Granger. Any messages you want me to deliver in town? I'm off to the store now."

"Thank you, George. I don't think so."

Callie could tell his offer had pleased the older woman, though. God bless George.

*God bless all of my family.* Even the youngest members of the Prophet clan knew how to put people at their ease. They also had a gift for making people like them—mainly because they took a genuine interest in others. Callie considered this Prophet characteristic a true blessing. She hoped she'd be able to use it to good effect with Becky Lockhart.

Speaking of Becky, Callie had no sooner bidden her brother good-bye and politely declined Mrs. Granger's offer of assistance in unpacking, when a tiny knock came at her bedroom door.

When she opened the door, her heart lit up when she beheld Becky, her hands clasped tightly, looking up at her with anxious eyes. *Poor little mite*, as Mrs. Granger might say.

Throwing her arms wide, Callie cried, "Becky! How lovely to see you! Would you like to come in and help me unpack?"

Instantly the hands unclasped and the aspect of anxiety vanished from the beautiful blue eyes. A huge smile lit Becky's features, and she all but leapt into Callie's arms. "Oh, yes! Please!"

So Callie carried Becky into her room and plunked her down on the fireplace rug. "This is a beautiful room, Becky. It's the prettiest room I've ever seen."

"Do you like it?"

"I love it."

The eagerness on the pert, pretty face made Callie's heart ache. The tyke was astoundingly anxious to please. Callie chalked it up to her trying so hard to please her father for so long.

"Say, Becky, I have something here that might interest you," Callie said as she walked over to the fireplace where odd grumbling noises could be heard issuing from the wicker basket. "But you'd probably better sit in that chair over there." She pointed to an ornately carved, straight-backed chair with a gorgeous embroidered silk cushion, shoved into the kneehole of a matching writing desk. She adopted a mysterious mien and waggled her eyebrows. "You never know what might pop out of this basket."

Becky's eyes went as round as pie plates. "You don't?"

Because the little girl looked a trifle worried, Callie dropped the mysterious stuff and grinned at her. "Don't worry, sweetheart. It's nothing bad. But it might be a little"—she paused while she attempted to come up with a good word to describe an irate Monster—"um, bouncy." She supposed that was as good as any.

Her uneasiness assuaged, Becky trotted over to the desk, pulled out the chair, and climbed up onto the seat. She looked tiny and sweet, and Callie watched her with a swelling in her heart. How could anyone not positively dote on such a pretty, well-behaved, darling of a girl? Again she longed to get Aubrey's attention—the thought of beating him with a stick appealed to her—and forcing him to focus on his daughter.

As if remembering lessons imparted by her late, lamented mother, Becky straightened her skirts and folded her hands in her lap. Callie thought her heart would burst with love and pity for this very proper, sober child. She asked softly, "All ready?"

Becky nodded. She looked extremely serious. "All ready."

"All right now. Hold on to your seat." She didn't realize until after she'd untied the rope ties and lifted the lid of the basket that Becky had taken her literally and unfolded her hands to grip the chair seat.

The emergence of Monster with a hiss and a spit was simultaneous with a gasp from his seated audience. He leaped out of the basket as if his legs were attached to springs.

"Oh, Miss Prophet!" Becky, unable to restrain herself, clapped.

Monster didn't like the clapping noise one teensy bit. He stopped dead still, arched his back, and looked for a second like a twenty-pound, jet-black and very furry porcupine with every single one of his multitudinous hairs abristle.

Callie said, "Oh, stop it, Monster."

"Monster?" The word was a breathless gasp.

Walking across the room, Callie held out both hands to Becky. She smiled her most comforting and charming smile. "It'll be *Mister* Monster to you, Becky love. Until he gets to know you. We have to maintain our decorum, after all." She laughed to let the little girl know she was joshing.

"Oh, Miss Prophet." Her eyes still wide, Becky gripped Callie's hand. "Oh, Miss Prophet, he's beautiful!"

The breathless quality of Becky's voice captured Callie's

attention. She watched the little face with interest. She'd never seen the child's eyes so huge or so fascinated. *Good*, she decided. The poor little thing needed to have something besides her loss to occupy her mind.

Speaking softly so as to disturb neither cat nor child, Callie said, "I hope you and he will like each other."

"I like him already."

Callie grinned. "Good. Believe it or not, he really likes to play. I have a ball he bats around like a baseball player."

Becky giggled. "Why's he called Monster?"

"It is sort of an undignified name, isn't it?"

Becky nodded.

"It's because he's so big. And also because when he came to live with me, I already had an elderly lady cat named Miss Naomi. Miss Naomi didn't like the invader at all."

"She didn't?" The girl sounded astounded.

"No, indeed. Miss Naomi didn't like sharing."

"Oh. Her feelings were hurt."

"Ex*act*ly. So, since he's so big and he sort of took over without waiting to be asked, I started calling him Monster."

"Ez*ack*ly," Becky repeated, nodding with understanding.

"They got used to each other after a while. Miss Naomi even started treating him like her own kitten."

Callie realized Becky had left off staring at Monster, and was now looking up at her. She smiled. "What is it, Becky? Do you have a question?"

Becky nodded. "Where's Miss Naomi?"

Oh, dear. The question took Callie by surprise. She could have kicked herself for not having thought about it before telling Becky about Miss Naomi. She had hoped that by bringing Monster with her, she would help Becky forget about death, not remind her of it. Still, it wouldn't do to lie. "Miss Naomi died last winter, sweetheart. She was almost twenty years old. That's pretty old for a cat."

"My mama was twenty-nine," Becky said gravely. "Is that old for a lady?"

Again, Callie's heart stumbled and ached. "No, sweetheart. That's not old at all. But your mama got sick. It was a terrible

shame." And if that wasn't an understatement, Callie didn't
know what was.

But Becky only nodded again, as if she were filing this
piece of information away to retrieve and study later. "My
papa said she was too young to die."

Lord in heaven. Fearing she'd cry if they continued to talk
about Becky's mama, Callie said bracingly, "It will probably
take Monster a little while to get used to his new surroundings, Becky, so I'm going to keep him in my room for a few
days. Cats don't like change much."

Becky nodded solemnly, as if she understood the cat's
qualms. "I don't, neither."

Instantly, tears sprang to Callie's eyes. She suppressed
them with ruthless severity. If she gave in to every impulse
of a soft nature that she experienced, she'd only turn Becky
into a cesspit of self-indulgence. There was a fine line between harsh abandonment and morbid pampering, and she
aimed to find and adhere to it. She had to, if she wanted to
help Becky.

Monster's hair had flattened out, although no amount of
inner serenity on his part could conceal his overall fluffiness,
and he'd begun a tentative, nervous inspection of his surroundings. Sitting on the desk chair, Callie picked Becky up
and plopped her onto her lap. She kept her arms around her.

"Let's just watch him for a minute. If he backs up to any
piece of furniture and starts to vibrate, I'll have to go grab
him before he causes any damage."

The notion that Monster might take it into his idiotic cat's
brain to mark a piece of hand-carved, imported, and undoubtedly wildly expensive Chinese teakwood furniture gave
Callie a spasm. She didn't think he would, as he'd never
marked anything at her house. She's spent many long hours
training him to use the sandbox when he'd first moved in
with her, as well, so she didn't anticipate any accidents. The
knowledge that life was unpredictable at the best of times,
however, and that cats were some of the most unpredictable
creatures in it, kept her vigilant.

"Why would he do that?" Becky whispered, keeping her

voice low evidently out of respect for the process they were observing.

Callie decided not to spoil the moment by explaining the odd and execrable behavior sometimes exhibited by male cats. Instead, she said seriously, "Sometimes cats just do things like that. It's not a good habit for them to get in to, so I'll want to nip it in the bud."

Becky only nodded again, thank goodness.

After a few minutes, during which Monster didn't do anything untoward, Callie said, "I think it's safe now. Would you like to help me unpack my things? I've an item or two you might be interested in."

"Oh, yes, please."

That the child should be so happy to help her do a job of work touched Callie's heart. Again. If this kept up, she'd become so attached to Becky she'd never be able to leave this house. The image of an elderly Callie Prophet, hobbling around with a cane and admonishing a grown-up Becky Lockhart to mind her manners made her giggle.

Becky looked at her curiously, but Callie only gave her a big hug.

# 3

Aubrey frowned when he heard Becky's squeal of delight issue from the room she'd begged he allot to Miss Callida Prophet. Pausing at the door to lean closer and listen, his brow wrinkled.

"Yes indeed, Becky."

Miss Prophet's voice, pleasant and with a smile in it, sailed out through the keyhole and into Aubrey's ear. He decided he liked her voice, although he wasn't at all sure he liked *her*. She was too young and too impertinent to be a proper nanny for his Becky.

The voice continued. "Alta, Florence, and I used to live in terror of our aunt Venetia. She's a *very* formidable dame."

"What's 'formable' mean?" Becky wanted to know.

In spite of himself, Aubrey smiled.

"Formidable means that she's the type of person around whom one always minds one's manners. She walks like this."

Aubrey wished he could see what Miss Prophet was doing now, because his daughter went off into shouts of laughter. The sound wrenched his heart. He hadn't heard Becky laugh like that since before Anne died.

"She walks like my great-aunt Evelyn!" Becky cried, still laughing.

"Oh, dear, I'm so sorry, dear."

Aubrey had to stifle a chuckle.

"And she talks like this," Miss Prophet continued. " 'None of your uppity ways, miss. Not here in New York, where proper manners prevail.' "

Miss Prophet's voice had taken on the broadest, twangiest, awfullest New York accent Aubrey had ever heard. Again, Becky shrieked with laughter. His own smile broadened.

"Oh, Miss Prophet! My tummy hurts from laughing!"

He could imagine Miss Prophet shaking her head in mock sympathy when she next spoke.

"Well, Miss Becky, if you laughed to Aunt Venetia's face, she'd have something to say about it. She doesn't approve of laughter."

"She doesn't?"

"No, ma'am. She thinks it's vulgar to laugh."

"Like my papa?"

Aubrey's smile evaporated abruptly.

A pause preceded Miss Prophet's next words. Aubrey didn't know if she was thinking about her answer or hanging something up. "I don't think your papa disapproves of laughter, Becky. I think he's just a little sad."

"His heart hurts," Becky said. "Like mine."

"Oh, sweetheart!"

Aubrey's ears detected a rustling of fabric, from which he gathered that Miss Prophet had picked Becky up and was hugging her. He entertained the nonsensical wish that he were a small boy and could be comforted by such means. But no such tender mercies were available to him.

Guilt stabbed at his heart when he thought about how unhappy Anne would have been to see him in this pathetic and pitiful state. Worse, she'd be appalled at how shamefully he'd been neglecting Becky.

With a sigh, he went on down the hall to his own room so he could change out of his riding clothes. He'd taken a trip to Santa Angelica to talk to Mr. Wilson about Miss Prophet. Unfortunately, Mr. Wilson had given her a sterling character reference, so Aubrey couldn't dismiss her on that account.

Not that he wanted to dismiss her if Becky liked her. He supposed he ought to give her a chance, even if she was too young, too rash, and too impudent, and didn't treat him with the proper deference.

Still, it galled him that Miss Callida Prophet didn't fit a single one of the images he'd formed of how a proper nanny should look and behave. He felt beleaguered by circumstances and very grumpy when he left his room.

All of Callie's clothes had been put away in their proper places. Her underwear had been commented upon by Becky, who didn't understand why Miss Prophet's drawers didn't have frilly lace edgings and elaborately embroidered flowers as her own did.

Callie had explained that when a young lady grew up, especially when she attained employment, she had, of necessity, to wear clothing that was more sober than frilly. She didn't mention the fact that she, although not dirt poor, couldn't afford the fabulously expensive clothing that Becky wore. She also didn't mention that she would rather see Becky in rags than living with a father who substituted frills for love.

Next, they'd fixed a sandbox for Monster. "Just in case he feels the need," Callie had told Becky with a wink.

The little girl had giggled merrily. Callie was glad to see her in such a happy frame of mind. And all because somebody who was willing to talk to her and listen to her had come into her life.

It wasn't right. It wasn't good. It was a crying shame that this little girl's life should have to be made bright by Callida Prophet, a stranger and a hired nanny. Callie wished she could smack Mr. Aubrey Lockhart about the head and shoulders with some kind of stick.

She pushed the thought aside and reminded herself of her promise to go easy on Becky's father. "All right, young lady, let's just see what your papa has in his library. I'll bet we can find something or other about New York."

Becky had been fascinated by Callie's stories of how she and her sisters used to dread trips to New York to visit their aunt. Callie had played up Aunt Venetia's sour side, with a prayer to her Maker for forgiveness. She didn't feel too guilty. Aunt Venetia really could be a beast without half trying, and Callie figured God would commend her for making this child happy, even if doing so involved telling one or two exaggerated tales about her aunt.

"You can show me on the globe where it is," Becky suggested cheerily.

"I can indeed." Providing Becky's papa wasn't ensconced in the room, in which case Callie planned to introduce a diversion. She didn't fancy running into Mr. Aubrey Lockhart until she absolutely had to.

The library door stood open, however, and there was no sign of Aubrey within. Callie heaved a gusty internal sigh. She wasn't afraid of him; it was only that she didn't want to tangle with him while she was so blasted mad at him. The longer she remained in Becky's company, the more firmly she believed the child needed her. More, she needed her father, the big lug.

Becky skipped into the room and darted over to a huge and beautiful globe standing on an ornamental teakwood stand.

"Here's Papa's globe. Can you show me New York?"

Callie joined her at the globe. "I certainly can. Can you show me where the United States is?"

Becky was happy to demonstrate her geographical knowledge. Before pointing out the United States, she reeled off the rest of the continents, much to Callie's delight.

"This one's Asia," the little girl said in a teacherish voice. "This is where most of my papa's business comes from. In China. See? This is China. Over here's India. He gets pretty things from India, too. He imports tea from both places."

"I see." Callie nodded soberly, although inside she was smiling.

"And this big one is 'Stralia. It's a big island, Papa says."

"I see."

"Papa says the English people used to send their criminals there." Becky shuddered eloquently. "*I* wouldn't like to live there with all those criminals."

"No, indeed." Callie didn't spoil Becky's moment by telling her that lots of the original settlers in the United States were deemed criminals by their British judges.

"And here's Europe. That's where Mama's ans'ters are from. Right here. In Wales."

"My goodness. That's very interesting, Becky. Do you know where your papa's ancestors came from?"

Becky nodded with vigor. "Yes. They came from another part of the same country. That's England. It's another big island, Papa used to say."

"Ah. The same place the criminals came from."

Becky looked up at her, shocked. "My papa isn't—"

Callie mentally smacked herself for being sarcastic about Becky's father in front of her. "Of course, he isn't a criminal." She made sure she sounded both positive and jolly. "I didn't mean it that way."

Still gazing up at her and looking puzzled, Becky said, "You mean it was a joke?"

A joke? "Well, sort of, although it wasn't a very good one. What I meant was that it wasn't only criminals who came from England, Becky. My own ancestors came from the same region. I think they originated in Scotland."

Becky's air of puzzlement didn't abate. "Where's that?"

Glad to change the subject, Callie showed her where Scotland was. "See? It's very close to England and Wales. They're neighbors."

"Oh. There are lots of countries close together there, huh?"

"There surely are. Do you know any of the other continents?"

"I know them all." The little girl sounded proud of her knowledge. Callie didn't begrudge her that; the poor thing needed to feel good about something.

"Can you show me?"

Nodding, Becky turned the globe. Callie noticed that she was very careful with it. Curious, because she'd also noticed that Becky mentioned her papa with regard to these geography lessons, she asked, "Was it your papa who told you where all the continents are, Becky?"

Becky nodded again. "Yes. He used to hold me on his lap and show me all the countries, too. He taught me lots."

"Ah. I see."

So. Mr. Remote hadn't always been such an old poop. Interesting.

"See? Here's Africa." Becky pointed. "People used to capture the natives and sell them to other people for slaves."

"That was very bad."

"Yes. That's what Papa said. He used to say slavery is one of the worse evils mankind ever thought up."

In spite of the dreadful topic, Callie smiled. She could almost hear Aubrey's voice coming out of his little girl's mouth. She jumped at the opportunity to mend a fence, too. "Your papa's right, Becky. Slavery is a great evil."

Becky nodded solemnly. "And here's Antarctica." She enunciated the difficult word slowly. "It's cold down there."

"Yes indeed."

"And where's the last continent, Becky?"

"Here!" Becky pointed her finger at it. "America! That's where we live."

"We sure do. Can you find Santa Angelica on the globe?"

Becky shook her head. "No. Papa said Santa Angelica is too small to show up on the globe. But it's about here." She pointed again. And she was right.

Callie was impressed. "Right you are. You're a smart girl, Becky."

"Papa said so, too."

It was almost always *Papa used to say*, Callie realized. She sighed. "Here, sweetheart, let me show you about where my aunt lives. New York City's a lot bigger than Santa Angelica, but I don't think it's big enough to show up on the globe, either. The world's a very big place. Here it is. This is where my aunt Venetia lives."

"That's way over on the other side of the country." Becky sounded surprised.

"It's a long way away. Three thousand miles, or thereabouts."

"That's a *real* long way."

"It sure is. And after you travel all that way, you have to see Aunt Venetia." Callie wrinkled her nose, and Becky giggled.

"So. Would you like to see if your papa has any books about New York or the eastern part of the United States?"

"Oh, yes!"

The excitement in Becky's voice made Callie happy. She was glad she'd applied and been accepted for this position. She might be a poor substitute for Becky's mother, but she was somebody, and it was already a great pleasure to pay attention to Becky Lockhart, who was a darling.

Callie and Becky searched the shelves. There were scads of books, some of which were novels. Callie presumed they'd been read and loved by Anne Lockhart and suppressed another sigh for Becky's loss. As she looked, Callie came across a shelf low to the floor that contained books written for children.

"Oh, look here, Becky. Here's a big picture book about the Pilgrims. That will probably tell us a lot about the people who settled in New York and thereabouts."

"I know about the Pilgrims."

Trying to sound casual, Callie said, "Did your papa tell you about them?"

Becky shook her head. "Mama used to read to me out of that book. It's all about the Pilgrims and early settlers." She delivered the last sentence in her teacher's voice.

Oh, dear. "Um, would you like me to find another book, sweetheart?" Above all things, Callie didn't want to stir up feelings of loss in her new charge. Becky'd had more than enough unhappiness to cope with lately.

"No. I like that book."

Studying her face, Callie decided Becky was telling the truth. The little girl even looked pleased that they'd be revisiting an old friend of a book.

"Good. Then let's sit over here by this window. I'll pull the curtain back for light."

Scampering over to the curtains behind a big, overstuffed chair, Becky pulled them back for Callie. "This is where Mama and I used to sit when she read to me."

Settling herself in the chair—which was every bit as comfortable as it looked—Callie patted her lap. "Want to sit here, Becky? Or you can sit on the arm of the chair if you'd rather."

If Mr. Lockhart ever found out she'd invited his daughter to squash his expensive furniture, he'd probably pitch a fit, she thought nastily. Then she took herself to task. Evidently he hadn't *always* been such a prune. According to the driblets of information Becky had let fall today, he'd actually been more or less human, once upon a time.

Ignoring the arm of the chair, Becky scrambled up onto Callie's lap. "I like the one about the Indians and Jamestown," she told Callie as she climbed.

"Jamestown was in what is now the state of Virginia, but if you'd like we could start there and work our way up to New York."

"Good. I'd like that."

"All right, then, we'll start with Jamestown." After consulting the index, Callie turned to page twenty-three, and started reading in a dramatic voice, " 'The first permanent British settlement was established in 1607. The coming of settlers to the New World, however, was not without dire incident. During their first hard winter, the citizens of Jamestown, in the Colony of Virginia . . .' "

Aubrey felt gloomy as he descended the stairs, intending to visit his library and do some work before he resumed brooding about his miserable life. He wished he could get over this. Not that he'd ever truly get over losing Anne. Such a thing was impossible.

But he could certainly use a little spirit and joy in his life. For two years now, he'd felt as if God had ripped his heart right out of his body. The wound refused to heal, and he was tired of it.

Although he hated to admit it, he believed that perhaps

he'd done his daughter a favor by hiring the rambunctious Miss Prophet. At least Becky's new nanny had made his little girl laugh.

"Which is a damned sight more than you've been able to do for the past couple of years," he lectured himself. "You ought to thank the impertinent busybody."

He reached his library and put a hand on the knob, then stopped still because he heard Callie's voice. Frowning, irked that she'd invaded his brooding room, he listened.

" 'After stopping in Amsterdam for several months, the British Pilgrims set sail for the Americas, landing in what came to be called Plymouth, in Massachusetts, in 1620.' "

Aubrey's heart stopped for a second, then started careening in his chest. A rage as red as blood rushed over him and receded into an icy lump. He'd heard those same words often in the past, but he'd never expected to hear them again. Hearing them now, read by Miss Callida Prophet, made him want to hit something.

When he entered the room and saw Callie, sunlight streaming through the window and glinting off her strawberry-blond hair, and Becky curled up cozily in her lap, he felt as if he'd been struck by lightning.

The feeling lasted approximately fifteen seconds, after which rage engulfed him again, much as if he'd been the victim of spontaneous combustion. *"What the devil are you doing?"*

Callie and Becky had both been engrossed in the story of the Pilgrims in Plymouth, and jumped as if the same bolt of lightning that had recently struck Aubrey had then changed direction and struck them.

"Papa!" Becky exclaimed, her blue eyes huge.

"Mr. Lockhart!"

Callie looked thunderstruck for about a tenth of a second, before fury overtook her alarm. Her arm went around Becky, and she gave the little girl a comforting hug.

Aubrey was too shaken to care that he'd frightened his daughter. He resented Callie daring to usurp a position as comforter to Becky. He resented everything about her. He wanted her to go away. When he'd heard Callie reading the same book Anne used to read, and had then seen her in the same chair Anne used to sit in, holding Becky in exactly the same way Anne used to do, all of his common sense had fled. The only thing he wanted from Callie was that she leave his room and his life.

"Get out of here." His voice shook with rage. He couldn't help it.

"Well!" Callie closed the book with a snap and, lifting Becky in her arms, stood up. "I guess we'd best take our reading elsewhere, sweetheart."

"Papa?"

Becky looked scared. As well she might, Aubrey thought with a sudden jolt of pain. He passed a hand over his face, beginning to understand how irrational his reaction had been, even if it had been unintentional.

"Becky," he said, and his voice trembled slightly. "I—I'm sorry, Becky. I—I—"

"Never mind." Callie's smile was as stiff and cold as an icicle. "We'll find more congenial surroundings, Mr. Lockhart. I'm *so* sorry we disturbed you."

The sarcasm in her voice and manner annoyed Aubrey. He wanted to say something, to further apologize to his daughter, but feared that, if he tried to, he'd shout. He'd already shouted. Shouting wasn't fair to Becky. He'd *really* like to shout at Miss Prophet. He'd like to tell her to get the hell out of his house and his life and never come back.

He was shaking when Callie marched herself and Becky out of his library and closed the door with a hint of a slam behind her. As soon as the room was clear of extraneous females, Aubrey lowered himself into his desk chair, folded his arms on his desk, buried his head in them, and proceeded to call himself as many foul names as he could come up with.

Never, in all her born days, had Callie met a more selfish, overbearing, crabby, and touchy specimen of humankind as Mr. Aubrey Lockhart.

It had taken her a good forty-five minutes to calm Becky

down after Aubrey's tantrum in the library. Whatever had caused him to roar at them like that?

Not that it mattered. He had no right—no right at all—to act like that in front of his daughter.

Callie and Becky had discussed the incident, although Callie'd had to do some prodding to get the little girl to open up. But, blast it all, the child needed to unburden herself.

The conclusion Becky and she had eventually come to was that Becky's papa didn't feel well.

" 'Cause he never yells at me," Becky said in a tiny, worried voice. "Maybe he's sick."

*He's sick, all right,* Callie thought indignantly. She said, "I suppose that's the answer. Sometimes when people don't feel well, they get grumpy. I know I do."

Becky looked up at her, alarmed. "Do you?"

With a laugh, Callie reassured her. "Don't worry, sweetheart, I'll never yell at you. Well," she added with a wink, "not unless you do something *really* bad."

She'd expected Becky to smile, or maybe even laugh a little at her wink, but evidently Aubrey's tantrum had bothered her a lot. "I won't," she said, far too seriously for a child her age. "I promise."

Normally, Becky's reserved, adult behavior would have brought a tear to Callie's eye. Today, however, it only served to make Callie even angrier and more determined to help the little girl.

As soon as she thought Becky had recovered enough to be left in the kitchen with Mrs. Granger and a glass of lemonade, Callie went in search of Mr. Lockhart. If it cost her the job she'd only just assumed today, she intended to deliver unto him a large piece of her mind.

The door to the library was closed. Callie suspected he was in there, wallowing in self-pity. She drew herself up as straight as she could, sucked in a deep breath, mentally uttered a prayer for strength, and rapped sharply on the door.

Immediately a sound of creaking hinges came to her, as if someone had been startled into sitting up suddenly. She hoped so. The man badly needed startling.

"Who is it?"

He sounded fretful. So be it. Callie was feeling rather fretful herself. Without answering, she turned the doorknob, pushed the door open, and walked into the room. She was pleased to see that Mr. Lockhart hadn't anticipated such a daring gesture from a member of his staff. When he saw who had dared invade his privacy, he scowled at her, but Callie just scowled right back.

"Mr. Lockhart," she said in her steeliest voice, "we need to talk about Becky."

He didn't stand as a gentleman should, but continued to sit sprawled in his chair, glowering for all he was worth, which was a good deal. This lapse in manners was not lost on Callie.

"What about Becky?" he barked, his voice full of anger and annoyance.

No quantity of barks was going to prevent Callie from fulfilling what she perceived as her duty. "You upset her terribly when you shouted at us earlier. It has taken me all this time to soothe her poor nerves."

"Hmm."

She pressed her lips together in fury before opening them again. "It's all very well for you to say '*hmm,*' Mr. Lockhart, but the fact is that your daughter is in a very fragile state right now. In case it's slipped your mind, she lost her mother just a year ago.

His glower deepened. "In case it's slipped my *mind?*"

Callie lifted her chin. "Yes. And in case it's slipped your mind as well, your daughter is only six years old. I understand that you prefer to languish in your own selfish grief and ignore hers, but you've hired me to care for her, and I shan't put up with anyone, even you, undermining my job."

"*You* shan't put up with it?" he goggled, incredulous.

As well he might. Callie could hardly credit herself with this stroke of boldness. She made a conscious effort to relax her hands, which had balled into fists. She knew her cheeks must be flaming, because she was burning with rage.

"No," she declared stoutly. "I shall not. In the few months I've known Becky, I've become very fond of her, sir. She's a darling, dear child, and she doesn't deserve such a father as you."

"Why, you—" Aubrey started to rise from his chair.

Callie trampled over whatever he'd been going to say, sensing that if she didn't get it out now, she might never have another chance. "I say that," she continued brutally, "not because I believe you don't love your daughter, but because I know your late wife would be horrified to see you neglect her as you are doing."

"My late wife," he said, and Callie could see his clenched teeth, "was a saint. You have no business to refer to her at all, young woman, and I won't permit—"

"Yes," Callie said, again interrupting, "I know. Your late wife was universally esteemed and admired. She was a woman of great love and humanity. It's a pity that she didn't instill some of the same qualities in you while she had the chance. It may be too late to redeem you, but I *still* won't allow you to bully my charge while I'm in your employ."

He'd risen to his feet and now towered over Callie. She wanted to shrink back and scuttle out of the room, but she wouldn't allow her fear of Aubrey's anger to overcome her mission. Becky needed her, and, more importantly, Becky needed Aubrey. As dramatic as it sounded, Callie perceived this confrontation as something of a battle for Becky's life.

"And what makes you think you're going to remain in my employ after this act of impudence, Miss Prophet?"

Callie had feared it would come to this. She supposed it was better that it happen now rather than after she'd been in the house long enough for Becky to form an even deeper attachment to her.

She took another deep breath and said a quick mental prayer before she started to speak. "I believe I shall stay in your employ, Mr. Lockhart, because however much you don't like me or want me here, you and your daughter need me. Although you have chosen to have nothing to do with your daughter—a rather blockheaded move if you ask me—you've evidently noticed that she needs someone upon whom she can rely. And that someone is me. So the way I see it, you've got two choices: either take care of your daughter by yourself, or keep me—someone your daughter trusts and cares about—as her nanny. Becky and I get along too well for you to dismiss me out of pique."

Aubrey roared, "Out of *pique*?"

Unflinching, outwardly—inwardly she'd flinched into a quivering ball of anxiety—Callie said, "Yes. Out of pique. You know you're doing your child a great disservice in ignoring her as you've been doing all these months. That's why you hired me in the first place. If you dismiss me now, you will be doing it for your own selfish reasons and disregarding Becky's welfare. I don't believe even *you* would sink to that depth."

She saw his chest expand with the lungful of air he drew in. He had a rather impressive physique, if one were in a mood to admire such things. Callie decided to ponder Aubrey's physique later. She stared straight back at him, daring him by her posture and her glittering eyes—at least she hoped they were glittering—to deny that what she'd just said was the truth.

He didn't. Instead, after standing for several seconds in a pose reminiscent of a great Indian on the warpath, he let his breath out slowly. Callie had no illusion that he'd calmed down though—it was clear from the dour look on his face that he was still as mad as flinders. "Get out of my library, Miss Prophet." His speech was measured, as if he were trying hard not to yell. "For the sake of my daughter, I won't fire you *this* time," placing special emphasis on the *this*. "But I warn you, I don't tolerate impertinence from my hired help."

"Of course not." Callie had to take a pretty deep breath herself. She didn't really want to say what she aimed to say next, but felt it would be to Becky's benefit to do so. Therefore, although it cost her an internal pang, she said, "And I didn't mean this chat—"

"Chat?" Aubrey snorted.

Callie chose to ignore his outburst. "I didn't mean it to be impertinent. You need to understand that when you yell at Becky for what seems to her no reason at all, you upset her." She went on, wondering if she was right. "I know that you love your daughter and want only what's best for her."

He nodded. She took some encouragement from that and continued her speech.

"Therefore, if you will think before you yell in the future, I believe it would be best for Becky."

He said nothing.

She waited.

He said nothing some more.

Taking this as a sign that she'd best not push her luck, Callie decided to do something she rarely did unless she was in the presence of her formidable aunt Venetia. She curtsied.

"Thank you, Mr. Lockhart. I shan't disturb you any longer."

Callie thought he said, "Good," as she headed for the door, but she wasn't positive. And she sure as anything wasn't going to ask him if he'd spoken.

*4*

Aubrey stood, quaking and staring at the library door, for several minutes after Callie Prophet exited the room.

How dare she? How *dare* she scold him about how he treated his own daughter? He couldn't believe she'd done such a thing. The vicious-tongued witch.

He wasn't sure if he was more furious because she'd dared to enter his sanctum and challenge him about his behavior or because she was right. Suddenly all the rage evaporated and he slumped into his chair, deflated as a pricked balloon.

"Damn it, she *is* right," he muttered to the empty room. He'd known it all along but, until Miss Callie Prophet barged into his life, no one had challenged him about his deplorable abandonment of his child. Aubrey loved Becky with all his heart, but, without Anne there to help him, he had no clue as to how to deal with Becky. Anne had been the one who'd bridged communications between himself and his child.

Dash it, he was a man. Men weren't supposed to rear children by themselves. That's why he'd hired the impossible Miss Prophet to begin with. Damn her.

Oh, he knew his reaction to seeing and hearing them in that chair had been illogical. But when he'd discovered them in the same chair Anne used to sit in, reading the book Anne used to read from, he'd undergone such a powerful wrench of agony he hadn't been able to stop himself. Not, of course, that his reason justified his shouting at Becky. He knew he shouldn't have done it. He wouldn't mind hollering at Miss Prophet for hours at a time, but Becky didn't deserve such treatment from the only parent she had left.

He was still brooding when Figgins sounded the gong to call the household to dinner. Aubrey had told Mrs. Granger before he'd hired Callie that the nanny was to be treated as a member of the household and would, accordingly, take meals with them in the dining room. He presumed the ever-efficient Mrs. Granger had communicated this message to Callie already, damn it, so there was probably no way he could avoid her. He dreaded seeing Callie at dinner and having to pretend everything was rosy between them.

If he'd had his wits about him when he'd considered hiring a nanny, he'd have made arrangements for the nanny and Becky to dine in the nursery together. That's the way most affluent families went about mealtimes. But Anne hadn't had any use for traditions that estranged her from her daughter and so the Lockharts had always dined together as a family.

Even after Anne's death, Aubrey had taken his meals with his daughter. They'd been strange, strained affairs, since he felt awkward around Becky, but he hadn't had the heart to banish her from the dining room because of his own deficiencies. He'd hoped a nice nanny would assume the role of facilitator between father and daughter.

But, dash it all, Becky's nanny wasn't supposed to have been Callie Prophet. Becky's nanny was supposed to have been a kindhearted, elderly lady with gray hair, false teeth, and a hearing trumpet.

Aubrey sighed as he shrugged into his jacket, straightened his cravat, and headed for the dining room. He felt rather as he imagined a convicted murderer might as he trudged to the gallows.

Miss Prophet and Becky were waiting for him in the sitting room leading into the dining room. He forced himself to smile at the two of them, although his smile for Becky was much easier than the one he drummed up for Miss Prophet.

She, damn her impudence, gazed with serene complacency at him and smiled as if she hadn't a care in the world.

Becky, rather tentatively, Aubrey thought, said, "H'lo, Papa. Mrs. Granger fixed chicken and dumplings for us tonight."

"Ah," said Aubrey as he tugged one of her braids, "your favorite, I believe."

The tension seemed to vanish from Becky's small body, and she grinned like the imp she could be—or used to be, when her mother was alive. "Oh, yes! I love chicken and dumplings. I asked Mrs. Granger to fix it special, for Miss Prophet."

Aubrey glanced at Callie. "Indeed."

Callie said, "Indeed. Good evening, Mr. Lockhart."

"Good evening."

If the world were a just place, thought Aubrey, Miss Callida Prophet would be an ugly, bucktoothed, weak-chinned, gangly specimen of womanhood, and well past her prime. As he'd been made aware of long ago, however, the world was far from just, and she wasn't any of those things.

In reality, Callie Prophet was a lovely young woman— well, to look at, he silently ammended. Her personality was another matter. If, Aubrey brooded unhappily, one were merely to look at her, one might judge her to be a cheerful girl with a friendly personality to match her bright eyes and gleaming blond hair.

Oh, but life could be a cruel deceiver sometimes, as Aubrey well knew. He had railed at God more than once for the many unkindnesses He had visited upon him.

And Becky.

Dash it, there he went again, forgetting about his daughter, and the struggles she had gone through as well. After holding a chair for Callie, Aubrey did the same for Becky, and tipped her a wink at the same time. She goggled up at him, and he had to fight a frown. Good God, was the poor child so unused to her father's jolly side that she perceived his wink as something rare and unseemly?

Well, and why shouldn't she? he instantly thought. He'd been mooning around the house like a lost soul for a year and more.

Hell's bells. As Aubrey sat at the head of the table gazing at his beautiful daughter, he was swamped with a sudden sense of hopelessness. He wanted so badly to reach out to her, to heal the damage he had inflicted upon her tender psyche, but he had no idea where, let alone how to start. Aubrey sighed inwardly as another thought hit him. Although it pained him to admit it, he was honestly glad that he hadn't dismissed Miss Prophet when she'd lectured him. If he had, he'd have made Becky even more unhappy than she already was, and that would have been ghastly.

"Would you like me to say grace, Papa?"

His daughter's trilling voice dragged Aubrey out of the pit of despair he'd managed to get stuck in. He glanced at her and forced another smile. "That would be very good of you, Becky."

It touched his heart when his little daughter obediently folded her hands, bowed her head, and said in her sweet, piping voice, "Thank you, God, for our chicken and dumplings. And thank you for sending Miss Prophet to live with us. God bless Mama in heaven, and Papa, and Miss Prophet. And Mrs. Granger," she added in something of a rush, leading Aubrey to understand she'd only just then realized she ought to bless the lady who'd cooked the food. "And thank you, God, for letting the Pilgrims come to America. Amen."

The first thing Aubrey noticed when he opened his eyes was the smile on Miss Prophet's face. He wished he hadn't. Her smile was lovely. Wrenching his gaze away from her, he said to Becky, "That was a very nice blessing, Becky. Thank you."

He'd suffered a slight pang when she'd mentioned the Pilgrims, recalling his temper fit earlier in the day. He'd been wrong to shout at Becky and Miss Prophet, although he'd sooner beat his head against a brick wall than apologize to Callie Prophet.

Callie seemed unfazed when she said, "Yes, Becky, that

was a very nice prayer. It's good of you to remember our founding fathers, too."

Becky, who was seated across from Miss Prophet at the large and imposing dining table, gazed at her with interest. "What's that?"

"What's what?" Callie asked. "Oh. You mean our founding fathers?"

The little girl nodded. Aubrey noticed how her blond braids caught the lamplight when they bounced. She was the image of Anne, God bless her. God, being the cruel fellow He was, had better not take Becky from Aubrey. That would be too cruel, even for Him.

He hadn't been paying attention to Callie's answer to Becky's question in regard to the founding fathers. His mind swerved to the present again, however, when he heard Becky ask, "But why don't they talk about our founding mothers, Miss Prophet? Didn't the ladies come, too, along with the gentlemen?"

There went Miss Prophet's smile again. And her green eyes did twinkle quite charmingly. Aubrey wished he hadn't noticed. Fortunately for him, Delilah, the maid who served the meals, ladled out a plate of soup, forcing him to drag his gaze from Callie.

"The ladies came, too, Becky, but the people who write history books generally tend to ignore women's contributions to progress, no matter which country's history they're recording."

"How come?"

"That," said Miss Prophet, smiling brightly at Delilah as she served soup before her, "is one of the mysteries of life."

"Thank you, Delilah," Becky said perkily as her own soup appeared in front of her. She picked up her spoon and took a sip before she spoke again.

"This is delicious soup," Callie murmured.

"It's real good," agreed Becky. "Mrs. Granger's a good cook." She set her spoon carefully on her plate. "You know what I'm going to do when I grow up, Miss Prophet?"

"No, I don't believe we've discussed that yet," said Callie, with her beautiful smile and her twinkly eyes. "Do you have plans?"

After spooning up another sip, Becky nodded. "I'm gonna write a history book about the ladies."

"What a brilliant idea!" Callie beamed at the little girl.

Aubrey glanced from one young lady to the other, feeling left out, as if Becky didn't need him anymore now that she had Callie. He cleared his throat, drawing their attention to him, and then he felt embarrassed. "I think," he said in a judicious voice, "that's a very good idea, Becky."

Becky grinned, pleased. "You do?"

She sounded surprised, which made Aubrey want to frown. Dash it, the girl acted as if she were afraid of him, and that was nonsensical. He'd never done anything to foster fear in his child. He'd always loved her. *Always.* In fact, now that Anne was gone, Becky was the most important person in his life. If he'd been a little distant these past few months, it was only because of circumstances.

He caught Callie eyeing him ironically and disliked her for it. A lot.


As Callie helped Becky dress for bed, she congratulated herself on surviving her first day on the job. It had been truly hellish at times, although Becky was a darling. Callie didn't think she'd ever want to leave Becky.

Becky's father, however, was another matter entirely. She was still amazed that he hadn't fired her earlier that afternoon when she'd confronted him about his bellowing fit.

As she folded back the bedclothes and Becky climbed into her pretty four-poster bed with its pink-and-white tester and counterpane, Callie said, "Would you like me to hear your prayers, sweetheart?"

"Yes, please. Mama used to hear my prayers every night before bed." Becky sighed deeply.

"Did she?" Callie sighed, too, remembering how her own mother had done the same for her. "Does your papa ever come up to hear them?"

Becky shrugged. "Sometimes. But most of the time, it's

Mrs. Granger who comes upstairs with me." A sad look passed over Becky's face only to be replaced seconds later with a glowing smile. "But now that you're here, you can do it."

"I'm very happy to be here, Becky, and I promise to hear your prayers whenever you want me to."

"I'm happy you're here, too." She wiggled into a more comfortable position on her soft pillows.

Good. That made two happy and one grouchy household inhabitant. Callie imagined she'd get along well with the rest of the staff. Most of them lived in Santa Angelica and she'd known them for years. She wished there was some way to get through to Aubrey.

With a small pang of guilt, she wondered if she'd been wise to confront him so boldly this afternoon. Once one confronted a man without mincing one's words, it generally took the rest of one's life to get him to climb down from his high horse.

On the other hand, Callie had perceived no other course of action. She couldn't, in good conscience, have allowed the incident to pass by unremarked upon. If she'd used subtlety, she knew good and well he'd have either ignored her or pretended not to understand. Therefore, she guessed she'd done the best thing for Becky, and that was what mattered. He'd probably hate her forever, but that couldn't be helped.

She didn't know why her heart ached a little at the notion of Aubrey Lockhart hating her, but it did.

"Miss Prophet?"

"Yes, Becky?" Callie scolded herself for letting her mind wander.

The little girl hesitated, then said, "Do you think Papa likes me?"

"Oh, Becky!" Callie scooped Becky into her arms and hugged her hard. "Of course, he likes you! He *loves* you. Very much."

Becky hugged her back without speaking for a moment. Callie, for perhaps the hundredth time that day, felt like crying. She settled Becky back on her pillows and stroked her cheek. "Darling Becky, your papa has suffered a lot, just as you have, because your mama got sick and died. I think it's taking him some time to adjust to not having her around."

"He used to laugh a lot," Becky admitted. "He doesn't laugh anymore. I guess it's 'cause he's not adjusting."

"Well," Callie said in a bracing voice, "we'll just have to help him learn to laugh again."

"How?"

Children could ask the most awkward questions sometimes. Callie admitted softly, "I'm not sure. We'll have to put on our thinking caps and try to find some way to make him laugh. Okay?"

Becky smiled up at her. "Okay."

"Let's hear those prayers now, young lady."

So Becky said her prayers, which included a lot of blessings for the grown-ups in her life, and Callie listened with a tear in her eye and an ache in her heart.

Callie Prophet had been living in the Lockhart mansion for a week, and Aubrey needed to get some work done. He could neither understand nor justify his compulsion to stand at his library window and watch Becky and Miss Prophet frolicking on the back lawn.

Although it was only midmorning, Miss Prophet had lugged out a big wicker picnic basket and set it under a tree. She and Becky were ignoring the basket at the moment, and were playing some kind of game that included a lot of running around and shouting.

His thoughts retreated into the past, and he recalled watching Anne and Becky together. Anne had been much more decorous than the rollicking Miss Prophet, but she and Becky had loved playing together. Evidently Miss Prophet didn't know the meaning of the word *quiet*.

Torn between amusement and irritation, Aubrey pushed the window up in order to hear better. The joyful sounds of laughter smote his ears. Becky had picked up a big stick and held it thrust out before her with her hands horizontal to the ground.

"They call me Little John," she roared, making her voice go as low as she could, which wasn't very.

"Little John? But you're enormous!" Callie propped her hands on her hips and adopted a swaggering pose. "Let me pass, you varlet."

Becky giggled. "Make me."

"All right for you, then I shall!"

With feigned menace, Callie strode toward Becky, who stood her ground fiercely and waggled her stick at Callie. The two met and engaged in a counterfeit battle that ended with Callie taking a tumble on the lawn. Her skirts and petticoats went flying, and Aubrey was privileged to a view of her shapely legs encased in plain cotton drawers.

In the time it took him to blink in astonishment, not untainted by appreciation, she'd popped up again and started shaking her fist at tiny Becky. "Why, you big overgrown scoundrel, you!"

"Aha!" cried Becky. "I bested you in battle, Robin Hood! How do you like *that*?"

Aubrey shook his head and wondered why he hadn't figured out what they were playing at before now. He'd been so engrossed in watching, it hadn't occurred to him that they were enacting the Robin-Hood-meets-Little-John scene from *The Adventures of Robin Hood*. Now he remembered that Becky loved to be read to from that book. Anne used to read it to her and now she'd obviously talked Miss Prophet into doing the same.

He was ashamed of himself for not having thought to read to his daughter before this. Reading only required his voice and some time. He wouldn't even have had to think of how to keep a conversation going. He'd only have had to read words someone else had already made up and written down. But he'd been too involved in his own grieving to read to Becky, and now she had Miss Prophet to do it and didn't need him anyway.

"Damnation, will you stop that, Aubrey Lockhart?" Hearing his own voice startled him. Yet the question that had prompted the command was a valid one, and Aubrey contemplated it as he gazed out the window and onto the happy scene.

Why did he always put the worst connotation on things? He turned away from the window and wandered to his desk. He didn't used to be such a dismal specimen of mankind. He seemed to have turned a corner somewhere in the last couple of years, however, and now it was as if he barred good thoughts at the door of his consciousness and only allowed the depressing ones to enter.

Frowning, he sat in his big chair and drew a ledger forward. He needed to get some work done.

Although he forced himself to concentrate, from time to time snippets of song and conversation came through the open window from Becky and Callie. They were having a marvelous time. Aubrey knew he had no right or reason to harbor this sense of ill-usage in his breast. It was his own fault if Becky turned away from him and clung to Miss Prophet, who was paying attention to her.

Dash it, he was jealous. What a lowering reflection.

Later, he heard the word "monster" every now and then and assumed the play had turned from Robin Hood to something along the lines of Frankenstein. Aubrey didn't know that he approved of Miss Prophet reading Mrs. Shelley's eerie book to such a young child. He might have to have a talk with her about it. The prospect made him grip his pen more tightly and grit his teeth.

Irked with himself, both for being distracted and, more, for being envious of Callida Prophet, he finally rose and walked over to shut the window. He *had* to get some work done.

Rearing children was women's work. He'd finally hired a woman to do it. He had no reason to be offended because she was doing it.

No matter how hard he tried, however, Aubrey couldn't rid himself of the notion that Becky's adoration of her new nanny would be easier to take if her new nanny were eighty-five years old and hard of hearing.

\* \* \*

Callie Prophet had been working as Becky's nanny—although it hardly seemed like work to her—for three weeks before Becky showed her the letters.

During those weeks, Callie had helped Becky write letters to her mother in heaven. She'd answered the letters she'd helped to write as well, feeling only a little bit guilty about continuing to do so. After all, she reasoned, it was important for Becky to know that at least *one* of her parents cared about her thoughts and feelings.

Becky's father certainly didn't.

Well, she temporized, forcing herself to be honest, it wasn't that he didn't *care*, exactly. Actually, he'd seemed a little less withdrawn lately. He might even turn human one of these days, although Callie wouldn't have laid any bets on the possibility. But Callie wanted Becky to be absolutely certain of her late mother's love.

Children were so apt to misunderstand the loss of a loved one, believing themselves to be somehow responsible for it. Therefore, Callie persisted.

The summer had started fading into autumn, the days were getting shorter, and the nights had begun to contain a decided nip. Callie and Mrs. Granger had got out the quilts that had been packed away during the hot weather.

It was eight o'clock, Becky's bedtime, and Callie had just brushed and braided the little girl's hair.

"You have the prettiest hair, Becky. It's just like your mama's." Callie didn't know that for a fact, although she imagined that when Anne was young, she had looked just like Becky.

"That's what Papa and Mrs. Granger say," Becky told her complacently.

Callie smiled. She said, "Your mama was a beautiful woman, inside and out, Becky. If you try hard, you'll be like her when you grow up."

"That would be nice."

Callie thought she detected a shade of dreaminess in Becky's voice. "Yes, it would."

"Everybody loved Mama," Becky acknowledged.

"Indeed, they did." Callie put down the hairbrush and patted Becky's shoulder. "There you go, young lady. Hop into bed now, and I'll listen to your prayers."

Becky was silent when she climbed into her bed and pulled up the covers. She scrutinized Callie's face with an intensity Callie hadn't seen before.

A trifle unnerved by the child's unusual demeanor, Callie asked, "Is anything the matter, Becky? Do you need to tell me anything or talk about something?"

Becky shook her head. "No." She pressed her lips together for a moment, then burst out with, "But you could help me, maybe."

Startled, Callie said, "I'd be happy to help you, sweetheart, but first you'll have to tell me what you need help with."

Spots of color burned in Becky's cheeks. She hesitated for another moment or two, then said, "I want you to read some letters to me. I can't read the big words."

"Some letters?" For goodness sake. Was Becky carrying on a clandestine correspondence with someone other than her mother? Callie knew the child was enterprising, but she couldn't imagine her being *this* enterprising. She was, after all, only six years old. "I'll be happy to help you, Becky."

Quick as a wink, Becky climbed out of bed, walked to her closet, and opened the door. With a glance back at Callie, she stooped, reached, and grabbed the handle of a suitcase that had been sitting on the floor since Callie's arrival in the Lockhart mansion, and, Callie assumed, for a long time before that. The little girl struggled to haul the suitcase out of the closet.

"They're in here."

"Would you like me to help you?"

Becky shook her head. "No, thank you. I can do it." She grunted. "I do it every night."

"You do? I didn't know that."

"Nobody knows. They're my secret." Becky had managed to pull the suitcase out of the closet. Now she sat in front of it and pressed the latch.

When she opened the lid, Callie saw a stack of letters, tied with a pink ribbon. It looked to her as though Becky had untied the ribbon and tried to tie it again, without much success. Little girl fingers had to learn ribbon-tying skills over a number of years. Six years wasn't long enough.

Callie experienced a sinking feeling in her stomach when Becky picked up the letters and trotted over to her bed. She laid them carefully on the pink-and-white counterpane and stood back. "I found these," she said simply. "It was after Mama died. I was sad, and I was walking around the house, thinking about things, and I found these in a drawer of Mama's desk."

Oh, dear. "I see. Um, they belonged to your mama?"

The little girl nodded. "My papa wrote them to her."

Good heavens. Callie wasn't at all sure she wanted to delve into love letters, if these *were* indeed love letters, written by the bereaved Mr. Aubrey Lockhart to his dead wife. It seemed so . . . intrusive. Snoopy. Sly, even.

"They made me feel better, so I put them in my closet and I read them after you tuck me in bed. Only I don't read as good as you do."

Becky handed Callie a couple of the letters. Callie took them, feeling more uncertain than usual. It wasn't proper to read someone's private correspondence. It was interfering and meddlesome. She turned the letters over on her lap so that the penmanship wasn't visible.

"They make me happy," Becky said simply.

Callie was lost. Although she knew she shouldn't, and that she would hate herself for what she was about to do, she took up the first letter and opened it. Becky climbed back into bed, snuggled against a pillow, folded her hands on the counterpane, and said, "He called her Annie."

There was wonder in the small voice. Callie swallowed hard. Oh, dear. Oh, dear.

Carefully unfolding the paper, she saw the firm, crisp, bold hand of a man. She cleared her throat.

She read. " 'My Darling Annie . . .' "

# 5

Callie lay in her own bed for hours that night after reading Becky two of Aubrey Lockhart's letters to his late wife. Becky had been wide-eyed and sparkling with joy to have all of the words pronounced for her. Callie herself had been fascinated, but not awfully joyful.

And now here she lay unable to sleep, tossing and turning, pondering the nature of love and loss. Every now and then she had to wipe a tear from her cheek.

She felt stupid. She also felt as if she'd done something inexcusably wrong.

But when Becky had told her that reading from the letters made her feel better, Callie couldn't have resisted if she'd tried. Actually, she *had* tried. A little. But not much.

Lines from the first letter echoed in her head: "Knowing that our love has created another life gives me a sense of awe, darling Annie. A child of ours. It is a blessing and a miracle."

Another letter left her in awe:

*My Darling Annie, When I hold you, the world falls away. Suddenly, miraculously, everything vanishes—*

*my fears, my worries, my sorrows—and I know only
you. Your lips. Your eyes. Your tender, trusting love . . .
I hope that you will never leave my arms. I know that
you will never leave my heart.*

He'd called his wife *darling*. Darling Annie. Aubrey Lockhart, who appeared to be as cold and distant as the moon
and the stars, had once cherished a woman and called her
*darling*.

Callie had never been as emotionally moved as she had
been when she'd read those letters. She'd been unable to read
more than the first two, because she didn't want to cry in
front of Becky. If she'd continued reading them, she'd have
been running like the Mississippi River in flood.

It amazed her that two people could adore each other as
Aubrey and Anne Lockhart had. They'd seemed in perfect
harmony, a sublime match made in heaven.

Callie didn't imagine that such genuine, deep, and abiding
love, complete with passion, respect, honor, admiration, and
happiness occurred very often in the world. She wondered if
her brother, George, and his wife, Marie, shared that same
kind of love. She supposed they did; the way they looked at
each other when they believed no one else was watching was
definitely a clue.

*My darling Callie.* She rolled the words around on her
tongue, but they didn't feel right, and the not-right feeling
depressed her.

She couldn't imagine a man cherishing her or ever calling
her his darling Callie. And it wasn't only because she thought
Anne a name with more harmonious potential than Callie,
either. The fact of the matter was that she'd believed for
some time now that she wasn't the sort of woman a man
*could* cherish, as she was far too independent and opinion-
ated.

Anne Lockhart had been a dear, gentle creature without a
spine or a single thought to call her own.

"Stop it this instant, Callie Prophet! Anne Lockhart was a
wonderful person, and everyone who knew her thought so,
too."

Appalled by her own mean-spirited critique—an unjust
and completely erroneous one, which made it even worse—
Callie turned over and slammed a fist into her pillow. It was
ridiculous to allow herself to be made melancholy by a couple of letters. It was stupid. Foolish beyond reason.

Oh, but when she recalled the passage Aubrey had written
in the second letter, she wanted to swoon:

> *My darling Annie,*
> *I can't find words to express the wonder I feel every*
> *time I see our beautiful daughter. And when I walked*
> *into the nursery this morning to find you and Rebecca*
> *together—well, I knew my life was complete in that*
> *instant. Thank you, my wonderful darling, for our Re-*
> *becca. She is the completion of our family. She is the*
> *perfect and magnificent affirmation of our love.*

Callie had long been under the impression, in spite of her
experience with her own father and brother, that most men
craved sons. It pained her to admit that she'd always assumed
her own father's evident pleasure in his daughters had sprung
primarily from the knowledge that he already had a son;
therefore, he was free to appreciate his daughters.

Yet Aubrey Lockhart, in his letters, hadn't even hinted at
being less than thrilled or at all unsatisfied with his daughter.
He hadn't once mentioned wanting a son next time, should
there be a next time.

Imagine that. Aubrey Lockhart happy. And about the birth
of a daughter, of all things. It didn't seem possible to Callie.
Yet she'd held in her own hand solid proof that he had, once,
been a happy man.

And then the joy of his life had withered and died, and
there hadn't been a single thing he could do to prevent it. It
was common knowledge in Santa Angelica that Aubrey had
taken Anne to innumerable doctors. He'd been to San Francisco in search of specialists. He'd even sent to New York
for a fellow credited with miracle cures of wasting illnesses.
Gossip had buzzed like a hive of honey bees when a spe-

cialist came all the way from Europe see Anne. But it had all been to no avail.

It didn't seem fair. As little as she liked the man Aubrey Lockhart was now, Callie did like the one who'd written letters to the wife he'd loved. Hang it, Callie knew as well as anyone that life was very rarely fair, but she still couldn't understand why Anne had been taken. So young. So infernally young. And so well loved. And now so horribly missed.

By the time she finally fell into a fitful sleep, Callie had stopped straining to hold her tears back. They ran onto her pillow even as she tried to figure out why she was crying. Was she envious of the love Aubrey and Anne had shared? Was she sorry she wasn't more like Anne Lockhart? Was she merely sad for Becky? Or for Aubrey?

And why did she feel such a strong emotional tug toward the man who'd written those letters? Callie didn't even *like* the Aubrey Lockhart she worked for. It didn't make sense to her that she should harbor such tender feelings for the Aubrey Lockhart he used to be. Her confusion hadn't abated by the time she fell sleep.

Callie felt heavy-lidded and sleepy the following day. Her dreams had been sappy and soupy, and she was mortified with herself that she'd allowed her emotions to dip so deeply into the realm of sentimentality. Sentimentality was all very well in its place, but this wasn't it.

As she stood behind Becky, who sat patiently on a tall stool in front of her dressing table mirror, Callie thought about how irrational she was being. "Pooh," she muttered as she wielded the hairbrush, trying to be careful so as not to pull.

"Pooh?" Becky giggled. "Why'd you say that? It's funny."

Grinning at the little girl in the mirror, Callie said, "I've been behaving foolishly, is all."

"You have?" Becky looked almost shocked. "*I* don't think you're foolish, Miss Prophet."

Callie stooped and deposited a quick kiss on Becky's

golden head. "Thank you, dear, but I fear everyone's foolish every now and then.

"Although," Callie ammended, "it *is* difficult for me to imagine your papa being foolish." Her illogical brain seemed determined to dwell on Aubrey this morning, as if it didn't have enough to do just keeping her awake.

Becky sighed. "Yes. He's not foolish."

Callie kicked herself mentally—Becky sounded so depressed, and it was all her fault. Hoping to cast Aubrey Lockhart in a better light, Callie said, "He's a very dignified gentleman." She reached for the two neatly ironed pink ribbons she'd laid out, to tie onto the tails of Becky's braids.

"He used to laugh a lot." The little girl sounded wistful.

"Maybe we can think of some good jokes that might make him laugh," Callie suggested.

"Do you know any jokes, Miss Prophet?"

"A few. My brother, George, likes to tell—"

Callie's sentence was cut short by a hideous screech, followed almost instantly by a sharply bellowed, "Damnation!"

Becky and Callie stared at each other in the mirror for approximately three seconds before they whispered, in a horrified duet, "Monster!"

Callie had already opened the bedroom door by the time Becky hopped down from her dressing stool and rushed to join her. They held hands and ran to the staircase, from whence the noises had issued.

They skidded to a halt at the top of the stairs, their heels folding up the lovely Chinese hall runner like a concertina. Aubrey Lockhart, enraged, glared up at them. Rather, he glared at Callie. Callie could tell, if Becky couldn't, that his anger was directed exclusively at herself.

"Did you bring that fiend into this house?" he roared at Callie.

She opened her mouth to speak, but Becky beat her to it. "That's not a fiend, Papa. It's Monster."

Aubrey sucked in about a bushel and a half of air, Callie presumed to prevent him saying something to his daughter that he'd later regret. Although she believed it was cowardly of her, she was grateful Becky had come with her. She wouldn't want to face Aubrey Lockhart in the grip of a temper tantrum all by herself.

Mrs. Granger and Delilah appeared at the door leading to the kitchen. Both women were wide-eyed. They'd evidently been startled by the noise, too. Callie didn't dare speak to them.

"You may call the thing a monster if you want to, Becky. A monster and a fiend are pretty nearly equivalent in my mind. However, whatever one chooses to call it doesn't answer my original question. Miss Prophet?" And with that, Aubrey turned and fixed such a dark stare on Callie that she had to bite her lip to keep it from trembling.

For someone who could write such beautiful love letters, Aubrey could sound awfully menacing when he chose to. Callie swallowed. Then, telling herself to buck up and that there was no reason for this unpleasantness, she lifted her chin. "I believe you just met my cat, Mr. Lockhart. I had believed him to be in my bedroom."

"That . . . *thing* . . . was a cat?"

"It's a big cat, Papa." Becky tried out a smile on her father, but it didn't last long. She tightened her grip on Callie's hand.

Again, Aubrey took a deep breath. Callie feared he'd done so because otherwise he would have bellowed obscenities or something equally horrid, and he didn't want to do so in front of his daughter. "You brought a cat into my house, Miss Lockhart?"

The way the measured words came out of his mouth gave Callie the impression that he was speaking through clenched teeth. She nodded her head. Then, considering a silent response too spineless, she added, "Yes." She deliberately omitted a "sir" after her "yes," because she didn't want him to get the impression she was afraid of him. Even though she was.

"You mean to tell me that this animal has resided within my home for three weeks now?"

"Yes."

"And did you obtain permission before you brought it here?"

She wished he wouldn't refer to Monster as *it*, but didn't press the issue. "Um, well . . . no." She thought about adding the reason she'd done so was because Becky had expressed a desire for a pet and Callie'd been afraid Aubrey wouldn't permit it, but decided she'd best not do too much explaining until he was in a better frame of mind—if that ever happened.

"I see." He closed his mouth and seemed to be undergoing some kind of internal struggle. When he opened it again, Callie feared for the worst, but was pleasantly surprised when he merely said, "And what is this cat's name?"

Callie licked her lips and wished she hadn't. She didn't want him to see how nervous she was. "Um, his name is Monster."

"Ah." Aubrey glanced at his daughter and then back at Callie. "I see. His *name* is Monster. Monster isn't a definition or a description."

Becky chirped, "*Mister* Monster, to you, Papa. Until he gets to know you."

"Mister Monster?" Aubrey's eyes glittered. Callie took this as a bad omen.

But Becky nodded, looking remarkably cheerful under the circumstances. She was a plucky girl, Becky. Unless she didn't know enough to be afraid of her father. "Yes. He has to get to know people before he likes them, but once he likes you, he's a real nice cat, Papa. He likes to play, too. He's funny when he plays."

The child was babbling the way Callie had feared she'd do if she succumbed to her panic. She gave Becky's hand a little squeeze, hoping in that way to stop her chattering.

"He likes to play?" Aubrey smiled at Callie.

Callie wished he hadn't; it wasn't one of the warmest smiles she'd ever received. However, since it seemed he desired her to explain the cat, she guessed she'd better. After clearing her throat, she plunged into an explanation that she tried to keep as coherent and unadorned as possible. Considering the dual facts that her heart was battering at her ribs like a congregation of maddened woodpeckers and her knees were knocking together like Spanish castanets, it wasn't that easy a job.

"You see, Mr. Lockhart, since my employment began the day after I applied for this position, I didn't have time to secure another home for Monster. It is also true that cats often take some time to adjust themselves to new surroundings. I could have left him at the home I was vacating, which is my family home, but then my brother or one of my sisters would have had to visit the house daily to take care of him. It was easier to bring him with me." She stopped talking because she'd run out of breath.

"I see."

She hadn't been counting or anything, but Callie didn't think he'd blinked more than once or twice since she'd started explaining Monster. Again she cleared her throat. She wished she could have gotten through this without exhibiting such obvious signs of nervousness, but she couldn't.

After giving him a nod, she continued. "He's a lovely cat, Mr. Lockhart. A sweetheart of a cat, really."

"He bit my foot." Aubrey said nothing more than that, but the words precipitated a definite palpitation in Callie's chest.

"He'll get to know you after a while, Papa, and he won't bite you anymore." Becky smiled sweetly at her father.

God bless the child, Callie thought dismally. Yet Becky's words were the truth. Therefore, she nodded her agreement. "Yes, that's so. He only attacks when he feels threatened."

"I see." Aubrey's eyes narrowed dangerously. "And I, while descending my own staircase in my own home, presented a threat to him? Is that the explanation?"

"Well . . . I suppose so. But it wasn't really his fault," Callie hurried to say. "After all, one can't expect a cat to understand the particulars of home ownership."

"I see."

Silence fell like an axed tree between Aubrey and Callie and Becky. To Callie's overstrained nerves, the silence seemed to stretch on for centuries. She felt prickles of tension in the air, and would have sworn she saw them, too.

"Please let Monster stay here, Papa," Becky implored at

last. "He's such a sweetheart, and he loves me. I love him, too."

As she watched Aubrey's gaze move from her own face—thank God—to his daughter's, Callie saw the change in his expression. The hard lines appeared to soften as she looked at him. The anger went out of his eyes, his mouth relaxed, and he unclenched his jaw. "You really like that animal, Becky?"

"Oh, yes, Papa. I love him lots."

"And you believe he will no longer attack me once he gets to know me?"

"Oh, yes, Papa! I mean no, he won't. Definitely not after he gets to know you."

Aubrey cast a scathing glance at Callie before returning his attention to Becky. "Would you be willing to introduce us, Becky? The cat and me, I mean."

"Oh, *yes*, Papa!" Becky released Callie's hand and dashed down the stairs, straight into her father's arms.

Callie knew she was probably evil to resent the ease and happiness with which Becky had abandoned her and run to her father. After all, one of Callie's main reasons for taking the position as Becky's nanny was that she had wanted to get father and daughter back on speaking terms.

Yet she did resent it. She turned to walk back to Becky's room—she had assumed the responsibility of tidying up after the little girl's morning toilette—when Aubrey's voice stopped her cold.

"Miss Prophet."

It sounded like the voice of doom, so dark and deep it was. Callie turned slowly, fearing what he might say next. He didn't look as if he'd taken a sudden liking to her, that was certain. In fact, he looked as if he totally disapproved of her. "Yes, Mr. Lockhart?" She *wouldn't* call him *sir,* no matter what.

"Won't you please come with us, Miss Prophet? Becky assures me that, while this cat of yours is now her friend, he's more comfortable when you're in the vicinity."

After shooting a glance at Becky, who was smiling up a storm and looked as if she were happy as a clam, Callie decided she was glad Aubrey had called her back. "I'd be happy to," she said. It almost wasn't a lie.

They discovered Monster in the drawing room, under a chair. Any other cat might have been said to be cowering. Monster, however, didn't look frightened. If one were to ascribe an emotion to his overall attitude, Callie feared it might be annoyance. Anger, perhaps. Disgust, too, maybe, a little bit.

"Good God." Aubrey, who had preceded the ladies into the room, stopped still when he'd barely cleared the doorway. That's when Callie spotted Monster.

"H'lo, Monster!" Becky said cheerily, although she didn't leave her father's side.

Monster didn't respond. He huddled under a straight-backed chair, his fur bristling, and his greenish-yellow eyes gleaming. Callie guessed that, while it might have been unkind of Aubrey to have said it aloud, he might be forgiven for equating Monster with a fiend. Those eyes alone were enough to cause alarm in a sensitive breast.

Callie was so accustomed to Monster, she didn't give a thought to the cat's glittering greenish-yellow eyes. Well, except at night, when she came upon him unexpectedly. Then, even Callie's innards might execute a leap or two of apprehension.

She wasn't sure what she should say under these circumstances, although she thought she ought to say something—anything—to diffuse the tension. "Um, I do believe he's relaxing after a trying morning, Mr. Lockhart. I think you frightened him."

"*I* frightened *him*?"

Callie wasn't sure, but she thought he'd sounded sarcastic on purpose. She tried to get mad at him for it, but her honest nature wouldn't let her.

"Watch this, Papa."

Becky, who had been standing between the two adults, threw something small, white, and round at the chair.

Aubrey said, "What the . . . ?"

But Monster, who knew a good game when he saw it, shot out from under the chair like an arrow from a bow, leaped on the white thing, which, Callie now discerned, was a crumpled piece of paper, turned a somersault, and started batting the paper ball in the air. He kept it aloft for several bats before the paper dropped to the Oriental carpet and rolled a foot or so. He leaped upon it as if it were a mouse, threw it up into the air, swiped at it with a furry black paw, connecting with a skill that would have done many a baseball player proud, and bounded after it as it flew across the room.

Becky laughed merrily. "See? He loves to play. But he's so big and black that you don't expect him to, so it's extra funny when he does."

Callie couldn't have said it better herself. She nodded, intuitively believing that Aubrey would rather not hear from her at the moment.

"Good God. I'd never have guessed." Aubrey sounded awed. "I didn't even realize the thing was a cat until you told me."

"He's a sweet cat," Becky said. "Look, Papa." She tripped over to Monster, grabbed the crumpled paper from between his paws, and threw it across the room. The cat charged after it and pounced again, making a tremendous thudding noise. Monster wasn't exactly a lightweight.

Callie noticed that Aubrey's head was shaking back and forth, not in denial, but in amazement, as if he were witnessing something strange and incredible. She guessed it wouldn't hurt to say something now.

"He's a very nice cat, Mr. Lockhart, although I'm sure he must have given you a start this morning. As you didn't know about him and all."

"A start?"

She didn't like the way he turned to peer at her. His eyes had gone narrow, and his expression was something like a grimace, but it was mixed up with incredulity, wonder, disapproval, and disbelief. "Um," she said, "Yes. I'm sure you must have been startled."

"Startled doesn't begin to describe my feelings on being attacked by an animal I didn't know resided in my home, Miss Prophet."

Oh, dear. "Um, yes, well, he doesn't usually bite people. Really, he doesn't."

Fortunately, Becky wasn't listening to this conversation. She was having too much fun playing with Monster to bother with grown-ups. Callie thanked her stars for small favors.

"I see. He undoubtedly objected to my stepping on his foot. Or perhaps it was his tail I trod upon."

"You *stepped* on him!" Callie cried. "Well, then, that explains it. He objects strenuously to being stepped on, Mr. Lockhart. I mean, you can't really blame him for that, can you?"

"I don't blame the cat, Miss Prophet."

"Oh." It pained her, but Callie said, "I'm very sorry, Mr. Lockhart. I ought to have asked if it was all right to bring Monster with me."

"Indeed."

"And—well—I should have told you about him."

"Indeed."

This string of "indeeds" irritated Callie. She snapped, "Although, anyone with an ounce of sense or warmth in his heart ought to have understood before now that his daughter wanted a pet."

"Indeed."

Fiddlesticks, there was another one. Callie guessed she shouldn't have spoken up. It was one of her many failings that she spoke her mind too readily. Feeling defensive and, worse, wrong, she said, "Becky loves Monster."

"Yes. I see that she does."

Aubrey left off staring at Callie, thank God, and returned his gaze to Becky and Monster. Becky was crowing with laughter, and Monster was performing like a circus acrobat. For such a large, heavy cat, he was quite agile.

Callie caught her breath when Becky threw the paper ball and it landed on a table on the other side of the room. With the quick reflexes that had recently been admired by Callie, the cat took a run at the table.

"No!" Aubrey shouted, sending Callie's trepidation sky-rocketing.

Aubrey darted like a sprinter across the room, barely

reaching the table before Monster landed on it. Callie clapped
her hands to her cheeks when she realized that Aubrey had
just rescued a magnificent Ming vase from destruction.

Whirling around with the vase in his hand, Aubrey spoke
in a controlled voice, to his daughter. "Perhaps you ought to
take that thing outside and play with it later, Becky."

"I'll take him up to Miss Prophet's room, Papa. He lives
there."

"I see." He turned to eye Callie with distaste. "We'll discuss the cat later, Miss Prophet. I believe it's time for my
daughter's breakfast."

"Yes," Callie said, and swallowed. "Yes, I believe it is."

Becky was out of breath when she scooped Monster off
the table and into her arms. "I'm sorry, Papa. That was my
fault about the vase. I didn't mean to throw the ball on the
table."

"It's all right, Becky." Aubrey gave his daughter what
looked like a genuine smile. "I'm glad you introduced me to
Monster." He returned his gaze to Callie, although his smile
didn't accompany it. "At last."

Oh, dear. "Yes, well, let's go take Monster upstairs and
wash our hands, Becky. I'm sure Mrs. Granger has your
breakfast all ready."

"All right." Happy and undaunted in the face of the
strained relations between the adults in her life, Becky lugged
Monster toward the door.

"We'll discuss this later, Miss Prophet."

"Yes, you mentioned that before. Thanks for the warning."

Blast. She shouldn't have said that. Callie helped Becky
carry the cat upstairs. She felt very low and achy around the
heart as she helped Becky wash her hands well and accompanied her into the breakfast room.

There, as on most mornings, a tempting repast was laid
out on the sideboard. Callie had her choice of eggs, bacon,
ham, chops, toast, and a variety of jams, jellies, marmalades,
and honeys. Not to mention the oranges and apples.

If she were to make a judgment based solely on earthly
merits, she'd have to admit that it was rather nice to be living
in the Lockhart mansion where there were wonderful break-

fasts to be had simply by walking into the dining room. And then there were the fully accoutered bathrooms on every floor, and hot and cold running water. Callie had never lived in such luxury. She wondered how long it would last.

A cat. The woman had brought a cat into his home. Without even asking.

If she'd asked, he'd have told her no, but that was no reason for her outrageous presumption. Aubrey could scarcely imagine the effrontery it took Miss Prophet to inflict a pet upon the Lockharts. After all, what if Becky had been allergic or something?

Or him. What if *he* had been allergic?

And then the damned thing had bitten him. *Bitten* him! And he'd only barely stepped on its tail. Unless it was its foot. Aubrey wasn't sure. It had all happened so fast. If he hadn't been glancing at the book in his hand, he'd have seen the . . . well, the *monster* on the steps and would have avoided a collision. As it was . . .

Well, it was unconscionable for Miss Callida Prophet to have brought the animal into his house. Unthinkable. Her behavior was truly execrable.

Aubrey entered his library in a towering grump, cursing Callie Prophet and the Fates. "*Why* did you leave us, Anne?" he all but wailed, after shutting the library door so no one could hear him talking to himself. "Why?"

As always, there was no answer. Neither Anne nor God nor the Fates, if Fates there were, ever answered his questions. He was, therefore, as bereft and alone as ever.

Folding up into his desk chair, he stared at the window giving a view of the lawn. Something occurred to him, and he said, "Oh. By God, *that's* what they meant." He shoved his chair away from the desk and stood.

After walking to the window, pulling the curtain aside, and gazing at the lawn, he recalled the time he'd observed Becky and Miss Prophet playing Robin Hood. He'd heard them talking about a "monster" later on that same day, and had assumed they'd been playing at Frankenstein.

"What a way of discovering a mistake," he growled.

As he turned away from the window and went back to his desk, he recalled the stupid cat turning a somersault as it tried to get at a balled-up piece of paper. He remembered the idiotic animal whacking the ball as if he were a crazed baseball player trying for a home run. He remembered Becky squealing with delight as the deranged feline, with his fluffy black tail trailing behind him like a cloud of dust, raced after the paper ball like a lion after an antelope, and pouncing on it as if it were making a kill.

Aubrey had been laughing to himself for probably thirty seconds—perhaps even a whole minute—before he realized what he was doing and stopped, appalled.

What in the name of holy hell did he have to laugh about? His wife was dead. His daughter was in the clutches of a mad nanny. A huge black cat stalked at will through the halls of his home. His life was ruined. It might as well be over. There wasn't a single amusing thing left for him in this horrible world, and it was a blot on Anne's memory to laugh under these appalling circumstances.

Then he remembered the cat juggling the paper ball like a circus performer and, while he didn't allow himself to laugh, he did grin.

# 6

Brisk winds had started to blow, there was a distinct nip in the air, and the leaves were threatening to turn color. School was about to start in the little village of Santa Angelica. It would be Becky's first school year, and Aubrey's heart hurt when he thought about how Anne would have enjoyed preparing her for the new experience.

But Anne wasn't here to see their daughter off to school. And Aubrey hadn't a clue as to how to prepare a child to endure the vicissitudes of the schoolroom. Rearing children, as he'd discovered a long time ago, was not man's work. Men generally didn't know how to go about it, and Aubrey was no exception to this rule. Oh, how he missed Anne during the days leading up to their child's first day of school.

He'd heard Miss Prophet telling Becky all about the Santa Angelica Public School, which she had attended as a youngster. The village was small, and its school consisted of two rooms and boasted two teachers, one an elderly man and the other a young woman. Miss Prophet said this made it twice as big as when she'd gone there. Becky had laughed when she'd said it.

Since Miss Prophet had been born and reared in Santa

Angelica; she knew the two schoolteachers personally. Aubrey had heard her detailing their different personalities in a humorous way, but one that left no doubt as to what she expected Becky to do in the way of discipline and paying attention. Aubrey thought she'd done very well in this regard, although he didn't tell her so.

He presumed the two teachers split their teaching responsibilities by age or sex or something. He hadn't looked into the matter personally, but had left everything to Miss Prophet who, unlike Aubrey himself, knew all about getting little girls prepared to face the challenges of education.

Miss Prophet had also sewn five dresses for Becky to wear to school. Aubrey hated to acknowledge her talents in the direction of fashion, but he'd done so, grudgingly, when Becky, her face radiant, had turned in front of him, showing off her new wardrobe one dress at a time. The dresses were quite fetching, and he'd gone so far as to thank Miss Prophet, who'd responded coolly and inclined her head a quarter of an inch.

Upon further acquaintance, Monster had *not* stopped biting Aubrey, but attacked his feet whenever he had the chance. As Aubrey went to his office on this chilly September morning, he had to leap out of the way of the pugnacious cat, who seemed to enjoy lurking under furniture and hiding behind corners and leaping on him unawares. The cat seemed to consider attacking Aubrey's feet one of the great pleasures in life. Aubrey disagreed, although he hadn't gone so far as to kick the beast yet.

He made it to his office after fending off the cat, removed his coat and threw it on the sofa, and seated himself behind his desk. As he did so, he growled, "*Mister* Monster, my hind foot. The animal ought to be dispatched as a menace to society. It's a menace to *my* society, however much Miss Prophet likes to say he's a benevolent creature."

He didn't mean it. If Monster were to go away, Becky would be grief stricken. Aubrey didn't think he could bear to see her unhappy again, although he wasn't altogether sure he approved of the renewal of her spirits having been accomplished by Miss Callida Prophet and an insane cat. He, as Becky's father, ought to have been the one who'd comforted her and soothed her grief.

With a sigh, Aubrey burdened his conscience with the same reproach that had bothered him for months and months: He'd failed his daughter. He, who should have showered her with tenderness and understanding during her time of great loss, had withdrawn into his own selfish melancholy and ignored her.

The unfortunate truth was, though, that he hadn't a clue how to deal with children. Not even Becky, whom he loved beyond anything.

However, Miss Prophet, for all her faults—and she had hundreds of them—had eased his mind, if not his conscience, a good deal when it came to Becky. He applauded himself for having had the forethought to hire a nanny. Miss Prophet might be the bane of his own existence, but she'd been Becky's salvation. In truth, when he didn't want to kill her with his bare hands, he appreciated her.

For several days now, it had been difficult for Aubrey to remove his thoughts from Miss Prophet and Becky and concentrate on his Oriental imports business, but he always managed to do it. He might know nothing about children, but he knew his business inside and out, and he aimed to do that right, if nothing else. Therefore, this morning, as every morning, he cleared his mind of irrelevancies—if his child could be considered an irrelevancy—and concentrated on Chinese vases, Persian rugs, Siamese wall hangings, and Indian teas.

He'd been working at his desk for an hour or two when Figgins knocked at the door and entered. Aubrey expected the butler would announce the arrival of Mark Henderson, his secretary from the San Francisco office, who made the trip to Santa Angelica every week in order to go over business affairs.

Aubrey was surprised, therefore, to see that Figgins was alone. He also bore a silver tray with a single white calling card in its center.

With a sigh—Aubrey didn't really go in for all this formality, but he didn't have the heart to tell Figgins to forgo it since he took such obvious pleasure in these traditions—

he took the card and lifted it to his line of vision.

He goggled. "Good God!"

"Sir?"

Aubrey realized he'd uttered an improper exclamation, and that Figgins undoubtedly deplored such a lapse. "I beg your pardon, Figgins. But . . . well . . . this card. Is she here? Now? Right this minute?"

"Yes, sir. She's awaiting your pleasure in the drawing room." Not a flicker of emotion showed on Figgins's face.

The same, Aubrey was sure, could not be said of his own face. "Mrs. Bridgewater? Herself? Here?" Pleasure, be damned. She could await that forever and her wait would be for naught. Aubrey, pleasure, and Mrs. Bridgewater would never occupy the same room at the same time.

"Yes, sir."

Oh, God. There could be no doubt about it. Figgins never lied. Nor could he be mistaken, having known Mrs. Bridgewater far longer than he'd known Aubrey, since she was Anne's father's sister.

Aubrey allowed his head to bow for a moment before he straightened and told Figgins, "Please have Mrs. Granger bring refreshments into the drawing room. Have somebody fetch Becky and her nanny." It was difficult for him to say Miss Prophet's name aloud. A small groan escaped him when he added, "I'll tackle Mrs. Bridgewater as soon as I put my coat on."

"Very good, sir."

Figgins left the room. It had always amused Aubrey that Figgins looked as if he were floating, so smoothly did he move. The man was so dashedly formal. Figgins's gait ceased to amuse him today, however. The promise of encountering Anne's least favorite aunt could smother anyone's enjoyment of life.

Anne Harriott's parents had been wonderful people. It stood to reason that it had been so, since Anne herself had been an angel. Their lives had been cut tragically short, as had their daughter's, although their deaths had been incurred in an accident five years before Anne's illness had begun. And, no matter the reason for this unusual visit, Aubrey was sure it augured a problem. Mrs. Bridgewater, Mr. Harriott's older sister, had missed the angelic Harriott family leaning entirely. She was an overbearing moose of a woman, and Aubrey didn't like her. Worse still, neither did Becky. The poor child was always cowed in Mrs. Bridgewater's presence.

Well, and why shouldn't she be? Aubrey was pretty much cowed himself when faced with the austere and disapproving Mrs. Bridgewater. Anne and he had started calling her Mrs. Bilgewater in private, although they never did so in front of Becky, fearing she might believe it to be the woman's real name.

He stopped to take a deep breath before he entered the drawing room. Old Bilgewater, he saw at once, hadn't bothered to sit, but stood before the fireplace, staring with censure through her eyeglasses at the portrait of Anne hanging above the mantel. Immediately, Aubrey's ire rose. If the old bat said one word about that portrait, Aubrey would give her a piece of his mind that she wouldn't easily digest.

However, he owed it to Anne's memory to be courteous to any of her relations, at least at first, so he said pleasantly, "Mrs. Bridgewater. What a nice surprise." An honest man, Aubrey nonetheless permitted himself the occasional social lie.

Mrs. Bridgewater turned in a regal manner—probably due to her corsett stays, Aubrey thought bitterly. Her eyeglasses glittered, giving her an even more forbidding appearance than she might have had without them. Aubrey had never seen eyeglasses have that effect on anyone but Aunt Evelyn Bilgewater.

She appeared to sneer at him. "Oh. There you are. I think you ought to remove this portrait, Aubrey. It can't be good for Rebecca to be reminded of her mother all the time."

If human emotion could be registered in terms of volcanic displays, Aubrey would have erupted. He didn't permit his fury to show, but merely said quietly, "Anne's portrait is precious to both Becky and me, Mrs. Bridgewater, and I won't be removing it any time soon."

The middle-aged matron snorted. "Well, you're a fool then."

Aubrey didn't respond to this blatant attempt to rile him. "Mrs. Granger is bringing us some refreshments, Mrs. Bridgewater. Won't you be seated? I've sent for Becky."

"I want to talk to you about Rebecca, Aubrey." She sat with a crisp crunch of black bombazine. "That's why I chose to take the arduous journey to this end-of-the-world place today."

She reminded Aubrey a little of Monster, the way her large body pooched out around the edges. However, Monster, even when attacking his feet, possessed a better nature than Bilgewater.

Her words froze his blood. Not that this human female buffalo could do anything with Becky without his permission, but Aubrey didn't fancy getting embroiled in a fight with her. He said, "Oh?" and smiled benignly. Because he disliked her and didn't care for the way she belittled Santa Angelica, he added, "Anne and I chose to live here in order to get away from the fuss and bother of the city. We loved it here. We both thought it would be better to rear children in the country than in the city. Fresh air, vigorous exercise, and all that."

She sniffed. "No accounting for taste, I suppose."

"Right." Suppressing the urge to throw at old Bilgewater's head the Ming vase he'd rescued several days earlier from Monster's attack, he muttered, "You said you wanted to talk to me about Becky?"

"Yes. Something must be done about her."

Good God. She sounded as if Becky were a species of vermin that needed to be exterminated. "What do you mean, 'done about her'?"

"She needs a woman around her, now that Anne's gone. She ought not remain out here in the hinterlands with only her father and the servants for company. She'll never learn how to take her place in society this way."

Trying not to grind his teeth, Aubrey said, "You needn't worry about that, Mrs. Bridgewater. I've hired her a nanny."

Bilgewater snorted. "A nanny! And what good, pray tell,

is a nanny? The child needs to be with her family."

"It sounds to me as though you think she ought to be removed from her family," Aubrey pointed out.

"Nonsense. I only want you to understand that a girl child needs to associate with female family members."

Still holding back a bellow, Aubrey said, "She's quite happy, actually. She's about to start school in a couple of days, and she's excited about it."

"School!" Mrs. Bridgewater's lips thinned and her nose wrinkled. "And where will she be attending school?"

Aubrey inclined his head, puzzled at the question. "Why, in Santa Angelica, of course. She'll be in the first grade, and she's quite looking forward to it."

"*Fah.*"

*Fah*? Why *fah*? Aubrey lifted an eyebrow. "You don't approve?" He might have expected as much. Bilgewater didn't approve of anything unless she suggested it.

The door of the drawing room opened, and Becky bounced in, a smile wreathing her darling face, Callie right behind her. As ever, when in the presence of his child, Aubrey's heart first hitched painfully and then gladdened. She reminded him *so* much of Anne.

As soon as the child spotted her least favorite great-aunt, her smile vanished and she stopped bouncing. Evidently recalling past encounters with this intimidating dame, she curtsied prettily and stood stock still. She glanced over her shoulder at Callie. Aubrey could tell she did so in order to gain courage, and his heart pinged again. She ought to be looking to him for aid and comfort, not her nanny.

He went over to her and took her hand. "Come here, sweetheart. Let's say hello to Great-Aunt Evelyn."

His gaze found Callie, who stood with folded hands beside the doorway. She looked as if she'd just steamed in from a hard gale, with loose tresses flying out from the bun on top of her head. As soon as she caught his eye focused on her head, she unfolded her hands and began patting at her hair.

Aubrey knew, because he'd studied her hair, that it wouldn't be subdued by such feeble efforts. For a second, he allowed his glance to take in the rest of her, and he re-

alized she had smears of dirt on her apron and even on her
right cheek.

Aunt Evelyn was going to love this. He gave Callie a
quick frown to let her know he wasn't pleased with her, and
again turned toward Mrs. Bridgewater. "Another curtsy
would be in order here, Becky," he said softly and with a
smile. He knew Becky was afraid of this woman, and he
didn't fault her for her astute assessment of human nature.
Anyone with an ounce of sense would be leery of Evelyn
Bilgewater.

"Good morning, Rebecca," Mrs. Bridgewater said. She
was as formal as Figgins, but not as good-natured. Even her
smile appeared sour.

Becky executed another curtsy. She was rumpled, too, Aubrey noticed with a sinking heart. Bilgewater was certain to
disapprove. "Good morning, Great-Aunt Evelyn," Becky said
dutifully, but without enthusiasm.

Mrs. Bridgewater scanned the little girl with growing dis-
satisfaction. "What have you been doing with yourself,
child? Your dress is a mess." Squinting through her spectacles at Becky she said, "And so is your face."

Becky shot a quick glance up at her father. Aubrey was
pleased at this indication that she hadn't completely detached
herself from him but still sought his guidance and approval
in uncertain circumstances. He nodded and smiled down at
her, hoping to give her the courage to relate whatever it was
she and Miss Prophet had been doing. She didn't disappoint
him.

"Miss Prophet and I were out collecting birds' nests,
Great-Aunt Evelyn."

"Birds nests? Have you been climbing trees, child?" Mrs.
Bridgewater clearly did not sanction such antics.

But Becky's enthusiasm for her recent outdoor pursuits
overcame her fear of disapproval. She said brightly, "Oh,
yes! It's autumn, you know, and the baby birds have flown
away. We've found tons of feathers, and so far we've collected a robin's nest and a tanager's nest and a blue jay's
nest. Miss Prophet can tell the difference between all kinds
of birds' nests." She sounded as if she thought Miss

Prophet's knowledge of bird life was the most amazing thing she'd ever encountered.

"Miss Prophet?" Mrs. Bridgewater's nose wrinkled as if she'd smelled something putrid. "Is that Miss Prophet?" Becky's great-aunt would never do anything so gauche as to point a finger, but she inclined her chin in Callie's direction, and both Becky and Aubrey turned to look at her.

Aubrey was surprised to see the color climb into the nanny's cheeks. He couldn't recall ever seeing her react in embarrassment to anything or anyone before this moment. He wasn't, on the other hand, surprised to see her lift her chin and look defiant, in spite of the blush in her cheeks. With a sigh, he said, "Will you please step forward, Miss Prophet? Let me introduce you to Becky's great-aunt."

"Certainly, Mr. Lockhart."

She never called him *sir*. Aubrey didn't especially mind, not having much of a craving for subservience, but he suspected her lack of sirs had devolved from her false opinion of him as a coldhearted son of a bitch, and he resented it. This wasn't the time to air family quarrels, however.

Although it cost him an internal twinge, he smiled at Becky's great-aunt. "Mrs. Bertrand Bridgewater, please allow me to introduce you to Miss Callida Prophet, Becky's nanny. Miss Prophet has been with us for approximately six weeks now." He didn't add that those six weeks had been fraught with lectures, cat bites, household noise, and his own personal squabbles with the nanny.

To Aubrey's astonishment, Callie dropped a curtsy. It was a good one, too, leading Aubrey to believe that the woman had been taught pretty manners some time in her past, even if she seldom exhibited them in his presence.

"How do you do, Mrs. Bridgewater?" Even Callie's voice was civil.

Aubrey suppressed his amazement. He turned to Bilgewater, wondering what the old bat would make of Callie Prophet. Not much, from the look on her face.

"*You* are this child's governess?" Mrs. Bridgewater raked Callie with a glance probably meant to wound. Aubrey frowned.

"I'm her nanny," Callie corrected her civilly.

"You're too young." Old Bilgewater brushed Callie away with one of her well-manicured hands. She turned to Aubrey. "I don't know what you mean, hiring a mere child to care for Rebecca, Aubrey. It's scandalous that so young a lady should be living here in this house."

Callie's mouth dropped open.

So did Aubrey's, but only because a fellow couldn't talk with his mouth shut. "Miss Prophet," he said in a voice of steel, "is fully qualified to be Becky's nanny." He was going to go on, explaining Callie's educational qualifications, but Callie took over.

"I should say I am."

To Aubrey's surprise, the nanny's face had drained of color. He'd have expected her color to deepen with fury.

"I have a degree from the Brooklyn, New York, Teaching Seminary for Young Women—*with* honors—and am fully qualified to teach school."

Bilgewater remained unmoved. "Then why aren't you?"

"Not," Callie said—and Aubrey detected a faint quiver, probably brought about by anger, in her voice —"that it's any of your business, Mrs. Bridgewater, but I chose to live in Santa Angelica in order to remain near my family. If I'd chosen to teach school, I would have had to move elsewhere, and I didn't want to."

"*Hunh.* Well, you're still too young to have charge of Rebecca." She turned back to Aubrey dismissing Callie this time without so much as a flick of her hand. "Aubrey, the child should come to live with me. I intend to take her to San Francisco with me. In the city, she will have the best of everything."

Her great-aunt's words had a galvanic effect on little Becky. She cried out, "No!" and rushed to grasp Callie's hand. From that position, she gazed with horror from Great-Aunt Evelyn to her father.

A pain spread through Aubrey's chest. He didn't like it that Becky had run to Callie instead of to him. And, although he'd been thinking only that morning about how Becky needed the supervision of a woman, and that he wasn't fit to rear her alone, and, while he'd thought for weeks now that Callie Prophet was too young to be in charge of his daughter, he flatly rejected Bilgewater's suggestion. Command, rather.

"Thank you, Mrs. Bridgewater, but Becky will be staying here. At home." He was relieved to see Becky relax slightly. She still didn't leave her nanny's side for his, but at least she gave him a quavery smile.

"Pshaw," Bilgewater huffed. "You're making a grave mistake, Aubrey. Anne would have wanted Rebecca to have only the best."

Before Aubrey could say a word, Becky piped up. "But I already have the best. Miss Prophet's the best. Honest, she is, Great-Aunt Evelyn."

"Nonsense, child. She's far too young. And your manners certainly haven't improved under her care." She frowned so fiercely at Becky that the little girl snuggled more deeply into Callie's skirts.

Aubrey didn't intend to take any more of *that*. "That's enough! I won't have you browbeating my daughter or my staff, Aunt Evelyn. And speaking of manners, I think you ought to work on your own before you complain about anyone else's. You have no business coming here and telling us how to live our lives."

It took Evelyn Bridgewater mere seconds to draw in so much air that she seemed to grow larger and to poof out, again reminding Aubrey of Monster. He presumed she aimed to use all that air in denying his accusation and in vilifying his morals and living situation some more, but an interruption prevented her. Thank God.

"Good morning, Mr. Lockhart. I told Figgins he didn't need to announce me, and I just— Oh."

Mark Henderson, Aubrey's secretary from San Francisco, stopped in the doorway of the drawing room, his hat in his hand and his youthful face cheery. "I beg your pardon. I had no idea you had company."

Mark, unlike Miss Prophet, could blush up a storm at the drop of a hat, Aubrey noticed. Yet he was glad for the interruption. There was no telling how the scene would degenerate if left to its own devices. "Come on in, Mark. This isn't a formal meeting." With an effort, he smiled and went over to shake the young man's hand. "How did you get here so quickly? It takes hours to get here from San Francisco, I didn't expect you until this afternoon."

"I drove to Santa Angelica yesterday afternoon," Mark said, recovering some of his composure. "I spent the night at that quaint little hotel in the village. It's a charming place."

Aubrey was proud of his restraint when he didn't so much as glance at Bilgewater to see how she liked Mark's commendation. "You ought to have stayed here, Mark. We have plenty of room. Here, let me introduce you."

Still red of face, but with his company manners firmly in place, Mark entered the room and smiled at Becky. "How do you do, Miss Lockhart?" He took her tiny hand in his and bowed over it.

"H'lo, Mr. Henderson," Becky said and smiled back.

This had been a ritual with them ever since Becky was big enough to walk. Aubrey smiled, enjoying the scene before him. He turned to Miss Prophet to see how she was taking in Mark's theatrics and his smile suddenly faded. She was giving Mark Henderson a look full of approval. She'd never once looked at Aubrey that way.

Mark stood up from his bow and glanced from Mrs. Bridgewater to Callie, where his gaze seemed to stick fast. Aubrey saw him swallow and forge onward.

"Mrs. Bridgewater, please allow me to introduce you to my secretary and right-hand man, Mr. Mark Henderson. Mark keeps the office in San Francisco operating on an even keel. Mark, this is my late wife's aunt Evelyn, Mrs. Bertrand Bridgewater."

With what looked like a struggle, Mark managed to tear his gaze away from Becky's nanny and focus it on Great-Aunt Evelyn. He bowed formally. "Very pleased to meet you, Mrs. Bridgewater."

"How do you do, young man?"

"And this," Aubrey said, although he didn't want to, "is Miss Callida Prophet, Becky's new nanny."

With less formality but a good deal more sparkle, Mark

bowed to Callie, keeping his gaze locked on her the entire time. "Miss Prophet. A pleasure."

"How do you do?"

Callie returned his bow with another perfectly executed curtsy. Aubrey noted, however, that she didn't seem to be as enthralled with him as he was with her, because she almost immediately returned her attention to Old Bilgewater. To Aubrey, it looked as if she'd like to take the woman up on her criticisms about her own fitness to be Becky's nanny and about Santa Angelica and argue with her for the rest of the afternoon.

Aubrey was about to intercede when Mrs. Granger entered the room bearing a tray with bread-and-butter sandwiches on it. Delilah followed her carrying a tray laid out with teacups and the best silver tea service. He breathed a sigh of relief. He hadn't much been looking forward to getting in between these two headstrong ladies.

With totally feigned joviality, he rubbed his hands together and beamed at the two servants. "Ah. Good. Mrs. Bridgewater and Mark, please make yourselves comfortable, and take some tea and sandwiches."

He turned to Becky and Miss Prophet, who still stood by, hand in hand. "Miss Prophet, perhaps you should return to your outdoor-activities. Or, if you and Becky wish to partake of refreshments, you might want to visit the soap and water first." He hoped Callie would be so offended she wouldn't take him up on the latter suggestion.

Since she stiffened all over like Aubrey's favorite pointer when eyeing a duck, he guessed she wouldn't. "Thank you, Mr. Lockhart. I don't think we will join you for refreshments. As you can see, we're not dressed for company."

"Yes. I did notice that."

He saw her bosom heave. He'd been observing her bosom fairly often of late, although he was sure he shouldn't. But, dash it, she was a pretty woman, however ghastly her personality, and he was a young man, even if he still grieved over the loss of his wife.

"Come along, Becky. You'd better curtsy to your great-aunt first and ask to be excused."

From the tone of her voice, Aubrey supposed she'd wanted to suggest that Becky chuck something at her great-aunt first, and then at her father. He would have smiled, except he didn't want to give Bilgewater anything else to fuss about.

Reluctantly, Becky released Callie's hand and walked over to her great-aunt. She gave another one of her pretty little curtsies. "May I be excused, please, ma'am?"

Old Bilgewater eyed her critically. "Very well, Rebecca. At least your manners haven't vanished entirely. Yes, run along now. I'll talk to your father more about the subject under discussion later."

Becky didn't like hearing that. She opened her mouth to protest, but Callie touched her shoulder lightly, shook her head, and reached for Becky's hand. Unhappy, but understanding that it wasn't a child's place to question the adults in her life, Becky accepted defeat and turned around. She wouldn't even have said good-bye to her papa if Callie hadn't reminded her.

Aubrey frowned after the two females as they left the drawing room, unhappy with Becky's defection. If it was a defection.

Perhaps Old Bilgewater was right about Becky. Maybe his daughter would be better off staying in San Francisco with Bilgewater and her unpleasant husband. If Aubrey sent her to live with them, she'd at least be glad to see her papa when he made it into the city.

He chided himself at once. These musings were merely the result of his selfishness surfacing again. He hadn't realized how large that side of him was until recently, when Miss Callida Prophet had come into his life.

Damn her. Before she came here to stir up the ashes, his life was miserable, but at least he understood it. Now he didn't understand anything.

His mood was not improved when Mark said, "What a remarkably pretty young woman, Mr. Lockhart. Did she come from the city?"

"No. She was born and bred here in Santa Angelica."

"My goodness. The country produces some interesting

specimens, doesn't it? I like Santa Angelica even better now than I did when I arrived yesterday."

Great-Aunt Evelyn snorted, clearly disapproving of the frivolous, not to say unsavory, tone of the conversation. Mark had the grace to blush once more and mutter something that was probably meant as an apology.

Aubrey wanted to kick Bilgewater down the marble front steps.

# 7

If there was one thing Callie didn't want to do, it was to take her evening meal with Becky's great-aunt Evelyn. The woman was a menace to society. Or, she amended, she was a menace to Becky and, by default, to Callie Prophet.

"I don't want to leave home and go to live with Great-Aunt Evelyn, Miss Prophet," Becky said in a small voice as Callie toweled her off after her bath. She'd even washed the child's hair so that the old crone wouldn't be able to find anything else to complain about in Callie's care of Becky.

"It didn't sound to me as though your papa wants you to leave him, Becky, so I don't think you need to worry about it."

Suddenly Becky turned, buried her face in Callie's apron, and threw her arms around her. "If I *do* have to go live in San Frisco, will you come with me?"

Fat chance. Touched by Becky's obvious affection for her, Callie said, "Please try not to think about it, Becky, sweets. I'm sure your papa won't let Mrs. Bridgewater take you away."

The poor little thing had begun to cry. Callie felt awful. She sat on the dressing stool, picked Becky up, and settled the child in her lap. "It's all right, sweetheart. Nobody wants you to go away. Honest."

"But Papa never even sees me anymore. He wouldn't even *notice* if I went away!"

If Callie had possessed one of those Edison phonographic machine things, she would have liked to record Becky's assessment of her father's behavior and play it back to him. This was all his fault, and Callie wanted to hit him for it.

Except that she feared she was thinking far too much—and too affectionately—about the other Aubrey, the one who'd written those beautiful letters to his late wife. The two different men refused to reconcile themselves in Callie's mind.

Which was probably just as well. She had no business mooning over anyone, much less the long-gone writer of love letters to another woman.

She also didn't like herself much for continuing to read the letters, even though they did seem to make Becky feel better when she did. Reading a letter to her before she pulled the blanket up and went to sleep seemed to calm her and help sleep come more easily.

Callie tried to tell herself that making Becky feel better was the most important part of her job, but she couldn't rid herself of the certain knowledge that reading another person's personal and intimate correspondence was a foul and quite probably wicked thing to do.

With a heavy sigh, she said, "Please don't cry, Becky love. Everything will work itself out. Don't forget that your unpleasant aunt will be leaving soon."

Sniffing and wiping her eyes, Becky withdrew her head from Callie's dampened shoulder and gazed up at her, nearly breaking Callie's heart. "Do . . . do you think Great-Aunt Evelyn is unpleasant?"

Drat her too-ready tongue. Already Callie was regretting having spoken the truth so freely in front of Becky, no matter how much she meant it. "Well, I didn't care for her upon first meeting her, although I'm sure she's a very nice person, really." *Liar, liar, pants on fire.* The childhood taunt flickered through Callie's brain, and she banished it instantly.

Becky shook her head and submitted to having her cheeks wiped by Callie's handkerchief. "She's not nice. Even Mama didn't like her."

"She didn't?" It often surprised Callie how much Becky remembered of her mother. She'd have expected Anne's image to have faded more by this time since Becky had been so young at the time of her mother's death.

"No. Mama always looked funny when Great-Aunt Evelyn was around. Sometimes she made funny faces behind her back."

Easy to understand. And one more indication that Anne Lockhart had been a splendid woman—small wonder Aubrey had worshiped her. Callie said, "I see. Well, we must be polite to her, even if we don't care much to be around her. Will you be extra polite at dinner tonight, and use your company manners, Becky?"

"Uh-huh. I will." The little girl brightened suddenly. "Unless Papa tells me to eat in the nursery! If he asks me to eat in the nursery, will you eat there with me?"

Her charge sounded so cheerful all at once that Callie laughed. "I'd be happy to. I'm sure we'd have more fun eating by ourselves in the nursery than with Great-Aunt Evelyn in the dining room."

Becky's mood slid downward again. "But if we eat in the nursery, I won't get to see Mr. Henderson, and I like him. He's nice, and he tells funny stories."

"Ah, well, I expect your papa will want you to dine with the company, sweetheart, so you'll just have to watch yourself so that you don't incur your great-aunt's censure."

"What's that mean?"

With another laugh, Callie explained. "That means you'd better be especially polite, or she'll come down on you like a boulder."

Becky loved it when Callie used the expressions she'd learned from her brother and his friends. She generally delivered them in "New Yorkese," too, which added to Becky's enjoyment and made her giggle.

As she slipped a pretty evening dress over Becky's head and buttoned her up, Callie started singing a song. Becky loved to sing, and soon the two of them were deep into the chorus of "Yankee Doodle."

As Callie brushed and braided Becky's hair, she reflected on how appealing the notion of taking a relaxed dinner in the kitchen with Mrs. Granger, Figgins, and Delilah sounded. The two of them could eat in pleasant, relaxed surroundings and then go upstairs to the nursery where they could start organizing their birds' nests and feathers. Such a happy prospect was thwarted by Aubrey himself. Callie's evening's doom was sealed with a knock at Becky's bedroom door.

Callie answered the knock and discovered herself face to face with Aubrey. She frowned and stepped back to allow him entry. He frowned at her in his turn.

In other words, things were normal. She said with as little inflection as possible, "Won't you come in, Mr. Lockhart?"

"Thank you, Miss Prophet. I shall."

As ever, he sounded vaguely ironic when speaking to her. Unless he was being downright inhumane, which happened often enough, he sounded sarcastic. Callie made a face at his back, then glanced quickly at Becky. She breathed a sigh of relief when she saw that Becky had not noticed Callie's immature lapse.

The poor darling child craved her father's love and approval so much, and Callie knew she ought to be glad when he made one of his infrequent appearances in the nursery or Becky's bedroom. Instead, she made faces at him. She sometimes wondered if she was destined to live and die an old maid because she couldn't control her deplorable behavior.

Becky spotted her father and ran over to him. "Papa!" She was overjoyed to see her father—which made one of them, Callie thought nastily.

He smiled and picked his daughter. "You're looking as bright and shiny as a new penny, Becky. All cleaned up, I see."

His daughter nodded vigorously, although Callie had to fight against making another face. Blast him. What did he expect, anyhow? If a child were to have any kind of life at all, she had to get dirty sometimes. Callie had deliberately chosen an old frock for Becky's bird-nest-gathering adventure, blast it. It's not as if they'd grubbed around in the mud wearing one of her brand-new school dresses.

"And Miss Prophet washed my hair, too," Becky told him cheerfully.

"I see. You look very pretty, Becky."

Was it Callie's imagination, or did a spasm of pain flit across his face?

Oh, pooh, she was just making things up, she decided at once. Aubrey was a tough enough nut to crack without Callie endowing him with pangs of deathless love and all that rot. No matter what those letters told her about the Aubrey that used to be.

"Thanks, Papa." Becky gave him an impulsive hug, which he returned.

Callie always felt a little left out whenever father and daughter expressed any sort of spontaneous affection. She knew the feeling didn't do her credit, but she couldn't help it.

"Dinner will be served in a little while, Becky, and I came in to invite you to join Mrs. Bridgewater and Mr. Henderson." He turned and eyed Callie. "You and Miss Prophet."

It was just like him, Callie thought bitterly, to thrust her into the midst of the enemy with little warning.

Becky didn't seem quite as cheerful as she had been when her father had first arrived. Nevertheless, she was an obedient child. "All right, Papa. Can I sit next to you?"

Callie's heart gave a little ache that Becky should want to sit next to him instead of next to her. It was a *very* little ache, so she didn't mentally chide herself too hard for being a petty, spiteful, mean-spirited, selfish weasel.

"Your great-aunt will be sitting to my right, sweetheart, and since Mark Henderson is our guest, he'll probably want to be on the left. But you and Miss Prophet may sit next to them. We won't have any leaves put in the table, and it's not going to be a formal dinner. You'll have a lot of opportunity to talk to everyone. I'm sure you and your great-aunt will have much to say to each other."

Becky looked stricken.

Callie muttered, "Oh, really?" under her breath, and then wished she'd held her flapping tongue.

Aubrey turned and gave her a look. She returned the look with one of her own, although she knew she'd been at fault. With a sigh, she decided she owed it to him to help him out during the unfortunate conditions prevailing that evening in the Lockhart mansion.

"Don't worry, Becky, I'm sure she won't be unkind," Callie said, although she knew no such thing.

Aubrey bridled, "Of course, she won't be unkind! She only has Becky's welfare at heart."

*Like hell,* Callie thought savagely. She seldom even thought profanities, and never uttered them aloud, but this was a special case. She said, "Of course."

Becky said with great urgency, "I don't want to go live in San Frisco, Papa. Honest, I don't. I'll try to stay clean. Please? I didn't mean to get dirty today."

Callie rolled her eyes. "Becky, it's all right. Nobody knew your great-aunt was going to show up today." She shot another look at Aubrey. "At any rate, no one told *me* if she'd written to announce her intentions."

"She didn't write." Aubrey sounded miffed with her. What a surprise.

Callie went on, "And you were wearing an old frock that was going to be tossed into Mrs. Granger's rug-making bag. I'm sure your papa isn't angry just because we'd been collecting birds' nests and got a bit messy."

At least Aubrey had the decency to agree with her. "Absolutely, Becky. Nobody's angry because you got your old dress dirty. Mrs. Bridgewater is just a stickler, is all."

Becky seemed eager to accept this, although she did ask, "What's a stickler?"

Aubrey laughed and gave her another hug. "A stickler is a person who doesn't think children should ever behave like children."

"Oh." A worried expression visited Becky's face. "Then I *really* don't want to go live with her, Papa."

"You won't go live with her, Becky. Please don't worry about that. I'll never send you away, I promise."

Well, thought Callie, and she gave an audible sniff, *that* was something, anyway.

Aubrey finished dressing for dinner early and went downstairs to eye the table arrangements. If he could help it, Old Bilgewater wouldn't be able to carry tales of his sloppy housekeeping back to San Francisco. Mrs. Granger had told Delilah to set out the fancy Wedgewood china that Aubrey and Anne had bought in England during their honeymoon.

With a sigh, Aubrey allowed his gilded memories to play in his head for several seconds before shoving them away again. He hated wasting the Wedgewood on Old Bilgewater, but he'd agreed with Mrs. Granger that he should, since Bilgewater expected to be served only the best, both in fodder and in utensils. The table looked all right to him, although he was no expert.

Anne had been the expert on such things. He sighed heavily as his heart gave a predictable tug. It always tugged when he thought about Anne and how much he missed her. She'd been the perfect hostess.

Perfect hostess. Perfect mother. Perfect wife. Damn the Fates for taking her away from him.

As he gazed at the head of the table and pictured the seating arrangements in his mind, he wondered if Anne would have approved of them. He'd heard her say often that tables should be set so that a man sat next to a woman and the woman next to yet another man. Therefore, he supposed, he ought to seat a female to his left, rather than Mark, no matter how much business he and Mark had left to discuss.

Not that this was a formal occasion. Far from it. It wasn't Aubrey's fault that Bilgewater had got a bee in her bonnet and hared out to Santa Angelica with the intention of depriving him of his daughter.

Nevertheless, Aubrey didn't fancy listening to any more criticism from her, and particularly not about table arrangements. Frowning, he guessed he'd better seat Becky next to himself.

Or Miss Prophet. His frown deepened as he thought about

Callie. Dash it, but she was a disturbing female. Aubrey wondered if she was one of those Sirenlike women who cast out invisible lures to draw men into their webs. Mark certainly seemed to be smitten with her, damn him.

Pressing a hand to his head, Aubrey told himself not to be irrational. The fact of the matter was that Callida Prophet was an attractive young woman with a quick mind, a good education, and a very good figure. She was in a perfect position to be married, in other words, and Mark would be a good catch for her. As much as he hated to admit it to himself, she'd be a good catch for Mark, too, with her education and her ability to deal with children.

He also hated admitting that Becky had bloomed since Miss Prophet had taken on the job as her nanny. And Aubrey *was* glad that Becky seemed so much happier now than she had before Miss Prophet had inflicted herself upon the Lockhart household.

Even the servants liked her. Figgins, who never said anything, good or bad, about anyone, had told Aubrey that Miss Prophet was a "fine young woman," for heaven's sake. *Figgins!* Aubrey had gaped in shock at his butler. He still felt rather like gaping, but didn't.

Aubrey was saved from further musings as Mrs. Granger, in her apron and with perspiration beading her forehead, hurried into the dining room. She seemed startled to find Aubrey there.

"Oh, Mr. Lockhart! I didn't know you'd be here."

"Just came in to inspect the table, Mrs. Granger. It looks splendid. I knew you wouldn't fail me in my hour of need." He gave her a conspiratorial smile, which Aubrey could tell she appreciated.

She returned his smile. "The late Mrs. Lockhart used to worry up a storm whenever Mrs. Bridgewater came to visit. That's why I came out of the kitchen to make sure Delilah hadn't forgotten anything on the table. I know Mrs. Bridgewater is quite the perfectionist, Mr. Lockhart."

"You mean she's a cantankerous old fusspot," Aubrey said with a chuckle. "I'm no expert, but the table looks all right to me. What do you think?"

The older woman straightened a napkin that hadn't looked like it needed it to Aubrey. "I do believe she didn't forget a single thing."

"Good. I suppose Figgins has taken care of the wine situation."

"Oh, yes, sir. The Burgundy's breathing right now."

As Aubrey had never understood the intricacies of table settings, still less did he understand the language of wine. He was glad Figgins did, or Aubrey would probably be written off as a bumpkin by Anne's relations. He rubbed his hands together and tried to appear the hearty host. "Splendid. I guess we're all set."

"Yes, sir. The roast beef's almost ready to take up. It has to sit for a few minutes before Figgins carves it."

"Ah." Although Aubrey's parents had been quite well off, they hadn't put on airs, and there were lots of things about high living that Aubrey didn't completely understand. Fortunately, he could afford to hire servants who did. "That's good."

With a nod, Mrs. Granger went on to say, "Figgins will sound the gong at a quarter to eight."

"Wonderful."

Mrs. Granger dipped a quick curtsy and left the dining room with a parting assurance that all would be well with the meal. As Aubrey watched her go, he wondered whether Miss Prophet knew about things like letting Burgundy breathe or a roast settle before it was cut. He guessed he should ask Miss Prophet if he really wanted to know the answer to that one. The thought of how she would respond— most likely she'd fix him with that cold stare that she had used when he'd yelled at her and Becky—both depressed and angered him. Which, in turn, upset him more because he didn't understand why he was thinking about Miss Prophet in the first place, let alone wondering whether or not she knew how to cook a roast.

"For the love of God, quit thinking about that wretched woman," he snarled at himself as he exited the dining room and entered the small reception room leading from the drawing room.

"Which wretched woman?"

Damnation. What was *she* doing here? Aubrey frowned at Callie Prophet, who sat on the sofa with Becky. They looked as if they'd been glancing through the large volume of birds as illustrated by John James Audubon and reprinted on colored plates. Callie stared back at him, her color high, and Aubrey had the unpleasant sensation that she knew perfectly well about whom he'd been lecturing himself.

"Look at this, Papa," Becky said, pointing at a colored plate in the book. "Here's a yellow-bellied sapsucker." She giggled merrily.

Aubrey's mouth twitched. "That's a pretty funny name for a bird," he admitted, choosing to ignore Callie's question.

She sniffed. "It seems to me that there are a lot of yellow-bellied members of lots of species running around loose these days, Becky."

"Really?" The little girl glanced up at Callie wide-eyed, and Aubrey saw that, as improbable as it seemed, Becky's insufferable nanny looked uncomfortable.

Callie muttered, "That was only a joke, Becky."

"And one in remarkably poor taste," Aubrey said unnecessarily. He wished he'd kept his damned mouth shut—not because he didn't mean it, but because making such prim and prissy statements made him sound like old Bilgewater. Aubrey didn't like to think he and Bilgewater had anything whatsoever in common.

"Good evening, all."

Aubrey turned to find Mark Henderson standing just inside the doorway, gazing at Callie. His chest tightened, although he couldn't have said why. He certainly wasn't jealous of Mark. Was he? The idea was more than Aubrey could stand to think about at the moment.

The only thing he knew for certain was that the poor boy had better be careful if he had intentions in that direction. Miss Callida Prophet would eat him alive if he got within wooing—rather, in her case, attacking—distance. "Good evening, Mark. Hope you're hungry. Mrs. Granger's putting on the dog tonight."

"She's putting on a *dog*?"

Becky's sharp cry made Aubrey swivel toward her again. She stared at him, horrified.

After shooting Aubrey a fulminating glance, Callie said soothingly, "It's only a figure of speech, Becky. Sort of like ton of bricks."

"It is?" Becky looked doubtful.

This was ridiculous. It also irked Aubrey that Miss Prophet had leaped to explain the expression to Becky before he could. "It only means that she's preparing an exceptionally good dinner for us tonight, Becky sweet."

"Oh. Good."

"Did you think she'd cook a dog?" Mark opened his eyes wide with mock horror. He shook his head. "I don't go in much for dining on dogs."

"Good heavens, no," Aubrey said, aiming for jolly and almost achieving it.

"Although a dog might be tasty with mustard," Mark added with a wink.

Aubrey guessed the wink had been for Becky's benefit, but it seemed to have been aimed at Miss Prophet. The woman did look remarkably pretty tonight. She wore a rust-colored evening gown with no frills, and had dressed her strawberry-blond hair in a loose pouf, à la Mr. Gibson. Tiny dangles that looked like amber adorned her earlobes, and she wore a simple amber pendant on a gold chain around her neck. The dress was modest and simple and perfectly appropriate. Aubrey couldn't understand why, thus clad, she made him salivate.

Mark, he meant. She made *Mark* salivate. Aubrey was immune to feminine charms. He hadn't glanced at another woman since he'd met Anne.

Good God, he'd clearly been under too much stress of late, if he was mistaking Mark's infatuation for his own. Frowning, he took out his silver pocket watch and squinted at it. "It must be about time for the gong to—"

The musical note of the Chinese gong permeated the atmosphere. Aubrey stuffed his watch back into its pocket and gave an internal sigh of relief. "Ah, yes. There it is."

"Good. I'm famished." Mark, still eyeing Callie covertly,

gave his waistcoat a playful pat. Becky laughed, as he'd intended her to.

Aubrey glanced around the room. "Where's Bilgewater?"

"Where's *who*?" Mark asked, astonished.

After a second's shocked silence, Callie burst out laughing. So did Becky, although Aubrey imagined she wasn't sure what was so amusing. He scowled at the nanny.

"I *said*," he said, lying through his teeth, "Where's Mrs. Bridgewater?"

"Oh," said Becky, willing to accept her father's word.

"Oh," said Mark, who wasn't, but who was game.

"Oh," said Miss Callida Prophet, who Aubrey guessed was neither willing nor game, but was putting on an act for Becky's sake.

Aubrey gave her a good glare to let her know he wouldn't countenance her spreading his slip of the tongue to his daughter or the household staff. She gazed back at him, her green eyes as innocent as a new day. In other words, she could lie as well as, or better than, he could, and she wanted him to know it.

"I believe I heard the gong."

The occupants of the sitting room turned at the sound of Great-Aunt Evelyn's voice. She stood in the doorway, majestically clad in a maroon taffeta dinner gown that dripped beads and fluff. Aubrey blinked at the vision of enormity taking up space in his sitting room before someone—he suspected Miss Prophet, who had stood and taken Becky's hand—poked him in the back and he started forward to lead the formidable personage—she looked like a deep-purple whale, actually—into the dining room.

Mark Henderson bowed at Callie. "May I escort you and Miss Lockhart in to dinner, Miss Prophet?"

Callie's smile for Mark wasn't lost on Aubrey, who kept an eye on her. He told himself it was to head off any outrageous behavior on her part but he couldn't quite make himself believe that.

"Thank you, Mr. Henderson. Becky and I would be happy for your escort."

"We sure would," Becky exclaimed happily. "I'm hungry!"

"Me, too," said Mark.

Mark took seating arrangements out of Aubrey's hand when he held out the seat to the left of Aubrey's for Callie. She sat gracefully, smiling at Mark the while. Aubrey, dealing with Bilgewater, gritted his teeth and bore it.

"And you, young lady," said Mark with his ready twinkle, "can sit beside me here on my other side." He held a chair for Becky as if she were a grown-up lady.

Becky smiled up at him. Aubrey could tell she was happy to be noticed by his young, handsome secretary, damn the man.

Blast it, what was wrong with him tonight? Why was he feeling this animus toward Mark, who was a very nice and obliging young fellow?

Aubrey saw the way Mark looked at Callie as he took his seat, and the reason for his sullen mood became clear to him. He didn't want Mark and Callie getting together. Not, of course, because he himself had any interest in the young woman, but because she'd leave Becky if she had the bad taste to marry someone. Aubrey felt better now that he'd cleared up that tangle in his mind.

Smiling at the company, he said, "Mrs. Bridgewater, would you care to say grace?"

"Certainly."

The old crone offered a blessing that sounded more like a command to God, and which lasted for what seemed like forever. Aubrey almost fell asleep before she droned an "Amen."

That was when he noticed that his daughter's nose only barely reached the table. He frowned. Blast it, they *had* forgotten something. "Becky, my love, where's your chair seat?"

Becky shrugged. "I don't know."

"I'll look for it, Becky," Callie said.

"Thank you, Miss Prophet."

Aubrey stopped being grateful to her as soon as she rose and began wafting gracefully around the room. He saw

Mark's hungry gaze follow her as she searched for the cushion Anne had embroidered for Becky's use three years before—a year before they'd found out the nature of her illness, which was only then beginning to manifest itself. Aubrey's heart gave a familiar spasm, and he frowned as Callie lifted the pillow from a chair shoved against the dining room wall.

"Here it is." She smiled at Becky.

For such an obstreperous female, she had a remarkably sweet smile. Aubrey, who believed that in a just world outer trappings ought to tell the truth, did not approve.

"Excellent," said Mark, who instantly rose to his feet to help her settle Becky onto her cushion. "There you go, Becky. Can you reach better now?"

"Yes, thank you, Mr. Henderson. Thank you, Miss Prophet."

The two said "You're welcome" at the same time, their voices blending into a melodious duet. Aubrey discovered he was grinding his teeth and forced himself to stop it.

Figgins entered the dining room at that moment, bearing the roast beef. Thank God. Aubrey didn't think he could tolerate any more overt displays of mutual attraction on the part of his secretary and his daughter's nanny.

# 8

Callie tried to spend most of her meal time taking care of Becky and being as unobtrusive as possible. She'd recognized symptoms in Mr. Henderson that spoke of his attraction to her, and she didn't know what to make of them.

She supposed she ought to be flattered. After all, he was a good-looking, personable young man with a good job and solid prospects. She knew she could do far worse than to make a match with Mark Henderson, but the sad truth was that she didn't give a rap if Mark Henderson found her attractive or if he considered her as unappealing as a barnyard mouse. As nice as he was, Callie was totally uninterested. She liked her job and didn't want to leave it. More importantly, she loved Becky and didn't want to leave *her*.

If she was to be ruthlessly honest with herself, she'd have to admit, too, that she'd allowed herself to become fascinated with the man who'd written those beautiful letters to his wife. She didn't feel like entertaining ruthless honesty this evening, so she avoided that one.

Besides, the Aubrey Lockhart who now sat at the head of this table bore scant resemblance to the one who'd written the letters.

*Stop it this instant, Callida Prophet.* For once, she obeyed her inner voice and turned her attention to food.

The meal was delicious and, although Mrs. Bridgewater—Bilgewater, indeed—landed the occasional verbal sock in the jaw to whomever she'd singled out to address at any given time, the conversation was lighthearted and friendly for the most part. Mr. Lockhart and Mr. Henderson exchanged stories about banking and the Oriental imports business. Mr. Henderson told two jolly stories that made them all—all but Mrs. Bridgewater, that is—laugh heartily.

Mrs. Granger had outdone herself with everything, including the dessert, which consisted of baked pears in a delicious brandy sauce. Callie felt as though she might pop after she'd swallowed the last bite of her pear.

"I can't eat any more," Becky announced when she was halfway through with her own pear.

"Young children ought to be made to finish their dinners," Mrs. Bridgewater announced.

Although it wasn't her place to reply to her employer's great-aunt, Callie said, "She isn't accustomed to eating such a large meal. I think she's done a very good job with this one." She smiled at Becky, who'd glanced worriedly at her great-aunt. *Great buffalo,* Callie would have called her.

Mrs. Bridgewater sniffed. "Nonsense. Children ought to be taught to finish whatever they're presented."

"Fiddlesticks, Great-Aunt Evelyn," Aubrey said. To Callie, it sounded as though he were trying to sound lighthearted, yet really wanted to knife the absurd purple female in her overstuffed chest.

Mrs. Bridgewater sniffed haughtily. "You're going to be the ruin of that child, Aubrey. Personally, I am not accustomed to small children being allowed to eat with guests in the dining room."

Becky looked stricken. Callie felt like punching the old goat herself, thus saving Aubrey the trouble of knifing her.

"We don't practice society manners here in the country, Mrs. Bridgewater."

Callie glanced at Aubrey quickly, surprised by the acidic tone of his comment.

"And Becky is my daughter, and I'm not about to banish her from meals just because some silly old tradition says I should."

Evelyn Bridgewater sniffed and fixed Aubrey with a decidedly dismissive stare. "I don't believe in relaxing one's standards merely because one lives at the ends of the earth, Aubrey."

A season of quiet fell, not unlike a blanket of snow, over the diners. It looked to Callie as if Aubrey was holding back a rude comment—but just barely. Finally Mark, who appeared rather uncomfortable, spoke up, bless him. "I, ah, think Santa Angelica is a great place to bring up children. It's small, true, but it's awfully pretty. It's probably the forest being so close that gives it a particularly charming and rustic air."

Callie beamed at him, producing a blush in him, which surprised her. "Thank you, Mr. Henderson. I think Santa Angelica is about as close to heaven as one can get while still on God's earth."

Instantly, she wished she'd held *that* comment back, too. She sneaked a peek at Aubrey and was relieved to note that he wasn't glaring daggers at her. Blast her tongue! If there was one topic she should have known better than to introduce, however obliquely, it was death and dying.

"It looks like a picture in my Bible upstairs," Becky offered. "I think it's the picture of the wedding at Canaan." She smiled at her father, who smiled back.

Relief flooded Callie so fast, she barely managed to suppress a heartfelt gust of breath. "My goodness, I should like to see that picture, Becky. I thought all those biblical places were sort of desertlike."

Mrs. Bridgewater sniffed again.

Before she could rebuke Becky, Mark, or Callie for blasphemy or something equally awful, Aubrey spoke up. "Shall we adjourn to the drawing room, everyone? I don't think Mark and I need to linger over port and cigars." He smiled. "Particularly since I don't like port and neither one of us smokes cigars."

"That's a mercy, at all odds," Callie muttered as she untied

Becky's bib. Again, she wished she'd bitten her tongue. When would she learn not to say every blasted thing that popped into her head? With the sigh she'd repressed earlier, she wondered if she was doomed to speak out of turn for the rest of her life.

A young lady ought to be able to hold her tongue when required, as she well knew. She'd obviously lived among friends and family too long; she'd forgotten her company manners.

"So glad you approve, Miss Prophet."

Aubrey's voice sounded like last year's fall leaves, it was so dry and crisp. She gave him an apologetic smile, which he seemed to ignore. She sighed again.

"Here, ladies. Allow me."

At least Mark looked as if he appreciated her. He gazed at her warmly as he held her chair. He still gazed at her warmly when he helped Becky from her chair. "Do either of you ladies play the piano? Perhaps we could have a musical evening if Mr. Lockhart doesn't mind."

"Not at all," said Aubrey.

He didn't sound as if he meant it.

*A musical evening, my foot,* Aubrey thought sourly as he held the drawing room door for Old Bilgewater. She waddled in, her enormous rear end reminding Aubrey of a schooner in high seas.

The young ladies knew how to play the piano, all right. They made more noise on the thing than Aubrey had known was possible before they'd done it. He'd always considered piano playing, unless practiced in the arena of a saloon or vaudeville house, as a genteel pursuit.

It had taken Miss Callida Prophet to show him how wrong he'd been. Not a day went by during which his ears weren't assaulted by raucous music from the nursery-room piano. At least they hadn't sullied the drawing room for their musical incursions.

Anne had used to play, too, but she knew what a piano was for. She and Becky had used to sing soft folk songs and pretty ballads. Never, in all the years of their marriage, had Aubrey ever heard a music-hall tune tinkle from Anne's fingers through the piano keys.

This was not the case with Miss Callida Prophet. While Aubrey wouldn't go so far as to accuse her of frequenting saloons and vaudeville houses by herself, she'd evidently learned a lot from her male relatives and acquaintances. If, as was customary for her, she played *There'll Be a Hot Time in the Old Town Tonight* or *Who Threw the Overalls in Mrs. Murphy's Chowder*, Aubrey might have to speak to her forcefully. Those two were among her and Becky's favorites, to judge by how often they appeared on their musical agenda.

"Do you play, Miss Prophet?" Mark asked.

Aubrey watched him closely. He'd always liked and appreciated Mark Henderson. Mark was the best secretary Aubrey had ever employed, and he'd taken on additional responsibilities with cheer and ability. Aubrey intended to promote him as soon as he thought he could find another acceptable secretary. He'd even envisioned a future partnership with Mark, should things work out that way.

At the moment, he was less than pleased with his secretary, however. He didn't approve of the way Mark was hovering about Miss Prophet. It wasn't right. It wasn't proper.

It was perfectly logical, damn it.

"Yes, Mr. Henderson. Becky and I both play the piano."

Miss Prophet's voice was quite musical. That wasn't proper, either. She ought to have a boisterous voice to go with her boisterous personality. But, as Aubrey had to keep reminding himself, life was unfair about the little things, as well as the big ones.

"Miss Prophet's much better than I am," Becky said cheerfully. "She's real good. She's only just teaching me."

"You're an admirable student, Becky. You ought to hear her play *Mary Had a Little Lamb*, Mr. Henderson."

A pang that could only be jealousy smote Aubrey when he saw Becky and Callie smiling at each other. Dash it, he ought to be happy that his daughter had found a good friend in her nanny. He passed a hand over his eyes and told himself that he *was* happy about it. It was only Old Bilgewater's intrusion into the peace and quiet of his life that had rattled him.

"Let's play one of our favorites, Miss Prophet!" Becky dashed over to the piano bench, opened it with both hands and a good deal of effort, and scanned the sheets of music inside.

Callie was close behind her. "Um, I think this evening will call for some more sober selections, Becky sweets. How about, um, well, let me see here."

Mark, standing far too close to Miss Prophet, Aubrey decided, leaned over to look through the music, too. "What do you have in there?"

"Oh, we have lots and lots of stuff," Becky said.

"Yes, indeed," confirmed Callie. "Mr. Lockhart has a wonderful selection of piano music in here."

Mark swooped. "Here's one I like! It's a funny one."

"Oh, I love that one!" Becky took the sheet music from Mark's hand and spread it on the walnut music stand. *The Cat Came Back.* She laughed.

Oh, yes, Aubrey recalled at once. They liked that one, too. Probably because of that damned cat Miss Prophet had inflicted on his household. *Monster* was a good name for him.

"Well, really."

Miss Prophet shot a glance at Bilgewater. "Um, perhaps we ought to start out with a folk tune," she said, thereby demonstrating a far better understanding of social proprieties than Aubrey would have credited her with.

"Sure," agreed Becky. "Want to sing *The Ash Grove*? I love that one. It's real pretty."

"Perfect, sweetheart." Miss Prophet withdrew a second piece of sheet music and placed it over *The Cat Came Back.* "Would you like me to play first, Becky?"

Becky settled herself next to Miss Prophet on the piano bench. "Yes, please."

Aubrey watched the two young ladies with a small ache in his heart. Anne and Becky used to sit exactly that way. Only Becky had been much younger then. She was growing up so fast. She was going to be seven years old in October. It didn't seem possible.

As Callie played the first few chords, Becky folded her hands in her lap and looked eagerly at the music. Mark leaned against the piano, a baby grand that Aubrey had bought for Anne on their first wedding anniversary, and gazed soulfully at Callie. Bilgewater sat in a chair as overstuffed as she was and watched with an expression of clear disapproval on her face. Observing it all, Aubrey wondered if his life would ever be happy again. He doubted it.

" 'Down yonder green valley, as streamlets meander . . .' "

The lovely old tune filtered through the memories in Aubrey's mind. Anne used to sing it, too. The ache in his heart cranked up a notch. Miss Prophet possessed a nice voice. Not nearly as nice as Anne's had been, but perfection happens so seldom in life that Aubrey didn't fault her for it. Besides, Anne's voice had been a lilting soprano. Miss Prophet sang in a lower range. In a choir, she'd be an alto, Aubrey supposed.

For a moment, he allowed himself to wonder how Anne and Callie would have sounded singing together. Fine, he'd bet, and he wished he could hear their duet.

But he tried not to dwell on impossibilities, so he set that thought aside almost as soon as it entered his head. Becky and Miss Prophet's voices blended together sweetly. When Mark entered the lists in a tolerable baritone, Miss Prophet smiled up at him without missing a note.

Dash it, how dare Mark do his wooing here, in Aubrey's house? Aubrey rose from his chair and marched over to the piano. He took a place against the piano on the other side from Mark, who had, Aubrey noted sourly, chosen to stand on Miss Prophet's side of the piano bench.

Becky smiled up at her papa, surprised and gratified unless Aubrey missed his guess, and he decided it was better this way. He, too, began to sing, in a musical bass. He and Anne had enjoyed singing together, especially at Christmastime, when they'd entertained family and visitors with renditions of favorite carols. His heart still ached as he sang, although the pain eased slightly the longer Miss Prophet played.

After *The Ash Grove*, she struck up an introduction of *My Wild Irish Rose*. From there, they went on to *The Red River*

*Valley*, and then Callie played the opening bars of *Lorena*.

After the last note of that venerable old chestnut had died away, Mark spoke up. "I think we ought to play something a little livelier now. How about *The Sidewalks of New York*?"

"Oh, yes!" Becky gazed big-eyed at Mark. "Miss Prophet does a splendid New York accent, Mr. Henderson. You ought to hear her. She's so funny!"

Laughing, Mark said, "I'd like to hear that."

"It's quite something." Aubrey smiled at Miss Prophet. From the frown she offered him back, Aubrey guessed his smile had been a little too catlike for her.

He glanced at Bilgewater, who glowered at him, as disapproving as ever. No surprise there. Aubrey wondered when she'd last approved of anything, and guessed that it was before his own birth. To hell with the old biddy. "I think that's a wonderful idea, Mark." To Callie, he said, "Strike up the band, Miss Prophet."

Becky laughed again. Miss Prophet's smile appeared rather strained. Nevertheless, she played and sang gamely. She *did* manage to produce a fairly credible accent, from what Aubrey recalled of his visits back East.

"Can we play *The Cat Came Back* now?" Becky asked after they'd nailed *The Sidewalks of New York* to the wall.

Miss Prophet sighed gently. "I expect so, Becky. And then, we ought to get you to bed."

Although Becky looked disappointed, she didn't argue. Aubrey wondered how one man—he—could have been blessed with such a combination of foul and good luck. Of course, the foul luck, Anne's death, had come about directly from his good luck, which had been attaining her in the first place. And the good luck of having such a glorious daughter as Becky was the result of that same good luck.

*Ah, Anne,* he thought suddenly, *why did you have to leave us?*

But there never had been, and never would be, an answer to that one, he knew.

Callie started playing *The Cat Came Back*. Aubrey, glancing at old Bilgewater, saw that she was now scowling hideously. He rolled his eyes and wondered how one woman could be so unpleasant. She must have gathered unto herself all the unpleasantness that had skipped the other members of the Harriott family. None of Anne's other relatives was a sourpuss.

The first verse of the song passed without incident. Becky's clear childish soprano chimed merrily along with Callie's alto and Mark's baritone. Aubrey decided to play onlooker during this particular piece. The three singers clearly enjoyed the chorus.

" ' . . . thought he was a goner, but the cat came back for it wouldn't stay away,' " they all sang, exhibiting various degrees of melodrama.

The singers were well into the second verse before Aubrey knew anything in his household, other than the usual, was amiss. They had just sung, "caught the cat behind the ear," when a shriek issued from the overstuffed woman on the overstuffed chair. Miss Prophet, startled, brought her hands down on the piano keys in a discordant, jarring note. Becky shouted, *"What!"* and Mark jumped at least a foot.

"Oh!" bellowed Bilgewater. "What is it? Oh, get it away from me!"

All of the singers swiveled to take in the spectacle of the maroon matron, eye to eye with a huge black cat, fluffed out to twice his normal size, which was immense to begin with, and with his back arched into the classic witch's-familiar pose.

Callie slapped a hand to her cheek. "Oh, no!"

Becky sat silent and stared, goggle eyed, at Bilgewater and the cat.

Mark, agog, muttered, "What the . . . ?"

It was, therefore, left to Aubrey to march across the drawing room carpet and reach for the cat. "It's only Monster, Mrs. Bridgewater." He tried to sound matter-of-fact.

Bilgewater's face had gone as purple as her gown. "A *monster*? It's a *cat*!" she screamed.

"Of course," said Aubrey. "Obviously, it's a cat." He turned and glowered furiously at Callie, who jumped up from the piano bench.

"Oh, dear. I thought he was upstairs. I'm so sorry, Mrs.

Bilge—ah . . . Mrs. *Bridge*water." She hurried over to Aubrey and the menace.

"It's only Monster," Becky piped up. "He's a nice cat. Honest, he is, Great-Aunt Evelyn."

Bilgewater rose from her chair like something out of a horror novel. A creature from a crypt couldn't have looked more dangerous, Aubrey thought. He thrust the cat into Miss Prophet's outstretched arms. "Here," he said. "Take this thing out of here."

"Certainly, Mr. Lockhart." Callie gazed in consternation at Mrs. Bridgewater, who was eyeing her and the cat as if they were Satan and one of his minions. She stammered, "I— I'm so sorry, Mrs. Bridgewater. Monster's usually shut up in my room during mealtimes. I don't know how he managed to get out."

"I have never," Mrs. Bridgewater said in a tone so frigid, the very air around her seemed to freeze, "been so insulted."

Before Aubrey could intervene with a conciliatory—or even a commanding—word or two, Callie spoke. "I find that very hard to believe, Mrs. Bridgewater. Especially if you speak to everyone the way you speak to the members of this household." She swirled around. "Come along, Becky. It's time for bed."

"Well!"

Aubrey watched with fascination as Bilgewater's already huge bosom swelled until he feared she might pop right out of her bodice. Fearing the result of such a happenstance—if there was one female whose bosom he had no desire to see, ever, it was Bilgewater—Aubrey finally found his voice.

Since he wanted Becky to be comfortable even more than he didn't want to see Bilgewater burst her moorings, he opted not to make her say good night to her great-aunt. He dropped a kiss on the top of her head and said, "Good night, Becky. Sleep tight."

He was glad he'd thought of his daughter first when she offered him a tentative, but visibly grateful, smile and said, " 'Night, Papa. I will, thank you."

She skipped out of the room with Miss Prophet and Monster, whose fur had settled back into its normal overly fluffy, but not bristling, state. Aubrey heard her say, "I don't know why Great-Aunt Evelyn doesn't like you, Monster. I think you're a *fine* cat." She sounded, in short, exactly like Miss Prophet.

Bilgewater's voice cut into his thoughts. "That woman ought to be dismissed, Aubrey. Immediately." Mrs. Bridgewater's voice shook with rage. "She's a terrible influence on Rebecca. She's impertinent and impolite and shouldn't have the care of such a small child. I have never been so insulted."

Aubrey sighed as his gaze left the retreating young ladies and fastened once more on his daughter's great-aunt. He deliberately narrowed his eyes and thought to himself exactly what Callie had so imprudently said aloud. He said, "Oh. Do you really think so?" in a tight voice. To himself, he added, *You must have met up with only extremely tolerant and insufferably polite people until now. And I'll be damned if I'll dismiss Miss Prophet just because you don't like her. Talking back to you is the first thing she's ever done of which I approve wholeheartedly.*

Bilgewater swelled some more. "Aubrey Lockhart, it is not my intention to remain in this house to be bedeviled by a hireling."

"Nobody's bedeviling you, Mrs. Bridgewater." Aubrey frosted his own voice to match hers. "You're the one who came here unannounced. We've done nothing but try to be polite to you, even when you threatened to remove Becky from her home and my care."

"I? Threatened you? *I?*"

Now her eyes had started to bulge. Aubrey had a momentary mental image of Great-Aunt Evelyn's inner self bursting out of her skin and clothes, and pieces of her flying all over the drawing room. He shuddered and made himself stop thinking such things.

"Yes," he said. "You. You threatened to remove my child from my care. And *I* shall never forget *that* piece of insufferable meddling, believe you me." He gave her a steely-eyed stare to show her that she wasn't the only one in the household who could be unpleasant if he chose to be.

"Never. *Never* have I been so insulted. Deliberately insulted. I'm ashamed to be related to you, Aubrey Lockhart, even by marriage." She deflated slightly and began moving toward the drawing-room door.

Mark, about whom Aubrey had forgotten entirely, darted to the door and bowed civilly to her. *Thank God for Mark,* Aubrey thought, even though mere minutes earlier he'd wanted to thrash him.

"Good night, Mrs. Bridgewater," Mark said pleasantly as she passed him—not unlike a steamer passing out of a harbor and into the open sea. Aubrey shook his head to clear it of these images that seemed to want to take it over. "Pleasant dreams."

She gave Mark a superior huff and stalked toward the stairway. Mark glanced at Aubrey and gave a shrug of his shoulders, as if to say, "I did my best. Guess I might have left out the 'pleasant dreams' part."

"You're a hero, Mark." Aubrey walked over to stand beside his secretary.

Together they watched Bilgewater navigate the hallway and tackle the stairs. Aubrey muttered, "I hope she makes it all the way to the top without giving out. I don't think the two of us together are strong enough to carry her to her room if she faints from indignation."

Mark grinned. "I'm afraid you're right."

But they needn't have worried. Mrs. Bridgewater managed to climb the entire stairway and make her way to the bedroom Mrs. Granger had prepared for her. Aubrey and Mark went to the foot of the stairs and listened. They both sighed with relief when they heard the bedroom door close behind her.

"Saved by the cat," Mark said, grinning.

"Saved?" Aubrey squinted at his secretary. "If you say so. I'm not so sure, myself."

"Heck, the cat got rid of her, didn't he? I was afraid she'd sit there and glare at us all night long."

Aubrey headed for the brandy decanter. "There is that, I guess. And I don't think she can remove Becky from my custody."

"Good God." Mark looked stricken. "She couldn't possibly do such a thing. Could she?"

"I don't think so. I am, after all, Becky's father, and I believe the courts take a dim view of great-aunts pilfering children from their parents' homes. No matter what Bilgewater seems to think." He poured out a stiff one and held out the snifter to Mark. "I think we deserve at least one of these."

"I think you're right." Mark took the snifter and inhaled the aroma of the fine old cognac Aubrey had imported from France.

Aubrey held out his glass in a toast. "To Monster."

Mark clinked his own snifter to Aubrey's. "To Monster."

The two men drank that tot of brandy and had another before they, too, went upstairs to their beds.

After he undressed and put on his nightshirt, Aubrey sat on the edge of his bed, buried his head in his hands, and reviewed the evening's events in his mind. When he got to the part where Great-Aunt Evelyn and Monster had stood staring at each other, he unburied his head and grinned. He wished someone would invent a camera that could capture such moments for all time. When he got gloomy, as happened too often these days, all he'd have to do would be to take out the picture of the confrontation and glance at it in order to cheer up.

The notion of Bilgewater attempting to take Becky from him wiped the grin from his face, however.

"The frightful old cow." He swung his feet up and stuck them under the covers. "Her gall and nerve are almost as immense as she is."

Even though he'd begun to steam under the influence of thoughts of Evelyn Bridgewater, Aubrey's bed was cold. He guessed it was time to haul out the bed socks Anne had knitted for him five years before. He'd never had to wear them when Anne was alive—or, at least, not until the last year or so.

With a sigh, Aubrey allowed his thoughts to drift. Remembering Anne and all of her charming and kindly ways always made him melancholy.

He feared Miss Prophet had been right about him. He had neglected Becky.

What a galling admission *that* was. Still, he had been unkind to Becky during this past year. He ought not to have become so entangled with his own feelings of loss. He should have been there for his daughter.

Well, he was aware of his failing now, and he'd do better from now on. He'd already begun to improve. Even Miss Prophet, if she were honest, would have to admit as much.

He recalled her parting words to old Bilgewater, and went to sleep with a grin on his face.

# 9

On Becky's very first day of school, Callie drove Becky to Santa Angelica in Aubrey's pony cart. Becky was as excited as Callie had ever seen her. She'd written a special letter to her mother the evening before, which Callie had promised to post, detailing how much she was looking forward to starting school.

*Mis Prophet nos the teacher*, the little girl had written. *And she says she is very nice.*

And that was the truth. Callie and Myrtle Oakes had gone all through school together. If Santa Angelica ever required the services of a third teacher, Callie had aimed to apply for it—until she'd secured her current position. Now she wasn't so sure she wanted to leave Becky in order to teach. At all odds, she and Myrtle were the best of friends, and they'd spoken often about how nice it would be to work together.

Aubrey had dragged himself away from his business long enough to wave at them from the massive front porch of the Lockhart mansion. He'd even carried Becky to the pony cart, kissed her, and wished her well on her first day of school.

The mid-September morning air felt rather chilly, so Becky wore a bright red sweater, knitted especially for her by Mrs. Granger, over the new blue-flowered school dress Callie had made for her. She looked charming, with her cheeks glowing from good health and excitement, and in her new shoes and stockings. Mrs. Granger had packed her a lunch, which she carried in her new tin lunch pail.

Callie could tell Becky felt grown-up. "Did you remember the apple to give to Miss Oakes?"

Becky bounced on the seat. "Yes, ma'am." Then she grinned. She and Callie had been practicing Becky's school manners, and *ma'ams* were new to her.

"Very good, Becky. I'm sure you'll be a wonderful student."

"I already know how to read and write a little."

"Yes, you do. More than a little, I'd say. I was impressed with your knowledge of letters."

"My mama taught me."

Callie was interested to observe that Becky no longer sounded sad and wistful whenever she spoke of her late mother. Of course, that might be the result of time helping to heal the wound, or the natural resilience of children. But Callie believed at least some small part of the little girl's recovered spirits was due to her own presence in Becky's life. Or at least she hoped so.

"You're already very good with your letters, Becky. I'm sure Miss Oakes will be pleased."

"Thank you. I hope I'll do well in school. I told Papa I'd try real hard."

*Hmph.* As if Aubrey cared.

Callie scolded herself for the uncharitable thought. Becky's papa was not a beast, even if he didn't behave the way she thought he ought. Not often enough, anyhow.

The closer they came to the village of Santa Angelica, the more children they saw making their ways to the tiny schoolhouse. Callie scanned the scene, hoping to find some of her nieces and nephews. Sure enough, they were almost to the outskirts of town when she spotted Jane and Johnny, her sister Alta's two youngest. She called out to them, and they trotted over to the pony cart.

Callie introduced the two to Becky, who smiled shyly.

"Can they come up with us?" she asked Callie in a whisper.

"Of course. Climb aboard, you two." She hoped Jane, who was a sweet child and just about Becky's age, would take Becky under her wing. Jane was a motherly sort, and Becky needed friends her own age.

Money was a valuable commodity, and Callie would never discount its importance in life, but the truth was that Aubrey Lockhart's fortune hadn't provided Becky with nearly enough playmates—or any at all, for that matter. The Lockhart mansion sat quite a ways outside of Santa Angelica, and the circumstances of her mother's illness, as well as the isolation of her home, had prevented Becky from striking up acquaintances with other children. Callie prayed that school, and perhaps Jane's friendship, would take care of the problem.

When they pulled up to the small schoolhouse, Myrtle Oakes and Mr. Millhouse, Santa Angelica's other, older, schoolteacher, were standing outside the door, greeting the children as they entered the classrooms. Myrtle waved to Callie, who waved back. Callie had visited Myrtle over the last weekend and told her all about Becky, so Myrtle was prepared.

Callie wanted to walk Becky to the schoolroom and see her settled, but she knew she oughtn't. The other children might take her concern amiss and start to tease Becky about being a "mama's girl," or something equally cruel. Since Becky didn't need to be teased about her mother almost more than she *did* need to make friends, Callie forced herself to sit in the pony cart and watch.

She was glad for her restraint, since everything worked out quite well without her interference. Jane and Johnny chatted merrily with Becky as they walked with her up to the schoolhouse. Both of Alta's children knew Myrtle, as well as the other children in town, so introductions were quickly and easily made. Callie was pleased to see Myrtle stoop to chat with Becky and gesture her into the schoolhouse, explaining, Callie imagined, where the children were to store their lunch pails and sweaters.

As soon as Becky, Jane, and Johnny disappeared inside

the tiny building, Myrtle waved at Callie again. Her smile told Callie that all would be well. As she slapped the reins gently against the pony's rump and headed for her sister Alta's house for a visit before returning home, Callie prayed Myrtle was right.

That evening as Aubrey, Callie, and Becky sat at the dinner table, it was all Becky could do to sit still. It looked to Aubrey as if, given a free hand, she'd pop up from her chair and begin dancing on the table. And probably sing an accompaniment. As it was, even with the sobering influence of Aubrey and Callie restraining her, she couldn't stop chattering about her first day at school.

He blinked at her after she'd rendered a particularly enthusiastic description of the lunch hour, which, apparently, had been vastly amusing and fraught with games and exchanges of various foodstuffs. Aubrey couldn't remember his first day of school very well, but he didn't think it had been so full of fun and delight.

"So I got to eat one of Jane's sticks of celery, and she ate my apple." Becky sounded pleased with the exchange.

"Is that so?" Aubrey glanced from Becky, seated on the right side of the dinner table, to Miss Prophet who sat on the left. He opted not to mention what he perceived as an unfair trade of food items, because he sensed Becky would be hurt if he did. "It sounds as though you enjoyed your first experience with school."

"Oh, I did, Papa! It was so much fun! And Miss Oakes started reading a *super* story to us!"

"Did she indeed?"

"Yes. It's all about an English boy who ends up on a pirate ship. And there's a mean pirate named Long John Silver and a parrot, and buried treasure, and everything."

"I see. Sounds like *Treasure Island* to me." Aubrey smiled at his daughter, glad that she was so happy about school. He'd been worried that she'd feel alone and left out, since she hadn't had much interaction with other children in Santa

Angelica. "And did you learn anything? Or did Miss Oakes read to you all day?"

Blast. That sounded as if he were being critical, and he hadn't meant it to. He was only curious. Not for the first time, Aubrey wished he had a way with children.

"Miss Oakes is a fine teacher," said Callie—Miss Prophet, he meant.

Blast it, Aubrey couldn't recall exactly when he'd begun thinking of his daughter's nanny as "Callie," but he wished he hadn't. "I'm sure of it," he said soothingly.

"Oh, yes, Papa. She's *super*. And she only just started reading us *Treasure Island*. She read through the first chapter today. It was Johnny who told me the rest of the story."

"I see. I trust that won't spoil the remainder of the book for you."

"Oh, no! I can't wait to hear more of it tomorrow." She fairly glowed at Miss Prophet. "And I like Johnny a lot. And Jane. She's *super*."

Aubrey assumed *super* was a word Becky had heard today, liked, and decided to adopt as her own. "I see. And who are Johnny and Jane?"

"They're Miss Prophet's relatives," Becky said complacently. "They're both super."

"I see." Aubrey glanced at Miss Prophet and wondered if her relatives were all as rambunctious as she. He didn't ask, since he didn't want to precipitate an argument. "And you say Miss Oakes got some teaching done, as well as some reading?"

"Oh, yes." Becky forked up a piece of roast pork. Before she popped it into her mouth, she said, "She taught us all about our ABCs."

"I thought you already knew your ABCs." Aubrey delivered the sentence with a smile, and then shot a peek at Callie, to make sure she knew he wasn't quibbling with the teacher's methods. She didn't even bother to look at him, blast her, but serenely chewed a bite of potato, her gaze fixed upon Becky.

"Oh, I do know them, Papa." Becky was obviously proud of her exalted knowledge. "Miss Oakes found that out right off because I could read a whole page in my reader without once stumbling over a word. Since I can already read and write, Miss Oakes said I can help her with the other children who don't know their letters."

"Good. That's good." Aubrey beamed at his daughter, glad to hear that the Santa Angelica schoolteacher possessed enough perspicacity to recognize his daughter's brilliance.

"It's very good, Becky," Callie said, agreeing with him for once. "But you must never act as though you consider yourself better than the children who don't know as much as you."

"But I am better than they are," Becky said, although Aubrey was sure she didn't mean it the way it sounded.

Callie smiled at her. "Of course, you're much better at your letters than the rest of the children. But that doesn't make you a better person."

"Oh," said Becky, but she still looked confused.

"You know how much you hate it when people lord it over you because they know things that you don't," Callie went on.

Becky nodded.

Aubrey wondered what the devil Miss Prophet meant by this "lord it over you" nonsense. He imagined he was about to find out.

"Well, then, think of how the other children will feel if they think you're trying to lord it over them because you've had an opportunity to learn your letters and they haven't. You don't want them to dislike you or think you're stuck-up, do you?"

"Oh, no!" It looked as if a light had just gone on in Becky's head. "I see what you mean." She nodded.

"I knew you would." Callie gave Becky an approving smile.

Aubrey, astounded, glared at her. She gazed back at him calmly and said, "Becky has been extremely lucky in some ways, Mr. Lockhart. She's had the undivided attention of her parents—well, until the last year, at least—and the good luck to have had someone work with her on her letters before she started attending school. Not all of the children with whom

Becky goes to school have been so fortunate."

"Fortunate!" Aubrey couldn't believe she'd actually said that.

"Fortunate," Callie repeated firmly. She smiled at Becky. "Don't you feel fortunate, Becky? To have learned so much before you started going to school, I mean. In other respects, of course, you weren't fortunate at all."

Becky, evidently unperturbed by Callie's choice of words or the veiled reference to her deceased mother, chewed thoughtfully and pondered the question.

Aubrey was about to take Miss Prophet to task for what he considered a series of ill-chosen comments—"fortunate," indeed!—when Becky beat him to it.

"Oh, yes. I see e*zack*ly what you mean, Miss Prophet. I am lucky to know my letters already. And I don't want them to think I'm stuck-up." Becky smiled brightly at her nanny. "I know what I'll do! I'll try to act just like you."

Aubrey didn't suppress his groan in time to prevent some of it from escaping. Callie cast him a withering glower.

"You never make me feel stupid." Becky seemed unaware of the disturbances going on between the two adults sharing the dining table with her. "I'll try to act like you when I help the other children."

"Thank you for the commendation, Becky," Miss Prophet said, shooting another meaningful glance at Becky's papa. "I appreciate it."

"Oh," said Becky, grinning up a storm. "I think you're *super*."

Aubrey decided to let his daughter's misapprehension about her nanny slide so as not to wound her.

Then again, he thought suddenly, perhaps Becky was right. As much as he hated to admit it, life *did* seem to have become less oppressive since Miss Prophet's arrival in his home. He gazed at Callie for so long, she finally stopped pretending not to notice, and frowned at him.

He grumbled to himself as he cut another piece of the delicious roast pork Mrs. Granger had served for dinner. Or, perhaps he'd been right about her in the first place. She certainly seemed to possess no understanding of the social divisions separating employer from employee.

Aubrey decided to forego the rigors of business after dinner that night. He'd enjoyed Becky's recounting of her first day at school, Miss Prophet had managed to get through the entire meal without irritating him more than twice or thrice, and he was feeling quite a bit more relaxed than usual. Besides, while he'd started immersing himself in business all the time in order not to dwell on his personal tragedies, he was getting sick of it.

He plucked *Treasure Island* from a high shelf in his library where he'd stuck it when he and Anne had first moved to Santa Angelica. Aubrey didn't remember exactly why he'd kept the book; he'd read it when it had first been published in 1883, even though he wasn't a child at the time, and had enjoyed it thoroughly.

Mulling it over now and remembering his first days in this house, when life had seemed pure and perfect and blessed, he seemed to recall thinking it had been a rousing and entertaining novel. He also recalled thinking that if he and Anne should ever have a son, it would be fun to read *Treasure Island* to him.

With a sigh, he turned the book over in his hands, staring at it. Life had been full of love and promise in those days. Now it was flat and dull.

Perhaps not dull. Not anymore. He smiled when his mind pictured how excited Becky had been at dinner.

Besides, he really needed to stop dwelling in the past. He'd loved Anne absolutely, but Anne was dead. He owed it to his daughter—and, he supposed, to himself—to stop wallowing in despair. After all, Becky needed him.

And, honestly, when he thought about it, it seemed more that he'd become accustomed to being unhappy than that he truly *was* unhappy these days. Grief had become more of a habit with him than a genuine emotion.

How strange. Aubrey took a moment to savor the possibility that he'd just hit upon something profound.

By God, he'd never even considered the concept that the appearance of grief might become a routine—not unlike thinking of oneself in a certain way. Aubrey wondered if Great-Aunt Evelyn Bilgewater thought of herself as a nice person, for example.

The ramification of this new discovery was too much to take in all at once, even for him in a contemplative mood. He decided to think about it later.

He took *Treasure Island* to the back parlor, poured himself a cup of tea, sat in his favorite chair, propped his feet on the ottoman, turned up the lamp, and settled in for a good read. He felt slightly childish at first, rereading this old book, but he consoled himself with the thought that Becky would appreciate him being up-to-date on her *super* teacher's *super* reading. He chuckled once before he lost himself in the foggy English coastline.

A knock on the door frame startled him out of the tavern he and Long John Silver had been sharing. Glancing up, he saw Miss Prophet standing in the doorway, her hands folded primly in front of her. How one person's hands could lie so eloquently, Aubrey had no idea.

Putting a finger in the book to hold his place, he said, "Yes, Miss Prophet? You wish to speak to me?"

"Yes, Mr. Lockhart. If you aren't too busy." She gazed pointedly at the book in his lap.

Aubrey felt his neck get hot. Good God, was he going to blush in front of this impertinent nanny just because he was reading a child's book? He steeled his nerves. "Please, have a seat." Because he couldn't think of a way to avoid the issue, he lifted *Treasure Island*. "Becky's chatter at the dinner table reminded me how good this book is, so I'm rereading it."

She smiled at him. Unless he was mistaken, which was quite likely, it actually looked like a genuine smile with no brittle edges to it. "Yes, it's a wonderful book, isn't it? I'm glad Myrtle decided to read it to the children, instead of something insipid. You can't fool children, you know."

He hadn't known that but opted not to say so. Instead, he murmured, "Who's Myrtle?"

"Oh. I forgot you aren't acquainted with very many of your neighbors, are you?"

Aubrey had been pretty sure she wouldn't be able to maintain her neutrality for long, and he'd been correct. Talk about brittle edges. He did not, however, snatch at the bait she dangled so tauntingly before him. "No. Since my business is in San Francisco, and since my wife was so sick for so long, I'm afraid I've never had much of a chance to meet many of my neighbors." He gave her a smile he hoped she'd choke on.

Miss Prophet did look slightly abashed, and Aubrey felt better for it.

"Yes, well, I'm sure I didn't mean to criticize."

"I'm sure."

She cleared her throat. "Actually, that's what I'd like to speak with you about this evening, Mr. Lockhart."

He looked at her blankly. "My neighbors?"

"In a way." She finally took his suggestion and sat in a chair some few feet away from his own. "Becky's seventh birthday is coming right up. In October. That's only a little less than a month away."

"Yes. I recollect the day of her birth quite well, thank you, Miss Prophet."

He saw her lips pinch together and wished he'd managed to contain the dryness of his tone.

"Yes, well, I thought it would be fun for Becky to have a birthday party."

"A birthday party?" Aubrey had never heard of a birthday party and to be honest, he wasn't quite sure what having a birthday party entailed.

Miss Prophet nodded. "Yes. I understand from Myrtle— Miss Oakes—and from my sisters and brother, that people are beginning to host small parties for children on their birthdays nowadays. It would be a wonderful way for Becky to get to know her classmates better, don't you think?"

"A birthday party. *Hmm.*" He frowned, not sure if he liked the notion. "Where would this party be held?"

"Oh, here, of course." She smiled winningly.

She looked charming—and not at all rowdy or impertinent—when she smiled at him that way. In truth, Aubrey found himself responding to her smile rather more heatedly than he approved of.

"A party to be held here." He tried to think of something other than her smile. "I see."

"I believe Becky would enjoy it a good deal, and the other children would come to understand that she isn't so different from them just because her father has more money than their fathers have."

Aubrey felt his eyes widen. "Do they think she's different for that reason?"

"I'm afraid so, Mr. Lockhart. While some of the adults who live in Santa Angelica have come to know you slightly, as they came to know your wife, whom they all liked and admired, Becky has been quite isolated during these past years. And they are very important years in a child's life, too. Miss Oakes and I have spoken of it often."

He didn't at all like the notion of Miss Prophet and Miss Oakes gossiping about him and his daughter—particularly since he knew good and well that Miss Prophet's part in the conversation wouldn't show him in a favorable light. He frowned. "Is that so?"

"Don't worry, Mr. Lockhart, I haven't given away any family secrets." She waved a hand in an airy gesture and gave him a look that came mighty close to a smirk.

He didn't think it was funny. "Of course not. How could you, since you don't know any?"

The look on her face puzzled him, but he didn't ask about it. It seemed strange, however, that her smirk should have vanished and been replaced by an expression of longing. She didn't give him the opportunity to think about it for very long.

"So, what is your verdict on this idea, Mr. Lockhart? May I plan to have a birthday party for Becky and invite several of her new friends?"

He frowned. The notion of a horde of small children dashing about his home didn't appeal to him very much. He knew, however, that he owed Becky a lot if he intended to make up for his neglect over the past year. More than a year, if he counted the days he'd spent worrying over Anne before she died. The sigh he sighed felt as though it had been wrenched from his toes. "Very well. I suppose Becky deserves a party."

Callie jumped to her feet. "Oh, *thank* you, Mr. Lockhart! I haven't broached the subject with Becky yet because I didn't want to disappoint her if you didn't approve of the notion, but I'll tell her first thing tomorrow."

"Fine, fine. You do that."

To his astonishment, Callie actually dipped him a curtsy before she turned and headed toward the door of the library. Aubrey watched the way her hips swayed and wondered if a nanny's hips were supposed to do that. He supposed that, all things considered, nannies had no more power to order bodies to certain specifications than any of the rest of the people in the world. It did seem, though, that, in a just world, she ought not to have such a superb figure.

There he went again, fretting about the injustice of life. He shook his head and was about to wrench his gaze from Callie's hips when she surprised him again by turning abruptly at the door. With one hand holding the jamb, she gazed at him for a couple of seconds. It wasn't a long time, but it was fully long enough for Aubrey to get a queasy feeling in his tummy.

Because he believed in facing problems squarely and not allowing them to fester or sneak up on him, he said, more sharply than was strictly necessary, "Yes? Is there something else you wish to discuss, Miss Prophet?"

"Yes. I mean, no. I mean . . . Oh, dear."

She put a palm to her cheek. Aubrey started to worry. She wasn't going to quit, was she? Not right after he'd acquiesced on the subject of a birthday party.

Birthday party. Whoever heard of such a thing? The world was becoming a more frivolous place by the hour.

"What is it, Miss Prophet?" He held his breath.

She flung a hand out. "It's nothing, really, Mr. Lockhart. It's only that—that— Mr. Lockhart, I apologize if I've been unpleasant to you on occasion during these past weeks. While, at first, I blamed you for neglecting Becky, I've since come to understand more fully the nature of your loss."

Aubrey stared at her and opened his mouth. Since he could find no words to fill it, he shut it again.

Callie, her cheeks burning pink, muttered, "That's all. I just wanted to apologize if I've been impolite to you, is all."

Before he could string two coherent words together, she fled, and he was left staring at the wall and the doorway out of which she'd just exited his presence.

"Good Lord."

*Treasure Island* lay forgotten on Aubrey's lap as he considered Miss Callida Prophet and her unusual personality. He'd never met anyone quite like her. She was a true original.

For the life of him, he couldn't drum up a single ounce of disapproval. And he tried.

Callie told Becky about her birthday party the very next morning. Becky approved wholeheartedly, and was eager to begin planning party games and addressing invitations.

Since Callie's duties weren't as strenuous as they had been, now that school had started, she spent that day looking through *The American Girl's Handy Book* in search of party games. She chatted with Mrs. Granger about an appropriate luncheon meal to serve a horde of seven- and eight-year-olds.

"I'll bake a cake, of course," said Mrs. Granger in a complacent voice. "Becky's favorite is a white cake with white icing sprinkled with coconut."

"Sounds delicious," said Callie, who didn't care much for coconut but was willing to eat anything if it would make Becky happy.

"And perhaps we should have an ice-cream dessert to go along with the cake."

"My goodness. Do you think that's going overboard?"

"I do not." Mrs. Granger looked stern. "That poor child deserves all the good things we can give to her, Callie, and you know it. I sincerely doubt we'll spoil her by feeding her friends cake and ice cream one day out of the year."

After the two women had wrestled with Becky's birthday

meal and throttled it to a standstill, she wandered off to peruse the *The American Girl's Handy Book* some more.

In truth, she was using the book as an excuse. The conversation she'd had with Aubrey last night wouldn't leave her alone.

So, he didn't think she knew any of the family's secrets, eh? Little did he know. Guilt enveloped her like one of San Francisco's famous fogs.

No matter how guilty she felt about reading Aubrey's letters to Anne, however, she couldn't make herself stop reading them. Every night, she read to Becky from at least one of the letters. That was bad enough, and she excused that part of her prying by telling herself it was good for Becky to know that her parents had deeply and genuinely loved each other and their little girl.

The part that made her feel really guilty was that, every night after she'd kissed Becky good night, she took the letters to bed with her and reread them. She occasionally wondered if she had some kind of emotional insanity that propelled her to read another woman's private and personal correspondence and to dream that the letters had been written to her instead of to Anne.

Not that Aubrey Lockhart or any other man would ever adore Callie Prophet the way Aubrey had adored his Anne. Callie was not like Anne in the least.

"Bother. The letters made Becky feel better. That's the important part."

She knew she was only trying to assuage her guilty conscience.

And she still read the letters. She even prayed about the matter, hoping to gain some guidance from God, since she was too ashamed of herself to ask anyone else what she should do.

Anyhow, she *knew* what she should do. She should confess to Aubrey that Becky had found the letters. She'd never be able to tell him that she herself had been reading them; that would be too humiliating. Even if she never made a full confession of her guilt, she should return the letters to Aubrey.

But she didn't. That night, as every night since Becky had first showed her the letters Aubrey had written to Anne, Callie read a couple of them.

The really awful, not to mention stupid, part of the whole pickle was that Callie was wildly jealous of Anne, a dead woman. She'd feared she might also have fallen completely in love with Aubrey through those same letters, which was not merely awful and stupid, but impossibly idiotic.

She also began to understand that, all by itself, life was plenty complicated enough. When a person did things she knew she shouldn't do, such as reading another person's private letters, she only made it more so.

And she couldn't stop for love nor money.

# *10*

To all outward appearances, life at the Lockhart mansion proceeded much as usual during the month following the beginning of Becky's first school year. Becky continued to blossom under Callie's care, the gardens at the mansion took on an autumnal cast, Figgins started talking about instructing the gardeners to lay in firewood for the winter and having the storm windows put up, Mrs. Granger and a minion hired for the purpose finished the yearly potting, pickling, and preserving, and Aubrey's business interests flourished.

Mark Henderson made his weekly visits to Aubrey's house on schedule. Mrs. Granger, when she wasn't preserving foodstuffs, continued to prepare delicious meals, she and Delilah kept the house tidy and dusted, and Callie continued to answer Becky's letters to her mother in heaven.

And then there was Mrs. Bridgewater.

"The damned woman's driving me mad," Aubrey told Mark one day as the two men sat in Aubrey's library office, sipping a preprandial sherry after slaying the day's commercial dragons. The mail had been delivered earlier in the day, and now Aubrey's insides tightened when he picked up the letter Figgins had just brought to him. He eyed the envelope with misgiving, recognizing the fiercely upright penmanship inscribed on it. He steeled himself to open the envelope and disgorge its contents.

"Is she still trying to get you to send Becky to live with her?"

"Yes. The infernal, interfering busybody." He shook the envelope at Mark. "I swear, I get a letter from her every other day."

Mark grinned. "She's a regular Tartar, all right."

"She keeps proposing new reasons Becky ought to move to San Francisco and live with her. She's driving me crazy with her constant meddling."

"Why is she so intent on having your daughter move in with her? I have to say that she doesn't seem the motherly type to me."

"Motherly! Maybe to a pack of hyenas she'd be an appropriate mother."

Mark's grin widened. "Besides, I should think she'd be glad Becky's got a papa who cares about her."

Aubrey scowled as he picked up the Chinese letter opener from his massive teakwood desk. He stabbed it under the gummed flap of the envelope. "She's not happy unless she has all the members of her family directly under her thumb. She's driven most of her relations out of San Francisco already, except those who can't escape because of their business dealings."

"Dictator in training, is she?"

"In training, hell. She graduated from the dictator college a long time ago. She could give the kaiser a run for his money." Lifting the folded paper out of the envelope, he flapped it open and eyed it with distaste. "Dash it."

"What's wrong?"

"She's holding out lures," Aubrey said glumly.

"Lures?" Mark seemed to be having trouble containing his amusement. "What sorts of lures?"

Aubrey didn't think it was funny. He waved the letter in the air. "Old Bilgewater's sister, Anne's *nice* aunt, Glenda, is holding a party in honor of her daughter's—Anne's younger sister's—engagement. Bilgewater wrote to ask us to attend."

"Well, that doesn't sound *too* horrible," Mark mused consolingly. "When's the party?"

"In a couple of weeks."

"Can you claim Becky's school duties prevent your attendance?" Mark looked thoughtful. "After all, you can't take a child out of school every time a relative has a party, can you? And you'll have to spend at least one night away from home if you attend a formal party in San Francisco, since it's a four-hour trip each way."

Aubrey, who had already noticed a diabolical trend in Bilgewater's efforts to wrest Becky from him, shook his head grimly. "She thought of that one already. The party's set for a Saturday night." Holding the letter in one hand, he smacked it with the other. "Damn her, she said she talked Glenda into holding the party on a Saturday instead of a Thursday just so that Becky and I can attend."

Mark didn't do a very good job of concealing his enjoyment of this situation. "Thinks of everything, doesn't she? Are you going to go?"

A feeling of savage frustration chewed at Aubrey's insides. Dash it, it seemed that every time he turned around, his sanity was being tried by one officious female or another. First Miss Callie Prophet thundered into his home and took it over, and now Old Bilgewater was trying to direct the rest of his life from San Francisco. "I suppose I have to."

"Why?" Mark sounded genuinely interested.

Slapping the letter down on the desk at his side, Aubrey growled, "Anne would want me to. Amalie was her favorite sister, and Glenda was her favorite aunt. Besides, Becky ought to become better acquainted with her San Francisco relatives. Most of them are quite nice. Bilgewater's the only clinker in the works."

"Look on the bright side," Mark suggested. "She can't live forever."

Aubrey shot him a quick grin. "True. And she's really more of an annoyance than a threat. She can't do anything to take Becky away from me."

With a shrug, Mark said, "There you go."

"Bah."

It was all so frustrating, though, no matter how little real power Bilgewater had. Until a couple of years ago, Aubrey Lockhart had believed himself to be in absolute control of his life. It seemed to him now that Anne's illness had been the start of a whole series of events some evil presence had sent to prove to him that life was outside his command. He hated feeling out of control.

Happy sounds of a child and a nanny at play—Aubrey thought he heard the fierce yowlings of a particularly devilish black cat a couple of times, too—wafted through the library window. Although the early autumn mornings and evenings had begun to nip at the edges of the remains of the good old summertime, the afternoons had so far remained warm enough that Becky and Callie played outdoors after school. Aubrey sometimes wondered what the devil they found to do out there for so many hours at a stretch, although he hadn't asked, for fear he might disapprove and thus instigate a squabble with the nanny. He was glad to know Becky was no longer lonely, in any event.

He rose from his chair and meandered over to the window, his hands clasped behind his back, and peered out. His daughter and her nanny seemed to be involved in some sort of craft activity involving tree bark, grass, and a variety of leaves, acorns, and other bits of flora. He squinted, but couldn't make out what they were doing with it all.

Monster, reminding Aubrey of an Eastern potentate in his silent, superior pose, watched the activity, his yellow eyes glinting in the fading sunlight. His tail switched back and forth occasionally, as if to remind anyone who might be watching that he was aware of the goings-on around him and was ready to take action if necessary.

Aubrey had been staring gloomily out on the scene for a few minutes when Mark joined him at the window. Glancing at his secretary, Aubrey was neither pleased nor surprised to see that Mark's gaze was directed not at Becky but at Miss Prophet. His infatuation with the woman remained untrammeled, apparently.

"I suppose I'll have to take Becky to the dashed party. Don't see any polite way out of it."

With a shrug, Mark said, "It probably won't be so bad, Mr. Lockhart." He cleared his throat. "Ah, will you be taking Miss Prophet along? To look after Becky?"

Aubrey gave his secretary a searching look. "I suppose so. I don't think I'm up to traveling alone with Becky. Not exactly in my line, if you see what I mean, taking care of children."

"Understandable." Mark nodded. He cleared his throat again. "Er, I might be able to lend my assistance, if you'd like me to. You know, to carry things and so forth. Becky and I get along very well. I might be able to help keep her amused on the journey."

Aubrey had to fight an urge to thump Mark on the jaw with his fist—which he unclenched as soon as he realized he'd clenched it. "Thank you." His jaw seemed to have frozen into a tight knot. He relaxed it, too, and told himself to be calm. Mark's offer was kindly meant. He was sure Mark didn't intend to seduce Becky's nanny. And, even if he did, what business was it of Aubrey's?

As if he sensed that something odd had crept in the atmosphere, Mark glanced at Aubrey with some confusion. "Well, I know it's difficult to travel with a child if you're not used to it. At least, that's what my sister Margaret tells me." He laughed uneasily. "She's got three, you know, and likes to take me along on trips to keep the kiddies entertained."

"Ah. No. I didn't know that."

"Well, she does. Er, when did you say this party is planned?"

Eager to wrench his thoughts away from the problem of Mark Henderson and Callie Prophet, Aubrey said, "Weekend after next."

"I can plan my visit out here on Friday instead of Wednesday that week, if it will help you out," Mark said hopefully.

Knowing he was being completely irrational and disliking himself for it, Aubrey gave himself a fierce inner shake and said, "Thank you. That would be great."

"Good."

Dash it, the man didn't have to sound so cheerful about it. Aubrey shot Mark a glare from under his lowered eyebrows, but Mark didn't see it. He was too busy gazing wistfully at Miss Prophet.

Both Callie and Becky were excited about their trip to San Francisco. "Papa says I've been there before," confided Becky, "but I don't 'member it much." She paused, and Callie thought she could see the gears in her little brain grinding. "I 'member fireworks, though."

"Fireworks?" Callie smiled at Mark Henderson as he took a suitcase from her and handed it to the coachman.

"I think you're remembering the Chinese New Year's celebration we saw a couple of years ago, Becky," Aubrey said.

Callie was startled when he thrust Mark out of the way and lifted a second suitcase from the ground near Callie. "That must have been fun," she said as she watched Aubrey brusquely gesture Mark to the back of the carriage.

"It was," Aubrey said curtly. "Here, Mark, why don't you help John strap these suitcases on the back of the coach so they won't fall off." He frowned. "Don't see why we have to take so dashed much baggage with us."

"It's because we have to bring day wear and party wear, Mr. Lockhart." Callie pitched her tone to sound cool and neutral.

*"Hmm."* Aubrey all but hurled a bandbox at Mark.

Eventually they settled into Aubrey's comfortable traveling coach, and John, the head groom at the Lockhart stables and today's coachman, clicked to the horses to let them know they could start on the journey. Callie and Becky sat on one side of the commodious coach, while Aubrey and Mark took their seats across from them. Becky's cheeks were pink with excitement.

"I can't wait to see San 'Frisco," she announced, settling back and folding her hand in her lap, in blatant imitation of Callie, who'd only sat thus because she was trying to look prim. She didn't feel prim. She felt as exuberant as Becky looked, actually. As much as she adored Santa Angelica, she also occasionally loved visiting the city.

"It should be fun," she said, keeping her tone sober. "And I'm sure you'll enjoy seeing your San Francisco relations again, too."

"I s'pose so." Becky sounded as if her San Francisco relations were the least of her concerns.

Callie tried to hide her grin. Mark didn't go that far. He laughed outright. "What gives me the feeling you're more interested in revisiting Chinatown than in revisiting your San Francisco relatives, Miss Becky?"

Becky laughed, too. "Oh, it's 'cause I am! I 'member the fireworks. They were so pretty. But loud."

"They were very loud."

This, from Aubrey, who had joined the fray, Callie noticed, after shooting Mark another malignant glare. She didn't know what the man had against his secretary. Mark Henderson seemed to be a very nice person, and he must be a good secretary or Aubrey Lockhart wouldn't keep him on his staff. Callie had learned by this time that Mr. Lockhart, the businessman, did not suffer fools gladly.

"I don't suppose we'll see any fireworks this time, Becky," Aubrey went on to say. "The Chinese celebrate their new year in late January or early February, I think. This is September."

"Oh." Becky looked disappointed, but she perked up almost immediately. "But can we go to Chinatown, Papa? I want to see the pretty lanterns Miss Prophet told me about."

Callie fielded one of Aubrey's grumpy looks, and gave it back to him with interest. "We'll have time for a little sightseeing, won't we Mr. Lockhart?" she said, knowing as she did so that she was courting a rebuff from Aubrey. He, after all, was the one in charge of this trek.

After seeing Callie's black look and raising her one, he said, "We'll see. We might have time, provided the Harriotts don't have plans for us all day tomorrow."

"I really do want to see Auntie Amalie," Becky said. "She's nice, and she writes me letters and sends me things."

Becky's aunt Amalie was the youngest of Anne's sisters,

and the one whose engagement they were on their way to celebrate. "She seems to be a very nice lady," Callie put in before Aubrey could say anything.

"She is." Aubrey frowned out the window for a moment and added, "I'm glad she's found a husband. I think the family was beginning to worry about her ever settling down."

Instantly, if not sooner, Callie took umbrage. "Do you believe the only successful life a woman can have is that of being a wife to some man, Mr. Lockhart?"

His head whipped around, and he scowled at her. Out of the corner of her eye, Callie noticed Mark Henderson giving the both of them a puzzled stare. She stuck to her ground, unwilling to give an inch in the issue of women's careers.

"I don't believe I said that, Miss Prophet." Aubrey sounded like he'd iced his words before flinging them at her.

She sniffed. "It sounded to me as if you thought there might be something wrong with Miss Harriott that she hadn't snared a husband before this time."

"Nonsense. I said the *family* had begun to worry, not I."

Callie gave him a *"Mmm,"* and didn't elaborate.

"My word, Miss Prophet, you sound quite ferocious. Are you an adherent of Mrs. Anthony's cause, by any chance?"

Callie had almost forgotten Mark was in the carriage with them, but she glanced at him now, trying to soften her expression for his sake. "I believe women deserve the opportunity to make their ways in the world, Mr. Henderson. So many of us are obliged to seek employment and I think it's a a shame there aren't more avenues open to women."

Mark nodded judiciously. Callie got the impression he was afraid to open his mouth for fear she'd slap it shut, and she silently chided herself. Just because Aubrey got her goat every living moment—and she feared she allowed him to do so for reasons unworthy of her—that didn't mean all men were beasts who wanted to hold women captive to their power.

She said gently, "I didn't mean to snap, Mr. Henderson."

Aubrey huffed, "He's not the one you snapped at. It's I to whom you ought to be apologizing."

Callie sniffed. "Nonsense. I didn't snap at you."

"Could have fooled me," Aubrey muttered.

"Fiddlesticks." She noticed Mark Henderson watching them with interest, and so swalled the rest of her retort.

The remainder of the trip continued along the same lines. Callie was glad when, several hours later, the carriage pulled up in front of a grand house on Nob Hill in San Francisco. She stared at the edifice, which looked even more like a castle than the Lockhart mansion in Santa Angelica did.

"My goodness. Is this where the Harriotts live?" Anne's family must be monumentally wealthy.

The coachman opened the door and flipped the stairs down. Without glancing at her, Aubrey lifted Becky, who had fallen asleep a couple of hours earlier. "This is my house, actually. We're stopping here while we remain in San Francisco."

"*Your* house?" Callie's eyes widened as she took in the full glory of the Lockhart's San Francisco abode.

"Imposing edifice, isn't it?" asked an amused voice at her back.

Callie jumped when Mark took her elbow to assist her out of the coach. "Er, yes. Yes, it's quite imposing." Since Aubrey didn't seem inclined to speak to her, she decided to talk to Mark, who was much more kindly disposed. "Is the house empty? I mean, do any of the Lockharts live in it? If there are any other Lockharts, I mean."

"No. Mr. Lockhart's grandfather built it with the money he dug out of the gold fields. Mr. Lockhart keeps it in case he ever decides to move back to San Francisco. I guess the place is of sentimental value to him."

"Sentimental value. I see." Callie could appreciate sentiment as much as the next person, but to maintain such a huge mansion in an expensive city for the sake of sentiment was going a bit far. She gazed at the huge house as she stepped from the coach, holding Mark's hand for balance. "Does he keep the place staffed when he's not here?"

"Oh, yes, of course. You've got to keep places like this occupied, at least by a skeleton staff, or they go to rack and ruin in no time flat."

"Ah. Of course." Mercy. Callie couldn't imagine having

the good fortune to be able to afford a single maid to help her keep up her own family's home in Santa Angelica. Staffing an empty house in the metropolis was beyond her comprehension.

"Of course, I expect he wants to keep it for Becky's sake, too. And in case he ever remarries."

Callie, whose feet had barely touched the ground, spun around and gaped at Mark. "Remarries? *Remarries?*" The possibility of Aubrey remarrying had never occurred to her. It made her insides crunch up painfully. "But—but— Well, his wife. I mean, he's so brokenhearted."

Mark shrugged. "You never know about these things."

Every feeling inside her rebelled. The notion of Aubrey Lockhart with a woman other than Anne—or herself—made Callie feel positively ill. Restoring her composure with some difficulty, Callie supposed Mark was right. She swallowed around a big lump in her throat. "Yes, of course."

"Besides, it would probably be good for Becky if he did remarry one of these days. A little girl needs a mother."

"Of course. Yes. Of course, you're right."

That being the case, Callie knew she shouldn't entertain the urge to scratch out the eyes of the mythical future Mrs. Aubrey Lockhart. It took some willpower to force her fingers to relax from the clawlike spasm Mark's words had precipitated in them. Unless the future Mrs. Aubrey Lockhart was Callie Prophet, Callie didn't want even to *think* about it.

She did, however, rather enjoy her stay in the Lockhart manse that night. She allowed herself to pretend, even though she knew she shouldn't, that the house was hers. Hers and Aubrey's. After they'd wed.

Oh, God. When had she fallen in love with him? And why? At first she hadn't even liked him. How had this happened? Was it because of the letters? Was it because her mind had begun to reconcile the Aubrey of the letters with the Aubrey of today?

"You're an idiot, Callie Prophet," she told herself right before she climbed into bed. She feared she'd hit the nail square on the head, too.

\* \* \*

Aubrey and Anne had visited San Francisco quite often after they moved to Santa Angelica. He used to love the city and all the hustle and bustle abounding there. Anne had loved visiting her family and showing off Becky to them. However, since Anne's illness, Aubrey had only wanted to bury himself in the country.

He assuredly wasn't looking forward to spending this weekend in San Francisco, although he was willing to endure it for the sake of Anne's favorite sister, Amalie. And Becky. Becky deserved to know her Harriott relations, most of whom weren't at all akin to the bulldozer Bilgewater, and they deserved to know her.

Nevertheless, he wasn't feeling awfully chipper when Becky bounced down the massive stairs of the old mansion on Saturday morning, full of energy and glee, chattering away like a magpie about visiting Chinatown. Miss Prophet, he noticed, was busily abetting her in this desire. And, unsurprisingly, so was Mark Henderson, who had eyes only for Miss Prophet, except when he was forced by courtesy to pay attention to someone else.

Suppressing the irrational compulsion to kick his secretary down the front steps of his lavish townhouse, Aubrey forced a smile for Becky. "Ready to see the sites, sweetheart?"

"Oh, yes, Papa! Miss Prophet says we can have lunch in Chinatown!"

"Does she?" Aubrey eyed Callie with disfavor.

Dash it, he didn't understand why the woman should look so blasted appealing all the time. Nannies were supposed to be elderly, gray-haired ladies with canes and hearing trumpets. Aubrey's sense of ill-usage grew each day that he was faced with the young, pretty, bubbly, and—worst of all—competent Miss Callida Prophet.

"It's not a long walk to Grant, Mr. Lockhart," Mark said cheerfully, patting his topper in place and twirling his walking stick. It seemed to Aubrey that Mark had arrived with the sun that morning, jolly as an elf, eager to join in the fun. "Becky told me she'd enjoy a good brisk walk."

"Oh she did, did she?" Aubrey sucked in a breath and told himself to stop taking exception to every blasted thing anyone said to him. A glance at Callie, who was drawing on her gloves, an operation that required her to bend her head so that he could only see three-quarters of her face because of the hair and hat, made him grind his teeth.

It wasn't fair. Nannies weren't supposed to make a man think of beds and silken sheets and dim lighting and so forth. They weren't supposed to make a man want to undress them—slowly and seductively, tasting the sweet, exposed flesh as they went about it. They weren't supposed to make a man want to remove the pins from their hair, run his hands through it, and watch that glorious strawberry-blond mass spread out over his pillows.

"You don't mind, do you, Papa?"

Aubrey started when Becky tugged at his coat sleeve. He glanced down at her, noticed the worried expression on her piquant face, and his heart melted. He dragged his mind away from what he'd like to do with Callie, and stooped to pick up his daughter. "Of course, I don't mind. Do you want chop suey?" He tweaked her nose.

Becky giggled. "That's a funny word. I want whatever that Chinese dinner is that comes with the crunchy noodles. You remember, Papa. You brought some to me a long time ago."

"It was a *very* long time ago," confirmed Aubrey, his mind boggling. "I'm surprised you even remember it."

It had been Anne's last trip to visit a doctor in San Francisco—before they'd given up and accepted everyone's mortal verdict. Aubrey, his heart aching and his world crumbling around him, had thought to bring Becky a treat. And she'd remembered it. His heart gave a spasm now, in reminiscence.

"I 'member it, Papa. Mama and I ate the noodles and laughed."

Aubrey felt like crying. His astonishment nearly overwhelmed him when he glanced at Miss Prophet and found her discreetly wiping away a tear. His heart hardened immediately. Dash it, he hated it when the woman showed herself subject to human sympathies. He preferred thinking of her as an unruly bumpkin. It was much easier to keep his urges under control that way.

Nevertheless, their sojourn in Chinatown wasn't at all unpleasant. Aubrey was happy to learn that Miss Prophet could behave in a subdued and ladylike manner when put to the test, and that she could control Becky's behavior with gentle hints. Of course, that was primarily because Becky was a practically perfect child. But, still . . .

He didn't like the way Mark seemed to fawn over Miss Prophet, but he had to admit that Miss Prophet didn't encourage him. In fact, if Aubrey had been Mark, he believed he'd have been quite discouraged.

Oddly enough, the more Aubrey watched Miss Prophet treat Mark like a younger brother and not like a potential lover, the more cheerful he himself became. By the time the four of them toddled into a Chinatown restaurant for a restorative bowl of soup and some chow mein, complete with crunchy noodles, he was in a remarkably good mood.

He'd expected this first trip to San Francisco since Anne's death to be one of wrenching memories and depression. But he discovered that it was difficult to be depressed when one's almost-seven-year-old daughter was in such a sunny mood. And, while he wasn't sure it was a good thing that he'd noticed, it was difficult to be prey to wrenching memories when one was accompanied by a lovely young woman with strawberry-blond hair, a rosy disposition, and a smashing figure, who seemed to be able to win the hearts of everyone with whom she came into contact.

She'd certainly won Becky's heart. And poor Mark was totally infatuated, even though Callie gave him no encouragement whatsoever.

It was while Becky was giggling over the piece of paper she'd discovered in the crispy rice cake bestowed on her by a fawning Chinese waiter that the notion of a possible second marriage started worming it way into Aubrey's consciousness.

At first he was appalled. A second marriage? After Anne? Impossible. His marriage with Anne had been perfect in every respect. They'd loved each other wholly and absolutely. Aubrey couldn't imagine loving another woman as he'd loved Anne. Theirs had been a match that had been, if not literally, at least figuratively made in heaven. He could never remarry. The very idea was absurd.

"Oh, look, Papa!"

His attention jerked back from the thorny tangle, Aubrey glanced at his daughter. "What is it, sweetheart?"

"I got a fortune!"

"Aha. And what does your fortune say?"

Becky squinted at the small print. "I can read it," she announced as Mark reached to take the slip from her fingers. Grinning, Mark withdrew his hand. "It says, 'You will soon be happy.' " Becky looked up at her father, her cheeks glowing with health and good cheer. "It's right, Papa. I'm happy right now."

Aubrey's heart hitched. "I'm glad, Becky. Very glad." He couldn't stop himself from glancing at Miss Prophet. He knew she was the authoress of his daughter's happiness, and he appreciated her for it, even if she did cause him many pangs and disconcerting moments.

Miss Prophet looked away quickly, leading Aubrey to surmise that she'd been staring at him during his interchange with Becky. *Hmm.* What did that mean? he wondered. Perhaps she didn't find him as repulsive as her sharp tongue might lead a fellow to believe.

He was undoubtedly only being fanciful.

Nevertheless, that evening, he made it a point to go to Becky's room in order to escort his daughter and her nanny to the cab he'd hired to carry the three of them to the Harriotts' party. He gave a soft rap on the door and called out, "Becky? Are you two ready in there? It's about time to be off." He kept his tone jovial to forestall Miss Prophet, who seemed an exceptionally defensive young woman, from taking his prompting amiss.

"All ready, Papa!" Becky sang back. She sounded cheerful, and that made Aubrey glad.

As for himself, he wasn't looking forward to the evening. Not only was it going to be difficult to meet Anne's family, most of whom he hadn't seen since the funeral, but he didn't anticipate anything of a jovial nature from old Bilgewater. With a sigh, he stood back, drew on his evening gloves, and waited.

The door opened at last, and Becky popped out. "You look as fine as anything, sweetheart!" Aubrey exclaimed, heartened by his daughter's spiffy appearance. She'd make a huge hit with the Harriotts.

"Miss Prophet made me this dress, Papa," Becky told him as she twirled in front of him.

"Good for Miss Prophet."

She did look darling. Callie had sewn her charge a blue taffeta confection, full of frills, flounces, and ribbons, with a deeper blue satin sash at the drooped waistline. It suited Becky to a T. The blue of the satin sash was almost the same color as her eyes. She also wore pristine white stockings, frilly drawers that Aubrey could see when she twirled, and black patent-leather Mary Janes.

Not even Old Bilgewater could take exception to her appearance. Her hair, Aubrey noticed with satisfaction, gleamed, and was braided neatly and tied with blue ribbons.

As if reading his mind, Becky said perkily, "Miss Prophet washed my hair and rinsed it with vinegar, too."

"Did she?"

Becky nodded. "She says vinegar takes away the soap res—res—something. It's a nice word for scum."

Aubrey nearly choked. "I see. I believe the word is 'residue.'"

"That's the one!" Becky confirmed.

"I see." He squinted at the open door. "And is Miss Prophet planning to join us anytime soon?" He regretted the acidic tone in his voice as soon as he heard it. He really didn't want to rile Becky's nanny this evening. He wanted the night to be as pleasant a one as it could be, under the circumstances.

"Oh, yes. She said she just had to grab her evening cloak."

"I see."

"Here I am," Callie said, out of breath. She barreled through the door, buttoning a glove and almost bumping into Aubrey. She drew herself up quickly and blushed. "I beg your pardon, Mr. Lockhart. I couldn't find my reticule, and then I couldn't get this silly glove buttoned."

Aubrey took a hasty breath and forced himself to be calm. "Think nothing of it, Miss Prophet."

This was bad. Very bad. It might even be terrible. Something was definitely wrong with him. He ought not to be having these improper impulses, and especially not toward his daughter's nanny.

Eyeing Callie sideways, Aubrey felt indignation swell within him. It wasn't right. And it wasn't his fault, either. He couldn't be called to blame if Callie Prophet got herself all dolled up until she looked good enough to eat.

Or, if not to eat, at least to bed.

The worst of it was that, if he were called to say exactly what he found in Miss Prophet's appearance this evening that might be calculated to make a man salivate, he couldn't name it. She was dressed in a sober gray evening dress, perfectly appropriate for a nanny escorting a charge to a formal evening party. She was neat as a pin and perfectly fashionable, but there not a thing about her that might lead an impartial observer to think she was casting out lures with the intention of reeling Aubrey Lockhart into her creel.

He felt lured anyway, and he resented it.

Fortunately for him, the Harriott home was not far from his San Francisco mansion, so he was able to worry about something besides his libidinous feelings toward Callie Prophet after a very few minutes of fretting over them. After that, he only had to field obnoxious comments from Old Bilgewater once or twice. The rest of the Harriotts liked him just fine.

As well they should. After all, it had been Aubrey Lockhart who had saved the entire clan from bankruptcy when he'd married Anne and redirected their investments onto a profitable path.

Anne's aunt Glenda was a lovely, good-natured woman, too. She'd taken Amalie under her wing when Anne and Amalie's parents had died. Aubrey found himself talking to Glenda a lot during the evening, and blessing the woman for being as unlike Old Bilgewater as a blood relation could be.

"Becky is such a darling, Aubrey. You must be very proud of her."

Aubrey sighed. "I am. She's the image of Anne, isn't she?"

Glenda eyed him speculatively. "Yes, she is. How are you getting along, dear?"

"All right."

"I'm sure you both miss Anne."

"Yes." Aubrey's lips tightened. He knew Glenda only wished for his happiness, but he couldn't bear talking about Anne. Glenda didn't press the issue.

The two of them watched Becky dance with Mark Henderson, who had kindly led her out onto the floor. "Mr. Henderson is an awfully nice man, isn't he?" Glenda asked with a smile.

"Yes." Aubrey discounted the times when he'd felt like whacking Mark for being infatuated with Callie Prophet, because he sensed those times weren't really Mark's fault.

"And Becky's nanny is a delightful young woman. She seems to have done Becky a world of good. She's quite pretty, too, isn't she?"

Aubrey stiffened. "Is she? I hadn't noticed."

Glenda eyed him more closely. "She's more than merely pretty, Aubrey. She's a blessing for Becky."

*"Mmm."*

He didn't appreciate Glenda's knowing chuckle, but when he turned to offer her a glacial and suppressing glance, her grin was so broad and so wise that he had to look away again immediately.

Later on in the evening, and against his better judgment, Aubrey asked Callie to dance a waltz with him. His state of mind was not eased by the discovery that she felt nearly perfect in his arms.

The only thing she could have done to ease his mind, in actual fact, was to have been Anne. And even Aubrey, no matter how much he wanted to, couldn't blame Callie Prophet for not being Anne.

# 11

Aubrey didn't know about this.

Two weeks had passed since Amalie's engagement party, and his mind hadn't been quiet once. It was in more of a turmoil than usual this morning at he gazed out on his small kingdom in Santa Angelica. At least it used to be his kingdom.

Right now, the rolling lawn on the north side of his house had been turned into another world. Miss Prophet had installed a huge open tent, under which rested two long tables, what looked like a million chairs, untold yards of colorful bunting, and perhaps a billion balloons. Aubrey couldn't recall ever seeing a more festive side lawn anywhere.

Worse than that was the specter of approximately ten matrons, all dressed to the teeth, and all exhibiting various degrees of formidability and fascination. Aubrey imagined they'd all come to Becky's party in order to say they'd visited the Lockhart mansion and seen for themselves the reclusive owner thereof. He felt rather like the protagonist of a Gothic romance novel.

The very least pleasing aspect of the arrangements was that of Great-Aunt Evelyn Bridgewater, who was at present holding court in the middle of the flock of mothers. Aubrey had resisted inviting her, but Callie had prevailed. She always prevailed, a fact that Aubrey didn't understand.

But when she'd said, "Mr. Lockhart, Mrs. Bridgewater is Becky's great-aunt, and she's sure to find out about the party. If you don't invite her, her doubts about your fitness as a parent will be reinforced in her own mind."

"And can you tell me why I should care what she thinks?" Aubrey had inquired frigidly.

"You should care," Callie had responded promptly, "because she's your late wife's aunt. I'm sure you don't wish to have the late Mrs. Lockhart's family believe you wish to sever communications with them, and you know full well that Aunt Glenda can't come because she's involved with Amalie's wedding plans."

Damn it, she was right. He'd never admit it. "I don't want to sever communications with them, and they know that! For heaven's sake, I went to that infernal engagement party, didn't I?" Aubrey had bridled. He'd even bristled. "It's only old Bilgewater I don't want hanging about."

With a smile she couldn't suppress, Callie had said, "Yes, but she seems to have been elected—or, more likely, she appointed herself—family spokesman. You know it as well as I do. Even the late Mrs. Lockhart knew it."

Aubrey had stared at her, befuddled, and she'd blushed. He'd been on the verge of asking her how she knew Anne had acknowledged Mrs. Bridgewater's status, but decided it wasn't worth the breath it would take to ask the question. Instead, he'd agreed, without any enthusiasm whatsoever, to invite Old Bilgewater to Becky's birthday party.

He guessed it was a good thing he'd done so, although he still had his doubts about how pleasurable the day was going to be for him. He had enough trouble dealing with one child, and that one his own daughter, whom he loved. He couldn't imagine getting along with a couple of dozen other children whom he didn't know at all, plus their mothers. Add Bilgewater into the mix, and it sounded toxic to him.

Callie had told him not to worry about any of the arrangements, that she'd take care of everything.

He didn't doubt it for a minute. She was exceptionally adept at organizing things. Not to mention people. After scarcely three months of tenure as Becky's nanny, she had the entire Lockhart household adhering to schedules and rules of her making. What astonished Aubrey was that, while he'd noticed her managing ways and faintly disapproved of them even as he became more closely attracted to her physical person, no one else in his household seemed to mind them in the least.

Whatever unique quality Miss Callida Prophet possessed, he'd concluded several weeks earlier that it was dangerous and not to be trifled with. He wasn't exactly sorry he'd agreed to host this party, however. He wasn't yet ready to give it his approval, either. Several days earlier, he'd adopted a wait-and-see attitude toward the thing.

He was waiting and seeing this particular Saturday morning, when the party was about to start. As he stood on the front porch of his mansion, waving at incoming carriages and wagons, steeling his nerves to join the herd of matrons under the tent and wondering if he looked as skeptical as he felt, he noticed himself growing grumpier and grumpier. A birthday party. Who ever heard of such a thing?

Callie Prophet, that's who.

"Isn't it wonderful, Mr. Lockhart? The only child who didn't accept Becky's invitation was Gloria Hurst, and that's only because she had to have a tooth pulled yesterday, and her jaw is sore and swollen today. Her brother, Billy, is here, along with their mother."

Callie waved a folded sheet of paper under his nose, which only served to irritate him further. He snatched the paper from her hand. "Yes. Thank you. I can see that we're going to be overrun with children and their mothers." He pitched his tone to sound as ungracious as he felt.

"Oh, stop being an old fusspot," Callie told him. Then, when he stared at her, she blushed. "I beg your pardon. I shouldn't have said that."

Aubrey could tell her apology was less than sincere.

"Well, never mind," she said into his silence. "*I* think this will be a wonderful party!" And she ran down the porch steps and into a cluster of children.

Aubrey watched her with mingled annoyance and fascination. For some reason, the notion of remarrying had been niggling at his conscious mind ever since they'd all attended Amalie Harriott's engagement party last month. He didn't seriously consider the prospect, because he couldn't imagine loving anyone but Anne.

Still, the prospect kept bothering him. And, really, when he thought about it rationally, it might be a good idea for him to remarry. For Becky's sake. She deserved two parents. A daughter, in particular, needed a mother.

*Who are you trying to fool, Lockhart?*

The truth of the matter was that Aubrey himself wouldn't mind a warm body in his bed every now and then. He was still a young man, and he possessed a young man's needs and desires.

Remorse stabbed him as effectively as if the god of guilt had heaved a lance and pierced his heart.

Dash it, remarrying would be a betrayal of Anne and of his marriage vows to her. So what if she was dead? Aubrey had loved her with his whole heart and soul. He couldn't imagine loving anyone else.

Not that marriage necessarily had to include love. Plenty of men remarried after their wives died because they needed mothers for their children. And, while it was true that Aubrey Lockhart could afford to hire people to look after his daughter, it might be better to have a wife to see to things. More secure, and all that. After all, wives were more or less permanent. Nannies and so forth were subject to the vagaries of employment.

Callie and several of the young matrons who had accompanied their children to Becky's party started singing a song that evidently went with a well-known children's game, since all of the assembled children grabbed hands and started walking around in a circle. Aubrey watched with interest. It seemed that there was an entire culture devoted to the rearing of children about which he was ignorant. This game, for example, seemed to be known by one and all. Except him.

And Old Bilgewater. Aubrey saw her lift her lorgnette—he presumed she'd chosen lorgnette over her spectacles today in order to appear festive—to her bulging eyes and watch the party game. It looked to him as if she disapproved, which was only to be expected. Bilgewater disapproved of everything. His attention returned to the children.

He stared when Callie, laughing merrily, picked up a little boy and whirled him around. Aubrey supposed this was part of the game, but it wasn't a decorous one. Callie's skirts flew up, revealing her plain cotton drawers. Squinting and wishing he had a lorgnette like Bilgewater's, he could make out that the bottom ruffle was not lacy, and that there seemed to be a blue satin ribbon as trim. Otherwise, they were as plain as dirt, and a far cry from the frilly underthings Anne used to wear.

Which brought his mind back to the matter of wedlock, and the benefits that could accrue to a man through the age-old institution of marriage. Damn, but Callie Prophet had a spectacular figure. She was built on more buxom lines than Anne, who had been tiny and ethereal.

So ethereal, in fact, that she hadn't been able to withstand the rigors of life on this earth. Aubrey, a pain in his chest, imagined her in heaven. Anne would fit into heaven without causing a ripple in the firmament.

Callie, on the other hand, wasn't the least bit ethereal. It was Aubrey's opinion that she was as sturdy as an ox. But more appealing.

"Appealing? Get a hold on yourself, man."

How long had it been since he and Anne had made love? He shook his head as he counted up the months. More than twenty-four of them, as Anne had been so terribly ill for so long.

*When I'm gone, please don't grieve forever, Aubrey. Find a nice woman to be a wife to you and a mother to Becky.*

Anne's words, as clear as the day she'd said them, entered Aubrey's head like the wind, fairly knocking him over with the recollection. He shut his eyes, remembering.

"Ah, Anne," he murmured, wondering why he'd forgotten.

The doctors had just rendered their verdict. All the doctors.

Even the ones Aubrey had imported from Europe and back east. Anne's illness was a cancer, it was inoperable, and it was killing her. Aubrey and Anne had just returned from their last fruitless trip to San Francisco. That night, he'd sat by her bedside, holding her hand, his heart throbbing with grief and the knowledge of impending loss.

Anne had accepted the news with much more fortitude than Aubrey had—probably because she'd known her illness was fatal from the beginning. Anne had been like that. Perceptive. Realistic. Aubrey had wanted to fight the disease, but Anne had known that fighting would only exhaust them both, and eventually come to naught. She'd begged him to accept her approaching death with peace and grace.

Then she'd told him to remarry. For his sake and Becky's—and her own. *I'll die happy if I know you'll take care of yourself, Aubrey. Take care of yourself and Becky. For me. Please. I want you to be happy.*

He'd forgotten that. During the past couple of years, he'd managed to forget everything but how awful it had been to watch her waste away. And suffer. She'd suffered agonies from the pain. At the end, she'd probably been addicted to morphine, but Aubrey didn't care. Better morphine than frightful torture from the cancer eating her up.

He shut his eyes for a moment, unable to bear the pictures memory was dredging up and presenting to his mind's eye. Damn it, he didn't want to remember Anne as that fragile, fading flower. He wanted to remember Anne as she'd been in the beginning: beautiful, lithe, graceful, full of gentle humor and boundless love.

And she'd told him to remarry. With a sigh, he opened his eyes and looked out on the lawn where the party was proceeding with vigor and energy. Callie spotted him, put her fists on her hips in a mock-serious manner, and shouted, "Come down from your throne, Mr. Lockhart! You can help us pin the tail on the donkey!"

"Yes, Papa!" Becky called out to him—and Aubrey couldn't recall the last time he'd heard her sound so ebullient. "I want you to play with us!"

Good God. Aubrey couldn't imagine a worse fate than

being in the midst of—how many were there? fifteen? twenty?—little children with whom he had no sympathy or ability to deal. And with Bilgewater looking on and censuring him, no matter what he did.

So why did he find himself waving back, smiling, and calling out, "All right, sweetheart. Where's this donkey of yours?"

"It's on the *treeeee*!" Becky had shouted with glee.

He was probably only crazy.

If he was crazy, he decided later, insanity might not be as terrible as he'd always heard it was. He actually, really and truly, had a good time playing with the children and Callie. Callie was the one who tied the blindfold over the children's eyes, but she appointed Aubrey to spin the children around so that each would lose his or her point of reference and head any which way with the donkey's homemade tail in hand.

Once Aubrey had to scamper out of the way or get the donkey's tail pinned on his own backside. Becky had squealed with delight. Instead of feeling foolish, he'd laughed as loudly and genuinely as everyone else present. Everyone except Bilgewater, that is.

He did, however, refuse to have himself blindfolded and spun around and then try to find the donkey's hind end. He might be crazy, but he wasn't *that* crazy.

Following pin the tail on the donkey, roller skates were passed around. Aubrey had given Callie free reign to purchase whatever she chose for the party, and she'd chosen roller skates. She'd said they could serve as party favors.

Rather cumbersome party favors, he thought now, although the children didn't seem to mind. Actually, to look at them and listen to them, the children were ecstatic. Their mothers were interested. Bilgewater disapproved, of course.

Aubrey, unwilling to put on roller skates and make a total fool of himself, retired to a bench under a tree. From this vantage point, he watched the proceedings with fascination.

Of all the women present, only Callie dared don the skates herself, although she offered skates to anyone who wanted them. She'd even smiled brightly at Bilgewater and held out a pair of skates in invitation.

"Don't be absurd," the old hag had said tartly.

Callie hadn't pressed the issue, but only smiled sweetly. Watching from under his tree, Aubrey had to give her credit. She wasn't intimidated by Becky's great-aunt. Bilgewater hated her for it, too. Her detestation was as plain as the huge beaked nose on her face.

It seemed that Callie didn't care an iota what Bilgewater thought of her. "I haven't done this since I was twelve years old," she announced with a laugh as she sat on a bench and plied her skate key.

"That's almost twice as old as I am," Becky told her.

Aubrey grinned, cheered to discover that a child of his loins could do her sums so well. Becky was good with her numbers and her letters, and she made Aubrey proud. Imagine that. For months, he'd been ready to vow he'd never be happy about anything again—but he was happy about Becky. And he was even sort of happy about this nonsensical birthday party, except for Bilgewater.

Callie, wobbling a little on her skates, lined the children up. "We're going to practice before we hold any races. I don't want anybody getting a skinned knee or a broken arm."

The children laughed, although Aubrey was pretty sure he heard a couple of horrified gasps from the mothers and Bilgewater sitting under the tent. He eyed them and thought how pleasant it was to have Callie in charge of Becky. Callie never succumbed to fits of the vapors or irrational fears.

Good God. Had he honestly just thought what he thought he'd thought? Directing his attention at Callie and her group of skate-encumbered children, he amazed himself by acknowledging that he had. And, what's more, his thought had been not only correct, but enlightening.

He supposed—although it was far too early in the game to make any decisions about the matter—that if he *did* choose to remarry he might do worse than to select Miss Callida Prophet as his bride.

Aubrey frowned. He was beginning to frighten himself.

Although, it was true, by marrying her he'd be precluding

her exit from Becky's life on the arm of another man. Mark Henderson, for example.

Such a sensible notion eased Aubrey's misgivings considerably. Yes, indeed, Becky was the only reason—Becky, and the honest acknowledgment that he was a young man who had certain physical needs—he'd ever consider marrying Miss Callida Prophet. Absolutely.

"All right, everybody, here we go!"

Callie's merry voice jolted Aubrey back to the here and now. He watched as a dozen or more children skated, with various degrees of agility and ability, on the paved drive that made a half circle in front of his house. A rose bed, the roses having been chosen years earlier by Anne, decorated the center of the curve. Even though it was October, some of the roses still bloomed. Seeing them reminded Aubrey of his late wife, and he started to feel guilty.

Even if he remarried, he'd never forget Anne. He swore it, to himself and to her.

He got the feeling Anne was looking down from heaven and rolling her eyes in exasperation.

"Look, Papa!"

Becky's excited shout jerked him out of the beginnings of the mood he'd been poised to sink into. He waved at her. "You're doing very well, Becky!"

"This is such fun, Papa! It's *super*!"

"I can see it is!"

Aubrey noticed several of the ladies under the tent glancing at him and then putting their heads together. Bilgewater was in the center of the group. Damn it, he knew what that meant: They were gossiping about him. Because of his money and his personal loss, the fact that he'd hired a local young lady to serve as Becky's nanny, not to mention the fact that Bilgewater hated him, he was undoubtedly a hot topic of conversation in Santa Angelica.

Because he didn't like the idea of being the subject of idle chatter, he decided to put a stop to it. Deliberately, he rose from his comfortable, shady bench under the tree and walked over to the tent.

All talk among the matrons ceased, as he'd figured it

would. "Good afternoon, ladies." He even nodded politely at Mrs. Bridgewater. "Are you and your children enjoying my daughter's party?"

A moment of absolute silence, broken only by the happy shrieks and squeals of the gaggle of children, greeted his question. Then pandemonium broke out as every single one of the mothers hastened to assure him that both they and their sons and daughters were delighted to have been invited to the Lockhart mansion for Becky's party. Bilgewater, he noticed, maintained a stony silence.

He gave a savage internal snort of derision. She only wanted to talk about him behind his back. She'd never say anything nice, about him or his daughter's birthday party, to his face.

"For, you know, Mr. Lockhart, that we all think Becky is such a dear child," one woman—Aubrey thought she was Mrs. Hurst, mother of a chubby boy with a surly disposition who was a terrible skater—told him.

Several bonneted heads bobbed up and down as other women nodded agreement.

"Indeed, she's a particular friend of my Sylvia," another woman said.

Squinting at her, Aubrey tried to remember her name and failed. He didn't recollect Becky talking about anyone named Sylvia. Nevertheless, he smiled at her. "Becky is enjoying school and meeting other children."

"She's a darling child, too. Callie's been so good for her. Don't you think so, Mr. Lockhart?"

Aubrey knew who *that* was. He smiled at Mrs. Frederick Watson, otherwise known as Alta, one of Callie's older sisters. He'd be damned if he'd admit that Callie'd been good for Becky, even though such an admission would irk Bilgewater and might be worthwhile on that account. Also, he didn't quite know the cause of his reluctance.

However, he honored it and said, "Becky's enjoyed getting to know Johnny and Jane, Mrs. Watson. I believe they've become quite close. And I know they were helpful to her during her first few days at school."

"Yes, I believe so. Jane is always talking about what she and Becky did in school."

The air of serene complacency with which Callie's sister said this annoyed Aubrey. He felt rather as if he and his daughter were being used by the matrons of Santa Angelica as some sort of prize to be flaunted. He cast a stern glance at Bilgewater, who ignored him and made a show of looking at the swarm of skating children.

"I do hope there won't be any accidents, Aubrey," Becky's great-aunt said in chilly accents. "They're awfully young to be roller-skating."

"I'm sure Callie knows what she's doing," Alta said, instantly jumping to her sister's defense.

Aubrey was curious to note that she'd evidently taken Bilgewater in dislike. He wondered if her reaction to the older woman was prompted by sincere feeling or by having been told about her by Callie. It didn't much matter, he reckoned. Anyone who *liked* Mrs. Bridgewater had to be foolish beyond imagining.

"Do you?" Bilgewater asked Alta in a *faux* sweet voice.

"Yes. I do."

Because he didn't particularly want to get involved in a cat fight, Aubrey said, "I'll wander down there and see what I can do to help Miss Prophet. There are a lot of children to keep track of."

Mrs. Bridgewater sniffed.

Alta smiled at him.

As he strode over to the circular drive, he wondered if the entire Prophet family was made up of imps and busybodies. He didn't appreciate the look of knowing intelligence on Alta Watson's face.

Damn them all.

"Look, Papa!"

Becky's happy shout captured his attention—thank God—and Aubrey turned to seek out Becky among the swarm of children. She was skating quite well, considering she'd never done so before. Her arms were flailing like the blades of a windmill, but she was rolling along nicely and without wobbling as many of the other children were doing.

"Don't forget that if you think you're going to fall, head for the grass!"

This sensible piece of advice had been screeched by Callie, who looked and sounded as if she was having every bit as much fun as her charges. "Good job!" Aubrey called to his daughter, even as he glanced around to find Callie.

Ah, there she was. She was going strong and looked as though she were keeping an eye on all the children at once. In spite of himself, Aubrey was impressed. Perhaps some people just had a way with children.

Anne seemed to have had a way with Becky, although, thanks to the miserable Fates, Aubrey had never seen her in any milieu larger than their very small family. He'd bet Anne would have loved to have hosted parties for Becky.

He couldn't quite imagine her dealing with a couple of dozen small children with the ease and stamina Callie displayed. No sooner had that thought struck him than guilt struck, too.

But, honestly, the fact that Callie possessed a stronger constitution and, therefore, more vitality than Anne wasn't something that shouldn't be acknowledged. If he was to be brutally honest with himself, Aubrey resented Anne's fragility like fire. If she'd had more stamina, she'd still be here and in charge of this birthday party. And Callie Prophet would still be driving her rural postal route.

He didn't know how he felt about that, but the twinge of pain that assailed him at the notion of losing Callie bothered him a trifle. Fortunately, perhaps, he didn't have time to dwell on it, because he was struck a great blow to his back in the very next instant.

"Good Lord! Oh, Mr. Lockhart! I'm so sorry!"

Aubrey, who had wheeled around so as not to lose his balance and fall on the concrete drive, discovered Callie Prophet in his arms. He stared down at her, unable to speak.

She stared up at him and seemed likewise stricken. She was also gasping audibly.

"Oh!" she cried after a second of doing nothing but residing there in his arms.

She felt quite good there, too, Aubrey noticed instantly,

as she had when they'd danced together. Then, naturally, he was nearly overwhelmed with guilt and frowned at her. "Miss Prophet." His voice was stern.

"Mr. Lockhart."

She couldn't seem to get her footing, perhaps because her feet were now strapped to roller skates. "I'm so sorry."

"Think nothing of it." Aubrey wondered if he looked as sour as he felt.

The fact was that having Callie in his arms fitted exactly into the train of thought he'd been riding all day long. And she also fitted exactly into his arms the way a woman should. At least, he thought grimly, the way a wife should.

"Dash it, stand up, will you?" he barked.

At once, her face lost its dazed expression. "I'm trying to stand up, blast you! I can't get the stupid roller skates to stop sliding out from under me."

"Oh, look at Miss Prophet and Papa!" came a trilling voice, full of laughter.

"Damn it, try harder," Aubrey commanded through clenched teeth.

"I *am* trying!" Callie said, obviously feeling abused and mistreated. "It's the stupid roller skates."

"Here." Aubrey allowed his hands to slide down her body until he gripped her waist. Although it had seemed a necessary maneuver when he did it, he regretted it. Her body was one he'd like to explore in more depth. If, of course, he were free to do so.

Because he was angry with himself and her, he gripped her waist perhaps too tightly. "Can you stand up now, dash it?"

"I can't get my feet to stay still," she said. Her teeth, too, were gritted together. Her cheeks had flushed a brilliant pink. Aubrey didn't know whether they'd done so from embarrassment or anger, although he suspected a combination of the two.

After they'd stood there, locked together, for entirely too many moments, Callie said, "All right. I think you can let me go now."

"Thank God," Aubrey grumbled. He didn't mean it.

"Miss Prophet! You bumped into Papa!"

Becky skated up to them, grinning broadly. She seemed to find the situation funny.

Aubrey didn't. He did, however, have enough sense not to show his irritation to his daughter, who was a total innocent. "I think she broke my back when she bumped into me."

Another peal of laughter issued from his daughter. Other children had started to surround them. Aubrey felt like a sacrificial lamb.

"Well, it's all because I was watching you, Becky," Callie said. Her voice sounded somewhat strained, but she was obviously aiming at humor. "You're a super skater."

"I love to skate!" Becky threw her arms around Callie's knees, almost sending them both over backward.

Laughing, Callie grabbed Becky and managed to keep both of them upright. "Careful, there, Becky! We don't want to end up in the hospital."

Becky giggled appreciatively.

Miss Prophet's aplomb, Aubrey noted with annoyance, seemed to have returned in an unseemly short period of time. Any female with proper sensibilities ought to have been embarrassed for a much longer stretch after such an embrace.

Not, naturally, that he'd have appreciated it if she'd succumbed to a fainting spell, hysterics, or a fit of the vapors.

"Come along, Becky. I think your papa doesn't appreciate creating a spectacle."

"Creating a spectacle?" Startled, Aubrey glanced up from the vision of Becky holding Miss Prophet's hand. As soon as his gaze lit upon the ladies in the tent, he groaned.

From Old Bilgewater through her lorgnette to Callie's sister Alta, all eyes were focused on the three of them. As he watched, Aubrey saw Bilgewater's lips move. A woman—he thought it was a Mrs. Finney—lifted a hand to her mouth as if to cover either a gasp or a giggle.

Whichever it was, Aubrey didn't like it. Furious, he took Becky's other hand. "Come with me, Becky. Show me how well you can skate."

"Super, Papa!"

He felt Callie's gaze on his back as he and his daughter left her presence.

# 12

Callie's heart rattled like a kettledrum, her mouth had gone as dry as the Sahara, and she couldn't seem to catch her breath. Her gaze flickered from Aubrey's back, where it wanted to remain, to the group of gabbling women under the tent.

They were talking about her. Her or Aubrey. Perhaps her *and* Aubrey. And for no good reason. Merely because she'd practically swooned with ecstasy when she'd found herself in his arms didn't mean anybody watching should have known about it. Even if they *had* known about it, they most certainly shouldn't be talking about it now.

If they were talking about it.

Another glance at the herd of mothers and Mrs. Bridgewater confirmed her unhappy assumption that they were talking about *something* fascinating. Callie knew that gossip about men and women was the most fascinating kind and, since there hadn't been any other couples to gossip about recently, she assumed she and Aubrey were the one on today's menu. What's more, they were being chewed and digested with great relish. Drat it.

She tried to arrange her face to show nothing but amiability, and hoped to heaven she didn't look as though she'd just undergone a religious experience. If her face told the tale her insides were singing, it would be all over town in a day or two that she was hopelessly in love with her employer. That, while true, would be too humiliating to be borne.

In order to nip scuttlebutt in the bud, and in an effort to get her hammering heart to settle down, Callie hummed a merry tune as she skated toward the chattering matrons who were at present buzzing like a hive of honey bees being besieged by a bear.

"Oh, Mrs. Bridgewater, I'm sure there's nothing shady going on between them."

Callie's eyes widened and her cheeks caught fire when she caught this comment, uttered by a woman in a yellow polkadot morning wrapper. Callie had always mistrusted polkadots. It didn't make her feel any better to know her mistrust had not been unmerited.

"Of course, there isn't. Callie's much too respectable and high-principled to do anything like that," Alta announced staunchly.

*Thank God for sisters.*

"Well, I have reason to believe you're both wrong. It's improper for a young woman her age to be living under the same roof with a single gentleman—if he *is* a gentleman. I've always had my doubts."

Callie stopped humming when Mrs. Bridgewater's voice, full of quivering malice and self-righteous indignation, smote her ears. She glanced up from the driveway—she'd been keeping her eyes on the pavement because she didn't want to take a tumble—and saw the elderly woman plying her fan with one hand and her lorgnette with the other. Her bilious green bombazine bosom had swelled to alarming proportions, and the gaze of every matron was fixed upon her face.

Bilgewater went on, "There's something obscene going on between them, and *I* think it's scandalous." The other women were so fascinated, they didn't notice Callie's approach.

*The horrid old cow!* Callie's heart stopped trilling instantly, and any slight remaining fear of swooning vanished like smoke. Lifting her chin, she skated swiftly the rest of the way to the tent. "What exactly do you consider scandalous, Mrs. Bridgewater?" she asked civilly, but in a defiant tone, plumping herself down on a bench and leaning over to remove her roller skates.

A silence as thick as cream spread throughout the group of mothers. Callie glanced up and swept the group with one of her most glittering smiles. She hoped it conveyed both her fury and her challenge. Alta swallowed, so Callie guessed it did a pretty good job. That her so-called *friends* should be gossiping about her hurt and infuriated her.

Mrs. Bridgewater lowered her lorgnette to her lap and frowned at Callie without their help. "Were you eavesdropping, Miss Prophet?"

"Not at all. I skated over and heard you talking about something scandalous. Since this is a little girl's birthday party, I couldn't conceive of anyone talking in front of the mothers of the children present about anything unfit for all ears to hear."

Somebody drew in a gasping breath. Mrs. Bridgewater's frown deepened. She sat up straighter, causing her corset—which was being called upon to perform yeoman's duty by holding in her excessive bulk—to creak ominously. "I merely said I think it's a pity that a child has to reside in a house where so little attention is paid to propriety."

Callie sat up, bringing her skates with her and setting them on the bench next to her so nobody could step on them and fall. "Oh? Who is this child and where is this improper house? I didn't think Santa Angelica had any of those."

Alta stifled something that might have been a giggle or a moan.

Up came the lorgnette. "You know very well I'm speaking about this house, Miss Prophet. It's improper for you, a single young lady, to have charge of Rebecca. And it's perfectly scandalous that you and Aubrey should be carrying on under her very nose."

One of the matrons uttered a stifled, "Oh, my!"

Callie was now so furious that it was difficult for her to unclench her teeth far enough to speak. "That," she said in a tone she'd never heard herself use before, "is a vicious, unkind, and slanderous statement, Mrs. Bridgewater. These ladies"—she swung her arm in an arc, taking in all of her friends—"have known me all my life. They also know Mr. Lockhart, and they knew his late wife. How anyone—and a blood relation, to boot—can accept a gracious invitation to a little girl's birthday party and then spend her time spreading salacious rumors about her host, is something I do not understand."

"Hear! Hear!" murmured Alta.

"And another thing." Callie had stood up by this time, and was leaning over Mrs. Bridgewater, who had somehow seemed to shrink in the last few moments. "How you, of all people, a relative of the late Mrs. Lockhart, could spread such malevolent calumnies about Mr. Lockhart is incomprehensible to me. That man is a saint. He adored his wife. He all but worshiped her. He was and still is devastated by her death. He hired me because Becky needed a female presence in her life. I may be a poor substitute for her mother, but at least I *care*, which you obviously do not, or you wouldn't be spreading such insulting prattle."

All of the women except Mrs. Bridgewater nodded. Mrs. Hurst had to draw a hankie out of her pocket and dash a tear away. "So sad," she murmured. "So very sad."

"You," Callie went on, pointing at Mrs. Bridgewater, "are a malicious harpy!" And, with that, she turned on her heel and headed back to the group of children. Offhand, she couldn't recall another time in her life when she'd been so angry. When Aubrey's voice came to her from behind a hedge of daphne, she was so startled, she almost shrieked.

"Thank you for defending me, Miss Prophet."

Whirling around, Callie saw that Aubrey was carrying Becky on his shoulders. It looked to her as if the little girl had been crying. She opened her mouth to ask what had happened, but nothing emerged.

Aubrey saved her the chore of finding her voice. "Becky fell down and skinned her knee, so I'm giving her a pony ride."

With a pathetic cross between a giggle and a sniffle, Becky said, "Papa's being the pony."

From somewhere inside her, Callie found the wherewithal to smile at the child. "Papas make good ponies, especially if you have a sore knee, don't they, Becky?"

Becky nodded.

"I think we ought to take you indoors and bandage your knee, sweetheart. What do you think about that?"

Another nod from Becky, this one accompanied by a sniffle.

Although she'd have liked to have spent a few more hours mentally beating Mrs. Bridgewater to a bloody pulp, as she deserved, Callie turned and waved to the group of women. "Alta! Becky hurt her knee and we have to go indoors to bandage it. Will you please keep this swarm of skating children from running wild for a few minutes?"

"Glad to!" Alta called back.

Several of the other mothers rose to assist her amid a sympathetic buzz and bustle, thereby leaving a wide empty patch around Mrs. Bridgewater. Callie was gratified by this show of support.

When Callie, Aubrey, and Becky entered the house, Mrs. Bridgewater was left to stew all by herself under the tent. Which, Callie said to herself, was merely appropriate. She wished a tree limb, or something heavier, would fall on her.

Aubrey and Callie took Becky to the kitchen and parked her on Mrs. Granger's utility table in the middle of the room. Callie wetted a clean rag and rubbed soap on it, while Mrs. Granger tutted and clucked over Becky, and Becky explained how her accident had happened.

"I skated into a bush," she said soberly. "And fell down on the pavement."

"What a very bad bush!" said Mrs. Granger.

Becky smiled up at her. "It's 'cause I wasn't looking."

"Well, then, perhaps the bush isn't so *very* bad," Mrs. Granger amended, handing the little girl a piece of bread and jam to help soothe her battered soul.

Callie tried not to look at Aubrey as she reached for the ointment and bandages.

Had he thanked her out there on the driveway? She'd been

so startled by his sudden appearance, she couldn't recall. And if he had thanked her, why had he done so?

"All right, Becky. Be a brave girl now. This will sting a little bit."

"I'll be brave." Becky swallowed the last of her bread and jam.

It tore at Callie's heart to see the twin trails of tears drying on the little girl's pretty cheeks. "Hold on to the edge of the table, Becky. Sometimes it helps to hold on to something."

"You can hold my hands, Becky," Aubrey offered.

Callie was pleased to see Becky instantly reach for her father's hands and hold on tight. Using the greatest care, she lifted Becky's drawers up over the bloody knee. "This doesn't look too bad, although I know it hurts, darling. I'll try not to hurt you any more than I have to."

"Thank you."

Holding the small ankle so as to avoid getting kicked should Becky react to the soapy rag, Callie concentrated on her task, trying hard not to hurt the wound.

"I really do thank you, Miss Prophet."

She glanced up quickly, and just as quickly returned her attention to the job at hand. After clearing her throat, she said, "For what, Mr. Lockhart?"

"For sticking up for me out there."

Oh, good God, he'd heard. Callie's lips pinched together for a second as anger against Becky's great-aunt surged through her. "That woman," she said through gritted teeth, "ought to be horsewhipped." Immediately, she glanced up to see if Becky was paying attention to the adult conversation. She was looking pretty worried and seemed to be concentrating on her knee, so Callie hoped her last intemperate remark had passed over her head.

Aubrey chuckled. He had a deep chuckle that did odd things to Callie's insides. "You're probably right. Didn't they used to do that to gossipmongers?"

"I don't know, but I wish they still did."

"What's a 'gossipmonger'?" Becky asked.

So much for her not following the adult conversation, Callie thought glumly.

She and Aubrey exchanged a glance, and Callie opted to answer the question. "A gossipmonger is a person who spreads gossip and tells tales on other people."

"Oh. Miss Oakes says people like that are bad."

"She's right," Aubrey said firmly. "Your teacher seems to have a good head on her shoulders, Becky."

"She's real nice." Becky winced as Callie plied her soapy rag.

"I'm sorry, Becky. I'm almost through here. Then we'll put some nice ointment on your poor knee and tie a bandage around it. Maybe I can find a colored ribbon to decorate it, and then you'll have a birthday knee!"

Becky offered a tiny laugh, although Callie knew she was in pain.

"A birthday knee," said Aubrey. "I've never heard of such a thing."

"It's better than a plain old bandaged knee," Callie said in defense of her idea.

"Oh, much better," he agreed, and Callie could tell he was amused rather than annoyed.

She felt slightly cheerier.

Ten minutes later, when the three of them emerged from the house, Becky's leg sported a pristine white bandage and two pink ribbons that went nicely with her new pink-and-white checked gingham birthday dress and ruffled white pinafore.

Alta had done a good job in organizing skating races among the children, but they all stopped skating when they spotted Becky. Several of the children broke ranks and began wobbling toward the porch. Becky bounded down the stairs as if nothing of a painful nature had ever happened to her.

"Looky! I got a birthday knee!" She bent her knee and lifted her leg to show off her bandage. Callie thought that if Old Bilgewater—as Aubrey called her—was watching, she was undoubtedly scandalized at such a brazen display of frilly drawers.

The other children swarmed around Becky, desiring to see the knee. Callie turned to look at Aubrey and discovered he'd turned to look at her. Their gazes held for a moment before

Callie wrenched hers away. "I guess she'll live."

"Looks like it," he said. "You did a good job. Your birthday knee was a brilliant stroke."

Unused to having compliments bestowed upon her from this source, Callie felt her neck get hot. She hoped like thunder she wouldn't blush. "It was, wasn't it?"

He chuckled.

Oh, but Callie wished he wouldn't do that. Every time he chuckled, dark, trembly feelings tumbled through her. It really wasn't fair that Becky had showed her those letters, she decided unhappily. If she'd only known the Aubrey Lockhart who lived in this house now, a year after his wife had died, she'd probably not even like him much, mainly because she considered he'd been beastly to his daughter, whom she loved.

But Becky *had* showed her those letters, and Callie had read them, and, horror of horrors, she'd now managed to fall in love with Aubrey the letter writer. Life could get tangled up at the drop of a hat, blast it, and Callie didn't approve.

Shortly after the knee incident, Mrs. Granger and Delilah brought out a delicious luncheon for the children and their mothers. And, of course, Mrs. Bridgewater, who seemed to have lost some of her starch. Watching her, Callie wished she could lose even more of it. In fact, if she'd go somewhere and lose her whole self, the world would be a better place.

However, that was nothing to the purpose, and Callie didn't dwell on it. She tried not to dwell on Aubrey, too, but was less successful.

Fried chicken, biscuits, potato salad, and Mrs. Granger's famous coleslaw were served up to the throng of children, all of whom had worked up voracious appetites as they skated. Their mothers also dined well, although a couple of them tried to pretend they weren't hungry. Callie knew better. Nobody could be not hungry in the face of one of Mrs. Granger's feasts.

After the luncheon had been consumed, Becky's favorite

white cake with coconut frosting was brought out in style by Aubrey, who carried it as if he were carrying a crown to a queen. Callie followed with a tub of ice cream that two of the stable boys had spent the morning churning. The *ooh*ing and *ah*ing that went on at the prospect of cake and ice cream made Callie's heart glow.

The afternoon's festivities came to a conclusion shortly after luncheon, and Callie found herself standing next to Aubrey and Becky and thanking the guests for their attendance at Becky's party. She felt not unlike a matron herself under the circumstances, and she experienced a yearning in her soul that it should be so.

Which was nonsensical. It was also dangerous, as she learned when she glanced around to find Mrs. Bridgewater giving her a glacial stare. Because she couldn't stand the woman and, even more, couldn't bear the notion of gossip being spread about herself and Aubrey, Callie smiled at her. Mr. Bridgewater sniffed and turned her face away. Callie rolled her eyes.

"I'm going upstairs to rest, Aubrey," Becky's great-aunt said during the departure of the other guests. "I'm sure I've never been to a more unruly children's party."

Callie had to bite her tongue in order to prevent herself from asking exactly how many children's parties the old hag had attended. Fortunately, Aubrey did it for her.

"Oh?" he said, his own eyes glittering ominously. "And how many children's parties have you attended, Mrs. Bridgewater?"

The woman sniffed. "Several."

"I see. Well, since most seven-year-olds have much more energy than adults of your years, I should advise you not to attend any more than you can avoid in the future."

Callie's mouth fell open in surprise at that smart thrust. She expected Mrs. Bridgewater to launch a counter-attack, but she didn't. She said only, "I believe that children should be disciplined," and marched into the house.

Becky reached up and tapped Callie's hand to get her attention, which was just as well, since Callie was wasting time watching Bilgewater and wondering how a person could get to be that way. She smiled at Becky. "Yes, lovie?"

"What's 'dis'plin,' and is it bad not to have it?"

Aubrey choked. "Ha!"

"Discipline is manners, sweetheart, and you have wonderful manners for a girl your age."

"Don't pay any attention to Great-Aunt Evelyn," Aubrey advised his daughter dryly. "She doesn't believe in having fun herself, and she wants the whole rest of the world to be miserable along with her."

Becky still looked puzzled. "But is it bad to have fun?" she asked in a small voice.

Callie fielded that one. "Good heavens, no! Having fun is the whole purpose of a party."

"Then I don't understand."

"Don't fret about it, Becky," Aubrey said. "Nobody understands your great-aunt. Your mama didn't understand why she's so grumpy all the time, I don't understand it, and I'm sure Miss Prophet doesn't understand it, either."

"True," Callie said, this warm feeling of inclusion she'd begun to harbor beginning to worry her. She didn't dare let herself get used to feeling as if she were part of the family; such a path was dangerous and might lead to sorrow and heartbreak should she have to leave this job for any reason.

Adopting her no-nonsense-nanny manner, as soon as the last carriage rolled away, she swooped down and picked Becky up. "I imagine *you*, young lady, could use a rest right about now."

"I'm not tired," Becky cried, appalled at the prospect of being made to take a nap. "Besides, I'm *seven* now!"

Aubrey laughed softly and chucked her under the chin. "You are, indeed, Becky. You're a big girl."

"Yes, you are," Callie agreed, severely lecturing her heart to stop pretending she belonged to this family. "But even big girls need to rest after exciting parties. I'm older than you are, and I'm exhausted. Although *you* may not need to rest, *I* do."

"Do I have to go to sleep?"

"No. I think we ought to go up to the nursery and read

and draw for a little while. That's rest enough for a seven-year-old, I think."

This news cheered Becky considerably. "Oh, good! I can draw with those new colored pencils you gave me."

"Brilliant idea," said Callie.

Aubrey smiled at the two of them. Callie felt as if she'd been purposely included in one of his smiles. The sensation threatened to knock her cockeyed for a second before she regained her composure.

He left them at the foot of the staircase and went in the direction of his office. Callie breathed a small sigh and put Becky down so that she could walk upstairs under her own steam. "You're getting too big for me to carry around much longer, Becky. You're as heavy as a sack of flour."

The little girl laughed and ran up the stairs, birthday knee and all. Worn out after the day's festivities—not to mention the planning that had gone into carrying them off—Callie followed more slowly.

Becky had already fetched some paper and her new colored pencils by the time Callie got to the nursery door. Personally, Callie could use a nap, but she'd had sufficient experience with young children to know it would be better not to force Becky to lie down. Better that she play quietly for a while and allow her mind to catch up with her body enough to realize it craved a nap, too. "Are you going to draw a picture of your party, Becky?"

The little girl nodded. "I want to send a picture to Mama. I think she'd like it that we went roller skating at the party."

Callie's heart squeezed. "I'm sure she would."

Nodding, Becky settled into a low chair and opened up the box containing her pencils. "I'm gonna draw a picture of my birthday knee, too."

"I'd forgotten all about your knee, sweetheart. How does it feel?"

"It's fine."

Callie saw that Becky was concentrating hard on drawing a picture, so she didn't press the issue of her knee. She was pleased that Becky didn't seem inclined to use her injury for sympathy as might have been expected of a child who'd been left to flounder without attention for an entire year.

She tried to drum up some indignation against Aubrey on Becky's behalf, but didn't have enough energy left after Becky's party. Besides, she's seen something today that made her wonder yet again if she'd been too hard on Aubrey.

He'd actually enjoyed himself once or twice during the party. Callie realized that for the first time his customary austere, haunted look had vanished and had been replaced by one of friendliness and interest—several times, in fact. She supposed he'd been used to looking friendly and interested before Anne took sick.

Perhaps he was beginning to put his grief behind him. Maybe he'd even turn human again, one of these days.

Which would be good for Becky. And perhaps for Callie, too.

Aubrey had intended to get some work done after Becky's party, but he found himself brooding over several other issues instead. He sat at his desk, drumming his fingers and frowning out the window, watching in a desultory way as the household staff dismantled the tent and removed the other vestiges of the day's festivities.

He wished the idea of remarriage would go away and leave him in peace. For some reason, once he'd allowed the notion to enter, it seemed to want to take over all of his thought processes. Dash it, what was the matter with him?

Then again, he thought, he oughtn't to be too hard on himself. After all, there probably wasn't a man alive who wasn't occasionally troubled by carnal impulses. Aubrey, neither religious scholar nor psychologist, had a sneaking feeling that men's carnal impulses were one of the reasons the institution of marriage had been invented in the first place. The good Lord had known what He was doing. Aubrey's own experience with sexual matters had led him to believe that if it were left to women to initiate such contact, far fewer children would be born into this sorry world. Heaven forfend that the race should die out.

He passed a hand over his eyes and railed at himself for

becoming cynical. Hell, he wasn't even old yet, and already he was thinking like an ancient, embittered man.

With the exception of Anne's death, if anything could be excepted from that, his life had been remarkably lucky. He had money, a successful business, two lovely houses, a beautiful daughter, and . . . and . . . and what?

And nothing.

"Dash it, man, stop wallowing. You've been wallowing for two years now, and it's unbecoming."

Not only that, but it wasn't fair to Becky.

Giving Becky a new mother, and one, moreover, whom she already cared for, would be doing Becky a good turn. And about time, too. If he married Miss Prophet, he'd be ensuring that she remained in Becky's sphere, too.

Heaven alone knew what might happen if Miss Prophet were left to her own devices. For all Aubrey knew, she'd allow Mark Henderson to sweep her off her feet and carry her away from the Lockhart abode. That would never do. Becky would be crushed.

Rather than see his daughter suffer another wrenching loss, Aubrey would make sacrifices. Hell's bells, he was even willing to sacrifice himself.

By the time Figgins sounded the gong to announce dinner, Aubrey had begun to feel quite noble.


Becky yawned hugely. "But I want to write to my mama tonight, Miss Prophet, because I want to tell her about my party."

"Very well, dear. We'll write to your mama." Every time Becky wrote to her mother in heaven, Callie experienced an uncomfortable sensation of compassion mixed with guilt. She wasn't sure which emotion was dominant. Either one all by itself was hard to stomach. Both of them together might have given her indigestion, except that Callie's digestion was superb and nothing did that.

"I want to say what we did. Especially the skating. Then I can send her the letter along with the pictures." Becky had drawn several pictures portraying her party. Callie could even tell what some of them were supposed to be.

She brought more paper and pencils to the child-size table on which Becky wrote her letters. The little girl was wearing her brand-new nightgown Mrs. Granger had given her, and the frilly cap that went with it. Delilah had knitted her some bed socks, too, so she was ready to hop under the covers as soon as she finished her letter and said her prayers. Callie made sure Becky said her prayers every night. Becky's prayers did something to ease Callie's conscience about all the things she knew she shouldn't be doing.

Concentrating hard, Becky wrote slowly. She was a bright child, and was unusually good with her letters, but her little hands were still slightly clumsy. Callie knew from experience with her nieces and nephews that young hands needed lots of practice when it came to these things.

"How do you spell 'roller skates'?"

Callie told her.

Several minutes later, Becky looked up and smiled. "All done. I think Mama will like this one." Her smile didn't fade, but an expression of concern entered her blue eyes. "I hope she will. I don't want to hurt her feelings by making her think I'm happy without her."

"Hurt her feelings? I'm sure you couldn't do that, Becky. Your mama loves you and understands how difficult life is for a little girl without her mother."

Becky nodded. "Good. That's what I think, too."

So Callie listened to Becky's prayers and tucked her in. She left the room with Becky's letter to her mother, which she opened as soon as she entered her own room. As she read it, her heart swelled, tears filled her eyes, and she wished she could talk to one of her sisters.

*Dear Mama,*

*Miss Prophet got roller skates for all the children at my birthday party. It was ever so much fun.*

*Mama, I love Miss Prophet very much. You don't mind that I love her, do you? I love you, too. And*

*Papa. But it's nice with Miss Prophet here. I am not
so lonsom anymore. Thats OK isn't it?*

*Love,*
*Becky*

"Oh, my land." Callie pressed a palm to her cheek and
plopped down on her bed, disturbing Monster, who growled
at her. With tears streaming down her face, Callie turned to
the cat. "Shut up, you. What do you know about anything?"

His feelings evidently hurt, Monster leapt from Callie's
bed and stalked across the room, but Callie paid no more
attention to him.

"Whatever should I do?" Callie whispered to her empty
room.

She answered Becky's letter to her mother in heaven, hoping to God that she was saying the right things, and begging
forgiveness from the spirit of Anne Lockhart.

Her feelings of oppressive guilt did not abate.

# *13*

Aubrey's feeling of nobility about the prospect of remarriage didn't last through the soup course at supper on the night of Becky's party. By that time, Old Bilgewater had taken over and directed the conversation along unpleasant lines. From nobility, in fact, Aubrey plunged headlong into sheer rage.

"What's more, Aubrey, I don't believe children ought to be indulged so shamelessly." Mrs. Bridgewater sniffed as Figgins served her soup. "Birthday parties, indeed. I've never heard of such a thing."

Fortunately, Becky and Miss Prophet had taken supper in the nursery this evening. Miss Prophet had pronounced Becky too exhausted from the stimulation of the day to be fit company at the supper table.

"Not while Mrs. Bridgewater is visiting," Callie had told him in the frank, down-to-earth way she had. "Because Mrs. B is sure to criticize, and I don't think Becky needs that. Not after having had such a splendid day. It would only spoil the pleasure of her party."

"I think you're right," Aubrey had agreed, although he hadn't wanted to. Not because he didn't want to agree with

Callie aloud, either, but because he hated the mere notion of dining alone with Old Bilgewater.

Now, however, as he eyed the woman over his own steaming bowl of soup, he wondered if this wasn't an opportunity in disguise. "Oh?" he said coolly. "What do you advocate instead? Keeping children in leg shackles and wrist manacles?" He smiled, showing a lot of teeth.

Bilgewater looked at him and huffed irritably. "For heaven's sake, Aubrey! What a ridiculous suggestion."

"Is it?"

"Of course!"

He took a sip of soup. Mrs. Granger, overworked already today, thanks to all the party preparations, had warned him supper would be a simple meal this evening. Simplicity to Mrs. Granger, however, meant something different from what it meant to Aubrey. She'd made up a delicious soup, and she'd already told him they were having a chicken casserole, using chicken and vegetables left over from the party.

After he swallowed and smiled at Figgins to let him know he approved of the soup course, Aubrey again directed his attention to Becky's great-aunt. He narrowed his eyes. "I see. So, you think it's ridiculous, do you?"

"Yes, it is. Of all the nonsensical notions I've ever heard expressed, that's the most nonsensical."

Aubrey doubted that Bilgewater could sound too much more emphatic. She looked as if she were taking on air in order to launch another assault. He decided to give her a large target to shoot at. "Oh? Then do you believe the suggestion that Miss Prophet and I are carrying on an illicit affair, which you proposed to that group of mothers, to be a less ridiculous suggestion, Mrs. Bridgewater?"

Bilgewater sat up with a jerk, precipitating a loud groan from her corset stays. "What? I beg your pardon?"

"I overheard what you said to those ladies, Mrs. Bridgewater. I thought *that* was pretty near the top of the nonsense pinnacle."

"I never!"

"Oh, yes you did. I heard you." Aubrey allowed his anger to show. He hoped she'd choke on it. "And let me tell you,

I do not appreciate your insinuations, blatant accusations, and snide comments."

After swallowing once or twice and huffing three or four times, Bilgewater seemed to regroup. Her bosom swelled ominously. "Well! What do you expect people to think when you carry on in such a blatant way?"

"Carry on? Carry *on!*" Aubrey opened his eyes wide, unable to believe even Great-Aunt Evelyn could spout such bilge.

"Yes! Living here with that—that—"

"Nanny," Aubrey supplied, breaking in with a loud bark that made Bilgewater jump. "Miss Prophet is Becky's *nanny*, Mrs. Bridgewater."

"Nanny, my foot."

"I don't understand you. You don't even know the woman, yet you're willing to blacken her name here, where she lives. You're not only willing, you're *eager*. And you want to take Becky and me with you!"

"Nonsense! I—"

Aubrey trounced on her words as if she hadn't spoken. "I've heard of brazen talk, Mrs. Bridgewater, but I've never witnessed it until today."

"What? Why, Aubrey Lockhart, of all the—"

"I think the ladies of Santa Angelica know Miss Prophet far better than you do. What's more, she came to me with a sterling character. There isn't a person in the town who doesn't speak highly of her."

He didn't bother to bring up the fact that Callie had actually appeared in his drawing room without any written references. Aubrey had found out soon enough what the neighbors thought about her. They liked her; therefore, he didn't consider his prior statement a lie. It might be a bit of a stretcher, perhaps, but it wasn't an out-and-out lie.

Mrs. Bridgewater, apparently giving up trying to break into Aubrey's monologue, lifted her chin and glared at him in defiance. It was, and Aubrey recognized it as such, the last-ditch effort of a person in the wrong who would rather die than admit it. Which gave Aubrey some pleasant ideas, but he'd never dare act upon them.

"I am only concerned about Rebecca's welfare, Aubrey Lockhart, and you know it."

He wasn't going to let her get away with *that*. "I do not know it, Mrs. Bridgewater. I know nothing of the kind. I fail to comprehend how spreading malicious gossip about Becky's father and the woman he hired to take care of her can contribute in any way whatsoever to Becky's welfare. It can only hurt her. You know it as well as I do."

"That's not so."

"It *is* so. You want to get Becky away from me, for some reason known only to yourself, and you're not going to succeed. I won't let you. Becky has a good life. It's neither her fault nor mine that Anne died, and you're not going to use Anne's death, which was a tragedy for both of us, to maneuver my daughter away from this house. Until I heard it for myself today, I didn't believe even *you*, of whom I've learned to expect almost anything, could sink to the level of spreading false and vicious rumors to achieve your own selfish goals. I learned my lesson, Mrs. Bridgewater. After you leave Santa Angelica tomorrow, I don't want you to visit Becky again. Ever. If you show up without an invitation, you will be turned away from this house."

The older woman's face had turned a startling purple during Aubrey's last speech, and he saw that her hands shook when she placed her napkin on the table beside her soup plate. For approximately ten seconds, he contemplated whether or not he should feel guilty. After all, gentlemen seldom, if ever, took ladies to task for anything. When he recalled how this miserable specimen of womanhood had tried to blacken his name and Callie's name among the matrons that afternoon, he hardened his heart.

She rose slowly and with much creaking of whalebone. "I have never," she said, her voice atremble, "been so insulted in my life."

"I don't know why it's taken anyone so long to call you on your nefarious career as a gossipmonger," Aubrey told her frankly. "The way you carry on behind people's backs, I'm surprised you haven't been shot out of the water long since."

"Slanders. Vile insults."

"Fiddlesticks. I speak only the truth. Unlike you, who, this very afternoon, slung around blatant lies about me among my neighbors," Aubrey pointed out.

"I did not tell tales!" she began, but Aubrey again interrupted.

"Balderdash. There's not a shred of truth in anything you said today. You made up tripe, hoping it would ruin my reputation and turn my neighbors against me. God alone knows why, unless you think that making me into a black sheep will cause me to relinquish Becky."

"Of all the—"

He waved a hand, effectively silencing her once more. "You're a witch, Mrs. Bridgewater. It's difficult to imagine you and Anne coming from the same family. On consideration, I think it's you who are the changeling, since everyone else in the Harriott family is very nice. You're the only freak in a good lot."

"Well!"

"It's no use *welling* me in that indignant voice, either. You stepped way over the line today. Perhaps no one else whose name you've blackened over the years has ever had the brass balls to point out to you the error of your ways—probably in some misguided attempt to maintain his or her sense of conventional decorum—but I'm not so nice."

"I should say not!"

"No, indeed. I'm honest. I prefer to call a rotten apple a rotten apple. And you, madam, are a rotten apple."

"I shall retire now." Mrs. Bridgewater's voice shook violently. She turned and started tottering toward the door.

"I'll have Mrs. Granger send you up a tray," Aubrey told her back.

"That won't be necessary."

"I'll do it anyway, on the off chance you can manage to take some nourishment," Aubrey said dryly.

"I'm sure I shan't be able to eat a bite. I have never been so—" But, perhaps recalling Aubrey's reaction to the last time she'd told him she'd never been so insulted in her life, Mrs. Bridgewater didn't finish her sentence.

She also ate everything that was on the tray Mrs. Granger had Delilah carry up to her.

Aubrey, not accustomed to calling a spade a spade, felt shaky after Mrs. Bridgewater left him alone in the dining room. He conducted a spirited dialogue with himself on the issue, and twice started to rise from the table and pursue Mrs. Bridgewater in order to apologize.

He didn't do it. Not only did he know he'd spoken the truth—perhaps a trifle brutally, but it was no more than the old harridan deserved—but he even received unexpected confirmation that he'd done the right thing from an unusual source.

Figgins, who came in to remove the soup plates, and who looked this evening more like a treasure from a taxidermist's shop than usual, paused with two soup plates in his gloved hands and turned toward Aubrey. He bowed his head for a moment before lifting it again and looking straight at his employer.

Such a breach of orthodoxy was most uncommon in this ancient retainer. Aubrey didn't know if there was a school for butlers, but if there was, he imagined Figgins could give lessons therein. Alarmed—he hoped to God Old Bilgewater hadn't suffered an attack of apoplexy or, more important, that nothing had happened to any of the servants—he said, "What is it, Figgins? Is something the matter?"

"No, sir. It's only—" He stopped talking abruptly.

Good God. Aubrey rose from his chair. "What is it? What's happened?" Fear roughened his voice. Had Delilah upturned the soup pot on herself and been burned? Had Mrs. Granger suffered some kind of attack? Good God, if any catastrophe had befallen Becky—

"It's not my place to say this, Mr. Lockhart, but I believe you should know that the household staff is delighted that you gave Mrs. Bridgewater a piece of your mind, sir."

His hands braced on the table, intending to shove himself away from it and race off to the nursery or the kitchen, Aubrey paused, blinking at Figgins. He wasn't sure he'd heard correctly.

Figgins straightened, something Aubrey wouldn't have believed possible before it happened, since he'd looked about as straight as a man could get before he did it. "As I say, sir, it's not my place to say so, sir, but . . . well . . . hooray for you." Figgins swallowed.

So did Aubrey, who still wasn't sure he'd heard correctly. "Er . . ."

"That's all, sir. I sincerely beg your pardon if I've given offense."

Aubrey sat with something of a thud. "Offense? Good God, no, you haven't given offense. In fact—" The humor of the situation struck him suddenly, and he grinned. "In fact, thank you, Figgins. And Mrs. Granger, too. And Delilah. And anyone else who's been made unhappy by Mrs. Bridgewater."

For perhaps the first time in his career as an ever-so-proper butler, Figgins smiled. "Very good, sir."

He left the dining room with a spring in his step. He was back to being his austere butlerish self when he returned with the main course.

That settled the matter for Aubrey. He wasn't going to apologize to Bilgewater. Let the witch suffer. Aubrey hoped she'd choke on his scold.

In the meantime, Aubrey planned what he needed to do in order to assure Miss Callida Prophet's continued residence in his home. For Becky's sake.

He didn't leap to the conclusion that he should marry her. Indeed, he pondered the matter all through the chicken casserole, taking his time and thinking hard.

She was good with the staff. Would the staff resent someone in her position becoming their mistress?

"Hell, she already rules the roost," Aubrey mumbled around a mouthful of chicken. He grinned as he swallowed.

An odd thing about Miss Prophet: She took over without anyone's being the wiser. For nearly three months now— ever since Callie's arrival in his home—Aubrey hadn't been troubled by servants' queries regarding what to do with the sour milk or whether or not to wax the parlor floor. The servants all went to Miss Prophet when Mrs. Granger had no answers for them.

Mrs. Granger herself consulted Callie whenever anything needed to be discussed. She never bothered Aubrey with anything anymore.

It was a relief, in fact, how much household nonsense Callie had lifted from his shoulders.

So. He could relax about the servants. Aubrey didn't think any of them would mind if he married Becky's nanny.

And then there was Becky. She adored Miss Prophet. Becky would probably be overjoyed if her papa were to marry her nanny.

By the time Aubrey finished the baked apple in cream Mrs. Granger had prepared for dessert, he'd made up his mind. He was going to march upstairs to the nursery and ask Miss Prophet to be his wife.

As he laid his spoon beside his apple dish, Aubrey frowned. He didn't want to offer the woman false coin. Although it wasn't terribly flattering to her, Aubrey sensed that he ought to be honest with her.

"Anyhow, she's too smart not to figure it out on her own," he reminded himself.

Ergo, he would not declare an undying passion for her.

Perhaps he ought not use the word "passion" at all, come to think of it. Truth to tell, he'd been harboring passionate feelings for Miss Prophet for weeks now.

Lust and love were two different things, however, and Aubrey vowed that he would not give her the chance to misunderstand him. He'd loved Anne. He could not, therefore, love Callie Prophet, who was so different from Anne that they might be members of different species altogether.

Callie was boisterous and exuberant, healthy and hardy. Anne had been quiet and reserved, frail and fragile. Callie was buxom. Anne had been tiny. Aubrey's heart hurt when he recalled their lovemaking. He'd always been so gentle and careful.

It might actually be a relief to bed someone who didn't look like she might break every time he touched her.

Instantly, he felt he'd been unfair to Anne.

Because his emotions were in such an abysmal turmoil, he decided to postpone any proposal until he got them under control. It wouldn't do to rush into something as permanent as marriage and discover after he'd tied the knot that he'd made a hideous mistake.

Therefore, he went to his library office in order to mull over the matter. He must have paced in front of his desk for miles before he decided he was going to do it. Before he dared trot upstairs and confront Callie, however, he thought he'd better practice. He hadn't had much experience with this sort of thing.

"Miss Prophet, I have come here to ask you to marry me."

No. That sounded stuffy and too dutiful. Even if he couldn't offer her love, he ought at least to sound as if he wanted to do the thing.

"Miss Prophet, would you do me the honor of becoming my wife?"

Gad, that was even worse. He had to say something that would get across the point that, while his heart had been Anne's for years and would continue to reside with her, he intended to do Callie justice. If justice was the right word. He couldn't think of another one at the moment and didn't want to get distracted, so he dropped the subject.

"Miss Prophet, I know we haven't always seen eye to eye." An understatement at best, but true. "However, I believe that you would make a good mother for my little girl." Good. Play on the woman's sympathy. Aubrey had no idea what Callie thought of him, although he had his suspicions, but he knew full well that she loved Becky. "Therefore, I would be honored if you were to agree to marry me."

Better. Not perfect, but better. Aubrey practiced several more variations on that theme before, after delaying as long as he dared, he told himself to brace up and get on with it. He sucked in a deep breath, decided it was now or never, and marched out the door and up the stairs.

Pausing before Becky's door, Aubrey raised his hand and would have knocked, but he recalled the possible lateness of the hour before he did so. Pulling his watch from his vest pocket, he squinted at it and took note of the time. "Eight forty-five. She's probably asleep."

He released a gust of relief before he reminded himself

that his duty was not just yet done. Blast. Why was Becky asleep? It might have been easier to propose in front of his daughter. At least Miss Prophet couldn't have berated him if Becky were there. Unfortunately, Becky was undoubtedly dead to the world by this time.

It had, after all, been a tiring day for a newly turned seven-year-old. A smile flicked across his mouth as he tucked his watch away. Then he stood and pondered some more.

If Becky was asleep, it was probable that Miss Prophet had gone to her own room next door. Would it be proper for him to knock at her door?

Stupid question. Of course it wouldn't. After berating Mrs. Bridgewater for spreading false and malicious rumors, he couldn't very well go and prove the demon woman right and barge in to Callie's bed chamber, could he?

No, he could not.

Damn it, so what now? A quick glance down the hall reconfirmed Aubrey's impression that no one else was about. Fortunately, Bilgewater's room was in the other wing of the house. Therefore, unless she was snooping, she wouldn't show up in this wing any time soon. He sucked in a deep breath, held it for a few seconds, and let it out with a whoosh.

"Nothing ventured, nothing gained," he muttered as he turned away from his daughter's bedroom and walked to the next door down the hall. He squared his shoulders, tugged at his vest and coat, made sure his tie was straight, and lifted his fisted hand, intending to knock softly—very softly—at Callie's door.

Callie sealed the envelope, addressed it to Becky, and sat on her bed with a thump. Her head ached and she felt drained and exhausted. And guilty. She must never forget the guilt that was her ever-present companion these days. This evening, however, she was especially tired.

"Too much excitement," she murmured, glancing around her room seeking Monster. But Monster wasn't there. Apparently, he'd taken her sharply spoken words of a while ago amiss; she didn't see him anywhere. "Blast the cat."

She was so weary after supervising Becky's birthday party and dealing with her tumbling emotions that she didn't feel like searching for the stupid animal. Instead, she undressed, scarcely finding the energy to hang her dress in the wardrobe. Then she donned her flannel nightie, brushed out her hair, and crawled between her sheets. For about a minute, she contemplated conducting a more thorough search for Monster.

"Bother Monster. Let him sleep wherever he wants to. What can happen to him indoors, anyhow?"

She was so tired, she later couldn't even remember rolling over and plumping her pillows before sleep claimed her.

"Dash it," Aubrey mumbled. He'd been tapping at Callie's door for what seemed like hours. It had probably only been a minute or two, but it was a nerve-racking business, attempting to propose to a lady. The least this one could do was answer her dashed door.

But did she? No. In true Callida Prophet form, she did not offer the least assistance to him in the matter. She let him stand out here in the hallway, in full view of anyone who cared to walk by, knocking at her door. "Damn her," he growled under his breath. Every other second, he peered around to make sure he was alone in the hallway. He was.

Being alone in the hallway, however, didn't solve the problem of the recalcitrant Miss Callida Prophet not answering her dashed door. He knocked slightly more sharply. Damn. This knock, which had felt rather timid when he did it, sounded like thunder in the silence of the huge house.

Tension was making him twitch. "One more time," he grumbled. "Then I'll quit for tonight."

He feared that if he didn't accomplish his purpose tonight, he'd lose his nerve.

Damnation, he never used to be a coward.

He'd never asked anyone but Anne to marry him, either, though, and his nerves were quivering as if they were attached to electrical wires. He and Anne had understood each other from the first moment they'd met. Proposing to her hadn't had this unsettling effect on him.

He rapped sharply twice and dropped his fist to his side. If she didn't open the damned door now, he'd just have to brace himself to spend a miserable, anxious night without having accomplished his purpose, and try again tomorrow.

Tomorrow was Sunday. Terrific. That meant the whole dashed family, including Becky, Miss Prophet, Mrs. Granger, Figgins, and Delilah, would attend the little Santa Angelica Methodist church. He'd see all the mothers who'd attended Becky's party and have to be sociable to Callie's brother and sisters. And he wouldn't have a moment to be private with Callie for hours. He wouldn't be able to ask her to marry him until the afternoon, after the midday meal, which was the big one on Sundays.

He didn't think his nerves would last until then.

When Callie's bedroom door opened, he was so startled he nearly jumped out of his skin. Callie stood, blinking, before him, her strawberry-blond hair tumbling around her shoulders, her eyes puffy with sleep, and her cheeks flushed from her pillow. She stared at him and uttered, "Mr. Lockhart!" in a groggy, shocked-sounding voice.

"Miss Prophet." For the life of him, he couldn't think of anything to say after those two words. All that practicing, and here he stood, tongue-tied as an adolescent boy at his first dance.

This was ridiculous. Aubrey took a breath.

"What is it?" Callie was holding her wrapper tightly closed at her neck, but she seemed to be waking up fast. All at once she looked frightened. "What's happened? Oh, what is it?"

"Er, nothing's happened," he said. Hell and damnation. He'd practiced for what seemed like ten years and now, when he was at the point of declaring his intentions, all of his carefully rehearsed words had flown right out of his head.

Callie took a step toward him, and Aubrey backed up an equal distance, berating himself even as he did so. This was no way to get the woman to marry him, dash it.

Looking up and down the hallway, Callie said, "Is it Monster? Has he done something awful again?"

"Monster?" What the devil was she talking—! Oh, yes. Aubrey remembered. Her damned cat. "Er, no, it's not Monster."

She stepped back until she stood just inside her room and stared at him some more. "What is it, Mr. Lockhart? Is something the matter?" Her eyes widened, and an expression of dismay visited her face. Her hands tightened on her wrapper. "Mr. Lockhart . . . ?" She licked her lips and looked scared.

Good God, Aubrey recognized that expression. She thought he'd come here for some sort of immoral purpose. Aghast, he hurried to say, "Miss Prophet, I need to talk to you about—"

A piercing shriek ripped through the air. It was accompanied by a yowl that would have done a lion in the jungles of Africa proud. Both Aubrey and Callie jumped several inches.

Callie pressed a hand to her cheek and whispered, "Oh, my land!"

Aubrey snarled, "Bilgewater."

Stopping only to pick up Becky, who had rushed to her own bedroom door and thrown it open, Aubrey raced toward the other wing of the house. He heard Callie racing softly behind him.

"What was that noise, Papa?" Becky rubbed her eyes and looked worried. "It scared me."

"I'm afraid it was that dashed cat," Aubrey said grimly. He yanked the hall door open and barreled through the uncarpeted gallery. He and Anne had planned to borrow an affectation from British nobility and hang portraits of their families in this gallery, but they hadn't gotten around to it. Aubrey hadn't had the heart to do anything with the big, empty room since Anne's death.

"Monster?" Becky's eyes widened. "What did he do?"

"I don't know, but he seems to have done it in your great-aunt's room."

"Great-Aunt Evelyn?"

"That's the one, all right." Aubrey's chest roiled with indignation and fury. That damned cat ought to be flung out a third-story window.

"Oh, dear." Callie was out of breath. "I hope that woman didn't do anything to Monster."

Aubrey, glancing over his shoulder, could scarcely believe that even Callie Prophet, of whom he'd learned to expect almost anything, had actually said that.

# 14

"Oh, get it away from me!"

Aubrey and Becky screeched to a halt at Mrs. Bridgewater's door, which had been slightly ajar when they arrived. Aubrey had flung it open wide.

Pulling herself up right behind them and peering around Aubrey's broad shoulders, Callie didn't think she'd ever seen a more pitiful sight. She would, however, have been hard-pressed to say which animal looked more pathetic: Monster or Mrs. Bridgewater.

Monster sat hunched in a corner of Mrs. Bridgewater's bedroom, his fur bristling, his yellow eyes glittering. Callie could tell he was upset, although she was pretty sure she was the only adult watching who felt sorry for him.

Mrs. Bridgewater sat in her bed, the bedclothes pulled up to her chin, her hair in wild disarray, the cap with which she'd covered it falling down around her right ear, and her eyes bulging. She was uttering tiny, gasping screams, interspersed with barely coherent words.

"The cat!" she cried, ending with a chuff of breath and another gasp. "The cat!"

Callie shoved past the stunned Aubrey, who still clasped

Becky tightly in his arms, and dashed up to the bed. "What happened?" she cried. "What's the matter?"

Mrs. Bridgewater took in several deep breaths, loosened the fingers of one hand from their grasp on her bedclothes, and pointed one of them, quivering, at the cat in the corner. "That—that beast bit me!" She sucked in air. "On the *ear!*"

"Good heavens." Callie turned around and looked at the cat. Realizing that her own wrapper was open, she fumbled for the ties dangling at her sides, and tied them without glancing at what she was doing. "Monster." She walked slowly up to the cat, holding out her hand in a soothing gesture. "What happened here, sweetie?"

"Sweetie! *Sweetie!* That animal *bit* me!"

Callie turned her head and frowned at Mrs. Bridgewater. "Yes, yes, we all know that by this time. But if you'll please stop yelling, I'm sure this will be over much more quickly."

She didn't pause as she moved toward the cat, but she did hear Mrs. Bridgewater's offended gasp. *Too bad*, Callie thought savagely. If the old biddy were a decent sort of person, Monster undoubtedly wouldn't have sought her out to attack when he found himself wandering the halls in a bad-cat mood.

Aubrey seemed to regain his senses all at once. He took a step forward. Callie, who wasn't looking at him, heard him because his tread was heavy. "The cat bit you? On the ear?" He sounded as befuddled as might be expected. "But, how . . . ? When . . . ?"

"It's my fault," Callie said with a sigh. "I should have looked for him before I went to bed, but I was too tired."

"Monster never bites you anymore, does he, Papa? It's 'cause he's learned to like you."

This pointed question and comment came from Becky, and both were salient, in Callie's opinion. "Of course, Monster doesn't bite Mr. Lockhart anymore, Becky," Callie said sweetly. "He only bites people whom he doesn't trust."

She heard Mrs. Bridgewater take in more air, and expected a flood of invective to follow, but Aubrey intercepted whatever comments she'd been about to speak. "Let's just get the animal out of here and get everyone to bed, shall we?" He sounded ever so stern and disagreeable.

Callie's stomach crunched up. Lord, Lord, she hoped he wouldn't dismiss her after this incident. If she had to leave Becky—and him—Callie wasn't sure she'd survive.

Though she'd never say so. "Come here, Monster. Come on, boy. Let's get you out of here."

Monster, who was a very gentle beast except when biting people, allowed Callie to pick him up. He hung like a fur cloak or a dead bear from her arms. He probably weighed twenty pounds, but Callie didn't even notice his weight. She turned, knowing she owed Mrs. Bridgewater an apology, no matter how little she wanted to deliver it. "I'm so sorry, ma'am. Please try to forgive me. It's all my fault for allowing him to wander around the house at night. He usually sleeps in my room, but I frightened him off earlier and then didn't go in search of him."

Mrs. Bridgewater stared from Callie to Aubrey, her lips working. Callie wondered how her eyes stayed in their sockets, they were starting so wildly. She certainly was in a state. The older woman's frenzy suddenly irked Callie. "It's only a cat, Mrs. Bridgewater. There's nothing sinister in him."

She saw Aubrey jerk his head to look at her, and she sensed he wasn't pleased with her. So what else was new? She pressed her lips together and vowed she wouldn't say another word unless goaded beyond endurance.

"I have never," said Mrs. Bridgewater, her voice shaking, "been in such a house."

"Well, you needn't ever be in one again," Aubrey pointed out reasonably.

Surprised by his callous words, Callie shot him a quick glance. He looked fairly callous, too. Good heavens, what did this mean?

Bilgewater took in air again. "Aubrey Lockhart," she quavered, "I am appalled at your indifference, both to the state of my nerves and to general appearances. Anne would have been horrified."

It was the wrong thing to have said. Callie saw it instantly, if Bilgewater didn't. Aubrey's eyes flashed fire. "Don't you dare," he said in a measured, deadly voice, "bring Anne's name into this. If you were any kind of benevolent force in the universe, this would never have happened."

That might not be strictly true, Callie thought, but she decided not to mention the fact that Monster did actually tend to bite people rather often. Most of the time, he was a darling, but he did seem to take dislikes to certain people. Not that she blamed him in this case.

"And now," Aubrey went on before anyone else could speak, "let's all get to bed, shall we?"

"I'm real sleepy," Becky announced, rubbing her eyes again.

"Yes, sweetheart, I'm sure you are."

Aubrey turned and left the room. Callie, glancing one last time at Mrs. Bridgewater, opened her mouth to offer a final apology, saw that her breath would be wasted, and lugged Monster out of the room. Although her arms were full of Monster, she took care to shut the door so that the cat couldn't return if he decided to finish his meal and dine on Mrs. Bridgewater's other ear. No sense in inviting further catastrophe.

She hurried to catch up with Aubrey and Becky, who were halfway to the gallery by this time. "Mr. Lockhart! Please, wait a minute."

"I'm taking my daughter to bed."

Oh, dear. His voice was cold and impassive, and Callie feared it boded no good to her. She hurried faster. "But, I wanted to say how sorry I am, Mr. Lockhart."

She heard his sigh, but he didn't turn around. "It's quite all right, Miss Prophet. I'm sure this is no more than we've come to expect in the past few months."

"That's not fair, sir!" Or maybe it was. It stung, though, and Callie didn't appreciate it.

He opened the gallery door and stood aside, holding it so that Callie could pass through before him. She did so, trying to look as dignified as possible in her nightgown and wrapper and with a fuzzy black cat dangling from her arms.

"No?" He smiled politely. "You'll have to explain to me what's unfair about it."

She pinched her lips together. "I shall."

"Good. But perhaps we can postpone the discussion until tomorrow. It's rather late."

Drat it. He was right. "Very well."

It wasn't until Becky was retucked in her bed and Callie had retreated, with Monster, to her own room, that she recalled the incident immediately preceding Mrs. Bridgewater's terrified scream. Now why, she asked herself, had Aubrey Lockhart been knocking at her door? She lay in her bed, trying to relax, and worrying about it for a long time.

Had he been going to try to seduce her? Callie's heart shriveled at the thought. She'd never have believed him capable of such a thing. No matter how many things Callie had against Aubrey, they all centered around what she perceived as his abandonment of his daughter. Callie had always until now—and she wasn't sure about now—believed him to be an upright, moral man with high principles.

She was feeling quite blue when she finally got to sleep.

Mrs. Bridgewater left the Lockhart mansion before breakfast the following morning. When Callie and Becky descended the stairs to eat breakfast before going to church, Becky's great-aunt was gone. Aubrey sat at the dining table, glancing at a newspaper when the two of them entered the room. He looked up and smiled at Becky. He didn't seem to notice Callie at all. She sighed, her heart heavy. And yesterday had been such a nice day, too. For the most part.

"Good morning, Becky. No lasting ill effects from last night's excitement, I trust?"

Becky ran up and kissed him on the cheek. He returned her kiss. Callie's heart squeezed.

"No, Papa. I went right back to sleep." She giggled. "Monster looked funny last night, sitting in the corner of Great-Aunt Evelyn's room."

"Indeed." Aubrey folded the newspaper and laid it beside his plate. Finally, he looked at Callie. "Good morning, Miss Prophet."

"Good morning, Mr. Lockhart." Callie tried not to stare at
him.

She wished to goodness he wasn't such a handsome man.
He always looked so neat and tidy, too. Never overdressed
or underdressed, but always appropriately attired, no matter
what the day was to hold. This morning, for instance, he was
wearing a sober black suit, perfect for church.

He always attended church, too, which Callie thought was
telling. After all, it was a father's duty to set an example for
his children. As much as she wanted to criticize him as a
father, and often did, she couldn't lay nonattendance at
church at Aubrey's door.

It was Mrs. Granger's custom to lay out breakfast on the
sideboard of a Sunday morning. Callie went to the sideboard
and picked up a plate. "Would you like some eggs and a
biscuit, Becky?"

"Yes, please. And bacon, too, please."

"Certainly. There's some of Mrs. Granger's good, home-
cured bacon right here. One piece or two?"

"One, please."

Callie scooped up a small portion of scrambled eggs,
plopped it onto Becky's plate, and set a biscuit and a piece
of bacon next to the eggs. She carried the plate to Becky.
"Would you like to say grace, Becky?"

Folding her hands neatly in front of her, Callie bowed her
head. Casting a sidelong glance at Aubrey, she saw him roll
his eyes, as if he could conceive of nothing more out of
character than the hoyden Callie Prophet asking his daughter
to say a morning prayer, and she pressed her lips together.

For heaven's sake, it wasn't *her* fault nothing had ever
happened in this mausoleum of a house before she'd arrived
in it! When she heard Becky say a perky, "Amen," she realized she hadn't listened to a single word of the little girl's
grace.

Some kind of nanny she was. Feeling grumpy and out of
sorts, Becky murmured, "Thank you, dear," and went back
to the sideboard to get her own breakfast.

It was only when she sat at her customary place at the
table that she noticed they were short one family member.

She glanced sharply at Aubrey. "Where's Mrs. Bridgewater?"

He smiled at her. It was a rather chilly smile, full of teeth and no feeling. "She opted not to dine with us this morning, but to go back to San Francisco as soon as she rose from her bed. I can't imagine why."

Callie huffed.

Aubrey continued, "John has taken her to the train station. She was complaining of a headache at the time."

"Oh." A stab of guilt smote Callie. She knew last night's fiasco was all her fault—and hated knowing it. Nevertheless, she knew how to set an example as well as Mr. Perfect Lockhart, so she said, "I'm very sorry I allowed Monster to get away from me last night. I trust Mrs. Bridgewater won't suffer any lasting ill effects from the excitement." She opted not to mention the bite.

A giggle from Becky surprised both of them. They turned to look at the little girl who grinned broadly. "I'm glad Monster bit her," she announced. "She's mean, and I don't like her."

Callie didn't know what to say to that. When she looked at Aubrey, hoping for some kind of guidance, she saw he wasn't helping at all. In point of fact, he was grinning back at his daughter.

This was no way to teach a child proper behavior. Unfortunately, Callie agreed with Becky on the Bilgewater issue. "Well," she temporized, "I should have kept better tabs on Monster."

"I don't know. It might have done Mrs. Bridgewater some good. I know it did me some good."

Callie blinked at Aubrey, unable to believe her ears.

"Me, too!" Becky said, and she giggled again. "It was funny, him sneaking in there and biting her on the ear."

Turning her head, Callie blinked at Becky.

"Sometimes it pays to be a cat," Aubrey said then, in a meditative sort of voice. "I mean, you can't get away with biting people on the ear if you're a human, can you?"

"No." Becky went off into a peal of laughter.

Callie, deciding there was no point in joining this conversation, muttered, "And some people call *me* unruly."

"They do, don't they?" Aubrey's grin was so devilish, Callie blushed.


Aubrey managed to be polite to all the inquisitive matrons he encountered after church and was proud of himself. He didn't feel polite.

Every time another mother greeted him, often with her stiff and stuffy husband at her side, he wanted to snap and snarl. He wondered if Monster had felt this same lion-on-the-prowl sensation in his gut when he'd stalked into Bilge-water's room last night, seeking prey. Aubrey's innards were heaving and twisting and giving him a terrible time, and the truth was that he wished he could bite every single damned one of those mothers on the ear. And their damned husbands and children, too.

Damn Callie Prophet and her damned birthday party. This morning he felt like a specimen in a science laboratory—a butterfly pinned to black velvet, perhaps. He got the feeling that every Santa Angelican in church that morning was talking about him behind his back. He'd managed to hold himself aloof from Santa Angelica society before yesterday's blasted party. Today he felt like fresh meat.

Perhaps because he intended to ask Callie to marry him as soon as he got the opportunity, he was particularly sensitive to atmosphere. In truth, his nerves were skipping like drops of water on a sizzling skillet.

He was probably only being fanciful. He did his best to appear nonchalant as hordes of his neighbors, most of whom had never spoken to him before today, came up to shake his hand and thank him for entertaining their children the previous day. He even remembered to smile most of the time. He felt like a limp rag when the Lockhart contingent finally escaped from the throng.

Both Callie and Mrs. Granger seemed to think the heightened interest in him was a good thing. Aubrey wanted to yell at them for it.

"It's so nice that you're getting to know the citizens of

Santa Angelica, Mr. Lockhart," Callie said, and Aubrey could hear the satisfaction in her voice.

"Indeed, it is," agreed Mrs. Granger, who also sounded cheerful.

"This will put the last of the rumors to rest," said Figgins.

*Rumors?* Aubrey, who was driving the wagon since Mrs. Bridgewater had taken the traveling coach, turned to stare at Figgins.

Delilah, who didn't seem to notice his shocked expression, said, "Well, you know, it's only because people make up stories when they don't know the truth."

"True, true. It's better that folks know the truth." Mrs. Granger's voice was a model of complacency.

It was Callie who finally laughed at him, as if she couldn't resist another second longer. Aubrey frowned at her.

"Oh, don't look so grumpy," she told him. She held Becky on her lap. The two of them made a lovely picture, with Callie in sober brown, and Becky in buttery yellow. Callie and Becky didn't look a bit alike, but they went well together, if one were only looking. Aubrey looked a lot. "There weren't any bad rumors," Callie went on to say. "People mostly talked about how sad it was about Mrs. Lockhart."

"I see." Aubrey still didn't like it. It wasn't pleasant to learn that one had been a topic of idle conversation among one's neighbors for months without knowing about it.

"But now that the mothers have met you and understand that you're only human, I'm sure their curiosity will be satisfied."

"Good God." This sounded dire to him. Whatever would happen when the townspeople learned that he and Callie were going to be married?

If, of course, she agreed to marry him.

But why wouldn't she? She'd be fixed for life if she married him, and would never have to worry about money again. Aubrey wasn't sure, because he hadn't really thought about it much and had never asked, but he suspected Callie might have had a difficult time making ends meet after her parents' decease. Why else would she have secured employment at the post office?

It was all he could do to sit through dinner at noon that day. He knew the food was good because Mrs. Granger was a superb cook and her Sunday dinners were always wonderful, but he couldn't taste a thing.

Offhand, Aubrey couldn't recall another single time in his life when he'd been as nervous about some impending event as he was about his impending proposal to Callie Prophet.

Callie brooded about why Aubrey had knocked at her door the night before all through the sermon that Sunday morning. She wanted to keep her mind on the sermon, but it was boring, and so she brooded. After church, outside events occurred to keep her occupied, thank heaven.

Fortunately, she had Becky to care for, so she wasn't able to fret much. When, however, Aubrey asked if she could please come to his office for a chat after dinner, she almost fainted. She wondered if he was going to reveal the reason he'd come to her door last night. One second, she hoped he would; the next second, she hoped he wouldn't. If he made an improper proposition to her, she supposed she'd have to leave his employ. She wasn't sure she could bear doing that.

Drat Aubrey Lockhart! The man was a fiend.

Unless, of course, he wasn't. For all Callie knew, he was going to propose another jaunt to San Francisco to visit Anne's relations.

Callie wished her nerves would settle down. This was awful. "Of course, Mr. Lockhart. I'll be there as soon I take Becky upstairs for her nap."

Aubrey nodded and left for his office. Callie watched his back until Becky claimed her focus.

"Do I have to take a nap, Miss Prophet?"

Forcing herself to pay attention to the little girl, Callie smiled at her. "You ask me the same question every day, Becky, and every day I give you the same answer."

"I know it, but I'm *seven* now."

"My dear, I'm almost twenty-seven, and I'd love to be able to take a nap every afternoon," Callie said. She swept

Becky up from the floor and into her arms, and was pleased when Becky laughed with surprise.

"When I grow up, I'm never going to take a nap," she announced.

"Pooh. I don't believe it. Grown-ups *always* want to take naps."

"How come?"

Carrying her charge up the staircase, Callie sighed. "I don't know, sweetheart. I guess it has something to do with responsibilities or something." And worry. Worry could tire a person out. Callie knew it for a certified fact.

Her footsteps dragged when she left Becky to her nap and went downstairs. She paused before Aubrey's office door in order to collect her wits, straighten her skirt, pat her hair, take a deep breath for strength, utter a brief silent prayer, and knocked.

"Miss Prophet?" Aubrey's voice sounded as anxious as Callie felt. Oh, dear, what did this mean?

"Yes," she said. "It is I."

"Please, come in."

She was about to do just that when the door opened, startling her, and causing her to jump about a foot into the air and sending her heart ricocheting around in her chest. Slamming a hand over it in hopes of settling it down, she felt herself blush.

"I beg your pardon," she said.

"I beg your pardon," he said at the same time. He recovered first. "I didn't mean to startle you."

She waved his apology away. "Oh, no, it's not your fault." It was her fault for being as nervous as a native facing a charging hippo, although she didn't add that part.

"Well, I didn't mean to startle you," he repeated. "Please, come in. There's something I'd like to discuss with you."

Discuss with her? Perhaps that meant he wasn't going to fire her. She hoped he wouldn't ask her to get rid of Monster, though. Not only would it break her heart and Becky's heart to be parted from the idiotic cat, but Callie had a feeling Monster would object. When cats objected to being moved from one location to another, they seemed to have an uncanny knack of returning to the first location. She wasn't sure Aubrey would understand that as the nature of cats, but would blame the cat's return on her.

Oh, Lord, there she went again: borrowing trouble. She came up with a smile and entered the room. "Certainly, Mr. Lockhart."

"Please, take a seat." He went to sit in the big chair behind his desk.

He looked terribly official when he did that, but Callie tried not to think about it. "Yes, Mr. Lockhart?"

Aubrey cleared his throat, slightly alarming Callie, who took it as a sign that his nerves weren't as settled as they generally were. All sorts of horrible reasons for his being nervous flickered through her mind in the second she had to think before he spoke.

"I've been thinking about a lot of things recently, Miss Prophet."

Callie's mind went blank instantly. She stared at him, unable to come up with anything to say to this comment.

Aubrey began drumming his fingers on his gleaming teakwood desk. "As you well know, life here at the Lockhart home has undergone many unpleasant changes in the last year or two."

"Er . . . Yes." The drumming of his fingers made her nerves skip.

"You seem to be getting along quite well as Becky's nanny."

Why had he suddenly changed the subject? "Um . . . Thank you." It occurred to her that she ought to say something more, so she tacked on, "Becky is a darling child."

A brief smile visited his handsome features. "Yes, she is, isn't she? That's one of the things I wanted to talk to you about."

"Oh?" She swallowed.

"Yes." Suddenly Aubrey shoved his chair back and stood, making Callie jump in her chair. Clasping his hands behind his back, he began pacing in a circle before the window.

Watching him, Callie wished she could do that, too. It might help calm her down if she could move around. Unfortunately, she was the nanny, and he was the boss, and she had to sit still until he was finished with her.

"Becky seems to be much happier lately than she was before you came to work here."

"Oh?" Relief flooded Callie so fast, it nearly washed her out of her chair. Perhaps he wasn't going to fire her or make her get rid of Monster.

"Indeed. She seems to have taken a shine to you."

"Oh—"

He held up a hand as if to ward off further comment, a gesture that was totally unnecessary since Callie had run out of words earlier in the day and hadn't found any since.

"I know, I know," Aubrey went on, "I didn't believe you were the right person for the job at first, but you've proved me wrong."

She had? Good heavens.

"I had originally believed an older woman would be best for Becky, but I can see now that you're the right person for the job. You're young and have enough energy to keep up with a small, active little girl."

That was nice, she supposed. "Thank you."

He brushed her thanks away. "No need to thank me. I'm only reporting my observations."

"I see."

He turned and looked at her sharply. "Oh, yes. I've been thinking about this for quite a while, Miss Prophet."

Obviously. Callie nodded. The thought crossed her mind that Mr. Lockhart might have suffered some sort of fit that had affected his mind and left him babbling. She banished it at once, sensing that a fit wasn't the present problem.

"When I added everything together, I decided perhaps a change was in order."

Whatever was he talking about? "Oh?"

"Indeed. Because, you know, one has to think of one's child as well as one's self when deciding these things."

"Oh."

"So it occurred to me that perhaps this might be an appropriate action on my part."

"I see," said Callie, who didn't.

"It really only makes sense. After all, you're already here in the household and you seem to get along with everyone. Indeed, it seems to me that the entire staff has begun to defer to you." Looking as if he were worried that this last comment might be construed by the eager-to-find-fault Callie, Aubrey hastened to add, "Which is good." He flashed her a smile.

She didn't respond with an answering smile. If her expression told the truth, it would be one of total befuddlement.

Aubrey's smile faded into a slight frown and he cleared his throat. "At any rate, it wouldn't be as if I were bringing a total stranger into the house."

Callie was now completely at sea. She hadn't a clue what he was talking about. If there was a point to this rambling, she was missing it. She watched him pace, wondering if she was being particularly dim. She hadn't slept much last night. Probably her reflexes and thought processes were slow today.

"I probably should get into the city more, too. My business is doing quite well, but it's not a good idea to run things at too great a distance, and this would solve the problem of someone being here to see to things around the house."

Callie strained her brain, trying to figure out what his point was.

"I don't like to leave Becky here with only the household staff to watch her." He turned and glared at Callie, who jerked with surprise. "And I'll be dashed if I'll turn her over to Mrs. Bridgewater."

This pronouncement wrung a startled cry from Callie. "Good God, no. No child should be given over to that woman."

He nodded. "Yes. There. You see? We aren't at odds about everything, after all."

"Er, no. I suppose we agree on that point." Because she was sorry to have misjudged him so badly at the beginning of her employment, Callie felt impelled to add, "I'm sure we agree on other points, too, Mr. Lockhart." She'd like to have mentioned a few of them, but her mind wasn't functioning right this minute, and she couldn't think of any.

"Yes, yes, well, we needn't worry much about those things. I am, after all, the master in my home and will continue to be so." He gave her a sharp look and resumed pacing. "I shan't be relinquishing my position here."

"Of course not." Good Lord, was he thinking of moving to San Francisco and leaving the rest of his household here? Callie's insides went cold at the thought of Aubrey leaving. And what would Becky do? She'd already been abandoned by her mother. Surely, Aubrey wasn't thinking of abandoning her, as well?

She recalled what she'd thought of Aubrey when she first moved in to the Lockhart mansion, and was ashamed of herself. She still believed he hadn't handled his wife's death well when it came to Becky, but when she'd moved into his home, she hadn't understood the true nature of his grief. She hadn't understood it, in truth, until she'd read those blasted letters.

Callie decided it would be prudent not to think about the letters at the moment.

"So, it wouldn't be a major change," Aubrey said, furrowing his brow and frowning harder. "I think there's been too much change in Becky's life already. Continuity is the answer. I want to be fair to my child." He shot her a mildly accusatory look. "Whatever you think of me, Miss Prophet, I do love my daughter."

"Of course you do," Callie murmured. "I know that, Mr. Lockhart."

He nodded. "Good. So, then, what do you think?"

Callie blinked at him. What did she think? "Um . . . About what?"

He looked at her as if she were feebleminded. "Why, what do you think of my proposal?"

Squinting at him and casting her mind back over the past few minutes, trying to find some kind of proposal tucked away in the fuddle of words Aubrey'd flung at her, Callie didn't. "Um . . . Well . . . That is, I . . ."

"Well?" His voice had taken on an edge, as if he thought she were dawdling over her answer for some reason beyond his understanding.

She gave up and decided to tell the truth. Lifting one hand, feeling helpless, and hating it—Callie didn't like not being in control of situations and people—she said, "I'm very sorry, Mr. Lockhart, but I don't believe I grasped the essence of whatever proposal you think you've made." Then she worried that he'd take her words amiss and get angry with her. But really, after thinking about it, she didn't think he'd been clear at all, and if he'd proposed something, she'd missed it entirely.

He stared at her as if she were being willfully obtuse. "For God's sake, Miss Prophet!"

Frustrated, but willing to keep her temper in check until it became obvious that he needed a piece of her mind, Callie murmured, "I'm sorry, sir. Perhaps I'm slow today. I, ah, didn't catch the gist of what you were asking me."

His stare turned into a goggle. "You what?"

She shrugged. "I'm sorry, Mr. Lockhart."

Aubrey flattened his hands on his glossy desk and leaned forward, his eyes blazing. "For God's sake, you fool, what do you think I was talking about? I just asked you to marry me!"

# 15

Aubrey had known Miss Callida Prophet to be rowdy. He'd known her to have a temper. He'd known her to be sassy, difficult, and just plain rude. But he'd never believed her to be an idiot before this minute.

He glowered at her and resented it when her mouth fell open in shock, snapped shut, and fell open again. He said, "Well? I shouldn't think you would find the position too unbearable. After all, you're fond of Becky, aren't you? You've told me you are."

She remained silent. She looked as if she were stunned, as if, instead of proposing marriage to her, he'd clubbed her with a blunt instrument. Dash it, what was wrong with the woman?

At last, she found some words. After she'd spoken them, Aubrey wondered why she'd bothered.

"I—you—I— You want to *marry* me?"

His eyes narrowed. Squinting at her, he wondered if perhaps he'd rushed his proposal. Thinking back, he couldn't recall clearly explaining all the particulars of his offer to her. Because he didn't want her to misunderstand, he stopped leaning on his hands and stood straight. Still frowning, he said, "I don't see that a marriage with me should disrupt your life too much. After all, you're already living under my roof, and you've established an effective relationship with my daughter."

"I—" Her eyes were wide. Aubrey read confusion in them, and something else he couldn't put a name to. "I'm Becky's nanny," she said. "I hadn't even considered being your—" She stopped speaking and gulped. "I hadn't ever considered being your wife."

He shrugged. "Well, consider it. It sounds merely logical to me. Convenient."

"Convenient?"

He cast about for a more useful word than that one, which didn't really convey his meaning, and came up with another: "It would provide continuity. I don't want to bring a stranger into Becky's life. She's suffered too many disruptions already."

Callie cleared her throat. "You want to marry me so as not to disrupt Becky's life?"

"Well . . . Yes." He nodded again, judiciously. "It only makes sense."

She stood, folding her hands at her waist. Aubrey had never seen her look so demure, and he didn't trust her. "It makes *sense*?"

"Yes. Certainly." Remembering at last that he hadn't explained the love angle to her, he said hastily, "I'm sure you understand that this is primarily a business decision on my part, Miss Prophet. You know—the whole world knows—that my late wife and I had a special union of like souls and like minds. You must understand that. But, while I can't offer you love, I can and will strive to be a suitable husband to you. You'll never lack for material things, and you'll have a daughter in Becky, whom, it has become obvious to me, you love."

"I see."

Was her voice shaking? Could be. After all, it wasn't every day she got a marriage proposal. Probably. Or maybe she did. What did he know about her personal life?

Suddenly, Aubrey remembered something else and felt his

neck get hot. "I would want for it to be a real marriage," he said quickly. "If you understand what I mean. I, ah, would like to have more children. Perhaps a son. Not," he hastened to assure her, for fear of rousing her feminist sensibilities, "that I want marriage only as a means of securing a son. I'm an enlightened man in an enlightened age and don't believe that female children are intrinsically of less importance than male children. You know very well that I adore my daughter. But Anne and I had planned on having a large family. We— Well, you know what happened."

"Yes," she said. "I know what happened."

They stood in Aubrey's library, looking at each other, until Aubrey's nerves jangled. "Damnation, will you stop standing there, staring at me? I just proposed marriage to you, for God's sake! Say something!"

She took a deep breath, which effectively drew Aubrey's attention to her bosom. It was a very nice bosom. He felt a surge of lust and anticipation. Dash it, Callie might be a difficult woman, but she was a remarkably well-built one.

Her cheeks now sported twin banners of fire. Aubrey guessed they betokened some kind of modesty on her part, although he wouldn't have thought she possessed much of that quality.

"Thank you, Mr. Lockhart."

Her voice was shaking. It didn't sound particularly grateful, either. Aubrey sharpened his gaze. "You're welcome."

"It was very nice of you to make such a—a—sporting offer."

"Sporting? A sporting offer? What the devil do you mean by that?"

Her smile chilled him. "I mean, I understand that you think you need a wife, Mr. Lockhart. I, however, do not believe I'm the woman for you."

He gaped at her.

She went on. "I must say that, until this afternoon, no one has ever given me reason to believe I'm a particularly compliant woman."

"Compliant? Dash it, you're impossible most of the time!"

"Exactly."

There were certainly lots of teeth in that smile of hers. It made Aubrey nervous and he glanced around for lightweight objects near her hands that she might possibly pick up and heave at him. He didn't altogether trust her mood. Nevertheless, he wanted to get at the bottom of this refusal, if it was a refusal. "I still don't understand. Do you mean to tell me you're declining my proposal?"

"It sounded more like a business transaction to me, sir. I exchange my body and soul for your pleasure."

"Pleasure? Good God, I didn't mean it that way! I want Becky to have a mother. I want her to have *you* as a mother." Confused and feeling increasingly misunderstood, offended, and desperate, he bellowed, "Confound it, she's *used* to you!"

She nodded. If her cheeks hadn't turned a bright crimson by this time, Aubrey might have thought she was completely unemotional. "I see. I understand why you might not want to—to break in another female, as it were. After all, Becky's suffered enough losses in her short life."

Thank God she was beginning to understand. He expelled a gust of breath. "Exactly. Yes. That's it exactly."

"I see. I fear I can't oblige you, Mr. Lockhart." She turned around and started for the door.

Aubrey goggled at her retreating figure. "You what? But—but— Callie, wait!"

She whirled around, stamping a foot in the process. "Don't you dare follow me," she commanded in a measured, ferocious voice. "I have never received such a—a—a *damnable* offer in my entire life. I can't believe even *you* are so lost to feeling that you'd think a woman would accept such a proposition as the one you just made me."

"Proposition? Dash it, I just proposed marriage to you!" This was impossible. It was irrational. It was, in short, exactly like her. "Damnation, I want you to marry me!"

"No, you don't. You want a built-in nanny and a general housemaid you don't have to pay for."

His mouth fell open. All of his words dried up, along with his thought processes.

"Well, let me tell you something, Mr. Aubrey Lockhart. I

wouldn't marry you if you were the last man on earth!"

She turned abruptly and stomped off, leaving Aubrey at a complete loss.

Then it struck him. He even slapped his head. "Henderson," he breathed. "She's in love with Mark Henderson."

Well, dash it. After briefly considering following her—and deciding against it as soon as the thought crossed his mind—Aubrey turned and wandered back to the window behind his desk. "Henderson." Something in his chest scrunched up and started throbbing.

Damn.

Callie walked all the way upstairs to her bedroom, opened her door, and even shut it behind her without slamming it. She'd turned the key in the lock and walked to the fireplace before the floodgates opened and tears of rage overcame her.

"Damn him!" she whispered harshly, startling the cat, who had been curled up on her bed, into lifting his head and eyeing her. His eyes looked golden in the afternoon sunlight coming through her window. Callie marched to the fireplace, lifted a Chinese ornament from the mantel and was about to smash it to the carpeted floor when she stopped herself.

"No sense breaking priceless Chinese ornaments," she muttered. "I'd undoubtedly have to pay for it, and I don't suppose a year's wages as Becky's nanny would cover the cost of the blasted thing."

She eyed the ornament with loathing. It looked as if it had been made from some kind of ivory. It was an intricately carved ball containing several other intricately carved balls that got progressively smaller toward the center of the thing. It was probably a masterpiece of artistry, but at the moment Callie's fingers itched to break it. And, after she'd hurled it to the floor, she wanted to grind the pieces under her feet until they were powder. Dust. Particles of trash.

Wheeling around, she stared at her cat, who stared back impassively.

"Oh, God, Monster, how could he?"

The cat didn't so much as blink at her. He only gazed upon her with his enigmatic cat's eyes gleaming. Callie sucked in a breath that scraped a throat that was already so tight it ached. When she let the breath out, it sounded like the dying gasp of sick duck.

"Oh, God."

Unable to deny her pain any longer, Callie threw herself facedown on her bed. Monster hissed, but he didn't jump up and run away. Callie appreciated his consideration, because she needed him just then. Grabbing him around his rotund middle, she buried her head in his soft fur and wept until she thought for sure her heart would shatter.

It was a heart already broken. It felt as if it had been smashed like that Chinese ornament would have been if she'd been less considerate. Damn him, damn him, *damn* him.

"I love him, Monster," she whispered several minutes later when she could gather sufficient breath. "I love him, and he just offered me a business proposition. As if I'm no more to him than a—a—" She couldn't think of the right word and pounded on the bed with her fist, thus offending Monster, who tried to get away, but she wouldn't let him.

"I'm a convenience!" she cried into his fur. "I'm here, and he wants me for Becky. For *Becky!*"

Monster muttered a low growl, but he didn't bare his claws or his teeth.

"Oh, God, I can't stand it."

Callie hadn't slept much the night before, and the emotional energy required to react to Aubrey's damnable proposition succeeded in draining her entirely. After sobbing her heart out for what seemed like hours, she eventually subsided into gasping hiccups before she fell into an exhausted slumber, still clinging to her cat, who immediately began smoothing his ruffled fur when Callie's grip lessened.

She had no idea how long she'd been sleeping when a quiet tapping came at her door. She sat up on the bed and rubbed her eyes. Monster, who'd given up thoughts of escape and, catlike, accepted the inevitable and napped along with her after licking his fur back into place, eyed her malevolently, his expression that of a cat sorely tried.

The tapping came again. "Miss Prophet?"

It was Becky. Callie suppressed a groan and stood up, staggering slightly. She must have been upset to allow herself to fall apart so absolutely. She cleared her throat, which felt raw. "Becky?" Good heavens, she sounded like a hoarse toad.

"Miss Prophet? Papa said you weren't feeling well. Are you sick?"

Callie had made it to the ornately carved teakwood bureau. The sight she saw in the mirror was so appalling, she groaned aloud.

"Miss Prophet?" The little girl sounded worried now.

Oh, Lord. None of this was Becky's fault. Callie refused to take her emotional distress out on the child. "Just a minute, Becky sweets. I'll be right there."

Aubrey Lockhart was rich enough to have installed hot-and-cold running water when he'd built his mansion, but that didn't help Callie at the moment, since the bathroom was down the hall. Fortunately, Delilah always filled the water pitchers in the bedrooms during her morning rounds. Callie was, therefore, able to pour some water into the basin and give her face a cold scrub.

When she glanced in the mirror again, she saw that the water hadn't done much good. Her eyelids were swollen up like pumpkins and about the same color. What she needed was a damp, cool rag and a good long nap or three.

That couldn't be helped. Resigning herself to lie to Becky—she'd never tell the little girl how her father had crushed Callie's self-respect and shattered her composure—she walked to the door and opened it. She smiled down at the child. "Come on in, Becky. I was, er, napping."

Becky looked as worried as she'd sounded. "Papa said you weren't feeling well. Are you sick? You look sick."

Wonderful, and not unexpected. "I, er, don't feel too well," she temporized.

The little girl nodded. "Papa said I wasn't to bother you, but I didn't think it would be a bother to ask you if you're sick."

"You're absolutely correct, sweetheart." *Papa said I wasn't to bother you, indeed,* Callie thought savagely. *He said you were sick.*

The brute. Callie wished Aubrey Lockhart were here—without Becky. She'd show him sick. She'd *make* him sick.

"Can I come in and sit down?"

"Of course, you may, sweetheart. Come right in."

Because Callie couldn't think of a single thing with which to amuse Becky, her imagination having been drained along with her emotions, she gestured to the bed. "Why don't you pet Monster for a bit. Maybe I can find a book to read."

Her head ached, and Callie felt about as much like reading as she did climbing an Alp, but it was the least stressful way she could think of to amuse Becky. "Um, can you think of a book you'd like me to read to you?"

Becky plopped on the bed and started petting the cat. "How come his coat's wet?" she asked.

Callie felt her lips tighten. "I don't know, sweetie. About that book . . ."

Becky's cherubic face took on a worried cast. "I don't know. Maybe we can find one in Papa's liberry."

If there was anything Callie wanted to do less than she wanted to read to Becky, it was to see Aubrey Lockhart again this day. She said cautiously, "Um, is your papa there, do you know?"

Becky shook her head, looking troubled. "He said he had to go out for a while."

Aubrey never just went out for a while. Callie didn't wonder that Becky was worried. "Did he say where he was going?" She'd never known him to visit the village saloon. She hoped he hadn't gone out to drink.

But no. It was she who was upset by the afternoon's events. Aubrey had no stake in her acceptance of his proposal—except that he'd have to find somebody else to propose to. He most assuredly wasn't heartbroken. Not like, for instance, Callie herself, whose heart felt as if it were being hacked at by several crazed woodsmen with dull axes. At the notion of his marrying someone else, that same heart suffered such a terrible spasm she pressed her hand over it in an attempt to soothe herself.

Becky went on, "He said he just wanted to ride for a while and think."

"I see."

If her blasted heart would stop aching so terribly, Callie might be able to think, too. Her heart didn't seem to want to oblige her, so she stopped trying to think and said, "Let's go downstairs and find a book, shall we?"

Nodding, Becky got off the bed. She didn't look very cheery, and Callie's heart gave another spasm. "Is something the matter, sweetheart?"

Becky heaved a sigh that was a good deal bigger than she was. "No. But you don't feel good, and Papa doesn't feel good, and it makes me not happy."

"Oh, Becky." Wounded to the soul, Callie stooped and picked up the little girl. "Let's see if we can make you more happy, shall we?"

Becky snuggled her head against Callie's shoulder and nodded. "Thank you, Mama. I mean Miss Prophet."

The slip of the tongue was so unexpected, it made Callie gasp involuntarily. A swelling of guilt shot through her, pausing to wrap its tendrils around her already battered heart. Offhand, she couldn't recall when she'd been more miserable.

Once they got downstairs to the library, Becky selected a copy of *Little Lord Fauntleroy* from Aubrey's bookshelves. Callie wondered if Aubrey would be rereading this book any time soon.

She told herself to stop thinking about Aubrey and concentrate on her reading. In this endeavor she was successful for seconds at a time, but her mind, like a bee seeking its hive, headed back to Aubrey.

Fortunately for her, Becky was content to be read to for the remainder of the afternoon. The two of them had a simple supper in the nursery, and Becky didn't object when bedtime came.

It almost killed Callie to read to the little girl from one of Aubrey's letters to Anne that night.

Callie expected herself to toss and turn for hours, and she did. The overwrought emotions of the day had exhausted her, but her buzzing brain didn't allow her body the comfort of sleep.

She wondered if she should have accepted Aubrey's proposal after all. Wouldn't it be better for her to be married to the man she loved, even if he couldn't love her back, than to pine away and die an old maid? A spinster?

Spinsters were often held up as laughingstocks. They were considered odd and unworthy. Spinsters were women who'd never captured the love of a man.

Telling herself to be honest, Callie admitted that there were exceptions. Miss Beadle, for instance, had been engaged to a man who'd died during the last days of the War Between the States. Tragic, that, and obviously not Miss Beadle's fault. Miss Beadle had captured the love of a man, but the love had been blighted.

Callie hadn't so far in her life captured the love of a man, unless one counted a couple of puppyish bouts of adoration, one from Michael Perry and the other from Sidney Hammersmith, through which she'd suffered several years ago. Michael and Sidney had been adolescents at the time, and Callie a bright, pretty young girl who never thought she'd one day be languishing, unloved, and on the brink of becoming an old maid.

Oh, very well. She supposed Mark Henderson might have paid her particular attention recently, but he was a child.

Callie didn't want to marry a child. She wanted to attract the love of a man. She wanted to be cherished, as Aubrey Lockhart had cherished Anne Harriott.

Fat chance of that ever happening.

On the other hand, even if he couldn't cherish her, Callie had no doubt that he would treat her with respect. And perhaps they could be friends. Friendship was a good thing. Friendship, from all Callie had read and observed, was a generally more solid foundation for a lasting relationship than mad, passionate love. That sort of love had a tendency to burn out rather quickly, according to all the sensible people she'd ever met.

The poets, of course, never said so, but poets were notorious as being an eccentric and unstable group, and for exalting the emotions and leaving common sense to languish, scorned. As she contemplated everything, Callie decided there was a lot to be said for common sense.

And then there was the fact that Aubrey had told her he wanted more children. Callie remembered him saying so. He'd even blushed as he did so, so she was certain she wasn't mistaken about that aspect of the afternoon's dreadful confrontation. It would be splendid to have her own children to shower her love on. And Becky. If Callie married Aubrey, she'd always be close to Becky. The mere notion of Aubrey marrying someone else and taking Becky away from her made Callie want to cry with anguish.

When she thought about it, since Aubrey didn't want her love, it might be comforting to be able to shower it on innocent children. Children's hearts were pure and open; they didn't know Callie wasn't worth loving.

Aubrey rode for hours after Callie refused his proposal of marriage. He was furious with her and with himself. But, dash it, when he considered his proposal, he couldn't put a finger on any part of it that had been disrespectful or unkind. He'd even complemented the woman, for God's sake.

And yet she'd rejected him. There had to be a reason for her to have done so. The only one that made sense to Aubrey was that she'd formed an attachment elsewhere. And, since he'd never seen Callie in the company of a man other than Mark Henderson, and since he'd never heard her name spoken of in connection with another man, Aubrey presumed the man she loved was Henderson.

His hands tightened on the reins, and he told himself to calm down. Just because Callie loved another man didn't excuse Aubrey's hurting his horse's mouth.

"Damn and blast," he muttered as he rode through the woods. He came out onto the dirt road leading to Santa Angelica, and he decided he might as well ride through the picturesque little village. Perhaps he'd see someone there who didn't hate him, as Callie seemed to.

Memories of Callie and of how she'd expressed her low opinion of him, as a father and as a man, flooded his mind as he rode. His mood alternated between fury and black despair.

"Damnation, why should the woman be so blasted attracted to Mark Henderson and not to me? What does he have that I don't have?"

His horse, the only one present to whom he might have been speaking, since there was no one else around, gave him no answer. Aubrey brooded on Mark Henderson versus himself as a possible husband for Callie Prophet, and he couldn't figure it out. Aubrey was Mark's employer, for God's sake. Aubrey was richer than Mark and just as good-looking.

He felt silly when the last notion crossed his mind. Aubrey had never dwelt on his looks, even though Anne had told him over and over that she considered him the most handsome man in the world. But Anne had loved him. Love colored one's perspective of life in all of his variations. Aubrey knew it, because he'd loved Anne with the same fervor.

"Damnation, man, stop dwelling on love. That part of your life is dead and gone." He braced himself for the pain that always followed thoughts of Anne and was surprised when it didn't come.

It was when he thought about Callie Prophet that the pain stabbed him. He didn't understand it. He did, however, greet the outskirts of Santa Angelica with relief. How pleasant, he thought bitterly, to be among people who didn't loathe him.

In fact, as Aubrey rode through the village, he was the recipient of several cheerful waves from those of his neighbors who recognized him. He smiled and waved back, and was sorry their overt approval didn't make him feel significantly better.

"Ah, Anne," he whispered when he cleared the village limits and was once again alone with his horse and his thoughts. "I don't seem to do anything right, now that you're gone."

He brooded about all the things he was no good at as he

rode back home. He'd have liked to stay out longer, but it didn't seem fair to torment his horse just because he himself was making a hash of his life.

Mrs. Granger jumped with alarm when Aubrey came through the kitchen door. He glowered at her. Dash it, did the whole *world* hate him? He'd thought it was only Callie who did. "It's only I, Mrs. Granger," he said coldly.

"Oh, Mr. Lockhart." Mrs. Granger pressed a hand to her heart as if trying to pat back a fit of apoplexy. "I didn't expect you to come through the back door, sir."

She smiled at him, and Aubrey wondered if he'd been the least little bit irrational in assuming she'd jumped because she hated him. He decided to give her the benefit of the doubt. "Sorry, Mrs. Granger. My boots are all muddy, and I didn't want to track it through the front hall." He gestured over his shoulder. "I left 'em next to the back door."

"Good, good," Mrs. Granger said, sounding complacent.

Aubrey took heart. Perhaps he'd overreacted. Perhaps it was truly only Callie who hated him. "Sorry I missed supper. Is there a chance of getting a sandwich or something?" He smiled, trying for one of the smiles he used to offer people with no trouble at all. His smiles used to be second nature to him, in the days when life was good. It occurred to him that he had to stretch to reach for them these days.

"Don't be silly, Mr. Lockhart." Mrs. Granger laughed. It sounded like a genuine, honest-to-goodness laugh, but Aubrey didn't feel competent to accept anything at face value today. "I have a plate of cold supper for you. There's a couple of sandwiches. If you don't want both of them, I'll just put one away in the icebox for tomorrow. And I fixed a fine salad and pickles, too."

"Thank you." Aubrey felt humbled in the presence of such goodness. "I didn't expect such bounty after I missed the supper hour."

She looked at him as if he'd lost his mind. "But you told me you were going out, Mr. Lockhart. It wasn't a surprise when you weren't here for supper."

"Oh." He'd forgotten that part of his afternoon. He'd been too busy fretting about Callie, he guessed.

Rather than dining on his sandwich, salad, and pickles in solitary state in his big dining room, Aubrey made himself comfortable at the kitchen table, after making sure he wouldn't be in Mrs. Granger's way.

She gave him another odd look. "Good heavens, Mr. Lockhart, you're never in my way."

Really? Glancing at her closely, Aubrey detected nothing but honesty on her kindly face. "Thank you."

Maybe, he thought, he was allowing his problems with Callie to color the way he viewed the rest of the world. Maybe it was Callie's fault, and not his, that she'd rejected him.

As he munched his sandwiches, he contemplated Callie, life, marriage, Becky, and remarriage. He'd come to no conclusion about anything by the time he'd finished his meal, thanked Mrs. Granger once more, and wandered to his office.

# *16*

Thank the good Lord the following day was a Monday, and Callie could resume her household chores—sewing for Becky, mending, tidying up the nursery, and planning educational opportunities for her charge—and try to forget about not becoming Aubrey's wife. And of having been asked to marry him in such an unromantic way.

"Convenience," she muttered as she brushed Becky's hair out in preparation for braiding it. "Bah."

"What's convenient?" Becky wanted to know.

What, indeed? Callie knew good and well *she* wasn't, no matter what Aubrey Lockhart chose to think. "Oh, nothing," she said airily. "I was just . . . talking to myself."

"But I'm here," Becky pointed out. "You don't have to talk to yourself. You can talk to me."

Callie laughed and leaned over to give her favorite child a quick kiss on her golden head. "You're right, sweetie. So, what do you think Miss Oakes has in store for you today?"

Becky took a deep, anticipatory breath and grinned. She adored school. A good deal of her enjoyment, Callie suspected, lay in her having been deprived of social contacts with children her own age for so long. Which was all Aubrey's fault, drat the man to perdition.

But no. She must stop thinking things like that. Aubrey had been laid flat by Anne's illness and death. If he hadn't been a perfect father during that agonizing period of time, he had at least eventually recognized his shortcomings in regard to his daughter's welfare and sought to correct them. Why else would Callie be here, brushing Becky's hair?

"I think we're going to start mem'rizing poems today."

"Aha. Miss Oakes and I used to loved memorizing poems when we were in school. Do you know which poem you're going to memorize?"

"Not yet. She's going to read us some, and then she'll probably have us go to the liberry or home and memorize one we choose for ourselves."

Callie didn't fail to notice that Becky had picked up on the proper pronunciation of the word "memorize." It made her heart ping every time she saw another indication of Becky's eagerness to please the adults in her life. Some children would have resorted to disruptive behavior in order to secure recognition if they'd endured Becky's losses. It was probably only pure luck that had given Aubrey so compliant and pleasant a child.

Luck or human nature. With parents like Anne and Aubrey, how could they fail to produce a practically perfect child? Callie reminded herself that cynicism was unbecoming in a young woman, and she told herself to stop being cynical instantly.

*Convenient, my foot.*

"I'll help you choose and listen to you recite, if you'd like, sweetie pie."

"Thank you!" Becky all but jumped up and down on her chair, so eager was she to get to school.

Breakfast was a less uncomfortable meal than it might have been, primarily because Aubrey had eaten before Callie and Becky came downstairs, and then taken himself off.

"Business matters," Mrs. Granger informed the two of them. "He's gone off to San Francisco for a couple of days."

"Oh." Becky sounded disappointed. "I wish he'd said good-bye."

The rat. The selfish, cowardly, daughter-deserting rat. Callie mentally gave herself a good whap upside the head and told herself she was in no position to judge another human being. That was God's job, and He was undoubtedly better equipped to handle it than she was. "Perhaps he . . . had to catch an early coach," she said, straining to find something nice to say about a father who could run out on his child merely because something rather embarrassing had occurred the day before.

"That he did," supplied Mrs. Granger, handing Becky a plate containing a flapjack in the shape of a bunny rabbit, alongside two small sausage patties. "He left notes for the two of you. A wire came from Mr. Henderson, you see."

"Oh." Startled, Callie looked at the housekeeper. "Did something bad happen?"

Becky glanced up from her flapjack, and Callie wished she'd kept her apprehension to herself.

"Oh, no," Mrs. Granger said, and Callie released a breath. "But Mr. Henderson had some questions, according to Mr. Lockhart, and Mr. Lockhart thought it better that he go to the city to take care of them." She flipped another pancake. "I don't recall the cable coming, but I napped yesterday afternoon."

"I see." So it had been cowardice after all, Callie thought unkindly. There had been no cable from Mark Henderson; she'd bet her teeth on it.

Then again, cowardice might have played some part in Aubrey's defection this morning, but when she considered the matter, perhaps he'd been right to remove himself. By the time he came back in a few days, perhaps the awkwardness inherent in the situation would have faded.

Maybe. As Callie ate her own flapjacks, in plain old-fashioned rounded shape, she decided she'd have to make up her mind about that later.

\* \* \*

Aubrey felt a little silly when he showed up in his San Francisco office late that Monday morning. Mark Henderson glanced up, registered his shock, and rose to rush over to him, fawning as if Aubrey had been a hundred and ten rather than a sprightly thirty-five. He frowned at his secretary.

"No need to pamper me, Mark. I'm not in my dotage yet."

Mark leaped back. "Good God, no, sir! I didn't mean to—that is to say, I only—"

Taking pity on him, Aubrey relaxed. "I'm sorry, Mark. Didn't mean to snap at you. Sorry I didn't let you know I'd be here this morning."

"I'm sure it's quite all right, Mr. Lockhart. There's no need for the owner of the business to apprise his subordinates of his every move."

Oh, Lord, now he'd gone and done it. He'd offended Mark Henderson, a superior employee, because he was embarrassed about having run away from home. Aubrey sighed. "Take a powder, Mark. I'm not conducting a spot inspection or anything. I just needed to get away from the house for a while."

Mark remained stiff for a second or two, then relaxed and offered a tentative smile. "Too many women?" he asked in a teasing tone.

Ah, that sounded so simple. Aubrey pounced on the suggestion as he'd seen Monster pounce on a paper ball. "Exactly. I'm as fond of women as the next man, but I need to escape every now and then."

Going back to his desk, Mark sat, still smiling, although with more palpable strain. "Is, ah, Miss Prophet causing you any problems, sir?"

"Miss Prophet?" Aubrey took his own chair, behind his massive desk, and gazed thoughtfully at Mark. Here, he had yesterday assumed, was the man whom Callie Prophet loved, damn him for daring to deprive Becky of her nanny.

Aubrey couldn't see it. Mark didn't appear any more lovable than Aubrey to Aubrey's eyes. He was a good-looking fellow, but so was Aubrey. Mark was smart, but Aubrey considered himself smarter. And he was a dashed sight richer.

After sighing deeply, he said, "No. She's fine."

"Ah. I see." Mark heaved a huge sigh, too. "She's an awfully pretty woman, isn't she?"

"I suppose so." Aubrey slid a pile of correspondence to the center of his desk. Lifting the first envelope and squinting at it, he said as casually as he could, "You seem rather fond of Miss Prophet, Mark. Should I be alarmed?"

"Alarmed?" Mark sounded genuinely shocked. "Good God, sir, no! That is to say—I assure you, I don't have any—I mean—"

"It's all right, Mark. I only wondered if I'd have to hire another nanny anytime soon. I have no business to pry into your personal life."

"But I don't *have* a personal life!"

Aubrey glanced up with interest and saw Mark's face flush. "You don't?"

Mark gave a shaky chuckle. "No. Well, not really. My sister's family generally takes up my time. I live with them, you know, sir. She married a capital fellow, and I've lived with them for six years now. I'm fond of their children, and enjoy entertaining them."

"I see." Aubrey hesitated, wondering if it would be polite to ask the question that had sprung to his mind. Then he decided he might as well. "Do you ever think about marriage, Mark?"

"Marriage?"

Aubrey's secretary was plainly startled by the question. His flush deepened. Aubrey was sorry to have embarrassed the boy, but he had an almost overwhelming need to understand Mark's relationship with Callie—if there was one. "Yes. You're a young, vigorous fellow. Do you ever think about marrying and settling down?"

After clearing his throat, Mark said, "Well, yes. Sometimes. But I don't want to rush into anything."

Aubrey nodded, trying for a judicial, contemplative expression but fearing his relief might be leaking through. "So, you haven't met anyone recently whom you'd consider suitable material for a life's mate for yourself?"

"Well . . . No. Not really."

Dash it, that was no answer. Well, it *was* an answer, but it wasn't the one Aubrey wanted to hear. He decided to be more blunt. "I wondered, after seeing the two of you together, if you might have an interest in Miss Prophet." There. He'd said it.

"Oh!" Mark's face had begun to regain its normal color, but it reddened again at once. "Miss Prophet?"

"Yes." Aubrey picked up another envelope and tried to appear nonchalant as he perused its contents. "Just a thought, is all."

"Oh. I see. Well . . . Well, I do think she's a charming woman," Mark said. "And she's quite pretty. She seems to be good with children. She'd probably make some lucky fellow an admirable wife."

Dash it, Aubrey didn't ask for a compilation of Callie's finer qualities. The longer Mark took in listing them, the more Aubrey feared he was going to confess to a secret engagement or something. He schooled his features to betray none of his irritation.

"But I don't think she'd give me a second thought if I didn't work for you, Mr. Lockhart. She's obviously head over ears in love with you, sir."

The envelope slipped from Aubrey's suddenly numb fingers, and he stared at his secretary. "She *what*?"

Mark started and paled. "Well, I— I mean, it seemed— I don't mean to say that you— Oh, dear."

Aubrey took three deep breaths and let them out slowly. He could scarcely credit what his ears had just heard. But his hearing was excellent, and he knew he wasn't mistaken. Mark, however, was.

"I don't believe you've judged her sentiments correctly, Mark," Aubrey said after a moment or two. "Miss Prophet . . ." Miss Prophet what? Miss Prophet hates his guts? Miss Prophet despises him? Miss Prophet considers him beneath her contempt? Aubrey didn't want to admit those things aloud. After fumbling around in his brain for a few seconds, he merely said, "I don't believe Miss Prophet entertains those sorts of feelings for me." In any way whatsoever.

"No?" Mark eyed his employer skeptically. "Well, sir, I'm sure you know best, but I've seen the way she looks at you."

Squinting at his secretary, Aubrey thought about Callie. No. Mark was wrong. "I've seen the way she looks at me, too," he said, trying not to sound as sardonic as he felt. "I can assure you that *love* isn't the word I'd use to describe it."

"No?" Mark remained unconvinced, Aubrey could tell. "If you say so, sir."

"Yes, I do say so." Dash it, this conversation was insane. "But how did we get onto this topic?" he said with asperity. "It has nothing to do with business."

A flash of annoyance passed across Mark's face. "No, sir, but you did ask."

"Oh. Right. I did. Sorry, Mark." Dash it. Aubrey told himself not to take his own problems out on his secretary. "I beg your pardon. Didn't mean to pry."

"Oh, no, sir. It's quite all right." His glance was shy. "I, er, appreciate you taking an interest in me, sir. Most employers wouldn't."

Embarrassed now himself, Aubrey said gruffly, "Nonsense. I value you, both as an employee and as a gentleman of integrity and intelligence, Mark. I care about your life and future."

God bless it, if he got any more maudlin, they'd both be weeping like babies. Aubrey gave himself a mental shake.

"Thank you very much, sir."

More embarrassed than ever, Aubrey rose from his desk. "I came to the city in order to see to a few things," he said mendaciously. "I'll be back a little later."

He escaped to Golden Gate Park, where he walked for two-and-a-half hours, after which time he felt capable of dealing with his business affairs again. His personal affairs were another matter entirely. But Aubrey decided to be patient. Patience had been his friend in business matters. It probably couldn't hurt in his dealings with Miss Callida Prophet.

His confidence in business affairs didn't, unfortunately, leak over into his feelings about Callie.

He did dare, however, to ask Mark in as casual a manner as possible how he planned to spend Christmas. It had occurred to Aubrey as he wandered around the park, not looking at anything in particular but pondering his own problems, that Christmas might be a good time in which to try to change Callie's mind about marrying him. All that warmth and good cheer. Fellowship. Merriment. That sort of stuff.

"Oh, my sister and her husband invite the whole family over on Christmas Eve," Mark told him. Aubrey didn't fail to notice the twinkle in his secretary's eyes, or the expression of fond memory on his face. "Christmas is a jolly time for families."

Exactly what Aubrey had been thinking. He and Anne hadn't had enough time together to establish very many Christmas traditions, but they'd enjoyed family get-togethers twice after Becky's birth. After that, Anne had been too ill to plan anything, and Aubrey had been too heartsick.

However, it might not be taken amiss, by Becky or the indomitable Miss Prophet, if Aubrey were to suggest some sort of family function. Christmas Eve sounded like as good a time as any, and Callie had already shown her good generalship when it came to organizing parties. Mrs. Granger would probably enjoy it, since her own family was back East somewhere and she considered the Lockharts her family. And Figgins, too. Delilah had family in Santa Angelica, so she probably would rather spend the time with them, but that needn't matter much.

Now if Aubrey could only figure out where to find a family. . . .

His own family consisted of himself and Becky. He'd be dashed if he'd invite Old Bilgewater, probably the only available member of Anne's family. The reason she was available was that nobody wanted her around, and Aubrey was no exception.

*Hmm.* He'd just have to think of something, was all there

was to it. Becky would enjoy a Christmas party, and it would give him an opportunity to show Callie a bit of the good life she'd be throwing away if she didn't marry him.

On the other hand, maybe he was just insane. On that happy note, Aubrey scowled, and went back to work.

" A Christmas party?"
     Callie stared at him blankly. Aubrey grew irritated. "Yes, a Christmas party. I understand Christmas parties aren't entirely unheard of, even in Santa Angelica."

Her own eyes flashed. "Yes, I have heard of Christmas parties, Mr. Lockhart." She sucked in a breath. Aubrey expected her to use it to scold him, but she didn't. "When would you like to hold this festive gathering?"

Her voice was so dry Aubrey might have thought she'd dipped it in alum before flinging it at him, if such a thing were possible. "I thought about Christmas Eve."

"I see." Her eyes narrowed. "Whom exactly do you expect would be available to travel to your home on Christmas Eve, Mr. Lockhart? That evening is generally held to be one for families gathering together. Even rich people can't expect everyone to drop their own family traditions when they snap their fingers, you know."

He glared at her. "Yes, Miss Prophet, I do know that."

Aubrey could see her better nature struggling with her desire to hurt him. He was surprised when her better nature won.

"I beg your pardon, sir. That was unkind."

He eyed her narrowly. "Yes, it was. I don't suppose you'd consider calling me 'Aubrey,' would you? And I could call you 'Callie,' and we might end up not hating each other eventually."

"I don't hate you!" Callie's cheeks bloomed with color. "I don't hate you," she repeated less fiercely. "You annoy me sometimes, is all."

She grimaced, and Aubrey watched with interest as another battle waged itself within her. She was an emotional woman, and not a little explosive. In which regard she was as unlike Anne as she was in every other regard. He waited for her emotional turmoil to settle.

At present they sat in his library. It was a blustery Saturday afternoon in late November, and when he'd looked out the window, he'd decided snow wasn't far off.

Becky was upstairs taking a nap. She'd come down with a bad cold two days prior and was happy to sleep the day away. When he'd gone upstairs to kiss her before her nap, Aubrey had noticed that Callie had lent her Monster to keep her company during her nap. Incomprehensibly to Aubrey, the dashed cat seemed to ease Becky's uncomfortable cold symptoms.

Aubrey had thought about his Christmas Eve party idea for at least a month before he decided it might prove to be a worthwhile one. He and Callie had established a comfortable rapport in the weeks following his rejected proposal. The first few days had been prickly, but the fact was that the two of them seemed actually to like each other. It was a big change from the beginnings of their relationship. Aubrey figured they'd overcome those initial misunderstandings through familiarity and mutual respect. The notion pleased him.

It could not be denied, either, that the longer he remained in the same house with Callie, the more he thought she'd make a good mother for Becky. And, although he disliked himself for it, he itched to get his hands on her, too. He tried to downplay that aspect of the situation, but it wouldn't let him.

He lusted for her. He desired her. A day didn't pass in which, at one time or another, he didn't have the urge to lift her in his arms and make away with her. He wanted to strip her naked and taste every inch of her. He wanted to take the pins from her hair and run his fingers through its silky mass. He wanted to bury his sex in Callie's hot, wet depths. He wanted to ravish her for forty days and forty nights, until neither of them could walk.

It was, he decided, a dashed good thing he sat behind his desk, so Callie couldn't see the evidence of his lust. She probably had no idea these thoughts crossed his mind every time he looked at her. He sighed and waited some more.

"I beg your pardon," Callie said stiffly when she spoke at last. "I know it's not my place to be annoyed by my employer."

He lifted an eyebrow. "Can one help it if one is annoyed by someone, employer or not?"

Her lips pressed together. "I suppose not. But you know very well that I have a temper. I should try to keep it better controlled."

"Wouldn't hurt," Aubrey agreed, and was interested to see her color flare up again. He smiled at her. "Face it, Callie, it's not in your nature to take things easily."

"I did not give you leave to call me Callie, Mr. Lockhart!" she cried, as if that were the point of the conversation.

"I, however, gave you leave to call me Aubrey, and I wish you would."

She huffed. "Oh, very well."

"Thank you, Callie." He smiled sweetly. It was odd, but he'd stopped taking her temper amiss some few weeks before he'd proposed. When she'd first come to his home in order to be Becky's nanny, her plain speaking and unrestrained moods had irked him. He now found them rather amusing. Refreshing, even. Nobody ever had to guess about where he stood with Callie Prophet.

"However," Callie went on, "that doesn't solve the problem of where you're planning to come up with a family for your family gathering. Do you have one? Besides Becky, I mean."

"No, I don't."

She gave him a hard look. "I hope to heaven you aren't thinking of asking Mrs. Bridgewater."

"Good God, no!"

"I'm glad of that, at all odds."

"My—and Becky's—lack of family is why I asked you to meet with me this afternoon, actually."

"Oh?"

"You know more people in Santa Angelica than we do. Do you know of any people who might enjoy getting together with Becky on Christmas Eve? People who don't participate in large family gatherings of their own, I mean?"

"You mean stray people?" Callie eyed him doubtfully. "Widows and orphans? People like that?"

He frowned, taking exception her choice of words. "I hadn't thought of it in those terms exactly, but I guess I did mean something like that."

"Well . . . Let me think."

He gestured, giving her leave. He had his own ideas on the subject, but hoped she'd think of them before he had to suggest them. She'd probably reject them out of hand if he did.

It didn't seem to be one of Callie's brighter days, however, and after he watched her brow furrow and her eyes narrow, and he practically read her thoughts as they sped through that agile brain of hers, she smiled briefly, then shook her head.

"I'm not having much luck, Mr. . . . Aubrey."

"No?" Dash it, why was she being dim today, of all days? "You can't think of any people in Santa Angelica who might like to have a family gathering here?" He glanced around his library. "This is a big house. It could hold a lot of people."

She hesitated for a second. "Yes. Yes, it could."

Aubrey gazed at her for several more seconds, then sighed. She wasn't going to help him out with this. It was up to him. He cleared his throat, steepled his fingers, and positioned them under his chin, hoping he looked merely thoughtful and not eager. "Um, what about your own family, Callie? I understand your parents are gone. Do you suppose your siblings and their spouses and children might like to gather here, en masse, as it were, to celebrate Christmas on Christmas Eve?"

Noting the expression of absolute shock on her face, Aubrey hurried on. "I mean, if they have other plans— That is to say, if they get together with others— I mean, I wouldn't want them to think I'm trying to encroach. It's only that Becky would . . . well, it would be a blessing, since she has no other relations who— That is to say . . ." He stopped trying to concoct a coherent speech and sighed disconsolately. Dash it, he'd made a perfect hash of it.

"My family?" Callie's voice was very small, quite devoid

of its usual robust inflections. "But—" She swallowed. "Do you mean it?"

"Dash it, of course, I mean it!" Aubrey decided he ought to be insulted, so he bridled. "I'm not in the habit of offering false coin, whatever you may think of me."

"I know that. It's just that the idea is so—so—" She broke off abruptly. "Actually, I'd thought about my family, too. We do like to get together on Christmas Eve, but nobody's house is really big enough for everyone, even though we all squeeze in together. We usually go to George's, since he lives in the middle, and the children enjoy playing outdoors, and he's in the country. Sort of."

"Oh? Well, then, perhaps this more commodious abode wouldn't be frowned upon as an alternative?" His anticipation was so potent, it was difficult to keep it from leaking into his voice. Oh, but the Prophets would be perfect for Becky! If any family on earth could provide Becky with the support a family was supposed to provide, they could.

Aubrey had noted before this that the Prophets were a singularly close family. Every time Callie got time off, she visited her family, often taking Becky with her. Becky clearly enjoyed the visits and had become close with a couple of Callie's nieces and nephews. Aubrey thought the Prophets were a good example of family-hood, if there was such a thing.

What's more, all of the husbands and wives therein seemed to blend right into the mix. Not unlike mixing cement with straw in order to strengthen building blocks, newcomers into the Prophet clan only seemed to intensify the family bond. Aubrey thought Becky could use such a family, and he appreciated their willingness to take her in. Adopt her into their fold, in a way.

He told himself he didn't care for his own sake, but he was pretty sure he was lying. He cleared his throat again. "Um, do you think they would go for it?" *Please say yes.*

Callie paused and then nodded, although she didn't look exactly positive when she did it. "I think they would. In fact, they'd probably love it." She gave him a saucy smile. "It's not every day the members of my family get to participate in Christmas jollifications in mansions, you know."

"This isn't a mansion," Aubrey said gruffly. "Anne and I built this house on a large scale because we had hoped to have a big family."

He didn't appreciate the expression of sympathy that suddenly appeared on her face. If there was one thing he didn't need, he thought sourly, it was to be considered pitiable by Miss Callida Prophet.

"Yes, of course," Callie said. She rose. "Thank you very much, Mr. Lockhart."

"Aubrey," he grumbled.

Her smile nearly dazzled him. "Aubrey."

The way she said his name, sort of caressingly and soft, had a remarkable effect on Aubrey's already unruly masculinity. It stiffened completely, dash it. Irritated by his own lack of self-control, he tried to sound casual. "So you'll take up the matter with your sisters and brother?"

"Yes, I will. Tomorrow, while Becky's at school." A troubled look crossed her face. "If she's well enough to go to school. I suspect she won't be. But I'm sure Mrs. Granger won't mind watching her for an hour or so while I extend invitations."

A little worried that his offer would be taken amiss by the proud Prophet clan, Aubrey said, "Please tell them I'd be grateful for their participation. I don't want them to think of this as a command performance. It's only that since Anne's death . . ." Damnation, since Anne's death, what? He feared he'd almost said something stupid.

"I understand," Callie said gently. "You felt lost and alone. It's difficult to pick up the pieces and carry on."

Shocked that she should understand so clearly, and express his feelings in such simple, straightforward words, Aubrey nodded and murmured, "Yes. Yes, I guess so."

She sighed. "I remember how it was when my parents died. It was awful. But at least I had siblings." She gave him another tender smile.

Aubrey resented that one; it was as if she were pitying him, and he didn't want her sympathy. What he wanted from her was—was— What he wanted was that she agree to marry him, is what.

Callie bade him good night and left the library, and Aubrey decided it would be better not to think about what he'd been about to admit he wanted from her.

After Callie left him, he brooded for a few minutes, then went upstairs to Becky's bedroom. She was awake, but not feeling well, and he sat on her bed and petted her with one hand and Monster with the other. He was touched by how much his daughter appreciated the gesture of love on his part.

"Thank you for visiting me, Papa." Her throat hurt, her voice was hoarse, and she sounded pathetic.

"You don't look like you're feeling very well, Becky," he said gently.

"I don't, Papa. I feel icky."

He was alarmed to see her eyes fill with tears. "Don't cry, sweetheart. You'll feel better soon."

"Indeed, she will," came Callie's voice, sounding efficient and cheerful at his back. He turned and saw her standing in the doorway, holding a glass. "I have some salicylic powders here, Becky, darling. They taste terrible, but they'll help you feel better. Mrs. Granger squeezed some oranges and I stirred the powders into the juice, so they won't taste *quite* as bad as they usually do."

Feeling unnecessary and in the way, Aubrey rose from his daughter's bed. "Right. When I was sick with the influenza last year, I remember how much salicylic powders helped me."

Becky appeared doubtful. She was, however, an obedient child, so she sat up resignedly. "I hate them," she said woefully as she wiped tears away.

Callie swooped down on her like a ministering angel. "I know you do, lovie, but they really will help you to feel better."

Becky's pretty mouth trembled, causing Aubrey's heart to spasm so fiercely, he decided he'd better exit the room. It wouldn't do Becky any good if her papa started bawling. Bending over and depositing a kiss on her forehead, he muttered, "Get better soon, sweetheart."

"Thank you, Papa." She sounded utterly wretched and pathetic, and Aubrey all but ran out of the room.

He spent the rest of his day in an unsettled mood. He read newspapers, went for a walk, contemplated going for a ride, decided against it, and ate dinner alone. Callie and Becky were dining upstairs in her bedroom since Becky was feeling so rotten. That meant Becky wouldn't be going to school tomorrow and he hoped that wouldn't cause Callie to delay extending Christmas invitations to her family. He knew he oughtn't to be as impatient as the notion made him.

"Dash it," he growled as he sat in his big desk behind his big desk. "You're an adult, man. Act like one."

His tiny lecture made him buck up slightly. He could wait until Becky was well without restlessness eating him up from the inside. Of course, he could. He was, after all, a successful businessman. Successful businessmen didn't get overwrought about such things as Christmas party invitations.

Feeling better, he contemplated reading a book versus looking at another newspaper or one of the periodicals that had arrived yesterday from San Francisco.

At last, he did neither. Instead, after considering it for a long time, he unlocked the bottom drawer of his desk for the first time in a year and a half, reached inside, and withdrew a bundle of letters. They were love letters Anne had written to him during the happy years of their short marriage. He'd tied the letters with a ribbon and stuffed them in his desk drawer some time after the fatality of Anne's illness had been diagnosed and, at last, accepted. Aubrey hadn't had the heart even to look at the bundle from that day to this. The mere thought of them had made his heart hurt.

Tonight, seeking answers to questions he wasn't sure how to frame, he set the bundle on his desk and proceeded to look at it for fifteen minutes. Then, with aching heart and trembling hand, he reached out, tugged the ribbon loose, and picked up the first envelope.

He stared at it for another several minutes, studying Anne's beautiful, elegant handwriting, before he lifted the flap and withdrew the letter.

*My Darling Aubrey*, the letter began. As soon as Aubrey read the words, something inside him gave way.

*17*

Callie didn't know how long she'd been lying in bed that night, alternately thinking, brooding, and trying to pound her pillows into shape. The dratted pillows felt like boulders under her head. She wanted fluff, not boulders.

"It's not the pillows' fault," she told herself sourly. "It's you, Callie Prophet."

Which didn't help her get to sleep. She got up after an hour or so, wet a washcloth, climbed back into bed, and pressed the washcloth to her eyes. If she couldn't sleep, she might at least try to refresh her looks.

It had shocked her when Aubrey said he wanted to invite her family for a Christmas Eve celebration. She knew he'd done it for Becky's sake, not hers, but the mere fact that he had done so at all had revived all of her feelings about him. And marriage to him.

In truth, she didn't even know if his marriage proposal was still open. For all she knew, he was busily seeking a wife elsewhere.

So vicious a stab of pain shot through her that she had to slap a hand over her heart. "Stop it this instant, Callie Prophet!"

Callie Prophet wasn't a wilting lily. She was as sensitive as the next woman, but she prided herself on her common sense and emotional stability. She hadn't been emotionally stable today.

When Aubrey had suggested inviting her family to a Christmas Eve party, she'd immediately and without thought envisioned herself as mistress of the Lockhart mansion. She'd seen herself, not as Becky's nanny, but as Aubrey's wife.

Yup, there she was, standing, in her mind's eye, at the head of the staircase, clad in a dress she couldn't afford in a million years, beaming down on her brother and his wife, and her sisters and their husbands, and everybody's children. But Aubrey could. And he'd probably be happy to buy her any number of lovely gowns, too.

One thing she could say for Aubrey: He wasn't a miserly fellow. In truth, he was just about perfect.

Except that he didn't love her.

She socked her pillow again. "Damn and blast! Will you stop being such an idiot, Callie Prophet? The poor man adored the only woman he'd ever loved. It's your stupid dumb luck that he met her before he met you."

Not that he'd have paid any attention to her if he *had* met her before he'd met Anne. Callie Prophet and Anne Harriott were worlds—universes—apart, personality-wise. And Aubrey obviously desired a more sober personality in a wife than Callie possessed.

Although, he *had* asked her to marry him.

"For Becky, you fool. Not for him." Callie turned over and shrieked into her lumpy pillow, knowing the sound would be muffled.

She wished Monster were here so she could hold his big, heavy, body close to her bosom and comfort herself that way. But Monster was busy comforting Becky this evening, and he couldn't be in two places at once. Besides, Becky needed him more than Callie did. Becky was genuinely sick. Callie was only an idiot.

If she kept this up, she'd be no better than Cissy Hammersmith, who was known throughout the village of Santa

Angelica as "Silly Cissy," for her romantic notions and extravagant emotional displays.

The comparison made Callie cringe. On the other hand, Callie would bet money that Cissy had never been asked to endure the trials Callie herself had faced and conquered. At least Cissy's parents were still alive.

Would being married to Aubrey be a trial to endure? Callie told herself to stop asking stupid questions. After another half hour or so, though, she decided she was being foolish to try to fall asleep when her brain refused to cooperate. She'd be better off going downstairs and getting a book to read. Reading might help to calm her mind and make her sleepy.

With that in mind, Callie got out of bed, slipped her robe on over the flannel nightgown Florence had given her last Christmas, stuffed her feet into her old, floppy slippers, and tiptoed out of her bedroom. She carried a candle, since the Santa Angelica Electric Company shut down at midnight, and she didn't especially want to fall downstairs and break her neck.

The door to Aubrey's library was closed, but Callie didn't think anything of that. He often closed the library door at night, probably because he worked in there and his desk was often messy. Mrs. Granger didn't approve of messes, and Aubrey didn't approve of Mrs. Granger or Delilah fussing with his papers.

She was shocked when she stepped into the room and saw Aubrey. He'd been sitting at his desk, with his head buried in his folded arms. He looked up when she entered, his face ravaged, his eyes red-rimmed and tortured.

"Aubrey! Good God, what's the matter?"

"Callie." He sat up, cleared his throat, and tugged at his vest. He'd discarded his jacket, which he'd hung over the back of his chair. His hair was disarranged, and he dragged his fingers through it.

She took a step toward him, propelled by a fierce longing to take him in her arms and hold him. She held back, knowing full well that it wasn't her place to offer solace to her employer. "What's the matter?" she asked again, hoping to help, even if she couldn't demonstrate physically what she felt emotionally.

He waved a hand over the papers on his desk. "Nothing. I—I was just going over some things. Letters. Old letters."

Callie's heart swooped and throbbed. "Letters?" Good God, if he'd discovered her secret, she was doomed. She should have confessed about those blasted letters months ago; it was too late now.

His sigh ruffled the papers. "Yes." He lifted one of them. "Letters Anne wrote me, oh, years ago. I, ah, haven't looked at them for a long time."

"I see." So. He hadn't discovered her dreadful secret. Her heart continued to ache, the knowledge that he'd sought comfort from a dead woman painful to learn.

Callie would have loved to comfort him.

He didn't want comfort from her.

"Um, I'm sorry if the letters, um, brought back painful memories."

He heaved a deep sigh. Shaking his head sorrowfully, he said, "The last two years of her life were so hard on her. She suffered so much."

Callie clutched at the neck of her bathrobe. The blood pumped painfully in her throat, and she wanted to cry. Ruthlessly, she suppressed her own emotions. "I'm sorry. It must have been hard—on everyone. You, too. And Becky."

He sighed again. "Yes. Becky." He sucked in an audible breath. "Oh, God!"

Callie was stunned when he covered his face with his hands and bowed his head. She heard him inhale hard, gasping breaths, and knew he was trying to keep from breaking down.

"Oh, Aubrey."

Forgetting that she was his employee, that she was Becky's nanny, and that he didn't love her, Callie gave up being strong for herself and rushed over to Aubrey. Thrusting her candle, willy-nilly, onto the desk, she fell on her knees and reached out to him. Her heart overflowed when he turned in his chair, threw his arms around her and drew her close.

"Oh, God, Callie, it hurts so much!"

"I know, I know," she soothed, wondering what she thought she was doing. But she couldn't push him away now. She loved him, he was in pain, and if she could offer this little bit of solace, she'd do it. She couldn't deny herself to him. She couldn't deny him to her. If the only thing she could do for him was hold him, she'd do it.

She hoped to heaven whatever happened now would be for the best.

What was he doing? Aubrey was only dimly aware that he held Callie in his arms. She felt so good there. So right. So . . . comforting.

Reading Anne's letters had hurt. Recalling the love they'd shared, the dreams they'd had, the way everything had withered just when life had been about to bloom into perfection.

The ink on the pages was fading now, but his memories wouldn't fade. He longed for the old days even as he desired a new life. With Callie.

And she'd come to him. Openly and freely. To give him solace in his time of need. He knew it. He knew he shouldn't take advantage of her big heart.

He also knew he needed her. Desperately. Wildly. In every way. "Please come to me tonight, Callie. Please. I need you so much."

She swallowed audibly. Aubrey tried to hold in the ghastly sobs that wanted to wrack his body. Every nerve in him strained with waiting for her answer. If she denied him this, he didn't know how he was going to get through the night.

After what seemed like eternity to Aubrey, she didn't speak, but let herself relax in his arms. Then she kissed him on the mouth, softly, sweetly, invitingly, showing him her answer with her body.

"God." He expelled the word on a breath of air that shook him from head to toe. Holding her face in his hands, he gazed into her eyes. He had a feeling his own eyes looked haunted, if not worse. Hers held only concern and something else he didn't feel qualified to name, although he thought he recalled seeing it on Anne's face.

Could this woman possibly love him? No. Of course she didn't. If she loved him, she'd have jumped at his proposal of marriage, and she'd rejected him absolutely. But she wasn't rejecting him tonight.

Cautiously, fearing she'd change her mind, but knowing he had to be sure, he whispered, "Are you sure, Callie? Are you sure?"

"I'm sure."

Her eyes were huge in the dimness of the library. When Aubrey had finished the last of Anne's letters, it had been nearly midnight. He'd remained in the library, unable to move long after the electric company shut down. He had no idea how late it was, but he knew he needed Callie tonight.

He feared he needed her even more than that, but he didn't dare open his heart. His poor, battered heart had been through too much already in its thirty-five years. Aubrey didn't think it could survive another wound like the one Anne's death had inflicted.

"Come with me, Callie," he said softly.

His legs felt wobbly when he stood, holding her elbow and helping her up. She staggered a little, too. Perhaps he wasn't the only one whose feelings were being battered tonight.

"All right." Her voice was small, but firm.

Aubrey almost dared to hope that what he was going to do wasn't bad—almost. Not quite.

He picked up the candle, and the two of them walked side-by-side up the big staircase. He and Anne used to walk—

But no. He needed to stop remembering what he and Anne used to do. He was with Callie tonight, and he owed her his full attention. When they reached his bedroom, he opened the door and stepped aside, giving her another chance to stop things while they could still be stopped.

She walked in. Aubrey considered her poise astonishing under the circumstances. She had to be a virgin. And she was going to be giving herself to him without the bonds of matrimony. Perhaps this meant she trusted him to do the honorable thing.

Funny. As many problems as he and Callie seemed to have with each other, evidently neither of them believed the other to be anything but honorable. Encouraging, that.

Of course, he would do the honorable thing. She wouldn't refuse him after he'd taken her maidenhood. Something akin to elation filled him. She'd marry him now. After tonight, she'd have to. And he'd never be alone again.

As soon as they were inside his room, he shut the door and turned the key in the lock. She still clutched the neck of her robe, but she turned and looked at him calmly.

"Are you sure?" he asked again, wondering at his sanity. If she backed out now, it would probably kill him.

But she nodded. "Yes, Aubrey. I'm sure."

He shut his eyes for a moment and thanked God for bringing Callie Prophet into his life. She might be irritating. She might drive him crazy. She might be as different from Anne as the day was from the night, but he sensed in that moment that she was his salvation.

*Dramatic,* he told himself. *Too dramatic.* But he couldn't suppress the feeling. He walked up to her and drew her close. "I'll be gentle, Callie."

"I know you will," she whispered.

Aubrey wasn't surprised by how well she fit into his embrace. Ever since Becky's birthday party, he'd been longing to hold her again. And he'd wanted to taste her. He did so now, covering her mouth gently with his own and caressing it, nuzzling it. He felt her relax inch by inch, until her body was molded against his.

His arousal was heavy and powerful and urgent, but he refused to hurry. Callie was saving his life; he owed it to her to be careful.

Her lips had softened under his, and she opened them willingly when he tasted them with his tongue. Slowly, carefully, he allowed his tongue to explore her mouth. She tasted wonderful. He recognized the faint taste of mint. She must use mint and soda when she brushed her teeth. Anne used to do that.

Dash it, he had to stop thinking about Anne! It would spoil everything if he started to feel guilty. It had been Anne who had urged him to remarry, he reminded himself almost desperately.

Fearing his mind would start working and ruin the moment, Aubrey deepened the kiss and pressed more urgently against Callie. He hoped to God his stiff sex wouldn't alarm her. Surely, she understood the basics of how men and women went about consummating a union. She was twenty-four years old, too old to be silly and impressionable. She wasn't a flighty adolescent, but a mature woman.

"Come to bed, Callie," he said urgently. "Come to bed with me now."

She obliged, leaning on him for support as he walked her to the big four-poster bed he'd shared with Anne until the last year of her life, when she'd had to sleep alone because of the pain.

"I—I've never done this before," she told him unnecessarily.

"I know, sweetheart. I know." Her confession, whispered and sounding as if she considered herself lacking somehow because she was unexperienced in sexual matters, touched him deeply. He lifted her up and sat her on the edge of the bed, then put his arms around her again, feeling a swell of tenderness toward her.

He kissed her tenderly and passionately, longing to lose himself and his sadness in her. He wished he could tell her he loved her, but of course he couldn't. He loved Anne.

She returned his kiss with an eagerness he hadn't anticipated. Her arms tightened around him, and he had a feeling she'd just surrendered everything to him and that she was now clinging to him for dear life—and trusting him with her essence.

It was a heady feeling, and Aubrey reacted strongly. Pushing her back onto the bed, he joined her there, pressing her into the covers and kissing her hard. "God, I want you." His voice sounded ragged to his ears.

"I want you, too," she whispered. "I love you."

The last three words were so soft, Aubrey wasn't sure he'd heard them. They rattled him for an instant before he realized he'd misunderstood her. He wasn't sure what she'd said, but he was positive it hadn't been a declaration of love.

Because he didn't want to get confused, he reached to thrust her robe aside. A smile touched his lips when he saw that he hadn't revealed much by the rash act. The flannel nightgown she wore was serviceable and perhaps even pretty, since it had tiny pink rosebuds embroidered around the high neck, but it was absolutely modest.

"How," he asked with humor, "does this thing come off?"

She smiled up at him. His heart turned a back flip and went all soft and mushy. "I'll do it."

And she did. As he watched, she sat up, reached to the back of her nightgown and pulled something. The garment slid down her shoulders. His eyes grew large when the fabric caught on her breasts. He'd ached to touch her breasts. To see them. To weigh them in his hands. He reached with those hands now, and gently slid the flannel aside.

There was little light in his room, but he thought he saw her swallow. She might have been blushing; he couldn't tell. "You're beautiful, Callie. Beautiful." He dragged his vest off and threw it aside. He heard it land somewhere, but had no notion where.

She murmured something that might have been thanks. Aubrey's ears were roaring from the blood coursing through his veins. He was so strongly aroused, his condition was almost painful. Gently, he lowered Callie to the bed and kissed her, deeply and thoroughly. He felt the tension flow out of her. Her arms went around his neck, and she held him tightly.

Life. For the first time in more than a year, Aubrey felt fully alive, thanks to Callie. She gasped when he drew his mouth from hers, and she gasped again when he feathered light, caressing kisses over her body.

She had a spectacular body. She was both taller and meatier than Anne had been. Aubrey didn't feel that he had to be as careful with Callie as he'd been with Anne, who'd been fragile and delicate. Not Callie. Callie was robust. There wasn't any fat on her, but there was lots of flesh. Soft flesh. Warm flesh. Beautiful flesh. Arousing flesh.

Aubrey felt every inch of it. And Callie reacted to his touch as no woman ever had. Soft moans and gasps told him how much she appreciated his efforts. Not that they were entirely on her behalf. He couldn't have stopped himself if he'd wanted to, which he didn't. Nor did he try.

He aimed to marry this woman. What did it matter if they consummated the matter beforehand? Not a whit. Thank God, thank God.

Callie's fingers, shaking as if with a palsy, lifted to his shirt buttons. "May I?" she whispered, as if she feared she was being too bold.

She couldn't possibly be too bold for Aubrey. He needed this, he needed her, and he needed her boldness. "Please do," he whispered back, his voice gone low and scratchy.

So she did. As soon as she'd finished unbuttoning his shirt, he shrugged it off and tossed it in the general direction of his vest, wherever that was. "I'll get rid of these," he said, reaching for the buttons to his trousers. His sex pressed against the buttons, impeding his progress, and he grew impatient. "Damnation."

"What's wrong?"

She sounded worried, so he smiled down at her. "Nothing's wrong. I'm eager, is all."

"Oh." She smiled back.

She had a pretty, saucy smile, and Aubrey liked it a lot. He liked *her* a lot, if it came to that, and his admiration rather surprised him. Callie was so different from Anne, they might be different species altogether. Yet he could appreciate both of them.

In a desperate hurry now—offhand, he couldn't recall the last time he'd been this aroused—Aubrey shoved his trousers down. His erection was so hard, it was difficult for him to bend over and remove his shoes and stockings and trousers, but he did it. And then he was free.

He fairly bounded back to lie beside Callie. When he took her naked body into his arms, she felt stiffer than she had before. His passion was so high, it took him an instant or two to realize she'd been staring with horror at his aroused manhood.

Damnation. He'd forgotten she wasn't used to this sort of thing. If she backed out now, he'd die; he knew it. "Don't be afraid, Callie." He tried to pitch his voice to a soothing timbre, but was afraid his desperation edged in.

"It might hurt this time, but it will never hurt again. I promise you. Don't be afraid," he begged.

"I—I'm not afraid," she said. Aubrey figured she'd just lied to him, but he didn't mention it. "Not really afraid, I mean."

"Good." He'd take her meaning as spoken, then. Trying to restrain his lust, he kissed her softly but deeply, hoping to feel her tension ease, as it had before.

No such luck. Nevertheless, she did relax a little bit, and Aubrey blessed her for it. *Take it easy,* he commanded himself. *Don't go too fast. She's a virgin.* He had to remember she was a virgin, or he might be rough. He wasn't accustomed to being able to be free to fondle and sexually tussle with a woman, Anne having been so delicate and all. He didn't want to hurt Callie because of his exuberance.

It occurred to him that it might be nice to have an exuberant sexual partner to wrestle with for the rest of his life. Pleasant, even.

But he didn't want to think about that now.

Aubrey was feeling more impatient by the second. If they didn't get on with this pretty soon, he'd explode. With that aim in mind, he caressed her hips and fondled her thighs and quickly made his way to the mop of dark blonde curls between her legs. She gasped again when he covered her hidden treasure.

"I won't hurt you, Callie," he growled desperately. "I promise I won't hurt you." Not after this time, anyway.

"I know you won't, Aubrey." She took the initiative this time and kissed him.

Taking that as a good sign, Aubrey dipped a finger between the soft petals of her femininity. She arched like a bowstring. He'd never witnessed so strong a reaction to his lovemaking. She was already wet, too. And hot. Thrilled by her passionate reaction, he kissed her deeply and gently as he plied his fingers. She bucked like a horse under his ministrations and gasped with astonishment. He pulled his mouth away from hers so he could watch her face.

"Aubrey!" His name was a quiet shriek. Her eyes were huge, and she looked to him as if she were in the throes of some kind of alien emotion. He was beginning to feel pretty good about this. Anne had never demonstrated such overt evidence of her pleasure, although she claimed to enjoy the marriage act. Callie's pleasure was obvious.

"It's all right, Callie. This is what it's all about."

"My God." She lifted the back of her hand to her mouth and pressed hard, Aubrey presumed to catch any other errant screams.

Her face and its changing expressions fascinated him. No prim miss, Callie. Not a bit of it. It was as if she couldn't help herself, and Aubrey found himself reacting with real satisfaction that was a part of, but different from, the sexual satisfaction he was experiencing of this, their first sexual union.

She was, in short, a pure joy to watch. She was a pure joy to be with. Marriage to Callie Prophet wouldn't be a hardship at all, if this was going to be a part of it.

When her climax came, Aubrey was almost as shocked as Callie. She grabbed his shoulders and screamed, "Aubrey!" Fortunately, the walls of his house were thick and her scream was partially muffled because the upper part of her body lifted off the bed and her face was buried against his chest.

It was more than Aubrey could take. Before her spasms of pleasure had subsided, he'd pressed her back against the bedclothes and guided his shaft to her wet, tight passage. With a shove, he was inside her—and Callie went perfectly still.

"Oh," she said in a sort of gasp.

Aubrey was holding himself back with all the strength he possessed. He squeezed his eyes tightly shut, he gritted his teeth, and he held himself rigidly away from her with his arms. He wasn't going to disgrace himself by spilling his seed instantly. Granted, it had been a long time since he'd made love to anyone; still, he owed it to his masculine pride to take more than a second or two in achieving his own satisfaction.

After a couple of moments, he dared open his eyes. Callie stared up at him, her eyes gone round, and all traces of pleasure vanished from her face. Damn. In spite of his promises, he'd hurt her.

"I'm sorry, Callie. It won't happen again."

"Oh," she said again.

*Ah, to hell with it.* Aubrey gave up on his pride, and everything else in the universe. He needed this more than he'd ever needed anything.

Taking the time to lean over and kiss her hard, he relaxed his arms and moved within her. He'd never felt anything like it. What's more, she moved with him. He couldn't recall ever having a woman react like this. Callie's body relaxed into his and Aubrey gave her a moment to adjust to the feel of him inside before he started moving again. He didn't want her to be in pain, but he was getting to the point where he couldn't restrain himself anymore.

He pumped, in and out. Harder and faster. Lord, Lord, Lord, it felt *so* good. Never had it felt so good. Never.

With a harsh cry, he hurtled over the edge, pumping his seed into her body. His climax seemed to last forever. Spasm after spasm racked him.

It was, bar none, the best sexual experience of his life.

He barely managed to stop himself from collapsing on top of her and smothering her with his weight. With his last ounce of energy, Aubrey sank to her side, still buried deep inside her. He never wanted to pull himself out. He took her with him, so that they lay face-to-face. He threw a leg around her to hold her there. He couldn't bear to lose her yet.

"Callie," he murmured, feeling proud of himself that he'd formed the word and even prouder that he'd said it aloud. He hadn't thought himself capable of speech.

"Aubrey," she said back. She quietly cleared her throat. "I—ah—didn't know it would be like that."

He cranked an eye open. She looked solemn. Aubrey wasn't sure that was a good sign. Although he didn't want to, he reached within himself and discovered the wherewithal to speak. "It won't be painful again, I promise."

There. That was good. Ease her worries. He allowed his eyes to drift closed again.

"It wasn't the pain part that I didn't expect," she said after a moment of silence.

He cranked the other eye open this time. "No?" He really, really didn't want to chat right now. He wanted to sleep. This was the first time in at least two years when he felt utterly drained. He knew he'd be able to sleep deeply and dreamlessly now. Thanks to Callie's generosity in allowing him this intimacy before they were married.

Recalling her generosity allowed Aubrey to summon an ounce or two of strength, and he told himself he could stay awake and reassure her, whatever this chattiness on her part betokened.

"No." He saw her swallow. "Before the pain. That's the part I hadn't anticipated."

Vanity swelled in Aubrey's chest unexpectedly. He opened both eyes and grinned. "Did you enjoy it?" She had. He knew she had.

"Oh, yes." She swallowed again. "Oh, yes, Aubrey. Very much."

"Good." Satisfaction spread over him like a warm blanket. "Good. I'm glad. So did I." He pulled her closer, shut his eyes, and went blissfully to sleep.

## 18

Callie wasn't altogether sure what had just happened. Oh, she knew she and Aubrey had made love. But she hadn't known it would be like *that*.

Good Lord, she'd completely lost her mind for a moment or two. The physical anticipation she'd experienced under Aubrey's relentless and expert ministrations had been almost unbearable, and then ecstasy had swept her clean out of herself and into another realm.

It's a good thing no one told little girls and boys about this sort of thing, or the human race would be completely out of control. Why, people would rut like animals.

She glanced over at Aubrey's sleeping form. He'd been very sweet, too. He hadn't tried to rush her or hurry her, and he'd been gentle. The pain had shocked her a little bit when he'd first entered her, but that was only because she'd still been tingling with the aftereffects of sexual satisfaction.

And then they'd been joined together as one. Tears sprang unexpectedly to Callie's eyes. She loved him so much. She wished he could love her, but she understood now, as she hadn't when she'd first come to live here, that a love like the one Anne and he had shared didn't come along often.

She'd marry him now, of course. He was too honorable not to renew his proposal after tonight. The notion of being wed to Aubrey, of being Becky's honest-to-God mother, and of being mistress of this grand property—and that amazing townhouse in San Francisco—washed over her. Oh, she'd like being married to Aubrey! She'd love it.

Guilt slammed into her so hard and so fast that she gasped, causing Aubrey to mutter something in his sleep. She brushed hair away from his eyes and thought about what she must do. She couldn't marry him without admitting that she'd been surreptitiously reading his private correspondence to his late wife for months now.

"Oh, Lord." Callie wished she'd had enough courage to make her confession earlier in their relationship, before things became so entangled. He might be miffed.

Very well. He'd almost certainly be miffed. Furious, even. It was bad enough that she'd read the letters in the first place. That she'd continued to do so went far beyond the pale. She ought to have gently explained to Becky that it was impolite to read other people's letters, and immediately taken the whole bundle, without looking at even one of them, and handed them over.

She hadn't done that, and now she had to face the consequences of her deceit.

Was deceit too strong a word? As she lay there, her body in a state of boneless satisfaction and her mind racing, Callie came to the glum conclusion that deceit was far from too strong a word. If anything, it was too mild for what she'd been doing.

Blast. Why should something that ought to have been wonderful in every way be spoiled?

Because she'd not been honest, is why.

Callie just hated it when honesty got in the way of a good pout.

But she was tired—exhausted, even—and sated with physical pleasure, and she loved the man who'd taken her to such unexpected heights of passion, and she was going to marry him. She was, in short, both happy and worn out, and eventually her brain ceased to torment her, and she went to sleep.

She awoke with a start when light poured into the room. Blinking into the light, she saw Aubrey standing at the window. He wore a beautiful burgundy robe and matching slippers, and he'd just pulled back the curtain. Now he smiled at her from the window, backlit by the sun, his tousled hair making him appear charmingly informal and entirely too handsome.

"Aubrey," came out on a gasp.

"Good morning, sleepyhead." He sounded friendly and unless it was her desperate wishes making her think so, even happy. She couldn't recall too many times since she'd come to live here that he'd sounded happy.

"I—I should have left," she stammered. "I guess I went to sleep."

He came over to the bed and sat beside her, taking the hand with which she gripped the bedclothes over her naked bosom and prying it loose. He lifted her hand and nuzzled her palm. "I'm glad you didn't leave me, Callie. That's the first good night's sleep I've had since . . . in a long time."

"I'm glad." He'd been going to say, *since Anne died*, but he'd caught himself. Trying to spare her feelings, Callie knew, and she sighed inside. "I slept well, too."

"Good." He rose, walked across the room, and fetched Callie's nightgown and robe.

He'd collected their clothes, Callie noticed, and folded them neatly on the back of a carved teakwood chair. She glanced around his room as she hadn't been able to do last night. It was a suite, rather, consisting of a sitting room with a large fireplace, a bathroom, and the room in which the two of them now were, his bedroom. Gorgeous. Perfectly gorgeous. And soon Callie would share it with him.

Or maybe not. The truth was that Callie didn't know what sleeping arrangements Aubrey had planned for them after they were wed. She guessed lots of couples had separate bedrooms. Perhaps there was another bedroom connected to this suite of rooms.

There was a lot she didn't know about the running of the Lockhart mansion, although she'd pretty much been doing it since she moved in. Mrs. Granger had admitted she needed help running such a huge place, and Callie had gladly stepped in to assist her. Yet, she knew nothing about the master suite.

"Here you go," Aubrey said, handing over her nightgown.

"Thank you." Callie slipped the nightie on over her head. She had to tie the ribbons at her throat, which made her cheeks feel hot. Usually, her nightie remained tied from washing to washing. Last night's activities had been exceptional. In more ways than one.

Aubrey sat on the bed again and leaned over to plant a kiss on her forehead. Callie felt herself blush furiously, and silently called herself all sorts of names. After what the two of them had done last night, there was no need to blush over so chaste a kiss as the one Aubrey had just bestowed on her.

"I trust you'll change your mind about marrying me now, Callie." He said it with a smile on his face, but his voice was serious. "I hope you will, because I think we'd make a good married couple."

She'd been concentrating on subduing her blush and tying her ribbons with fingers that wanted to tremble, but she glanced up at that. "You do? Really?"

His smile relaxed some and appeared more genuine. "Really, I do. You've already earned Becky's undying love, and I—have a great deal of admiration and—and—affection for you."

Affection. Well, that was nice, wasn't it? "Thank you. I—have affection for you, too." Had she admitted her true feelings last night? She entertained a dreadful feeling she had.

"So, would you like a formal engagement and a big society wedding in San Francisco, Callie? Or would you be willing to have a smaller ceremony here in Santa Angelica? I understand that a young woman getting married for the first and, I trust, only time might prefer to do the thing grandly, but . . ."

He allowed the sentence to trail off, but Callie understood. He didn't want to go through another huge, messy wedding ceremony. He'd done that once, with the woman he loved. Callie supposed she was a poor substitute for the perfect and ethereal—and dead—Anne.

The truth was, however, that she'd never fancied herself as a blushing bride marrying the man of her dreams in front of thousands. She didn't care for crowds; she preferred gatherings of comrades. She'd be pleased to be wed in the little Methodist church in Santa Angelica with her family and friends surrounding her.

"I'd rather have a small wedding here in town, Aubrey. It would be more comfortable for me."

He nodded, but his eyes narrowed. "Are you sure? I don't want you to sacrifice any dreams on my account, Callie. Truly, I don't."

She believed him. In fact, her throat tightened so painfully with unshed tears and love that she could scarcely squeeze words out. "I'm telling the truth, Aubrey. I think I'd faint dead away if I had to endure a huge San Francisco wedding."

He lifted an eyebrow. "Somehow I can't imagine you fainting dead away at anything, Callie Prophet. You seem mighty indomitable to me."

Indomitable, eh? Well, who knew? Maybe she was. Or maybe she'd only had to shoulder too much responsibility too early in her life. On that note, she swung her legs out of the bed, wincing slightly when the muscles she'd used for the first time last night protested. "Good. Then that's settled."

"Yes. Except for the timing. I'd . . . well, I'd like to get it—that is, I'd like to do it fairly soon, if that's all right with you. Giving you plenty of time to get a dress and a wedding party together and all that." He frowned. "I'm not sure what all goes into this sort of thing, but I know that women have to do a lot of work and organization beforehand."

She grinned. "Yes, they do. I recall my sisters' weddings, and my brother's. My sisters ran themselves ragged. My brother only had to watch his future bride running herself ragged, along with her mother. Her father watched, too."

"Please don't run yourself ragged, Callie. I'll hire whatever help you need." He walked up to her and put his arms around her.

The gesture seemed so spontaneous and genuinely fond that Callie again found herself close to tears. This was ridiculous. She had to get herself under some kind of control.

Becky. If she thought about Becky and her nanny duties, she could climb out of the swamp of emotions that seemed to want to smother her. She did return his embrace, and with enthusiasm. She couldn't help it.

It felt so good to be in his arms. She rubbed her cheek against the velvet of his robe and sighed deeply. "I've got to go see how Becky's doing, Aubrey. She felt truly terrible yesterday, poor thing."

"I'll go with you," he offered, allowing his arms to slide, but taking up her hand. "We should tell her the happy news. She'll be pleased."

"Yes," Callie said after thinking about it for a second or two. "I believe she will be." And that eased her mind some. Until she remembered those blasted letters, and then she felt guilty again. "Um, maybe we ought to wait and see how she's feeling."

Aubrey complied easily, which led Callie to believe he didn't care one way or the other. And why should he? He wasn't harboring any guilty secrets, after all.

Becky was still sick. She'd been crying, Callie saw at once, and she was tossing fretfully in her bed. As soon as the door opened, she cried out in a pathetic voice, "Where have you been, Miss Prophet? I'm sick."

"I'm so sorry, darling. I'm here now." Rushing to the bed, Callie glanced at Aubrey and saw that he shared her concern for the little girl. She gave her head a little shake, and he seemed to understand its meaning: They'd save their news until Becky felt better.

"You're still sick, pumpkin?" Aubrey's deep voice drew his daughter's gaze. Her cheeks burned with fever, and she nodded soulfully.

"Yes, Papa. I feel icky."

He smiled at that. "I'm sure you do, and I'm sorry Becky." After leaning over to kiss her hot forehead, he glanced at Callie. "Is there anything I can bring you, Callie?"

"Yes, please. If you could bring some water. And maybe a glass of orange juice, if Mrs. Granger has any oranges left. I think I'd better have this little trouper take another dose of salicylic powders."

"I don't *want* to!" Burying her face in Callie's bathrobe, Becky started crying again.

Callie knew she only did so because she felt wretched, and she held her tightly, rocking her back and forth. When she glanced up at Aubrey, he appeared worried. "Don't fret, Aubrey. I believe it's only a bad cold. Maybe a touch of influenza. Myrtle told me that some of her other students were ailing. She says this always happens this time of year."

"Good God," Aubrey muttered as he turned to do his errand. "I didn't know school was bad for one's health."

Callie chuckled.

Becky sniffled and knuckled her eyes. She watched her father leave her room and turned to Callie. "Why'd he call you Callie? And you called him Aubrey, too."

Fudge. Callie wished they'd been more careful. Yet it probably didn't matter much. She wasn't going to spring the news on Becky until she did so accompanied by Aubrey, but she could prepare her. "Your father and I are good friends, Becky. We decided it was silly to call each other Miss and Mister."

Becky's fevered cheeks pressed against Callie's shoulder, and Callie felt the little head nod. "Can I call you Callie?"

*Why not?* Callie thought. She'd like Becky to call her Mama, but couldn't very well tell her so now. Besides, Aubrey might not like it. She sighed. "Of course, you may, sweetie."

"Thank you, Callie."

A coughing and sneezing fit followed Becky's thanks, and after producing a clean hankie, Callie hugged her more tightly. "Poor Becky. I'm sorry you feel so rotten, sweetie."

"Me, too." Becky sniffled disconsolately.

"After you take your powders and I eat breakfast, why don't I bring up some books, and I can read to you when you feel like being awake. But when you want to sleep, please tell me, because that's the best thing to do."

"All right."

She didn't sound enthusiastic about Callie's plan of action, but Callie chalked up her lack of interest to her illness. She was surprised when Mrs. Granger bustled into the room a few minutes later, since she'd expected Aubrey.

"Mr. Lockhart's changing into his clothes," the house-keeper explained. "I told him he had no business in the sick-room."

"But I want my papa!" Becky wailed.

"Tut, child," Mrs. Granger said. "He's coming right along. He needs to change his clothes because he's going to ride to Santa Angelica and fetch the doctor to come out here and see you. He can't very well do that in his bathrobe and slippers, now can he?"

Slightly mollified, Becky sniffled some more. "I guess not."

"I expect they'll bring back a dose of quinine for you, too."

"I'm glad he's going to get a doctor. Which doctor do the Lockharts use?" Callie took the glass of orange juice from Mrs. Granger after the older woman had stirred in the powders.

"Dr. Marshall comes when there's a need. Well, except for—well, you know, Callie."

"Yes. I know." Except for illnesses outside his scope, such as the late Mrs. Lockhart's illness. "Here Becky, let me hold the glass, and you sip the juice."

Every time Callie turned around, Anne's tragic death seemed to slap her in the face. But that's the way life worked, she told herself with a dash of practicality borrowed from some hidden cache of sanity still dwelling inside her. She went on to remind herself that she wouldn't be the first woman in the world to marry a man because he needed a mother for his children. Love didn't necessarily add happiness to a marriage; Callie had lived long enough to learn *that* much.

Why, just a few years ago one of Callie's dearest friends had married the man she loved, and he'd turned out to be a miserable specimen. He drank and ran around with other women, blamed it all on Sylvia for not being perfect, and even hit her occasionally. Sylvia had finally left the brute and returned to Santa Angelica.

Fortunately, there'd been no children to suffer from the

separation—or from the marriage—but Sylvia's reputation had been marred. Divorce was an ugly word, but as far as Callie was concerned marriage to a man like Sylvia's exhusband was a far uglier fate than divorce. And, in the end, Sylvia had married Mr. Ambrose two year ago, primarily because Mr. Ambrose needed a woman to care for his children. The last Callie had heard, the couple were doing very well, and Sylvia was much happier than she'd been in her first marriage.

Callie wasn't unanimously supported in her opinion about divorce being preferable to a bad marriage—or, in Sylvia's case, a dangerous marriage. Still, Callie had done what she could for Sylvia, remaining her friend and not avoiding her as some folks did. It really wasn't fair.

But, there. It was silly to be thinking about men like the one Sylvia'd had the misfortune to marry for love. Callie already knew that Aubrey had been an exemplary husband to his Anne, and, even if he couldn't love Callie, she knew he'd be a considerate husband to her.

That would be enough for Callie. It would have to be. "Can you drink any more juice, sweetheart?"

"It tastes horrid!"

Callie lifted the glass away a second before Becky's hand would have knocked it out of her own. This show of temper was a product of Becky's illness, Callie knew, and was uncharacteristic of the usually compliant child. "I know, sweetheart, but you need to drink it because it will make you feel better."

"I like plain orange juice," Becky wailed. Tears welled in her eyes and spilled down her cheeks. "That tastes icky!"

Callie felt awful for her. "Maybe Mrs. Granger can get you a fresh glass of juice, sweetheart. To drink after you finish this one."

"I'll run right downstairs and squeeze another couple of oranges." Mrs. Granger suited her action to her words, and whirled around to go downstairs to her kitchen. She called back, "I'll bring some breakfast for you, too, Callie."

"Thank you." Returning her attention to Becky, Callie

said, "There. Now you finish this, and you'll have some good-tasting orange juice in a jiffy."

"I don't want to."

She sounded too pitiful for Callie to be angry with her over the rebellion. She was about to try to jolly her into drinking the rest of the medicine-laced juice when Aubrey returned, dressed for the road.

"What's this I hear about my girl not taking her medicine?" He pitched his voice to sound mockingly severe, but Becky evidently heard the steel in it.

Whimpering miserably, she lifted her huge eyes and gazed at her father. If that look had been directed at her, Callie figured she'd melt, but Aubrey was made of sterner stuff. Becky's pretty mouth trembled. "But it tastes horrid, Papa."

He smiled at her, and Callie decided if *that* look had been directed at her, she'd also melt. Merciful heavens, but she loved that man. How strange, considering how much she'd disliked him in the beginning.

"Why don't we let Callie wash up and get dressed, Becky, and I'll force that stuff down your throat?" Aubrey winked at Becky, but it didn't help much. She started crying again, softly.

Callie looked up at him, a question in her eyes, but Aubrey nodded. "Go on, Callie. Mrs. Granger's fixing your breakfast and squeezing some more oranges. I hate to rush you, but I want to get to Dr. Marshall as soon as I can. You'll probably feel better after a wash up. After all . . ."

He didn't have to finish his thought, because Callie understood perfectly. Instinctively, she lifted her hands to her hair, which probably looked like she'd swept a floor with it. Her face felt hot when she arose, Becky still held in her arms. "Right. Absolutely. Here. You'll probably have to strap her down."

Becky threw her arms around her father's neck and buried her small face on his shoulder. "He *won't*! Don't strap me down, Papa! Please don't."

"Callie's only teasing, Becky," Aubrey said in so loving and gentle a tone, Callie would have swooned if she'd been the type of female who did such things.

She did stare, though, for far too many moments. When Aubrey sat on the bed and lifted an eyebrow at her, she realized she was in a trance and jerked out of it, swirling around and dashing for the door. "Right. I'll hurry. Be right back."

"Take all the time you need."

She heard the laughter in his voice. It made her want to cry. Which only went to prove what a besotted fool she was.

Aubrey had been absolutely correct, however. She felt much better after she'd taken a quick bath—praising the Lord the whole time for having allowed people to discover the benefits of indoor plumbing—brushed and knotted her hair into a French coil, and donned a clean frock.

She was a little disconcerted to discover bloodstains on her nightgown. They were mere spots, really, and could probably be chalked up to her monthly courses having started during the night. God alone knew what Delilah would make of any blood stains on Aubrey's sheets, but Callie couldn't very well take the time to do anything about the sheets with Becky feeling so poorly.

With a sigh, she decided she and Aubrey weren't the first couple—and undoubtedly wouldn't be the last couple—who'd anticipated marriage by a few days or weeks. She didn't know when Aubrey wanted to wed, but he'd mentioned sooner rather than later, which suited Callie.

First, however, they had to get Becky well.

And Callie had to confess about having read his letters to Anne. She didn't want to. But she'd rather be pilloried in the Santa Angelica public square than begin marriage with the man she loved with a big guilty secret on her conscience.

Perhaps he wouldn't be as upset as she feared he would be.

"Not very likely," she muttered as she glanced in the mirror to make sure everything was in place and buttoned, and that her hair wasn't lopsided where she'd pinned the coil up. "He'll probably hate me." Or at least be angry.

With a sigh, Callie knew she couldn't very well blame him if he did get angry with her. She'd be pretty darned annoyed if anyone read her private correspondence. And she'd be downright furious if anyone read her love letters. Not that she had any to read.

Bother. She was borrowing trouble again. Making only one further detour, down to the library, where she quickly selected *The Adventures of Tom Sawyer, Adventures of Huckleberry Finn*, and a volume of Edgar Allan Poe stories, she darted up the stairs, taking them two at a time, and hurried to Becky's room. She felt much more the thing when she entered and saw Aubrey's smile of approval.

"Excellent," he said, standing. He'd settled Becky back into her bed. "You look lovely this morning, Callie."

And, by gum, he walked over and gave her a quick kiss on the cheek. Callie felt herself blush. "I'm glad you made me take the time," she muttered, feeling outrageously shy.

"Yes, well . . ." He turned and rubbed his hands in a gesture, Callie supposed, meant to instill confidence in and support to his sick child. "I'm going to town now, Becky, and I'll be back as soon as I can be with Dr. Marshall. Do you remember Dr. Marshall, Becky? He came to our house when you had the measles."

Becky, whose tiny flushed face looked pathetic against her sparkling white pillowcases, nodded. "Yes. He gave me awful-tasting medicine."

Aubrey chuckled. "I expect he'll do the same thing today, sweetheart. That's what happens when we get sick. We have to take awful-tasting medicine to get better."

"I brought you some books, Becky," Callie said. "Maybe reading a rousing tale of adventure will make you feel better."

"Maybe." The little girl didn't sound precisely positive about it.

"Or," Callie said, giving her a sly glance, "after your papa leaves, maybe I can read you another scary story by Mr. Poe."

"Poe?" Aubrey looked startled.

"Oh, yes!" Becky said, sounding less than ghastly for the first time in two days. "I'd like that a lot!"

Aubrey frowned doubtfully at Callie. "You read the child Edgar Allan Poe stories?"

She beamed at him, although what she really wanted to do was throw her arms around his neck and kiss him silly. "Absolutely! I loved them when I was Becky's age, and she loves them now. Kids love to be scared, Aubrey. Don't you know that by this time? That's why they adore hearing ghost stories." Because Aubrey's bemused expression was making her heart palpitate, she turned back to Becky, trying to look cheerful and chipper—which wasn't too hard, under the circumstances. "Isn't that right, Becky? Don't you and your friends enjoy listening to scary stories?"

Becky nodded, her blue eyes dull this morning, but her lips smiling at last. "Yes. I love a scary story. As long as Callie stays with me until I fall asleep."

Callie was surprised when Aubrey said, "You call Miss Prophet 'Callie'?"

"I told her to," Callie told him quickly. In a whisper, she added, "She noticed when you called me Callie, you see."

Taking her arm, he led her to the door and spoke softly, "Perhaps we should tell her about our upcoming nuptials. Perhaps she'd like to call you . . . Mother."

Not, Callie noticed, *Mama*, but *Mother*. Well, that made sense, she supposed, although her heart hurt a little. "Why don't we wait," she suggested, thinking of those damnable letters looming in her conscience like a mountain. "After she feels better might be a more appropriate time."

"If you say so." He didn't sound concerned, which suited Callie fine. Turning so that Becky could hear him, he said, "I'll be back as soon as I can be, sweetheart."

"Bye, Papa," Becky said in her hoarse, squeaky voice.

Callie noticed the tears had started again by the time she got back to Becky's bed. Poor baby. Even short, temporary abandonments were hard to take when one was a small child and feeling poorly. They were hard for grown-ups to take, for that matter, but adults were at least supposed to have better control over overt displays of their feelings than were children.

"Did you finish taking your powders, sweetheart?" she asked gently, brushing hair back from Becky's hot forehead with her hand. She noticed the empty orange-juice glass on the night table.

Becky nodded. "Papa made me."

"Has Mrs. Granger brought up your good juice yet?"

This time the little girl shook her head. "Papa told her to wait until you got back so your breakfast wouldn't get cold."

"That was nice of him." It was unnecessary, however. Becky's health was more important than Callie's breakfast, although it was a consideration on Aubrey's part that Callie hadn't anticipated.

"I s'pose he'll tell Mrs. Granger you're back when he goes downstairs," Becky added.

"I suppose he will."

He did. It wasn't long before Mrs. Granger entered the room with a tray loaded with good things to eat, Callie's breakfast as well as morsels to tempt the invalid.

Callie made a good breakfast. Becky's throat hurt too much to allow her to do much more than swallow a couple of bites of oatmeal with raisins, brown sugar, butter, and milk. The orange juice stung her ailing throat, but she seemed to crave it, so Mrs. Granger sent one of the stable lads to the Venable farm, where Mrs. Venable always kept a supply of fresh oranges on hand.

"We'll give you all the orange juice you can swallow, Becky," the housekeeper said. She looked worried.

Callie wasn't. She figured it was only a bad cold. Maybe a touch of influenza. The powders and quinine would help, and with a lot of rest and good, fresh fruit and juice she imagined Becky would be well in a week or two. One couldn't rush these things.

Aubrey returned with the doctor in less than an hour. Dr. Marshall was a tall, thin, gray-haired man with a jovial manner and a way with children. He managed to tease a laugh out of Becky, prescribed fresh juice, salicylic powders every four to six hours, and a dose of quinine immediately.

"I'll return this evening to check on the invalid. If she needs another dose, I'll give it to her then, and I'm going to bring along a medicated salve to rub on her chest. We don't want her lungs to become infected."

"Thank you, Dr. Marshall."

The doctor smiled down at Callie, who was helping Delilah change Becky's sheets since her fever had made them damp. "You're certainly looking splendid these days, Callie. This job as Becky's nanny, difficult as it must be, seems to agree with you." He tossed Becky a wink to let her know he was teasing.

Callie grinned back at him. "It's rugged, Doctor. Persuading this child to behave is a sore trial, believe me."

"Is not!" exclaimed Becky hotly, but she grinned.

"Aye, I've heard about her wild ways." He leaned over and deposited a kiss on Becky's head. The little girl was seated in the overstuffed easy chair in her room and hugging a stuffed bear to her chest while the grown-ups changed her bed linen. Monster, who had been sharing her room, had vanished under the bed as soon as Dr. Marshall entered it. "You rest, Becky, and you'll be feeling better in a few days. You have a nasty cold, but it's not fatal."

"Thank God," Aubrey whispered from a corner of the room.

As if he'd only then remembered such jests weren't necessarily funny in this household, Dr. Marshall cast a swift glance at Aubrey, looked embarrassed, then cleared his throat. "Yes. Well, I guess I've done enough damage here for one morning. You sleep a lot, Becky, and take your medicine, and I'll come back this evening to make you miserable again." He shook his finger at her in a mock show of sternness. "And don't forget to gargle with warm salt water. None of your shirking, Miss Lockhart, do you hear?"

"I hear." Becky grinned at him again.

"Then I guess I'll take my leave now. Got other folks to see. There's a lot of this nasty cold going around."

"Bye, Dr. Marshall," Becky said, sounding as if she liked him even if he was the purveyor of awful-tasting medicines.

"Thank you, Dr. Marshall." Aubrey came forward and shook the doctor's hand.

"Yes, thanks a lot, Doctor," Callie called from behind a flapping sheet.

"Thank you, Dr. Marshall," said Delilah, making it unanimous.

As they left the room, Callie heard Aubrey say, "I think Mrs. Granger has a piece of cake for you in the kitchen, Doctor."

The voices faded, and Callie thought how lucky she was to be here, in this household. It was so pleasant to live in luxurious surroundings, not to have to handle everything all by herself, to be able to call the doctor any time one needed a doctor, and never have to worry about money. It was to be her fate, and she was grateful to her Maker and to fate in general.

She'd love being married to Aubrey. She loved him. She loved Becky. Life couldn't get much better.

The letters loomed like a high wall in her conscience, and she resolved to take care of that matter as soon as might be.

# 19

But Callie's confession wasn't made that day or the next, nor the next after that. Becky's flu got better slowly, but she was a mighty sick little girl for several days. Dr. Marshall continued to call twice a day, and Callie didn't like to leave Becky's room for any lengthy period of time.

Every time Callie left, even for a few minutes, Becky became fretful, and she herself worried. She even set up a cot in the room so that she could keep tabs on Becky overnight.

Monster shared Becky's room as well, much to Becky's appreciation. It seemed to soothe her misery to have a big, fluffy cat to hug.

Aubrey paid many tender attentions, both to Becky and to Callie. Callie appreciated them—and him—more than she could say. He was a genuinely kind man, so unlike the man she'd initially believed him to be that Callie's conscience grew heavier and heavier as the days passed and she didn't tell him about the letters.

Mrs. Granger bustled in and out of the room several times each day, bringing food, medicine, glasses of warm salt water, juice, sympathy, and platitudes. Aubrey had told her the good news about his impending marriage, and she was fairly bursting with pleasure, both for Callie's sake and the sake of the Lockhart household.

"Because, you know, Callie, the poor man's been in such a state during the past couple of years. You'll be good for him. You've *already* been good for him and Becky. And for the household, as well."

"Thank you, Mrs. Granger. I hope I'll make him a good wife."

"Nonsense, child. You'll make him a fine wife. I know he loved his Anne, but he needs someone to take care of things for him, and he's quite fond of you."

Fond. Right. Exactly what Callie wanted to hear. She took the tray Mrs. Granger had prepared for the invalid. "Thank you."

Not that she expected anything more from Aubrey. He respected and liked her. She'd known for ages that she wasn't the type of woman a man could cherish. At least she'd be able to share Aubrey's consideration and affection.

So why, she wondered, did her heart feel so heavy as she carried the tray up to Becky's room.


During Becky's illness and convalescence, Aubrey had a lot of time to think about things. He thought about Becky, he thought about Anne, he thought about his life in general, and he thought about Callie. A lot.

Every time he saw her, a jolt of awareness and desire washed over him. At first, he chalked up this strange phenomenon to the fact that he and she had recently shared a very satisfying sexual liaison. It was the first sexual liaison Aubrey had experienced since long before Anne died, and he'd been more than ready for it.

As the days passed and he observed Callie and Becky, and Callie and Mrs. Granger, and Callie and Dr. Marshall, and Callie and Delilah, and Callie in general, he came to the slow and reluctant conclusion that it wasn't mere sexual passion that so fascinated him about Becky's nanny.

If he didn't watch himself, he'd be falling in love with the woman.

The first time that idea struck him, the Saturday after he and Callie first made love, guilt followed so swiftly on its heels that he had to run away and hide in his library office.

For the love of God, he'd loved Anne. He couldn't possibly love Callie Prophet. She was nothing in the remotest degree like Anne.

*Aubrey, dear, use your common sense for a moment, please.*

Anne's voice wafted through his brain as clearly as if she'd spoken the words herself. Aubrey stiffened. He even glanced around his library, wondering if someone might be playing a nasty trick on him.

But he was alone in the room. Anne's voice had been a curious aberration in the atmosphere and nothing more or less than that.

Or perhaps it had been a particularly strong memory. But why would she tell him to use his common sense?

He'd remembered not long ago that Anne had told him to remarry. On her deathbed, yet. Was it possible that, had she lived, she also would have told him it was possible for a man to love two dissimilar women at different times in his life? Aubrey knew full well that his love for Anne remained as strong as it had ever been. Could he love another woman— Callie—as passionately as he'd loved Anne, even though they were as different as night was from day?

"Good God." He paced to the window behind his desk, yanked the curtains aside, and peered outside.

Autumn had fallen, accompanied by the season's first hard freeze, and the leaves had turned a couple of days ago. They were falling in waves from the trees today. Aubrey watched mulberry leaves catch the sun and drop like flakes of gold to the yellow grass. He employed a team of gardeners who raked the lawns daily, but they couldn't keep up with the steady rainfall of autumn leaves.

The almonds and walnuts were ripening. A hard wind would come along soon and start knocking them down. Then Mrs. Granger would begin making fruitcakes and cookies for Christmas. Becky was particularly fond of a cookie Mrs. Granger made that featured both nuts and bits of chocolate.

Aubrey liked them, too. Those cookies were a highlight of the entire year in the Lockhart household.

He sighed and forced himself to think about love. He hadn't thought about love as an emotion removed from Anne and her life and death, for years. If ever. Perhaps he'd never thought about it.

What was love, anyway? Affection, certainly. And sexual desire. That was important in a marital relationship. Aubrey didn't approve of men who kept mistresses, and he wouldn't be one of them; he didn't care how fashionable such affairs were in some circles. He liked to keep what was his; and he didn't believe in double standards. Besides, he didn't move in those exalted social circles, except peripherally, and he didn't want to.

But what else was involved in love besides affection and desire? He thought hard, his hands clasped behind his back, and his eyes focused on the beautiful grounds of his home. Shared principles, he supposed. And complementary goals in life. He imagined he and Callie had those in common. What about need? Did need play a part in love?

He often felt as though he needed Callie Prophet, rather like a plant needs water. It bothered him some to admit it, but he did. If she left, it wouldn't only be Becky who was devastated by her absence; Aubrey would be, too. In truth, if she left, he'd be crushed.

By God, losing Callie would hurt as much as losing Anne.

The realization stunned him, and he blinked into the autumn sunshine, almost afraid. He didn't like knowing he needed her this much; there was too much that could be lost when a person began needing another person, and he wasn't sure he was up to the perils. He tested his new understanding cautiously.

He'd been contemplating it for some time, and had reluctantly come to the conclusion that he really *did* love Callie and was almost willing to risk the need, when a soft knock came at his library door. He turned, saying, "Come in."

His heart lit up when he beheld Callie, smiling at him from the doorway. By God. It really *must* be love. He smiled back at her and walked to the door, impelled by, well, love, he supposed, to touch her. He took her arm and said, "Come in, come in, Callie. How's the patient?"

*Not very loverlike,* Aubrey scolded himself. He'd been much better at this sort of thing with Anne. But Anne had been a different sort of person. Receptive. Gentle. Callie was more prickly. She was self-sufficient and didn't impel a man to pamper her. With a sigh, he told himself he'd learn how to express himself with her.

"She's much better," Callie said, gazing at him with what Aubrey was startled to recognize as adoration.

Could *she* love *him*? It seemed unlikely, given her opinion of him when they'd first met.

On the other hand, he vaguely recalled her saying something about loving him that night they'd made love. That night now seemed centuries ago. Given the state of his sexual arousal every time he saw her, he hoped they'd be able to remedy his deprived state soon.

"What's that you have, darling?" he asked, noticing for the first time that Callie held a cardboard box that looked as if the lid didn't fit very well from the box being overfilled.

"I need to talk to you about a few things, Aubrey. Including this."

She didn't meet his eyes when she sat. Faintly puzzled, Aubrey went behind his desk and sat as well. "Oh? What is it, sweetheart." The endearments fell from his lips like the mulberry leaves falling from the tree.

Was he really becoming the besotted lover? Whereas not long ago—minutes ago, even—the notion would have brought with it feelings of guilt, now it pleased him. He sensed Anne's approval, and began to feel even better.

"Um—" Callie stopped speaking and swallowed.

Aubrey tilted his head, bemused. Callie wasn't generally at a loss for words. "What's the matter, Callie? You can tell me." He hoped his smile conveyed his newly recognized love.

He was startled at the tormented expression in her eyes when she finally lifted her head and gazed at him. "I have a confession to make, Aubrey."

Good God. "A confession?" What in the name of heaven

could she have to confess to him? Unsettled, but hoping she was only being dramatic, he tried to tease her. "I hope you're not going to confess to murder or anything of that nature, Callie, because I won't believe you."

A smile flickered and died on her face. "No, I'm not a murderess."

"I didn't think so, although after experiencing your temper a couple of times I couldn't be sure." He grinned, hoping to lighten her mood.

"No. It's not that." She gulped again and lifted the box. "Among other things, it's this."

"Oh?"

"Or, rather, these."

Aubrey put his elbows on his desk, steepled his fingers, and propped his chin on them. She was very nervous. This looked as though it was going to take some time unless he prompted her. "Go on, Callie. Whatever it is, I'm sure we can resolve it."

Maybe she was going to confess to having had a torrid affair with someone when she was younger; someone who'd seduced and abandoned her, perhaps. She wouldn't be the first young woman to suffer such an indignity, and it would explain how she'd managed to remain single for so long. She was too precious to avoid matrimony unless there was a pretty good reason for it.

Although the thought of Callie succumbing to the lures of some Lothario made Aubrey wince, he decided he couldn't hold such an affair against her. Not if she truly regretted it. After all, she was an emotional creature, and if she'd been young . . . Well, he would forgive her; that was all.

But, wait. He frowned, recalling that she'd been a virgin when he'd deflowered her. Ergo, evidently he'd been the first Lothario to have taken advantage of her. He frowned, not liking the scenario his brain had just produced. It had to be something else.

She lifted her chin in that characteristic gesture of defiance that used to irk him and now made him want to laugh out loud. "You know I used to work the postal route in your neighborhood."

"Yes."

"Well, I got to know Becky then."

"Yes, I know. You told me, and so did Becky."

"Yes, well, there's something I didn't tell you."

Uh-oh. Aubrey braced himself. "And what is that?"

"You were grieving over your loss." As if against her will, her chin lowered. She stared at the box in her lap. "Becky started writing letters to her mother, your late wife."

Aubrey's gaze narrowed as he tried to make sense of this tidbit of information. "She . . . what?"

She lifted her chin again and forged onward. "She started writing letters to her mother. In heaven."

"Good God."

"Yes." Callie nodded. "I felt sorry for her when she gave me the first letter."

"I can see why." Guilt entered uninvited and began nibbling at Aubrey's vitals. "I, ah, wasn't very good company for some time after Anne died."

"Yes. I know."

He frowned and opened his mouth to deny culpable intent, but Callie spoke before he had a chance.

"I know you were having a terrible time, but so was Becky. I felt sorry for her, so I took her letters home, read them, and answered them."

"You answered Becky's letters to her mother?" Aubrey gawked at Callie.

"Yes." Firmly. As if she were defending her position. "I couldn't bear the thought that Becky, who is the most darling child in the world, would write letters to the mother she loved and lost and never have them answered." She turned mutinous. "It's not as if she could turn to *you* for comfort, after all."

*"Touché."* After the first shock had passed, Aubrey began to see some humor—and a lot of pathos—in the situation. "In truth, you probably eased her mind a good deal." He felt benevolent after he said it, as if he were granting absolution.

"Yes, well, they did seem to ease her spirits some."

"So. You knew my daughter quite well before you came to work here as her nanny, I see."

Callie nodded and swallowed. "Yes."

This didn't seem so awfully bad. It pricked Aubrey's pride some to know his daughter had felt compelled to turn to a stranger for assistance during a time of great stress in her life, but he admitted it had been a God-awful time for all of them. He knew the household staff had suffered, too.

And, he admitted, he guessed he was glad Becky had found someone in whom to confide—even if she didn't know it wasn't her mother, but Callie, who was reading and answering her letters. That was a bit . . . Aubrey couldn't think of an appropriate word. Underhanded was too harsh. Intrusive, perhaps. But Callie's interference had been for a good cause, and it had helped Becky, and that was the important thing. He supposed.

"Well," he said at last. "I'm glad you found a way to ease Becky's mind, Callie. That was a bad time for all of us."

"Oh, I know it, Aubrey!" Lifting her chin again, she gazed at him earnestly. "And I'd never have done it if Becky weren't so young to have suffered such a wrenching loss. She was so unhappy. I couldn't stand to let her wait and wait and wait for answers from her mother. I just couldn't." She brushed tears away.

Aubrey felt vaguely manipulated, although he knew he shouldn't. It wasn't like Callie to stoop to feminine wiles like tears. She'd sooner knock him over the head with a brick as cry in front of him. The thought made him grin. "It's all right, Callie. I'm glad you answered those letters. They helped Becky, and that's the important thing."

"Yes, well . . ." Callie gulped. "There's more."

"Oh?" For some reason, Aubrey experienced a creeping sense of dread.

"Um, Aubrey, Becky found these letters some time ago." Callie lifted the lid of the box in her lap and held up a letter with a hand that shook slightly. "She, ah, had been trying to read them."

"Letters? More letters?" All thoughts of Callie and her letters from Anne vanished instantly. His gaze sharpened. "What are those? Not answers to the letters she wrote to her mother in heaven, I presume."

She licked her lips. "Um, no. They're letters you wrote to your wife while she was still alive."

For a second Aubrey's mind went blank. He didn't comprehend, although the sensation of slithering dread intensified. Squinting, he said, "I beg your pardon?"

Callie sucked in a breath Aubrey heard from where he sat. She stiffened her spine and looked him in the eye, as if she were gathering her courage like a cloak around her. "They're letters you wrote to Anne, Aubrey. Love letters. Becky found them and read them at night. They made her feel better after Mrs. Lockhart died, to know that you and her mother had loved each other, and loved her."

She seemed to run out of steam. Aubrey still didn't understand. "Love letters to Anne? From me?" He and Anne had been used to writing each other letters, and Aubrey supposed they might be classified as love letters. He and Anne had assuredly loved each other. He held out a hand. "May I see them, please?"

"Of course." With a jerky gesture, Callie plopped the box on his desk and shoved it toward him.

He glanced into the box, open now that Callie had lifted the lid. Frowning, he said, "Yes, I see. What of them? I don't think I wrote anything indelicate in them."

She heaved an exasperated breath. "It's not that, Aubrey. It's . . . it's worse than that."

He cocked an eyebrow. "Worse than that? What's the matter, Callie. Spit it out, please, because I'm no mind reader."

"I read them."

He blinked at her, uncomprehending. "You what?"

"I read them." She took another deep breath. "I did more than read them. I kept reading them. I—I—I don't know why. It was wrong of me."

All of the good feelings Aubrey had started to harbor about Callie Prophet suffered a magnificent shock and began crumbling around the edges.

"You read my letters to Anne?" He felt numb.

She nodded, bowed her head, clasped her hands tightly in her lap, and whispered, "I kept reading them. They—they're so beautiful. I don't know why I read them. I knew I shouldn't. It was like a compulsion. It was wrong of me. Very wrong."

Numbness fled. A sense of violation and rage consumed him in a flash.

"So that's how you managed to weasel your way into my daughter's heart."

His voice had gone low and cold. He didn't feel cold. Inside, flames of fury had started to consume the remnants of his good feelings for Callie. He felt plundered. Infringed on. Burgled. "No wonder you knew exactly how to get around my defenses, Miss Prophet. You knew my most intimate secrets, didn't you?"

Aubrey had never seen Callie cower before. She wasn't the cowering type. Yet she seemed to cower back in the chair now. She also flinched. "It wasn't like that, Aubrey. Truly, it wasn't. I—I don't know why I read the letters. But they were so—so beautiful."

"They were written to the woman I loved," he said in an even voice that chilled the air around him. He couldn't understand how his voice could sound so cold, when inside, he'd never been so incensed.

"Yes," she said in a tiny voice. "I know they were."

"You had no business reading them. No right."

She hung her head. "I know."

"You read my innermost thoughts. You learned exactly how to manipulate me, didn't you?"

Her head whipped up, and she stared at him, so pale she appeared ghostlike. "No! No, it wasn't like that! It's because—because—" The breath she took sounded like a sob. "It's because I'd never known a man could love a woman so much. The letters—they were so beautiful."

"They were private." Aubrey's fury was so potent, he shook with it. He didn't know what to do. He felt betrayed. He felt as if his whole world had been smashed to smithereens—again. Only moments earlier he'd been happy for the first time in two years, and now, with this box of letters and Callie's so-called "confession," his happiness, short-lived, had been shattered.

She lifted her head and watched him warily. "I'm so sorry, Aubrey. I was very wrong. Entirely wrong."

"Yes," he said. "You were."

"I'm so sorry." Tears began to fall from her eyes, and she wiped them away with an impatient gesture. "I was so wrong."

As he observed her, he felt as if he were watching a play. Her tears were only part of the act, and he resented them. He felt foolish, as if he'd been handled by an expert puppeteer. A mistress of her art. He'd never have believed Callie capable of such a—a wicked deception.

Yes. It was wicked, the deceit she'd practiced on him. She was wicked. How strange. Even from the first moment he'd met her, when he'd actively disliked her, he'd never have believed her capable of so rank a deception. If nothing else, he'd always believed her to be honest and possessed of a certain integrity.

Not any longer. Fearing his calm would crack and that he might become violent with her, Aubrey drew the box of letters closer to him and carefully replaced the lid she'd put on the desk. "We'll discuss this later."

"But— Oh, please, Aubrey, don't hate me. Please!"

"Hate you?" He gazed at her, his insides in such a turmoil, he couldn't distinguish one emotion from the other. "I don't know." He gave her a grim smile. "I'd just begun to believe I loved you, the more fool I."

He could scarcely believe his eyes when she grew even paler than she'd been before. "You—you love me?"

In the very most icy voice he could summon, he said flatly, "Not any longer."

"Oh!"

It was a cry of anguish, and Aubrey didn't care. He felt wrung out. Depleted. Crushed. Deceived.

For the second time in his life, he'd allowed himself to love a woman—and he'd lost her. This loss was as bitter, albeit for a different reason, as the loss of Anne.

This time he'd been a jackass, and the knowledge was hard to swallow.

Callie rose from the chair. She looked shaky. He didn't

care about that, either. She was a jade. A doxy. A manipulative bitch, and he hated her.

"Aubrey . . ." Her voice faded.

He only looked at her.

With one last, "Oh!" she whirled around and fled from his
presence.

Aubrey rose from his chair, walked stiffly to his office
door, shut it, and turned the key in the lock. He walked back
to his chair, sat, and stared at the box of letters for a good
two or three minutes. Then, with an anguished, "Oh, God!"
he buried his face in his hands and commenced to suffer,
feeling the pain, his heart hurting as if it were being ripped
in half by sharp, poisonous talons.

It had been even worse than she'd feared it would be. Callie
ran to her room, shut the door, locked it, and stood leaning
against it, her whole body shaking with sobs.

"Idiot!" she raged at herself. "You *should* suffer. You were
totally at fault."

She'd eased Becky's life and soul, she reminded herself.

But she'd used deceit with which to do it. She should
have—should have—

Callie didn't know what she should have done, but she
knew good and well she should never, ever, ever have read
Aubrey's private correspondence to his late wife. It was a
despicable thing to have done, and she hated herself for it.

With a moan, she flung herself face forward on her bed—
no, not *her* bed, Aubrey's bed. Everything in this beautiful
house was his. She had no part of it.

She might have been part of it. If she'd had the gumption
to hand over those letters when Becky had first told her about
them. She oughtn't to have read them, not even for Becky's
sake. It would have been the perfect time to explain to the
little girl that some things were private. Surely Callie could
have eased over the situation and still have gained Becky's
love and trust.

But she hadn't. She'd sunk to wicked depths of subterfuge,
and continued to read those beautiful letters.

"Oh!" The memory of the beauty contained in Aubrey's letters to Anne stabbed at Callie heart like tiny pitchforks. Which was no more than she deserved. She hated herself.

She hated herself almost as much as Aubrey now hated her.

And he'd said he'd come to love her. The memory of his words made Callie cry harder.

"Idiot," she cried into her bedclothes. "Fool! Wicked, deceiving fiend!" In fact, she didn't spare herself a single epithet as she continued to rage against herself.

Callie had been acting as nursemaid to Becky for a week now. She hadn't slept much, and she'd suffered agonies of worry for Becky's sake, and her own. The guilt she'd piled up during the last week, since she'd agreed to Aubrey's proposal of marriage, had interfered with her waking and sleeping hours almost more than Becky's illness.

She'd also been deprived of Monster's comforting presence, since he'd abandoned her room for Becky's. Callie believed it was no more than she deserved for being such an evil, wicked person. She wouldn't blame the whole world if it despised her.

Eventually she sobbed herself into a restless sleep. She woke slightly when Mrs. Granger knocked at her door, but she didn't stir. She didn't want to talk to the kindly housekeeper. She didn't want to sully Mrs. Granger's presence with her evil essence.

After another light knock and another pause, Callie heard Mrs. Granger mutter, presumably to Delilah, "Poor lamb, she must be dead to the world. She's worked so hard lately."

Callie couldn't hear Delilah's answer, but from the tone of her voice she knew the maid was agreeing with Mrs. Granger's opinion of her. If they only knew.

If they only knew, they'd hate her, too.

On that note, she shut her eyes and slept some more.

When she awoke again, night had fallen. Callie staggered to her feet and made her way to the window, where she pulled the curtains aside and gazed outside. There was no moon tonight, and fog, which occasionally crept over the landscape, seemed to thicken as she watched it.

Callie knew what she had to do. The knowledge had come to her as she slept.

"I'll write a note to Becky, and one to Aubrey," she decided.

The electric company had turned the power off, so Callie presumed the night was far advanced. Lighting the lamp on the mantel, she squinted at the clock. "Three-thirty."

So. Dawn was a little less than a couple of hours away. She could write her notes, pack, and make her escape before the household stirred. Good. Callie didn't think she could face Aubrey again. And she knew she couldn't take leave of Becky. Such a parting would be too painful for both of them.

"Notes. I'll write notes."

She'd also leave Monster with Becky. It was going to be hard enough on Becky to lose her nanny. Callie wouldn't deprive her of her cat, too. She might be wicked, but she wasn't quite *that* bad.

It took Callie an hour to write her notes because she wanted to be sure to phrase everything just so. That didn't leave her much time to pack. She managed, imperfectly, and with no regard for wrinkles. At a quarter to five, she crept down the back stairs of the beautiful mansion she'd come to love. She still had forty-five minutes to make her escape. Aubrey didn't get up until seven-thirty or eight, so, even if Mrs. Granger would be up and about at six, nobody would know she was gone until Becky awakened. She'd been sleeping late because of her illness.

Callie knew she could get away completely before she was missed.

It was a cold, miserable, foggy walk down the long, long drive to the road to Santa Angelica. Callie had no idea what she'd tell people when she turned up back at her family home.

She'd think of something, but she knew it wouldn't work very well. Everyone would wonder. Rumors would probably fly.

With a sigh, Callie decided that was no more than she deserved for deceiving Aubrey for so long.

Not that she'd really *deceived* him, she told herself. At once, her conscience slapped her.

"You did, too, deceive him, and you know it, Callie Prophet. You had no business reading those letters. And if you felt compelled to read them once, you ought to have turned them over after that one time. For heaven's sake, it's a felony to tamper with the U.S. Mail! You did worse than tamper."

Again, the less principled side of her nature tried to give her an excuse by reminding her that Aubrey hadn't used the U.S. Postal Service for most of the letters, but had left them for his wife. There were no postmarks on them.

"Stop caviling this minute, Callie Prophet!" Callie sniffed, disgusted with herself.

"Merciful heavens, it's foggy," she muttered, trying to keep her feet on the road and not wander into the woods. The fog had become so thick it made the trees look as if they'd been wrapped in cotton fluff, and it muffled every sound. Callie could neither see nor hear anything through the heavy cloak of thick, gray, dismal moisture.

No birds chirped. No squirrels chattered. The enveloping silence, like the enveloping fog, added an even greater degree of loss and solitude to her solitary trudge to the village and away from the scene of her disgrace. And away from her love.

It was no more than she deserved, to have to walk this road alone and in the fog. She deserved worse than that.

*If you'd been honorable, you might be marrying the man you love. But you weren't, and now you've not only lost Aubrey, but you've lost Becky as well.*

The notion of losing the two people she loved most in the world was such a miserable one that Callie couldn't contain her tears. She was surprised she had any left.

Stopping and setting her suitcase on the roadway, she fished in her pocket for a handkerchief with which to dry her eyes and blow her nose. She was irked with herself. This was all her fault, and if she was now suffering, it was no more than she deserved.

She didn't hear the milk wagon until the horse loomed out

of the fog directly in front of her. She didn't mean to scream any more, probably, than the horse did, but scream they both did.

Horrified and frozen in place, Callie saw the animal rear. She saw its iron-shod hooves, which looked to her startled brain like huge clubs, coming down straight at her out of the air.

After that, her world went black.

# 20

Aubrey lay in bed for hours after Callie's confession. At first his anger and sense of betrayal kept him awake. After those two bitter emotions had burned themselves to a slow simmer, he began to wonder about lots of things.

He still resented Callie's having read his private correspondence to Anne. Those letters had been written out of love to the person Aubrey had cherished more than life itself. Indeed, if he could have arranged things to suit himself, he'd have gladly sacrificed himself for Anne. The good Lord knew, Becky would probably have been better off with Anne than with him, if fate had insisted she lose one parent.

On the other hand, after his fury cooled, he sort of understood why Callie had read them.

"Bah! She had no right."

True, true.

However, if reading those letters had assisted her in understanding his and Becky's anguishing loss, he guessed the action, however underhanded it had been, had worked for some good.

"Conniving bitch."

Even in the feverish acme of his rage, Aubrey knew that

wasn't so. He'd accused her of being manipulative and
treacherous, but he didn't really believe it. Not Callie. She
had many faults, but disloyalty and deviousness weren't
among them. Far from it. She was more apt to lambaste a
person to his face than to sneak around behind his back. She
was more apt to demand than try to manipulate. Not for her
the behind-the-back tactics of a Bilgewater.

Hell, if she'd been *really* devious, she'd never have confessed her sin in the first place. Even in his shock and anger,
Aubrey had registered her honest contrition. She'd been
ashamed of whatever compulsion had prompted her to read
those letters.

It had startled him to know that it had been Becky who'd
initially found the letters and tried to read them. If Callie
were to be believed, Aubrey's own daughter had asked Callie
to read the letters to her. Said they gave her comfort. Made
her feel better.

Aubrey's heart squished slightly.

He'd been awfully hard on her. Aubrey couldn't recall
seeing Callie cry very often, but she'd cried when he'd been
berating her. Ripping her into bloody strips was more like
it. It had infuriated him when she'd tried to excuse her behavior, because he hadn't believed there to be any excuse
for it.

Maybe he'd been a little too hard on her. After all, she'd
been trying earnestly to help Becky overcome the loss of her
mother.

And she'd been writing letters to Becky, posing as Anne,
in heaven. In spite of himself and in spite of the unhappy
reality of Becky's life that had prompted her to do such a
thing, Aubrey grinned into the darkness.

She was a clever little minx, and no mistake. But he really
couldn't see Callie Prophet doing something like answering
Becky's letters to heaven in an elaborate and crafty scheme
to worm her way into his house and heart. She simply wasn't
that sort of person.

Hell's bells, when she'd first come here, she'd hated him
and had made no bones about it.

And now she claimed to love him.

By damn, when he thought about that part of this whole fiasco, an unreasonable and totally irrational feeling of pride crept over Aubrey. She loved *him*. Callie Prophet, who was twenty-four years old and had probably been courted by dozens of lovesick swain, loved him, Aubrey Lockhart.

And Aubrey would give his all if he were called on to do so in a wager that Callie didn't love him for his money. Indeed, the only things she seemed to want to spend his money on were items of use to Becky.

"A birthday party," he muttered. "Whoever heard of such a thing?"

By the time Aubrey's brain finally quit whirring and allowed him to sleep, he'd pretty much decided he owed Callie an apology. True, she'd been wrong, but he'd been wrong in attacking and condemning her so thoroughly. Two wrongs, as Aubrey's mother had tried hard to teach him when he was growing up, did not make a right.

He'd talk to her first thing in the morning. He told himself so as his eyes closed and sleep claimed him.

By that time, though, it was very late. Aubrey had spent a restless week fraught with worry over Becky, sexual frustration resulting from his one liaison with Callie, and suppressed excitement from keeping his engagement to Callie a secret from Becky, who was going to be elated when she heard the news.

The morning was creeping on toward noon, therefore, when Aubrey was startled awake by his bedroom door being flung open and by Becky flying into the room in tears. She was waving a letter in her small hand and between her sobs, she gasped out words that Aubrey didn't understand at first.

He sat up and rubbed his eyes. "Becky! Good God, child, what's wrong?"

"It's Callie!"

That's what he thought she said, at any rate, and his heart chilled. "Callie?"

"Miss Prophet!"

Becky hurled herself at him. Even with his body and brain still lagging behind his reflexes and struggling to emerge from sleep, he caught her up in his arms. "Miss Prophet?"

This was no good. He could do better than repeat everything she said. He cleared the frog out of his throat and tried again. "What about Miss Prophet, sweetie?" He hugged Becky hard.

"She's *gone!*"

It was a more-or-less incoherent wail of distress, but Aubrey caught the words, and his heart stuttered. He shook his head, trying to clear it of sleep webs. "What do you mean, she's gone?"

Becky dropped the paper she'd been holding, wrapped her arms around her father's neck, and gave herself up to heart-wrenching sobs. She didn't answer him, and Aubrey maneuvered one of his hands free and picked up the paper.

He read the missive with growing distress:

> *Dearest Becky,*
>    *I'm afraid it's time for me to go away, love. Please take care of your papa. He loves you very, very much. I love you, too, but I find I can't remain in your home any longer. Please remember that I love you, Becky, and I will miss you awfully. I'm leaving Monster to help you get better.*
>
>                                                *Callie*

"Good God." The paper fluttered from Aubrey's numb fingers, and he hugged his daughter more tightly.

She'd gone. She'd left him. She'd left Becky.

She'd left Monster, for God's sake.

What had possessed her to do such a drastic thing?

"Good God," he repeated, understanding all too well what had possessed her.

She'd believed him when he'd told her she was a no-good cheat, is what had happened. She'd believed him when he'd said those hateful things. She'd believed him.

This was all his fault. His daughter's broken heart—twice broken, now—could be laid at his own fumbling feet. He'd all but driven Callie away, all but had her pilloried in the public square and whipped at the cart's tail.

And she'd written Becky a letter. The impact of that struck Aubrey finally, and he wondered if she'd penned a missive for him, too. Suddenly, the compulsion to search for it assailed him and, holding Becky firmly in his arms, he swung his feet over the side of the bed. He needed to find Callie's letter to him. Surely, she'd written him a letter, too. She *had* to have written to him. She couldn't have hared out of his life without leaving so much as a note behind.

He wouldn't let her leave, anyway, if it came to that. "Come on, sweetheart. Let's get dressed and look into this matter."

"She's gone," Becky whimpered. She'd exhausted herself with crying and clung to Aubrey like a limpet, hiccuping and gasping and giving the occasional coughing sob.

"We'll get her back," Aubrey told her with more brightness and confidence than he felt. "We'll find her, sweetheart."

Becky pulled her face away from his shoulder and looked him in the eye. It hurt Aubrey to see pain and misery reflected in her puffy red eyes, still streaming with tears. "You promise?" she asked in a shaky voice.

"I promise."

And he'd be damned if he'd break a promise to Becky.

He found Callie's letter to him in the first place he looked. His heart hurt as he read the words:

*Dear Aubrey,*

*I'm so sorry. I can't tell you how sorry I am to have violated your trust. I was wrong, it was a bad thing I did, and I pray that someday you'll find it in your heart to forgive me. Please try to find another nanny for Becky. It's not my place to advise you, but I think a young woman with lots of energy would be best. You probably don't believe me, but I love you and Becky with all my heart. God bless you both.*

*Callie*

Callie hurt everywhere. She wondered if she was in the throes of a particularly bad dream.

Steel-shod hooves loomed out of the shadows of her brain, and she flinched. The flinch aggravated the assorted aches and pains in her body, and she groaned.

"She's coming around, Doctor."

The voice came to her through the fog shrouding the countryside. What did it mean? Callie couldn't figure it out, and she hurt too much to devote a lot of thought to it.

"Good. I'd hoped she would. That's a good sign, although she's not going to be out of the woods for a while."

A muffled sob filtered through the mud in Callie's head. Now why was someone crying?

She realized it had been one of her own sobs she'd heard and was surprised. Callie almost never cried in front of people. Then she heard another sob, and knew it wasn't her own.

Good heavens, why was everyone crying? It seemed very strange to her.

"Oh, Dr. Marshall, please, *please* save her."

Lord on high, that was Alta! At least . . . Callie strained to think, but her head hurt too much. She was pretty sure that had been Alta's voice, but Alta never sounded like that, as though she were terrified and alarmed and sad.

"Don't spare the treatment, Doc. I'll pay whatever it'll cost."

George! That was George! For heaven's sake. Callie couldn't figure this out. What was he offering to pay for?

"And we'll help, Dr. Marshall."

And that had been Florence! Mercy, what on earth was going on here? Callie couldn't remember the last time she'd heard all of her siblings sounding so upset about anything.

Oh, yes. She remembered now. When their father died was the last time. The thought of her father dying made her want to weep, but she hurt too much to spare energy for more tears.

"I'll do everything I can," came Dr. Marshall's voice out of the void. "What about Mr. Lockhart? Has someone been in touch with him?"

Callie's brain screamed *No!* but her mouth wouldn't work. Silence settled on the room after the doctor's question.

At last Alta spoke. "I, uh, don't know. Something funny's

going on there, Dr. Marshall. Callie had her suitcase with
her. She appeared to be walking to town."

"I don't know what's going on," said George, sounding a
trifle more hearty. Actually, he sounded rather belligerent.
"I'll go there and find out what happened, you can bet on it.
He shouldn't have allowed her to walk to town in that fog.
What was the man thinking?"

No, Callie's brain pleaded. *It wasn't his fault I left like
that.* She realized she'd probably been precipitate in her departure, although it hadn't felt like it at the time. Actually,
she couldn't remember the particulars, but she was sure she'd
had a good reason for not telling Aubrey about her departure.

"Please don't make trouble, George."

That was Florence, the peacemaker of the Prophet clan.
Florence wanted everyone to get along. Always. No matter
what.

"Well, but we really must tell him. For all we know, he
gave Callie leave to do something, and she was taking a little
holiday. Or something." Alta didn't sound sure of herself.

"You're going to have to leave the room now, folks. I
need to examine her further. The concussion's a bad one,
and I'm not sure if there will be permanent problems resulting from it. I also need to check for other injuries, and I
don't care to have an audience."

Thank God. If Callie had to be examined by a doctor, she
didn't want her brother and sisters peering on.

"After I assess her condition in more detail, I'll see what
I can do to ease her pain."

"Is she in pain?"

Callie could tell Alta was crying when she asked the question. She'd like to have answered her. She was in horrible
pain. She'd never been in such pain. She couldn't get her
muscles, nerves, and brain to cooperate, however, so she remained silent.

"I don't know," Dr. Marshall said, sounding worried.

Callie didn't like to hear the doctor sound worried.

"How can you tell?" asked George.

"I can't. If there's nerve damage, she might not feel anything. If—if the blow to her brain was severe enough, she might remain in a coma."

"No!" It was a chorus of three.

The hooves came out of the fog at her once more, and she flinched again.

A horse. She vaguely recalled something about fog. And a horse. And screaming.

Yes. There had been screaming. She'd screamed. And the horse had screamed. How funny. A horse screaming.

"Good God, she's smiling!" George. Callie felt him leaning over her.

"Does—does that mean anything, Doctor?" Alta, too, leaned over her.

"Oh, please, Doctor, tell us she'll be all right!" Florence joined the other two of Callie's siblings.

"I can't tell you anything until I've examined her." The doctor sounded as if he were losing patience. "Will you please leave the room so that I can get this done?"

"Oh, she looks so terrible! I'm so afraid for her!"

"Don't cry, Florence." Alta was crying, too, although Callie wasn't sure Alta knew it.

"Come on, Alta and Flo. Let's get a cup of tea or something. Let Dr. Marshall do whatever he has to do." More grimly, George added, "I've got to get a message to Lockhart."

*Lockhart. Not Mr. Lockhart.* Oh, dear, George was angry. He was blaming Aubrey for whatever had happened. If only she could remember. Callie tried to remember, but was again unsuccessful.

"Thank you," the doctor muttered. He sounded cranky, but Callie thought she detected an underlay of apprehension. She didn't think that was a good sign.

She heard a whoosh and a bang, and she flinched yet again. These loud noises played the very devil with her headache.

The doctor said, "For the love of— What are you barging in here for, Mr. Lockhart? And you shouldn't have brought Becky out in this weather. She's only recently recovered from a bad bout of influenza and needs to be resting, not running around in the cold autumn air."

Good Lord, it was Aubrey and Becky. Callie exerted every ounce of her inner strength to open her eyes and look at them, but none of her organs wanted to obey her commands.

"Callie!"

Aubrey. He sounded scared. Bad. Very bad.

"Miss Prophet!"

Becky. She sounded scared, too. Oh, dear.

Bother. It was all too much for Callie. She decided she'd just have to figure it out later. At the moment, she thought sleep would do her more good than thought. So she went to sleep.

When Aubrey and Becky had arrived in Santa Angelica in his surrey, Aubrey had gone to the post office, bought some stamps, and asked casually if Callie had been in to chat with her former coworkers. When Mr. Wilson had looked grave and told him about Callie's accident, Aubrey's heart had stopped beating for a moment. Then it had raced. He'd scooped Becky up, forgotten all about the stamps and the horse and buggy waiting for them outside the post office, and headed at a run for the hospital.

Then, when he'd seen Callie lying there, her face a deathly white except for the stark, livid bruises that bled into her hairline and seemed to Aubrey to be silent accusations, he'd almost fallen down on his knees. Only the fact that he still held Becky in his arms had kept him upright.

George Prophet had come to his rescue, taking his arm and leading him to a chair.

"Here, Mr. Lockhart, sit down here. Callie's been in an accident."

"An accident?" Becky, still not entirely recovered from her recent illness, began crying weakly. "What happened? Will she be all right?"

"We hope so, sweetie pie." George, bless him, had smiled encouragingly at Becky.

Then Callie's sisters had assisted their brother in coming

to Aubrey's rescue. Alta, whose house was situated closest to the hospital and whose children were friends of Becky's, offered to take Becky to her house. "I'm sure Jane and Johnny will be pleased to play with Becky."

Smiling, she held out a hand for Becky, who resisted, clinging to her father and staring at the bed where the doctor, hands on his hips, glared at them all.

"Will you please leave the room?" Dr. Marshall said severely. "I have to examine Miss Prophet."

Aubrey stood up abruptly. "Yes. Thank you, Doctor." He turned to Alta. "Thank you, Mrs. Watson. That would be very good of you. I—I need to know what happened and what the doctor thinks needs to be done."

George took his arm again. "Let's go out to the lobby so Doc Marshall doesn't start throwing things at us. I'll explain everything while Alta takes care of the tyke."

"Thank you." Aubrey felt as though he were walking through quicksand as he left the room. He wanted to stay. He wanted to shake Dr. Marshall until he explained fully and exactly what was wrong with Callie and assured him that she'd be all right. He clung to Becky as if she were his last link to the earth. She felt like it, even though he knew Alta's suggestion had been a sound one.

He nearly collapsed onto the sofa when they got to the hospital's lobby. Glancing at each of the Prophets in turn, he collected his emotions enough to say, "What happened? That bruise on her face is—is—" He swallowed, recalling the bruise with horror. "Well, it looks awful."

"Is she hurt?" Becky asked in a small voice, still hugging her papa tightly.

Aubrey hugged her back. "I'm afraid she must be, sweetheart."

George passed a hand over his eyes. "It's like this: From what we can figure out, she was walking along the road from your place to the town. The fog was thick this morning, and she evidently neither saw nor heard the milk wagon. According to Simpson, the driver, the horse and Callie scared the spit out of each other when they met up in the middle of the road. Don't know why in hell she was walking in the middle of the road."

"George," Florence said softly.

Aubrey figured she objected to his saying "hell." Aubrey didn't. He felt like saying worse than that.

George sighed. "Sorry, Flo. Anyhow, when Callie and the horse met, the horse reared, and one of its hooves struck her coming down."

"Good God." Aubrey shut his eyes, unwilling to picture Callie in such pain and distress. Yet she was. "Good God."

"Will she be all right?" Becky asked again, her voice even smaller than before.

George smiled at her. Aubrey realized that all the Prophets had fine smiles. Friendly smiles. Smiles that invited openness and friendship. A marvelous quality, that. Funny it should have taken him so long to recognize it.

"We're not sure yet, Becky. Dr. Marshall has to examine her. She has a concussion."

"What's a 'cussion?"

After exchanging a glance with George, Aubrey answered his daughter's question. "When a person gets a knock on the head, sometimes it makes the little blood vessels inside break and the brain swell. That's called a concussion."

Becky's eyes went wide with alarm. "You mean her brain's bleeding?"

"We don't know yet, Becky," George said.

Florence tried to stifle a sob, but didn't quite succeed. Alta patted her on the shoulder and said, "Dr. Marshall will do everything he can, Becky. What we all need to do is pray for her. Pray hard. God hears people's prayers, you know."

Aubrey could have argued with her on that subject, but didn't want to. At the moment, and in spite of his own experience, he decided to believe what Alta said.

"Has she been conscious at all?" he asked after a short spate of silence.

George shook his head. "No. Not yet." His voice sounded gravelly, and he cleared his throat. "The doctor says if she doesn't regain consciousness pretty soon, it might mean . . . Well, it'll be encouraging if she does, I guess."

"Right." Aubrey pondered this.

Again silence descended on the glum company. Becky sniffled audibly, and Florence sniffled inaudibly. The only reason Aubrey knew she was crying was that she kept wiping her eyes with a handkerchief.

At last Alta spoke. "Becky, I think it would be better for you and your papa if you were to come home with me now. It's about lunchtime, and Jane and Johnny will be coming home from Sunday school. They'll be so pleased to see you, and you can eat with them and play this afternoon." She glanced at Aubrey. "And I think you'll also feel better this afternoon. Callie said you've been very sick, you poor thing."

Becky nodded solemnly. "I had 'fluenza."

"Indeed, that's what Callie said." Alta swallowed, and for a moment, Aubrey feared she might start crying, too.

She didn't. Instead, she arose from the chair in which she'd parked herself and came over to Becky with her hand outstretched. She spoke to Aubrey. "Is that all right with you, Mr. Lockhart? I expect you and George and Flo and their families to come to my house for supper tonight, too. It won't be a fancy meal, but it will save everyone else having to cook when we're all so—" She sucked in air. "When we're all so worried."

"Thank you, Alta." Florence's voice wobbled so much it was difficult to make out the words. "I want to stay here."

"I'd better go home for a little while. Have to report to Marie and the kids. Marie will probably want to help you with supper, Alta."

Alta nodded. "That's fine, George. Send the children too. Might as well have a whole herd of them as one or two."

Aubrey marveled at the dynamics of this family. They were so easy with each other. And they seemed to accept and give help with equal facility. He wasn't quite accustomed to such easy relationships. It occurred to him that the Prophets were, in a way, a blessing of a family, and he was momentarily overwhelmed with gratitude that they should have blessed his life and Becky's.

Realizing he was on the verge of blubbering, he pulled

himself together and squeezed Becky. "I'll see you later, sweetheart. Have a good time with your friends." He gave her a smacking kiss on the cheek.

"Please tell Callie I love her, Papa," Becky said as she reached for Alta's hand. "And tell her to get better. Dr. Marshall made me better. I bet he can make her better."

Two tears trailed down Becky's cheeks, and Aubrey reached out to wipe them away. "I will, Becky. I'll tell her." He gulped and shut up before he could make a fool of himself.

George, Alta, and Becky left the hospital's lobby. Aubrey walked to the door and waved to his daughter until she disappeared from his sight. When he turned, he saw Florence watching him. He inspected her face, trying to decipher the expression.

Did she hold him responsible for Callie's accident? He was. He blamed himself. If he hadn't been so damned huffy with her, if he hadn't said such accusatory things to her, if he hadn't vilified her so viciously, she wouldn't have run away. She'd still be in his home, tucked away safely.

God, he loved her. For a moment, Aubrey covered his face with his hands, wishing with all his heart that he'd had the openheartedness to have told her so instead of condemning her.

But, no. He'd gotten so entangled with his grief over Anne that he hadn't even recognized when the grief had eased and the habit of grief had taken over. And he'd blamed Callie for curing him! What an ass he was.

"I'm sure Callie won't blame you for the accident, Mr. Lockhart."

Florence's voice, soft and oddly like Callie's, only less vibrant, filtered through his misery slowly. When he understood what she'd said, he lowered his hands and gazed at her. "I—I think it's my fault she was on that foggy road this morning, Mrs. Blanchard. I—we had an argument."

"I figured it was something like that." Florence gave him a quavery smile. "She loves you, you know."

"Oh, God." Aubrey shut his eyes and stood there, unable

to move, wishing he could trade places with Callie. He deserved to hurt; she didn't.

Florence patted the sofa cushion next to her. "Come and sit by me, Mr. Lockhart. I think you ought to know what Callie thinks of you and Becky."

He knew what she thought of them. She loved them both. With a sigh, Aubrey moved to the sofa and sat. At least Becky deserved Callie's love. He sure didn't.

"You know, Callie used to write to Becky before she went to live with you. She told us about it, although she swore us to secrecy. Poor Becky used to write letters to her mother in heaven and Callie answered them because she couldn't stand thinking that the poor little girl's letters would otherwise go unanswered."

"She told me." Aubrey's heart felt heavier than it had since the day of Anne's funeral. If it got much heavier, it would weigh him down forever.

"Yes." Florence sighed. "Callie's a funny girl." She laughed softly. "Well, of course, she's not a girl any longer. But I think of her as one because she's the youngest."

Aubrey nodded. He wasn't in the mood to talk.

"She's had several offers of marriage, you know, but she didn't accept any of them. Said she didn't want to marry anyone she didn't love. Since she moved to your house she's been telling me that she guesses she isn't the sort of woman a man could cherish. I don't know where she came up with that one, because she's the loveliest girl, and has the kindest heart in the world."

Aubrey knew where she'd come up with it. Guilt smacked him in the conscience, making him cringe.

"Bobby Collins wanted to marry her just this last year," Florence went on, sounding reminiscent. "Callie laughed and told him he'd get over it. He said his heart was broken, but Callie didn't believe him. I guess she was right, because he proposed to the Zellweiger girl just this past week, and they're planning a wedding in the spring."

Aubrey didn't care. His fear for Callie was gnawing at his innards. Between fear and guilt, he wasn't sure he'd survive until the doctor came out of Callie's room. He wanted to barge in and demand to know what the prognosis was.

Florence rambled on. Her gentle voice had a calming effect, which was a good thing, since it kept him from rampaging through the hospital and tearing his hair out. "She is the youngest, you know, and she was hit hardest when our mother died. She's very sensitive."

*Oh, God. And he'd all but flayed her alive last night.* He buried his head in his hands and was startled when he felt Florence's hand on his shoulder.

"Please don't despair, Mr. Lockhart. She's a strong girl. If anyone can survive such a blow, it's Callie."

Aubrey only stared at her, wishing he could do as she'd suggested. But the thought of losing the second woman he'd ever loved was too difficult to bear, and he despaired in spite of Florence.

# 21

"Ohh." Callie tried to lift her hand to her aching head, but it wouldn't cooperate. She felt as if her body had been pumped full of something very heavy. Lead, perhaps. She heard what sounded like a rustle of skirts and opened her eyes. Her eyelids felt heavy, too.

"Miss Prophet," a soft, sweet voice said, sounding tentative.

Callie tried to agree, but didn't have any luck. She tried again and managed to croak, "Yes." She wanted to ask where she was and why she hurt so badly, but such a complicated communication was beyond her at the moment.

"Do you hurt?"

Stupid question. Because her head hurt so much and she feared she'd only make it hurt worse if she nodded, Callie whispered, "Yes."

"Doctor gave me instructions to give you another dose of morphine if you were in pain if you woke up, so I'll be right back with it. Then I'll run to get Doctor, because he's been very worried about you." The rustle of skirts came again, retreating this time.

Who in the name of mercy was "Doctor"? Callie wondered. Dr. Marshall? Why did this person call him "Doctor"? And what was this *if* she woke up nonsense? And why was this woman giving her doses of morphine? Morphine was pretty strong medication for a headache.

When she thought, her head throbbed, so Callie decided to save all of her questions until later. She did wish she knew where she was and why she hurt so terribly.

"Here we go," came the voice.

Maybe it belonged to a nurse? But why would she be attended by a nurse? And, if she was being attended by a nurse, who was paying for it? She didn't remember much about anything, but she seemed to recall she'd done something bad to Aubrey. Her heart joined her head in throbbing, and she wished she hadn't thought about Aubrey.

Thoughts fled when the woman lifted Callie's head, precipitating a flood of anguish throughout her entire body, and especially her head. She felt stupid when tears leaked from her eyes and trickled down her cheeks. Callie Prophet didn't cry for no reason, but she was crying now, from pain, and she felt silly about it. She'd always been strong. Something very bad must have happened.

The nurse lowered her carefully to the pillow once more, and Callie could do nothing but suffer for several minutes. She was vaguely aware of the skirts rustling away from her bed.

Everything went black for a period of time, and when Callie opened her eyes again Dr. Marshall was looming over her. Seeing him surprised her. "H'lo, Doc."

Was that her voice? It sounded odd.

She was reassured slightly when Dr. Marshall grinned at her. "Howdy-do, Miss Callida Prophet. I can't tell you how happy I am that you've opened your eyes at last."

"At last?" Whatever did that mean?

The doctor nodded, so Callie guessed his phrasing hadn't been a mistake. "You've been out cold for a week now."

A week! Good heavens! "What happened?"

"You, dear lady, had a confrontation with Billy Simpson's Clydesdale. You lost."

"B-Billy Simpson? But . . ." Billy Simpson drove the milk

wagon. How could Callie have annoyed Pete, Billy's huge horse, so badly that Pete had clobbered her?

Dr. Marshall patted her shoulder and turned away, presumably to do something of a doctorly nature. "It wasn't anybody's fault, Callie. It was too foggy to see anything that morning."

That was minutely reassuring, Callie guessed, although why she should have been out in the morning fog was still a puzzle. Evidently, she was still *in* a fog. She decided that was an amusing thing to say, so she did. "I think I'm still in a fog, Doctor."

He chuckled, which made the pain of speaking almost worthwhile. "You're getting your spirit back. That's good, Callie. We've all been very worried about you."

If whatever had happened had occasioned this much pain, Callie guessed she'd have worried about herself, too, had she been in any shape to do so. "What happened?" Had she already asked that?

Oh, yes. She had. But Dr. Marshall hadn't given her a satisfactory answer.

"Billy's horse and you ran into each other on the road to town, and you scared the horse as much as he scared you, I guess. Unfortunately, he's bigger than you are, and has iron-shod hooves. According to Billy, the horse reared up and hit you with a hoof when it came down again."

Ow. No wonder her head hurt so much. Callie pondered Dr. Marshall's explanation for several seconds. The longer she pondered, the more amazed she was. "I'm lucky to be alive, I guess. That's one big horse."

Dr. Marshall's grin was broader when he turned and loomed over her again. "You're *very* lucky to be alive. And your family and Mr. Lockhart and Becky have been camped in here and in the hallway for days now, worried about you."

Callie seized upon the name that struck her with the greatest force. "Mr. Lockhart?"

"Mr. Lockhart. He's been practically living in your room, Callie. He's paying for everything. Even called in a trauma expert from San Francisco." Dr. Marshall's grin took on an ironic twist. "And I didn't even resent it. I know how worried he's been."

Callie blinked up at him. "The trauma expert?"

"No, you goose. Mr. Lockhart."

"Oh."

"He left you a letter for when you're well enough to read it."

"A letter?"

Wait a minute. Wasn't it letters that had gotten her into trouble with Aubrey in the first place?

Oh, Lord, yes it was. Callie shut her eyes and tried to think, but couldn't. All she knew for sure was that she'd read Aubrey's letters to his dead wife, they'd been so beautiful that Callie had fallen in love with Aubrey, and she knew full well no man would ever love her as Aubrey had loved his Anne. His "Darling Annie."

What was worse was that Callie didn't blame Aubrey. Not a bit. She'd be furious with anyone who read her private letters, too. Bits and pieces of her last day and night at the Lockhart mansion began finding each other and adhering into a coherent picture in her brain. Ah, yes. She'd made a fool of herself, Aubrey had been justifiably angry, and Callie had run away.

That must have been when she'd encountered Billy's horse. She had a vague recollection of fog. And unhappiness. And loss.

And if that wasn't a dismal thought, she didn't know what was.

"Why did Aubrey come here?" she asked, curious. If he hated her, he wouldn't have chased after her, would he? Callie could more easily understand him paying for her care, because he was a kind man, even if he didn't like her any more.

"You'll have to ask him, Callie."

As Callie had been thinking, Dr. Marshall had been checking her pulse, examining her head—which required a good deal of pressing at a tremendously sore spot above her right eye—and pressing his ice-cold stethoscope against various regions of her chest. She probably should have been embarrassed, but she was too weak.

Dr. Marshall straightened, and held out a hand so that Callie was staring straight up at it. "How many fingers am I holding up, Callie?"

"Five, but three are bent. There are only two straight out." She wondered if he wanted her to be so literal.

He only smiled some more, so she guessed it was all right. "Right. How about now? How many fingers are straight?"

"Four. Your thumb is still bent."

"Excellent. How about now?"

"None."

"Good. And now?"

"Three." This was the strangest test Callie had ever been asked to take, but she wasn't up to questioning the doctor about it.

"Perfect. You're progressing nicely. How do you feel, Callie? Do you think you can sit up?"

Sit up? Callie tested the notion and found it disagreeable. On the other hand, she'd been promised a letter from Aubrey and, while it might contain horrid news, it might say something conciliatory. Maybe they could at least be friends, even if he'd never renew his offer of marriage.

Her eyes began to fill with tears. Shoot, when had she become such a weeping lily? Since the horse beaned her, she guessed. "Sure," she said, and started struggling. Instantly, her body and head protested.

"Wait a minute, Callie," Dr. Marshall said. "You can't do it on your own. Let me help you."

Thank goodness. Callie was glad for the doctor's assistance. "I don't think I've ever felt so weak," she admitted.

"Small wonder."

With the help of Dr. Marshall and a nurse—Callie wondered if it was the one who'd spoken to her of morphine—Callie maneuvered herself into a sitting position. The nurse fluffed pillows at her back, and Dr. Marshall settled sheets and blankets over her.

When she looked at the bed, she saw very few wrinkles. Evidently, she hadn't done much tossing and turning during her stay in—"Where am I?" she asked suddenly.

"You're in the Santa Angelica Hospital, Miss Prophet," the nurse said. She looked familiar; Callie recalled seeing her in town a couple of times, although she'd never really met her.

"How long have I been here?"

"Seven days," the nurse answered.

Dr. Marshall had started fiddling with his little black bag. "And I don't mind telling you that we were afraid you wouldn't pull through for a while."

"Oh." Sounded serious. No wonder she hurt so much. "Um, did you say there was a letter for me?"

The doctor chuckled again. "There are lots of letters for you, my dear, although I'm sure there's one you're asking about particularly." He shut his bag with a snap. "Too bad your sister Alta finally managed to persuade him to go to Alta's house and get some sleep. Otherwise, he'd be here now. Did I tell you he's been practically living in your room?"

"Um, I think so."

"Even made us put a cot in here so he could stay overnight. Didn't trust the nurses to see to you properly, I guess." Dr. Marshall went back to Callie's bed and winked at her. "Although, I think there was probably another reason, too."

Probably wanted to scold her some more, Callie thought peevishly. She didn't care to be the object of speculation of so nice a man as Dr. Marshall.

Besides, Callie had ruined any chance of a romantic liaison with Aubrey because she'd allowed herself to behave in a despicable, sneaky way. She sighed, and realized her chest hurt, too. "Did the horse kick my chest?"

She saw the doctor's eyes open wide. "Good God, no. If he had, he'd probably have crushed you. I keep telling everyone that it's a good thing he only kicked your head, since that's the hardest part of your body." He laughed.

Callie didn't think it was especially funny, but she managed to produce a smile.

"I'll get your correspondence, Miss Prophet," the nurse

said, and bustled off to return in a moment, bearing several letters.

Listening to the nurse's white skirts rustle, Callie vaguely recalled hearing that noise a lot recently. Seven days. Good heavens.

Finally Dr. Marshall left the room and, after puttering around the room for another little while, during which time Callie wanted to shriek at her to go away, the nurse left, too. Alone at last, Callie shuffled through the several letters the nurse had set on her lap. She smiled at one that was addressed to her in Becky's distinctive, childish hand.

But that wasn't the one she wanted to read first. Dr. Marshall had mentioned a letter from Aubrey. She found it at last and picked it up, her heart pounding in a cadence with her head.

Aubrey had sealed it with wax, and Callie broke the seal with trembling fingers. She was surprised by how long a missive it was.

"Blast!" She was so weak, in body and heart, that the tears started flowing again. She wiped them away impatiently. "How can you read if your eyes are full of water, you idiot?" she asked herself.

Before an answer had occurred to her, she'd spread the sheet and lifted it so that she could read it without bending her head, which hurt abominably. She could hardly believe her watery eyes when she read the salutation.

*My Darling Callie . . .*

"Oh, my," Callie whispered. She read on.

*Please forgive me for hurting you, darling. I love you very much, Callie. I was a fool for not recognizing how special you are before now.*

"Good heavens." With growing wonder, Callie wiped more tears away and continued reading.

*If you can ever forgive me, I pray that you will consent to marry me, darling Callie. I need you. Becky needs*

*you. We both love you and, I think, you might learn to
love me. I know you love Becky.*

"If I could *learn* to love him?" Callie stared at the words,
wondering if her tears were getting in the way of coherent
reading. But, no, that's what he'd written, all right. Rereading the prior couple of sentences, she noted that he'd said
he loved her, too. Good heavens.

*Please get better, Callie. Get better and come back to
us. I will love and cherish you forever, my darling.*

He'd cherish her? Aubrey Lockhart would cherish Callie
Prophet? "Oh, my," she whispered, reading on.

*We can be married as soon as may be, love, and we
can celebrate Christmas with your family in the home
we share. Please, please, Callie, come back to me. I
love you.*

> *Aubrey*

Callie had to turn her head into her pillow before her flowing tears could make the ink on Aubrey's letter run. She
wasn't going to let anything happen to this letter. Ever.

When Aubrey silently pushed open the door to Callie's
sickroom, he expected to find her sleeping. When he
saw her sitting up in her bed, weeping, his heart flipped over
and turned to slush. "Callie!"
    Her face streaming with tears, she lifted her face and
looked at him. "Aubrey."
    "Oh, God, Callie! What's wrong?" He ran to her bedside.
Nurses had been scolding him for days now about his disruptive ways, but Aubrey didn't care about what the nurses
thought of him. He cared about Callie. Sliding to a noisy
stop beside her, he took up her hands. They were full of
paper. He looked more closely and saw his letter.

Had his letter made her cry? What had he said in it? Hadn't he declared his love? Had he said something oafish and crude? Lord, Lord, why couldn't he do anything right anymore?

"Oh, Aubrey." The words came out thick and watery.

He sat very carefully on the edge of her bed and kissed her hands. The paper tried to poke him in the eye, but he wouldn't let it. "What's the matter, Callie? Did I write something awful? I didn't mean to."

"No, Aubrey. Your letter is beautiful. Absolutely beautiful." Her voice broke and a new flood of tears washed her face.

As tenderly as he could, Aubrey wiped her cheeks with his handkerchief. "I love you, Callie. I love you beyond anything. I love you as much as I've ever loved anyone."

"Oh, Aubrey!" In spite of how much it must have hurt her poor battered body, she threw her arms around his neck. "I didn't think you'd ever love any woman but Anne."

Good God, he was going to cry, too. How humiliating. Swallowing hard, he managed to say, "I was an ass, Callie. I loved Anne, sure. I love Becky. And I love you—madly and passionately. I didn't realize how much love I had locked away inside me until you found the key to my heart."

Aubrey thought she said, "That's the most beautiful thing anybody's ever said to me," but wasn't sure, because her words were muffled by tears.

"Marry me, Callie. Please marry me. As soon as may be."

"I will, Aubrey. I love you so much!"

"Thank God." Aubrey thought he might just live through the day after that.

As soon as may be was the day before Christmas Eve. A fully recovered Miss Callida Prophet was united in holy matrimony with Mr. Aubrey Lockhart in the tiny Santa Angelica Methodist Church, with the Reverend Mr. Pinker reading the sermon. Everyone in the village attended the wedding, which meant there weren't enough seats in the church. Folks didn't seem to mind standing.

All of Aubrey's San Francisco relations attended the nuptials, too, including Anne's relatives. Only Mrs. Bridgewater, who claimed to be suffering from a nasty cold, didn't make the trek to Santa Angelica. Aubrey, Callie, and Becky, not to mention Mrs. Granger, Figgins, and Delilah, were surprised by the old cow's unexpected consideration.

Becky Lockhart served as Callie's maid of honor, thus preventing Callie having to make a decision between Alta and Florence, who served as brides' matrons. Mark Henderson, who stared rather wistfully at Callie during the ceremony, served as Aubrey's best man. George Prophet escorted Callie down the aisle and gave her away, acting as a suitable replacement for the Prophets' deceased father.

Monster watched from the choir loft, Becky and Callie having decided he deserved to attend the wedding ceremony.

A gala reception was held after the service at the Lockhart mansion, which was decked out in royal style for a Christmas wedding. Mrs. Granger hired several girls from the village to help her cook and decorate. Florence, who had a knack for such things, made and decorated the cake, which Mrs. Granger didn't resent too much, since she had plenty of other work to do.

Callie made a radiant bride in her ivory poplin wedding gown with pearls worked into an orange blossom design and scalloped sleeve caps. She'd had the gown made of ivory poplin since she didn't think she could honorably wear white. No one seemed to notice her choice of colors, especially since her attendants wore red velvet, in honor of the season.

Aubrey was more handsome than Callie had ever seen him, in his black cutaway coat and black trousers. She'd never in her life seen George arrayed so elegantly and was hard-pressed not to giggle as she walked down the aisle on his arm.

At the reception, Callie and Aubrey led the dancing with a waltz. Mark Henderson danced most often with Becky, but he managed to sneak in a few dances with Callie, too.

Callie and Aubrey exchanged letters that night, before they went to bed. Callie's read, *I love you, Aubrey.* Aubrey's read, *I love you, Callie.*

And they did.